MW00830408

THE SCIENCE OFFICER
OMNIBUS 2

BLAZE WARD

KNOTTED ROAD PRESS

The Science Officer
Omnibus 2
Volumes 5-8
Blaze Ward
Copyright © 2018 Blaze Ward
All rights reserved
Published by Knotted Road Press
www.KnottedRoadPress.com

ISBN: 978-1-943663-67-5

Cover art:
Copyright © Philcold | Dreamstime.com - Alien Space Base Photo

Cover and interior design copyright © 2018 Knotted Road Press

Never miss a release!
If you'd like to be notified of new releases, sign up for my newsletter.

I only send out newsletters once a quarter, will never spam you, or use your email for nefarious purposes. You can also unsubscribe at any time.

http://www.blazeward.com/newsletter/

CONTENTS

THE DOOMSDAY VAULT

THE LAST FLAGSHIP

AUTHOR NOTE: THE WAR OF THE PIRATE CLANS

When I wrote the fourth Science Officer story, *The Pleasure Dome*, my goal had been something lighter and not nearly as angry and dark as *The Gilded Cage* had turned out. I had been planning on writing and publishing a whole series of Science Officer novellas in 2017, with the eventual goal of finishing off that thing I have always called Season One.

I started writing seriously again in 2005, after a number of dead ends and events gone astray. The first thing I did when I set my mind to fiction again ended up being a series of stage plays, most of which aren't any good. But they were cathartic, and that was enough at the time.

Rough period in my life. Most of you have no idea, and I will probably never tell anyone the whole story. Even Fabulous Publisher Babe™ only knows pieces.

But it introduced me to Ray, who convinced me to start writing screenplays instead of theater. Different tone. Different rules. Different skills. Have a bunch of those in a can, just waiting for the funding fairies to sprinkle me with pixie dust. Might even happen one of these days. Weirder shit has.

One of the things Ray taught me was thinking in serial, like a television show where you can tell longer arcs, contained within a series of episodes. He took me back to my comic book days, or RPG's. For comparison sake, the amount of story contained in a 24,000-30,000 word novella (ala Science Officer, et al) works itself out to roughly the amount of story you would have if you were writing forty-two minutes of a television show, which is what a one-hour drama actually works out to in this country, when you add in the commercial breaks and credits at both ends.

So in my head, The Science Officer has always represented a single arc of story, spread out over a couple of years, but building on one another. For the BBC, a series is eight to twelve episodes, give or take, whereas in the US, it is usually 22-26, depending.

So I was set to pick up the story of Javier and Djamila and Zakhar where I left them off at the end of *The Pleasure Dome*. Svalbard spoke to me, with the vault of old seeds intended to keep things from going extinct. That's the sort of place a lunatic botanist pirate might enjoy.

But I wanted a bigger story. One of the things that irritates the hell out of me as a reader is when you have a character in a series who never changes. Never grows up. Never learns from her mistakes.

That's not a human thing. It might be a nice bit of genre fiction, but I hope readers are more sophisticated these days, and can pick up those little bits and references that go back to an older story. 'Mina has been gone since the end of *The Gilded Cage* (#3), but Javier still thinks about her. Others remember her and put her lessons in life to use.

It's what humans do.

So I wanted to write a bigger story. And I knew I was running eight episodes, so I had four more to cover, and could tell you something that big, but it needed to be compact. Each Science Officer story that I publish will be 24,000-30,000 words. (And yes, #9 will break that, but that's because I'm telling three, separate short stories and binding them under one 26,000 word cover and title. Exception proving the rule, and all that.) I don't want to write novels, because it is too easy to get bogged down. When you have 24k words, you have none to spare on aimless sub-plots that don't do anything.

Chop them out and go like hell.

At the moment I am writing this (Oct 2017), both *The Doomsday Vault* and *The Last Flagship* are out and being read by you. *The Hammerfield Gambit* and *The Hammerfield Payoff* are up for pre-order, but won't come out yet for a bit, so nobody knows what happens but me, Fabulous Publisher Babe™, and my awesome copy editor. Not even Matt W, the guy who does my audio books, has caught up with me yet.

I do wrap up this story. As you are reading this, it must be 2018 finally, and all four are out. Hopefully folks are enjoying them. Big arc. Big story.

Big changes brewing. For everyone.

I have a stack of notes for what will be Season Two. Eight more stories ((#10-#18, plus the transition collection that will be #9 when I write the other two stories).

I want to approach them slowly. I enjoyed writing five Javiers this year, but I need a break. So I plan to put out a couple each year for a bit, unless I start getting stalkers demanding more Javier, which is what happened in 2016 that put this book in your hands. Heh.

I won't spoil the fun for you, other than to point out that yes, I am aware that #7 is a cliff-hanger story. Think of it as the season-ender, followed by the kick-off episode, just like your favorite TV show does. I had serious considered dropping #7 and #8 two months apart, but Fabulous Publisher Babe™ assured me that I would start getting death threats if I did that.

And who knows, maybe I'll do a Season Three as well, if people really like these stories that much. One can never tell. And I do have fun. Just want to keep having fun doing them.

Hopefully, you will agree, after you read all the way to the end.

shade and sweet water,
blaze
West of the Mountains, WA

PS: Conversation with a fan last night where he mentioned that one of his favorite series authors just dropped #33. Yeah. So I can do a bunch more Javier if I want, and not feel weird.

ALSO BY BLAZE WARD

The Jessica Keller Chronicles

Auberon

Queen of the Pirates

Last of the Immortals

Goddess of War

Flight of the Blackbird

Additional Alexandria Station Stories

The Story Road

Siren

The Science Officer Series

The Science Officer

The Mind Field

The Gilded Cage

The Pleasure Dome

The Doomsday Vault

The Last Flagship

The Hammerfield Gambit

The Hammerfield Payoff

Doyle Iwakuma Stories

The Librarian

Demigod

Greater Than The Gods Intended

Other Science Fiction Stories

Myrmirdons

Moonshot

Menelaus

Earthquake Gun

Moscow Gold

Fairchild

White Crane

***The Collective* Universe**

The Shipwrecked Mermaid

Imposters

THE DOOMSDAY VAULT

PART ONE

BOOK THIRTEEN: CALYPSO

PART ONE

JAVIER ARITZA GLANCED up from the complicated electronic board that made up his duty station as Science Officer aboard the private-service, semi-piratical, Strike Corvette *Storm Gauntlet*. The bridge around him was quiet but poised. The walls were kinda gray today, but the crew wasn't.

Leaning forward, as his mother would have said.

Angry sharks smelling blood, as his first captain, back in the *Concord* fleet days, might have phrased it.

Javier turned his head far enough to make eye contact with Captain Zakhar Sokolov, seated atop his command throne chair at the rear of the chamber, everyone else in front of him where he could track them like an omniscient being.

"I don't want to hear it, Javier," the man growled. It would have been under his breath, but everyone on the bridge probably heard it in the empty stillness. "In fact, if you say it again, I'm going to start a curse kitty and charge you a quarter drachma every time you mutter it. We'll use that to fund orphanages, or something."

Even seated on his command chair, like a king atop a throne, it would be easy to mistake the captain for merely average. There wasn't much that made Zakhar Sokolov stand out. Mid-fifties. Typical Anglo skin color. Shaved head. Salt and pepper Van Dyke. Average height. Average build.

Javier grinned at the thought. Then he dug into a pocket for a coin and flipped it noisily into the air with his thumb in the captain's direction.

"This does not feel right," Javier announced, having paid good money for the privilege. "I realize we're only expecting to ambush a broken-down, half-blind freighter, but my recommendation would be to go in fully silent, and use extraordinary measures, since you don't want to leave."

Give the man credit. Javier got to watch Sokolov count to ten before he sighed quietly. And he pocketed the coin.

"Based on?" Sokolov asked in a voice used to dealing with an annoying, rambunctious eight-year-old in the backseat.

"While you've been watching for the big, bad wolf, I've been scanning the planet below us," Javier retorted, trying to not sound too smug about things.

You know, just slightly smug, without totally overdoing it.

The ship's dragoon, Djamila Sykora, gave him a good dose of stinkeye from her station across the bridge, but nothing she had going today was going to dent his mood. Not even a 2.1 meter tall, killer-Amazon, bad-ass, close-combat specialist known as the *Ballerina of Death*.

Sokolov didn't even speak, just posed a question with his face. A sad, put-upon, dad-face.

"The place was terraformed," Javier continued. "But it was done early on, during the Resource Wars era. And it didn't work. Life never really took, and it will probably revert to being a dead rock in another hundred thousand years or so."

"And?" Zakhar cast the word into the space between Javier's thoughts.

"There is nobody down there," Javier replied. "No lights. No radio signals. Nothing. And any time you spend on the surface you should have supplemental oxygen handy, as well as a warmsuit, because it is comparable to living at three-thousand-meters elevation, barely above freezing water, in the best places. The farther you get away from the equator, the worse it gets."

"Somebody is paying us good money to hijack a cargo," Zakhar observed.

Sokolov turned on that captain's charisma thing Javier had never managed for more than five minutes at a time.

He was *The Captain*, all of a sudden.

Javier nodded, an evil grin forming on his face.

"Those people are not delivering that cargo to anyone on *Svalbard*," Javier replied.

A beam of electricity seemed to connect the men, the only two here that had been trained, once upon a time, at the *Concord* Academy at *Bryce*.

"They're meeting someone," Zakhar said, mostly to himself. "And nobody mentioned that to me."

Javier just nodded.

"Alert Status One," Sokolov ordered in a hard voice. "Engage full stealth mode. Now."

Suddenly, the bridge sounded like a *Concord* warship going into harm's way instead of a civilian pirate sneaking around.

Javier flipped a single switch on his board that shut everything down to passive scans only.

He might have been sand-bagging the old man. After all, *Storm Gauntlet* had stolen all the sensor packages from Javier's old probe-cutter *Mielikki*. Right now, even on passive, his scan capabilities were probably better than most front-line warships in active mode, let alone freighters.

He had already mapped one hundred and fifty-three minor moons and major asteroids moving around in the darkness between planets.

"Nav," Sokolov continued. "Find me a different orbital path immediately. Your choice. Not here."

The pilot, Piet Alferdinck, nodded and began to play a complicated piano concerto on the board in front of him.

Javier repressed a sigh. His old ship, *Mielikki*, had been piloted by a full AI package, a *Sentience* named Suvi. In fact, Javier had been the whole crew.

Well, him and four chickens.

He missed that.

One of these days, he was going to see a great many of the people around him hung from a high yardarm in low gravity for cutting Suvi's ship, her corpse, apart. He had only barely managed to smuggle her personality chips out in a bucket of chicken feed and then pour her into his sensor remote, a planet-side surveying tool about the size of a large grapefruit.

There were days that young lady liked to remind him how much greater she used to be. But she had to do it quietly. If the pirates found out about her, they'd probably execute him in a heartbeat, regardless of the number of times he had saved their asses.

What they did to her after that wouldn't be worth mentioning.

"Stealth mode engaged, Captain," a voice called.

Deep. Male. Surprisingly smooth. Kibwe Bousaid, the captain's executive assistant and general do-it-all.

"Stay alert, but stand down to a small crew footprint under the science officer until we have incoming signals," the captain called, rising from his station. "I'll be in my office."

He took two steps and then pivoted to face Javier.

"We were hired to do a job, mister," Zakhar intoned seriously.

Javier nodded once, just as serious. He might act like a goofball most of the time, but there was absolutely no margin for error when the trap you had set might suddenly turn inside out on you.

PART TWO

Javier kinda enjoyed being in command, as long as he didn't have to actually do anything captainy.

About half the bridge crew had departed with the captain. Paperwork, certifications, stuff.

The dragoon, Sykora, had stayed put, but she was busy knitting. He would have guessed it was a sweater for herself, if pressed. She had laid out one whole back piece like the tanned hide of her latest victim. It didn't help his state of mind that she was working in a dark, almost umber-colored, yarn, about the color of his skin if he didn't get enough tan.

She probably knew that.

As long as she and her cannibal tendencies stayed on that side of the bridge, he'd be fine. They'd all be fine.

A chirp brought Javier back to the present.

Somebody had dropped out of jump a long ways out from the planet. From the sensor signal, they had pinged the planet and the inner system pretty hard while they waited for their drives to recharge.

Javier didn't know the exact model of ship coming, but that was a commercial scanner pulse, and not anything military. Nor a Particularly good one, either.

He assumed a dead-average everything for the freighter, and then down-graded that assumption by ten percent, them being smugglers.

Only the military ever had enough money to keep everything tuned, unless you could bribe techs at bases with fresh fruit cobbler, like Javier always had.

Back when *Mielikki* had a full botany station growing things year round.

Back before Sokolov had turned him into a slave.

Even *Janissary* was just a fancy title for what he did.

Javier flipped a coin in his head, then went ahead and brought the ship back to full readiness with a triple bell.

Sykora was already watching him like a hawk, but she nodded, then took the time to fold up her knitting carefully, instead of stuffing it randomly into the bag so she could get to one of her pistols quickly.

The woman was a violent psychopath, but she was a professional about it.

Sokolov emerged from his office about the same moment the passive scanners picked up a new signal and beeped intermittently until Javier silenced the alarm.

"What do we have?" the captain asked as he took his grand chair.

Other crew filed in at the same time. Warfare might be imminent. Or plunder.

"Commercial freighter," Javier replied, reading the signals the intruder was happily emitting. "I'm guessing a Kallasky Engineering Mark IV *Windwagon*, when she originally rolled off the factory floor."

"And Creator only knows what she looks like now," Zakhar said.

If there was a more customizable light freighter hull in the galaxy, Javier hadn't met it. Kallasky had made this model to be turned into almost anything a new owner desired. And do so cheaply, with whole modules that could be plucked out like seeds and interchanged from a standard parts catalog.

"She should have been in for a major engine tune at least six months ago," Javier said, studying the readouts.

For a supposed pirate/smuggler, the vessel was a wealth of signals intelligence. Most of it was garbage, but the sheer volume said something.

Mostly that they weren't trying to hide.

Which really did not leave Javier with a good feeling.

From the looks of the people around him, they agreed.

"What do we have?" Zakhar asked.

"She's above us now," Javier said. "Her last jump was conservative, and she's moving down to insert into an equatorial orbit, but doing it slowly."

"Any sign of a second vessel?" Zakhar inquired.

"None," Javier replied. "You're sure these people are supposed to be smugglers?"

"That was the task we were assigned," Zakhar said.

Javier nodded, but mostly as a placeholder.

Assigned.

He already knew that while Zakhar Sokolov owned the pocket warship, the man also belonged to what the more lurid news organizations liked to call *Pirate Clans*. If you had the money, the connections, and the need, you could hire *Storm Gauntlet* to do things, usually with plausible deniability.

One of these days, Javier decided, he might need to know a great deal more about how that whole underworld thing worked.

Rather than ask another stupid question, Javier routed one of his screens over to Sokolov's station. He watched the captain look down and study it intently for almost a minute.

Zakhar finally looked up with a very sour taste in the set of his mouth.

"The name *Calypso* mean anything to you?" Javier asked in an innocent voice.

He watched Zakhar look the name of the vessel up in the encyclopedia.

"Greek myth?" the captain asked.

"That's the origin," Javier agreed. "It's also a fairly common name for ships engaged in scientific research. Aquatic, predating starflight. Transponder identifies the ship as the property of the University of *Uelkal*."

"Considering how much someone paid for us to be here, I can't imagine a screw-up of that magnitude slipping through," Zakhar observed. "So you're probably right and it might be a trap."

Javier nodded grimly.

There were times when he would have settled for being wrong. This was one of them.

Zakhar nodded as well.

"Nav, when they get into their orbit, hide us above them in the gravity well, full stealth," he said. "If they move, notify me. Otherwise, we'll wait to see who shows up to play."

THE TEA MUG appeared at his right hand, almost by magic.

Javier refused to look, though; fully aware that the ship was still inhabited by evil pixies, carefully disguised as wardroom stewards.

Green tea from the color. Chewy, from the way it seemed to swirl with its own whirlpool when he finally looked down.

Javier steeled himself.

He took a sip. Perfection, itself.

Javier knew he was doomed.

A day had passed since *Calypso* had made orbit. *Storm Gauntlet* perched above them, like a hawk on a thermal hunting an oblivious pigeon.

The only thing that had broken the monotony was the amount of sensor data he had added, as *Calypso* had spent their whole time pinging the planet loudly with a sensor package almost as good as the pirate had.

The planet was dead as a doorknob. No question about it. But Javier could have done a full survey thesis just from his notes in the last twenty-four hours. It gave him something to do while he waited for that other shoe to drop. Everybody forgot how dull the waiting bits could be, even if you were walking a tightrope over a lava bed.

His board chirped happily. Around him, the skeleton bridge crew woke up from whatever they were doing.

After a moment, the guy watching the gunnery boards nodded at him. He was a tall, gawky kid with dark, brown skin and instincts almost as good as Sykora's. Just the person to babysit the big guns while they waited for something.

"Breakaway confirmed, sir," Thomas Obasanjo said. "*Calypso* has launched a shuttle."

Javier sounded the summons.

Sykora had apparently been in the day office with Sokolov, as she emerged one step behind him and took up her station.

"Good news," Javier smiled his most innocent smile at the giant woman.

"I doubt it," she sneered back at him.

"Oh, no," Javier disagreed with a smile. "They just launched a shuttle that's headed for the surface. You might get to go down and shoot people."

The way her eyes sorta gleamed told Javier all he needed to know about the woman's state of mind. Just as frustrated at the inactivity as he was, but at least she had a hope of being able to do something.

Nobody was going to rescue *The Science Officer*. Not even evil, wardroom pixies.

"I thought you said there was nothing down there, mister," Sokolov prodded.

"There isn't," Javier agreed. "And I've just spent a day reading their scanner logs to prove it."

"How did you read their scanner logs?" another voice intruded as she entered the bridge from another hatch.

Mary-Elizabeth Suzuki. Gunner extraordinaire. Dark hair and dark eyes. Lousy poker player. Pretty good dancer.

"I know what frequency they pulse on," Javier replied as he watched her walk. She was tall and skinny and a joy to watch move, or hold dancing. "That same signal comes back and we can capture it. I know enough major surface features now that everyone on both crews could have something officially named after them."

"Irrelevant." The captain did his Captain-thing. He speared Javier with an inquisitive eye. "Why?"

"How the hell should I know?" Javier asked. "You're the experts at being pirates. Maybe he has to go bury treasure? You know, *X marks the spot?*"

"Very funny," Sokolov replied.

The captain turned to Sykora, still all spit and polish formalness.

"Djamila," he commanded. "Organize a ground team. We'll pounce on the ship, and Del can insert you on top of them before they can hide or destroy anything."

She got that look in her eyes. Javier knew he was doomed.

"Don't forget your toothbrush, Mister Science Officer," she crooned at him. "You'll be joining us."

Javier already knew that. But he'd also take more than just a toothbrush on this trip.

This might be the day when he finally got to kill that woman.

PART THREE

In his sixty-five years in this galaxy, Delridge Smith had seen and done pretty much everything, he figured. Hell, in most places, the statute of limitations had even expired, but he'd never gotten around to comparing stupid feats with Aritza. Let that poor kid think he was a debaucherous pig. Del still made Javier look like a Nature Scout by comparison, if you went back far enough.

He ran a hand through the gray stubble on his head and then the neat, trimmed, white beard he had affected.

These days, all Del wanted to do was fly. Sokolov had offered him the ultimate gig: piloting a pirate assault shuttle. And letting him decorate it himself. All the adventure and craziness, with far less risk of someone over there being good enough to take him down on anything except luck.

'Cause when your luck was up, that was that.

Everyone else today was wearing gray and green splotch patterns as he looked out from the bridge hatch, down onto the shuttle's transport bay. Good to blend in, down on the surface.

Del's entire wardrobe consisted of baggy gray pants with pockets on the thighs, and a rainbow of fourteen different bright, floral-print shirts of an ancient style still called *Hawaiian*.

Del watched the science officer organize himself while Sykora and her pathfinders packed guns and backpacks.

Javier had brought the larger of his two drones on this drop.

14

The armed one.

To an abandoned planet.

Considering how many guns Djamila had, just on her person alone, to say nothing of the rest of her team, Javier didn't need any guns.

Need.

From the look on Aritza's face when he thought nobody was looking, it wasn't an accidental choice.

"Djamila," Del said, getting her attention quietly, even across the noise of people humping bags up the landing ramp of his assault shuttle. "Since this is an unknown situation, I'd feel more comfortable if you were manning the turret on the way down."

She fixed him with a look that just spelled out how little the woman understood poker.

"Del," she replied, almost exasperated. "There's nothing going to jump us. Even Aritza cops to that one."

"Humor an old man" Del implored her politely.

The girl and the science officer, put together, had only a few more years in this sky as Del did himself. And he'd seen a great deal more stupidity and combat than probably most of the crew.

Ah, the adventures of youth. But, any crash you can walk away from, regardless of which mountain you slammed it into first.

Del pulled out his clipboard and started the fourth page of his pre-flight checklist as Sykora gave a machine gun of orders to her people.

Even Aritza looked curiously in his direction.

Del just smiled serenely. Three more pages to go.

Task complete and landing bay finally settled, Del joined Djamila on the shuttle flight deck and brought the beast to full power.

Delridge Smith only had a few superstitions at this point.

The assault shuttle had no name.

None.

Nothing he had flown in the last twenty-five years had gotten a name. All his previous fighters and shuttles, the ones with names, had ended up dead in pieces somewhere. Better to not tempt the Fates on this one. They had apparently appreciated his effort.

And he liked his flight deck decorated like a Merankorr brothel, all pink and frilly, with faux fur and glitter paint on the walls. It went with his loud shirts and the Caribbean music he played, all steel drums and wood pipes.

That comforted him when he was doing crazy things.

Del settled into the flight chair and locked everything in place, both hands on multi-function controls that let him do everything without moving more than ten centimeters.

It was a really excellently designed ship. And tough enough for anything he had tried to put it through. At least so far.

"What are you up do, Del?" Sykora asked over the private comm channel as she brought the turret live and cycled it through its paces.

"You two are fire and oil," Del replied. "I would prefer not making someone clean blood off of my transport deck. You will never get the smell out. Trust me, I've tried."

Give her credit. The dragoon didn't play stupid. They had been comrades for several years now.

"It won't be today, Del," she replied.

"Probably," he agreed. "But I don't ever see you two making peace."

"Why should we?" she snarled at him.

Del knew he was pushing. Only the captain really had an inside gig to talk turkey with the woman, but Del could play the part of the grumpy, old man at least well enough to make her listen.

"Things would be a lot less tense for the rest of us if we weren't worried about becoming collateral damage in your little feud," he replied. "I realize that you two have never noticed that in your blind ambition."

Silence. Hopefully introspection, and not her throwing the headset across the open space as a prelude to stomping up from the gun deck and punching him.

She might do that.

Just in case, Del brought all the power live and stood the little shuttle up on its toes. With any luck, Djamila would stay strapped in until she calmed down.

"Bridge, this is the shuttle," he said into the comm. "Ready whenever you are."

"Roger that, Del," Zakhar replied. "Stand by."

Del watched the feed from the mothership.

Storm Gauntlet was a heavily modified Strike Corvette, an escort upgraded as a squadron leader once upon a time, and then retired out of *Concord* fleet service a generation ago when all the aftermath stopped aftermathing. When old warships like this and old warriors like Del got put on the shore for good.

She was more than enough to handle a single light freighter sitting below her in the gravity well, looking the wrong direction. Just in case, though, Del knew the captain would power everything up and race down at her, waiting for a good, solid firing solution from the Ion Pulsar to completely disable the wee beastie of a vessel, so the big, bad pirates could dock with her and hold her in orbit.

Nothing worse in the world than watching your prize fall out of the sky as all the crew bails out in lifepods and everything you hoped to steal burns up. Nothing more embarrassing, either.

Nothing went wrong today, either.

Hawks on pigeons.

On his primary screen, Del watched *Storm Gauntlet*'s B-Turret, the one with the double ion cannon, light that poor freighter up with fairy fire, a reverse St. Elmo's Fire bringing ruin instead of divine protection from the storm.

"Shuttle, you are clear for launch," Sokolov's voice came over the com. "Good hunting."

Del acknowledged then maneuvered the beast through the shield lock and into open space like a salmon climbing for spawning season.

One quick look at his boards showed nothing in space above him, and only one interesting spot on the entire, damned planet, roughly forty degrees south latitude on the leeward side of a big continent.

The spot where *Calypso*'s shuttle had gone to ground.

Del pushed the nose of the vessel over and jammed the throttle open. Assault shuttles were designed to go hot through an atmosphere.

Let's get you before you get away, and see what secrets you have to hide.

PART FOUR

Javier had felt the shuttle powering up, back up on the ship, and deliberately pulled every one of his straps extra tight. Del Smith probably thought the look in his eyes was reassuring.

Javier knew better.

The atmosphere had parted like the Red Sea, under protest, wailing like a hungry *ban sidhe* on a dusty, August night as Del took her in hot and crazy.

Not a surprise. Del was already crazy.

On the feed from the flight deck, the marble turned into a map, and then a skyscraper's window. Perched on the edge of a cold promontory overlooking a vast, icy valley.

From this approach, Javier could see the big, flat ledge, about halfway up one of the mountains that made up the basin. And the cave that appeared to open up behind it.

There was a small cargo shuttle nose-out and butt-in on that ledge, but no movement Javier could see.

And considering how sneaky the Assault Shuttle was swooping, those folks might not know there was anything wrong down there, other than sudden silence from orbit as *Calypso* went dark.

"Landing party, this is your captain speaking," Del's bored voice emerged from the speakers. "Please stow your gear and place your tray tables in the upright and locked position. Our target appears to be cold, and we will be on the ground in ninety seconds."

Javier settled for popping his knuckles and beeping Suvi to make sure she wasn't locked into one of her video games, ignoring the outside world.

"Are we there yet?" scrolled across his board on the little remote's controller with a sad face.

Javier's cover story, of upgrading and automating his pair of survey drones to make them more autonomous, worked to let her have to spend less time pretending to be listening to him, and more time flying. At the same time, they still had to make sure nobody realized she was in there.

If Sokolov found out, Javier was most likely a dead man and she would be a slave.

"Almost," Javier typed back. "Prepare for high winds and precipitation."

"You stay warm," she sent.

Trust his AI sidekick to go all motherly on him when they set down on a new planet.

But Javier checked anyway. A mask with supplemental oxygen hung around his neck, just in case. The warm suit under his pants and jacket was currently dialed up halfway, since Del had kept the landing bay chilly.

Javier went ahead and dialed the suit up to compensate for zero degrees Centigrade outside. The change wouldn't be instant. However, it would be enough to keep him warm when they got on the ground.

Everything else was in his backpack for now, except the "flight controller" for the drone hanging on his belt. Adding a "voice controller" function just meant he could talk out loud, not that Suvi would answer with people around.

A good-enough halfway measure today.

Impact.

Del must be feeling his oats today.

Usually, Del's landings were feather soft. This was one hard, and the bay door was already halfway down.

At least the dragoon hadn't felt the need to light the shuttle up with her cannon as she got close.

Javier would have lost that bet.

Sykora came pounding down the steps from the flight deck at a fast jog, pausing just long enough to count noses before she went down the ramp into the bitter cold at a dead run, battle rifle out. Both pathfinders ran behind her: Sascha with the nice hips and Hajna with the long legs.

Half-a-dozen male gun-bunnies followed, apparently intent on invading Guatemala.

"Probe. Access Command Mode," Javier said aloud, just in case anybody was listening besides him. Del was the only person still on the ship. "Exit shuttle and begin scanning. Defensive perimeter, please."

Translation: Make sure nobody is sneaking up on us. Shoot them if they do.

Javier unbuckled and stood slowly, stretching everything as Del appeared.

"Not in a rush?" the ancient pilot drawled.

"Let her absorb any incoming fire," Javier replied, slinging his pack. "They aren't going anywhere. I'm just here for buried treasure."

"Come again?" Del asked.

"Long story," Javier cast over his shoulder as he shouldered the backpack and tromped down the ramp, happily last.

Suvi hovered overhead in her dangerous little globe, like the eye of doom.

Calypso's shuttle wasn't smoking, so they had apparently opened the door at the top of the ramp, instead of blowing it apart with explosives.

You never knew with these yahoos.

One man guarded Del's hatch. Another protected *Calypso*'s shuttle. Javier assumed the rest were aboard the other ship, scaring people.

They were good at that.

Something caused him to look to his left as he emerged. Buried treasure, maybe.

Pirates always needed a secret place to hide things.

X marks the spot.

The cave was only about forty meters deep. There was a bank vault door back there, fit for *Jotunheim*.

Seriously, seventeen, maybe twenty meters high. Ten wide. Turning on Javier-sized hinge pins.

And completely invisible to all the scans he had done or intercepted from orbit.

Groovy.

Javier ignored everyone else and wandered that direction. The dragoon and her mob could catch up. Plus, Suvi was faster and more dangerous than Djamila Sykora, on any day.

Not much snow in the cave, for all the slushy ugliness out on the ledge. Mostly what swirling winds might deposit if left to their own devices, like a bored eight-year-old.

However, any snow that remained had been scraped off to one side when that giant door had swung open recently. Like, say, in the last hour, probably about the time that the assault shuttle had slowed down to sub-sonic speeds as it got close.

Javier wandered close. Ambled, more or less.

He wasn't willing to admit that the door impressed him. Not after trying to figure out how to steal the *Land Leviathan*, but his subconscious mind kept wanting to show him the evil giants lurking on the other side of that huge door, just waiting for a little mouse named Javier to knock.

Not a single beanstalk in sight.

At least the door controls were at a human scale, off on the right side. Simple little ten-key keypad, with individual buttons the size of his palm. Javier assumed they were meant to be pushed by hands in mitts, or handy elbows.

And someone had etched the control sequence into the metal panel just above the numbers. Obviously, it was meant to be opened by strangers who were intelligent, while keeping wildlife outside.

Briefly, he wondered why nobody had put a *Sentience* in the system, but then he remembered where he was.

Even the most carefully programmed AI would go utterly nuts from boredom given enough time alone.

Nope. Better to have a stupid system here, and rely on humans.

Was it well-enough engineered that some future star-faring species might come along and open the thing? Humanity hadn't found anything more sophisticated than lichens and simple plant life, anywhere, but that didn't mean nobody else was coming along.

Fermi might have been wrong today, but the galaxy was a big place and forever was a long time.

The flight controls on his hip chirped.

"Should we wait for the dragon lady? It might be dangerous, or something," Suvi typed with all the sarcastic insolence he had programmed into her.

Javier grinned and typed.

"Buried treasure, young lady," he typed back. "What if I don't want to share with the other pirates?"

His reward was a blinking smiley face, flickering quickly and randomly around the spectrum.

Truly, Suvi could be a goof.

Javier keyed the four digit sequence and listened as heavy bolts slowly retracted into the mountainside. The door began to move slowly outward beside him.

What was the worst that could happen?

PART FIVE

Zakhar had been way more adventurous in his youth.

Time was, he would have been happy to swap Javier places and go romp around on a strange planet looking for treasure and having adventures.

Becoming a starship captain, and then an entrepreneur, had cured him of some of his crazier ideas.

Okay, maybe tempered them enough so that he could live vicariously through the stories of other people getting shot at and nearly falling off cliffs.

Dry socks and fresh coffee was a happy trade-off.

It had been two hours since they had captured the freighter. One hour since Del and Djamila had landed and secured the shuttle. *Storm Gauntlet* had undocked from *Calypso*, but left a skeleton crew aboard, having found only three people over there to capture.

Zakhar hadn't let the bridge crew relax from Javier's ideas of paranoid sneakiness, though.

An *Osiris*-class Strike Corvette like *Storm Gauntlet* was only a little warship, as military vessels went. Pulse Cannons in Turret A fore, and Turret X aft for balance. Turret B had been refitted with an Ion Pulsar to capture ships instead of destroying them. Four smaller batteries with twin pulsars as defensive weapons on the front and rear flanks. She was mostly an escort that had been upgraded in service as a squadron leader, but nothing dangerous to big warships.

Hell on wheels against the average freighter, though.

Calypso had been stunned unconscious at the first shot from the Ion Pulsar. Mary-Elizabeth was an expert at that sort of thing. A couple of follow-up shots had just been gilding the lily, but there were no penalties for overkill in this business.

All a victim had to do was randomly trigger their jump drives to escape, even from this deep in a gravity well. It usually got you away, and if you stayed quiet, you probably could buy enough time to repair the drive matrix configurations to escape clean if your engineers were any good.

Smart crews would program an emergency jump for that exact purpose.

Hell, he'd only caught Javier Aritza in the first place because the man had dropped out of a jump almost on top of *Storm Gauntlet* and was stuck in the middle of recharging.

Bad luck for Javier. Maybe good luck for Zakhar.

His crew had been almost as broken down as their ship when the science officer first came aboard. Zakhar looked out over his bridge and considered what life might be like as a retired, former pirate.

Javier fixing the life support system had injected a spark into the crew that had been missing. Since then, he had become an officer that the crew would follow.

Now, if I can only figure out how to get him to stay after he has paid off his debt, which is coming up all too soon. Maybe I'll charge him extra to buy back his chickens and arboretum. Something.

Zakhar day-dreamed about taking a desk job somewhere.

Anywhere.

Someplace where he wasn't a pirate warlord, a slaver, and a wanted criminal. Maybe take Djamila with him and sell the ship to Javier, so those two could finally be separated and not have to kill each other.

A person could dream, right?

"Sir," a voice intruded on Zakhar's happy little fantasy.

Tobias Gibney. Gunner's Mate. Also, pretty damned good with the sensors when Javier wasn't around. He was short, skinny, and pale. And so quiet about his past that nobody knew anything about the man, except which planets he adamantly refused to ever take leave on.

Zakhar looked over.

Gibney had an angry look on his face, but it seemed to be pointed inward. It usually was.

"Go," Zakhar prompted.

"I've got a weird signal return," Gibney finally said. "I'd say a sensor ghost, but I know how good our scanners are. Science Officer would have spotted something going that far off beam a while ago and fixed it."

Yeah, Javier would have.

Not much brought out the nerdy professionalism in that man. Having better eyes and ears than any warship in service was high on that list, though.

Zakhar checked his boards. Everything was still in stealth mode, passive sensors only, but drinking in as much data as they could and filtering it according to the paranoid tendencies of one Mister Javier Aritza.

The chances of a false positive were technically above zero, but not by enough to actually count in anything but horseshoes and hand grenades.

"Where?" Zakhar asked in a tight voice.

Once upon a time, he had been a captain in the *Concord* Fleet. Warrior. Commander.

Right sneaky bastard.

Being a pirate hadn't taken any of that away from him.

Calypso was orbiting in front of them as they went, a little below and off the port bow. A silvery object close enough to be a very detailed model on a twenty-zoom telescope, but not so close as to present a maneuvering risk.

Good ship handling was still one of Sokolov's hallmarks.

"Higher plane. Sixteenth of an orbit ahead," Gibney chopped off his syllables like slicing carrots.

A-yup. Right where I'd want to be to start an attack pass. If I was running silent and trying to get close enough to ambush someone. Come to a dead stop relative to everything and let them come up under me before I uncloaked.

A genius admiral had once said that the difference between a good commander and a great one was fifteen seconds.

Which meant reacting immediately instead of dithering.

"Comm," Zakhar snapped his command voice across the entire bridge. "Break radio silence and order *Calypso* to emergency jump and then go silent. Bring all shields to maximum settings now."

"That will void our cloak, sir," the comm yeoman stated.

"Acknowledged," Zakhar said. "Tell Del to go silent as well. Nav, as soon as *Calypso* confirms, trigger our jump. Up and out. Get me clear so Engineering can start putting us back together. Drop us back to full cloak and total silence as soon as we come out of jump."

Things started happening immediately, at least here.

Calypso blinked out of existence. The ship was in good-enough shape, and the crew over there capable. They could get it all to rights in a couple of hours. Three or four light-hours of empty space took a long time to quarter, if you were looking for a silent needle in an empty haystack.

Storm Gauntlet surged with power as every generator was suddenly dropped into line and paralleled.

Above and ahead, *something* appeared. The mystery bird got off one salvo that hit home on the shields with a mighty sledgehammer, but not a second one. Not the dangerous one.

And then *Storm Gauntlet* jumped.

Darkness.

Emptiness.

Otherspace.

Back.

Everything went back to dimness as *Storm Gauntlet*'s crew hid, silent mice in the cupboard. Down below, Engineering would be a kicked-over ant's nest of activity as the jump matrix went sideways from too much gravity, too close. An average crew could fix it in six hours. On an average day his Chief Engineer, Andreea Dalca could probably do it in three.

Hopefully, this was a better-than-average day for her.

The captain over there had been good. But he had made a mistake.

I would have fired everything from under the cloak and let it collapse, rather than trying to bring it down cleanly. It would regenerate just as well as the jump matrix.

The difference had been not getting a second, full broadside from a battle frigate-sized Raider. One hit had gotten home hard. The second would have done damage, had Zakhar still been there.

Zakhar checked the readout. He even knew the vessel that had tried to kill them.

Ajax.

One of the enforcers for Walvisbaai Industrial.

Officially, the competition.

If the many pirate clans could be arrayed on a spectrum from good to evil, Zakhar would put his bosses, the Jarre Foundation, somewhere closer to the nice end.

Walvisbaai was about as bad as it got.

There was no chance in hell that they just happened to be out here in the middle of nowhere, all stealthed up and ready to attack.

Piet glanced over from his pilot's seat, but remained silent. The smile in the man's eyes was enough. He didn't have to actually say it out loud.

Javier had been right.

It was a trap.

PART TWO

BOOK FOURTEEN: SVALBARD

PART ONE

As the humongous door waddled open and lights on a single overhead track came on, Suvi sent a soft ping on a weird, ultrasonic frequency down the big atrium. Just the sort of thing for annoying the hell out of bats.

She didn't figure there were any on this planet, anyway. And if there were, better to find out what sort of mean bastards might have colonized an iceball in the middle of nowhere, early, right?

Tunnel. Straight for a bit, back into the soul of the mountain. Inclined at exactly seven degrees for the four hundred meters she could scan. Either the tunnel hairpinned at that point, or there was another door blocking things.

Because the outside air was just at freezing, she had transformed her regular black, skin-tight, leather flying-suit gear into fur-lined pants, snow goggles, and a parka made from a hideously-pink polar bear.

You could do anything when you were an AI. You just had to dream silly enough.

Suvi maneuvered her armed gunship through the door and looked around. Javier was following her lead, and the corridor was empty, but it was still twenty-seven meters tall, perfectly round if you had cut off the bottom third. Probably bored that way, and then all the pipes and wiring put in underneath before they built a new floor.

Weird, but humans did things that made no sense, even to themselves.

Because she could, Suvi decided to fly this mission on the ceiling. She left fourteen centimeters of clearance above her, tilted her nose down and imitated one of those flying cops tracking speeders with a radar gun as she moved at Javier's relaxed pace.

And because there might be carnivorous bats around, she unlocked the pop-up pulse pistol turret the bigger drone had on the bottom ring. Probably heavy enough to knock a moose on his ass.

Girl needed to be prepared.

The big cathedral door began to close behind them with a hooting sound, probably designed to remind stupid humans to move out of the way. She had to dial down her audio sensors a little, and throw in a filter, or it would have been extra annoying. Kinda the reverse of what she had just done to the bats.

Javier was mostly watching her feed as she let every scanner and probe she had make as much noise as it wanted. She hadn't found anyone, so if they were here, they were really good at hiding.

Or they were ghosts.

She was pretty sure none of Javier's wardroom pixies had followed him here.

Not yet, anyway.

"Anything?" Javier asked.

"Moles don't tunnel straight," she typed back. "Space dragons?"

That got a laugh out of him, which was good. Javier had been too tense lately. Probably needed to get laid more. You never knew with organics, but that seemed to be his go-to remedy, since he didn't drink with nearly the audacity of some of his old stories.

Thirty seconds after the outer door closed, the light flickered out, but Javier had apparently been expecting it. He had a flashlight out and on. Good enough for him to see, and she didn't need to add anything.

The inner door, when they got there, was just as grandiose as the outer one. In better shape, since it didn't have the added exposure, but cut to exactly the same dimensions. Someone had forged both simultaneously and put them here.

What the hell did you hide on a dying planet in the middle of nowhere? And why would it need to be this big?

Suvi took a quick spin through the encyclopedia she had finally convinced Javier to upload, but nothing jumped out with an answer.

Javier approached the inner door and took off his gloves as she watched. He stashed the flight controller in his backpack and studied the big door.

Hmm. Temperature was warmer here. Already three degrees ambient, and the door itself was nine degrees. Was there a volcano on the other side of that wall, or something?

Javier stepped to the side and entered a different four-digit sequence to open this portal.

Interesting that they didn't use the same one as the outer.

No, strike that. Absolutely illogical. And thus, human.

The door beeped once and started to open.

The hallway lights came on again.

Because she was above it, Suvi had a great view of the interior, while still being kinda invisible up here.

And that was good, since there were a dozen guys on the inside, armed to the teeth.

Javier had no chance to move before he was suddenly at the wrong end of the problem, but at least he never looked up at her. And the visible guns were all stun models, as near as she could tell.

"Don't move," one of the closest guys said.

"Yeah, I kinda figured that," he replied.

"Who are you?" the stranger asked.

"Just a guy," Javier said.

And then they shot him.

PART TWO

THE JUMP HADN'T BEEN as far as Zakhar had hoped.

Hopefully, it was still far enough.

That was the problem with triggering an emergency jump. By its very nature, it would be a random distance, in a random direction, since the drives were not capable of factoring the extreme curvature of space-time once you got too close to a planet.

Still, it had worked.

Storm Gauntlet had gotten clear before *Ajax* was able to lock on and hit hard enough to get through the shields.

However, now was when things got dangerous.

Calypso would be staying as dark as a hole in space, waiting either for orders, or to make their escape if *Ajax* took out *Storm Gauntlet*. Either way, he didn't have to worry about them. An unarmed freighter had no business being around here, so they would be moving away as quietly as they could. He'd already set up a rendezvous with the prize crew, for exactly this sort of surprise.

At the same time, the ground team was trapped on a very hostile planet. With an enemy overhead.

Zakhar wasn't sure if their best outcome would be to be abandoned here forever, or to be captured by a bunch of goons from Walvisbaai. Certain death versus the possibility of something worse.

The control boards, at least, were promising.

Engineering was on the ball. Drive tuning would be accurate within an acceptable limit in under an hour. Piet was flying. Mary-Elizabeth had the guns. Even Gibney was doing nearly as good a job as Javier at the science officer station.

And now, to sail into harm's way, against an invisible opponent.

"Ahead one quarter," Zakhar ordered. Just enough to get them in the right direction, having already killed their inertia.

Time to get sneaky.

Zakhar studied the various readouts at his fingertips.

Ajax had been a purpose-built pirate ship, rather than a retired and refurbished old warboat like *Storm Gauntlet*. She was bigger and meaner, but most assuredly not built to the same standards for durability. That was expensive to engineer and fabricate, and like most pirate ships, *Ajax* would be relying on an overabundance of firepower for such a small hull.

Hell, at the end of the day, *Ajax* could probably go toe-to-toe with a destroyer for a little bit, before the bigger ship's mass began to tell. But that wouldn't do Zakhar any good today. These two vessels were capable of pounding each other into scrap at a fairly even pace. Sykora and Aritza were still trapped on the planet below.

The edge he had was in his sensors. Already, Gibney had managed to spot the other vessel once. After all, the cloak function wasn't perfect, nor invulnerable. Just an energy shield that masked nearly all emissions behind a blanket of randomness.

Nearly being the operative phrase here.

Could they do it again?

Zakhar's ability to rescue Djamila, from this trap he had stepped into, hinged on it.

What was the best way to out-think the other guy?

Zakhar glanced over at Gibney, face down and studying everything intently, as if Javier was leaning over his shoulder offering suggestions.

Yeah, there was an inspiration.

When in doubt, do something crazy.

"Piet," Zakhar continued, as if not a moment had passed. "Plot an insertion orbit that runs on an oblong angle."

"How oblong?" the pilot actually looked over his shoulder with a concerned face.

"Del landed forty degrees south?" Zakhar asked.

Piet nodded carefully.

"So forty-five south, fifty-five north," Zakhar concluded. "And keep it extremely high."

Just the unconscious recoil that shook Piet's whole body told Zakhar just how offended a well-trained pilot would be with such a course. Which was the whole point. He would never think of something like this on his own, so he wouldn't be expecting it.

Out-think the other guy.

Everyone else plotted orbits that ran parallel with the equatorial plane, usually at some latitude that put you directly overhead of some important terrestrial target below you. That or an orbital insertion that let you cover the whole planet as you went pole-to-pole with it turning beneath you.

This was the sort of thing Javier would have thought up.

"Why this orbit, sir?" Gibney asked, trying to wrap his head around the kind of craziness that usually emanated from the science corner of the bridge.

Probably afraid it was contagious.

"I want him to fly below us at some point, Tobias," Zakhar replied. "Our sensors are better than his, so if we can get him to shadow part of the planet, we'll see him."

"Then what?" Mary-Elizabeth chimed in from the gunner station.

"Still working on that part," Zakhar said. "Feel free to offer ideas."

"Roger that," she replied.

Zakhar opened an internal comm channel.

"Wardroom," he said quietly. "Prepare to feed the bridge crew lunch and dinner in place, please."

He closed the channel and got to thinking.

How do you beat a bigger enemy, when all he has to do is just stop you from saving your people?

PART THREE

UNLIKE DEL'S ASSAULT SHUTTLE, the pilot from *Calypso*'s shuttle hadn't stayed aboard after the other group had landed.

Or if he had, he had found a really good place to hide. One even Djamila couldn't find.

She finally considered it good enough, for now.

Her team had cleared the vessel about as quickly as anyone could have managed. Certainly, they would have been on the podium, if this had been a competitive event. The after-action report wouldn't have many deductions.

She left Sascha and Hajna aboard the vessel as a precaution and went outside to gather up the strike team. The two girls were good scouts and pathfinders, but the six boys were more linear.

The men were for the times when charging a machine gun nest really was the best solution.

Del was standing in the hatchway as she emerged back into the brisk air.

"Where's Aritza?" she called, looking around.

He smiled at her, and pointed back to the tunnel.

Damn it. Was that man incapable of ever acting like an adult?

"Lock everything up, Del," she ordered, signaling her men to join her, battle rifle held casually pointed downrange.

The first door was better suited to be a flight hangar, even if it was built like a bank vault, except that it was just too narrow for anything big enough to be dangerous. Still, someone was obviously intent on hiding something down here, or it would have shown up on scanners.

Aritza wouldn't have been capable of keeping out if he saw something like this. Just like he wasn't capable of not walking right into what was obviously a trap, instead of waiting for backup.

Hopefully, he had finally met with that tragic accident she had always been meaning to arrange, whatever Del thought to the contrary.

Six men, and her. Good enough.

Everyone was prepared. Del had already started withdrawing the landing ramp upwards. Aritza's sensor drone would be nice about now, but had obviously gone inside the deathtrap with him.

Hopefully, it had survived enough that she could make use of it in the future. After he was dead.

The panel was obvious. Human designed. Set into a stone façade. Door opening outward from a plug frame, where outside overpressure would just drive it deeper into a narrowing face and let it survive much greater pressures than just resting in place would allow.

Good architecture for defense.

She checked the keypad and noted that someone had permanently carved a four-digit numeric sequence above it.

Her men had squatted into a defensive formation. Well spread-out against grenades. Covering front, sides, and rear. Every weapon was hot, judging from the fingers carefully not touching triggers.

She moved to one side and pressed her bottom flat against the cold wall. Given the confines, Djamila slung her rifle and drew the pistol on her hip. She transferred it to her left hand, multi-dimensional ambidexterity having always been one of her greatest assets, and keyed the button sequence with her right.

The behemoth beeped and began to open.

Inside, Djamila found a vast cathedral empty. Her men were strung out behind her as they moved, carefully covering everything.

The overhead light falling dark was a surprise, but only for a moment. Lights on barrel rails came on, as well as the one on Djamila's pistol. It made everyone a target, but there wasn't much they could do, unless they wanted to abandon the science officer, or go back for night gear.

Leaving that punk would have been a happy solution, but she still had to find the crew that had come down with the shuttle in the first place.

Knowing Aritza, he had already found them and was drinking and having a wild, uproarious time.

Fortunately, the corridor had smooth walls, so nothing was in a position to ambush them, unless they came from a hidden door. And her men were just waiting for that.

It didn't feel like a home, the kind with comfortable side corridors. More like a doomsday vault, where *Neu Berne* High Command had once burrowed into a mountain to hide from orbital strikes that had never come.

Almost half a kilometer in, Djamila found a second vault door, an identical copy of the first, athwart her path in the darkness.

A woman's voice came out of the dark sky.

"Dragoon Sykora," Djamila heard a modulated voice that almost sounded like an angel. "You are in extreme danger."

PART FOUR

JAVIER ALWAYS FOUND it hard to distinguish between a good, morning-after hangover, and getting blasted unconscious with a commercial stun rifle. Strange ceilings, weird smells, and total strangers around him didn't help sort anything out.

"Where am I?" he groaned.

Maybe groaned.

It might have come out as a general blur of syllables. That was a common side effect of both kinds of mornings.

"Ah, you are awake," a man's cheery voice cut through the gunk coating Javier's mind.

Javier opened his eyes anyway.

A fat, cheery elf with a white beard hovered in the air above him.

No, leaned over.

I'm flat on my back on the floor.

The pain was fading, so Javier leaned towards the stunner theory. A hangover that good usually lasted a day or so.

"Who are you?" Javier strung syllables together as he sat up, pulled more or less into a sitting position by the elf.

"Dr. Alex Mornan," the annoyingly-joyful elf replied as he turned into a middle-aged, pudgy, pale-skinned Anglo. "Chief Scientist aboard the Star Yacht *Calypso*. And you might be?"

Calypso?

They were in a small room with a dozen other folks, a big conference table, gray stone walls, and what looked like a locked door.

Oh. Crap. Quadruple cross, at least.

"Navarre," Javier lied.

He needed to have a life after piracy. The fewer people that could connect one Javier Aritza with acts worthy of execution by *Concord* authorities, the better.

"Have you any idea what might be the affair with our erstwhile captors?" Mornan asked.

It took Javier's semi-scrambled brains a second to parse all that back into something comprehensible. It didn't make any sense a second time, either, but he remembered the hard look in the eyes of man who had been hiding inside the vault, just before that jackass pulled the trigger.

"It's a trap," Javier said finally. "We were lured here under false pretenses. What are you doing here?"

False enough pretenses. Ambush a freighter. Hijack the cargo. Get paid.

Obviously, someone had other plans.

"I see," the elf said dubiously. "We were making our annual delivery to the vault, and were greatly surprised to find armed men waiting for us. We've been locked in this compartment for over an hour now. Were you with them?"

"Vault?" Javier asked innocently. "My brain is still scrambled. What's in the vault?"

"Seeds, my good man," Mornan replied. "The future of galactic ecology. This is *Svalbard*. We're standing in the Doomsday Vault."

Seriously? That *wasn't* an old wives tale?

Javier had heard rumors of such a thing. Empty, habitable world. Mountain hollowed out and filled with every kind of plant seed known to humans, regularly updated so that no earth-derived species ever went extinct.

He had joked about raiding the place, back when he was flying survey jobs for the *Concord Fleet*, just to expand his arboretum.

Apparently, it really existed.

Who knew?

"*Svalbard?*" Javier faked. "Of course. My pardon for the holes those pirates seemed to have left in my memory."

"Smashing, my dear chap," Mornan beamed. "What brought you here?"

Javier let the older man pull him the rest of the way to his feet as he thought furiously. The others watched, but stepped back, like he was in the ring with the smaller man.

Not a happy vision, but not much he could do about it.

"There were rumors…" Javier let his voice trail off. "I have been working on a variant of a Terran gooseberry that fixes a variety of useful trace vitamins and minerals with just enough of a secondary euphoric that eating a handful guarantees the average human blissful sleep without narcotic side effects or withdrawal. It dries with seventy percent potency, as well as surviving fermentation that yields a low alcohol wine perfect for long-term shipping."

Javier was able to identify the five professional botanists in the group by the rapt attention they paid, while the others seemed to glaze over at his words.

Always know your audience.

"Go on," Mornan had lost his reserve and leaned forward breathlessly.

"I've bred the root stock too narrowly," Javier admitted with a flash of guilt in his tones. "I was hoping to find something here that was hardy in an 8A climate so that I could cross-pollinate without hybridizing the daughter generations, to stabilize the breed. Then I take it to an agricultural university as a breeding project."

"What are your berries like?" a woman on his left asked sharply.

It suddenly felt like he was defending a thesis. Might be.

"Shockingly pink," Javier grinned at her. "About the size of a good table grape, up to possibly a snooker ball if growth conditions are perfect. Four seeds symmetrically arrayed from the center. Good, juicy flesh. Skin firm enough to handle transport, without being so thick that it turns into a pain to bite through."

"Have you considered…" she started to say, when the door opened.

The man with the hard eyes was standing there. He pointed an angry finger at Javier.

"You," he commanded. "Come with me."

Javier shrugged and turned to the elf.

"Dr. Mornan, it has been a pleasure to meet you," he said. "Pardon me. I'll be back as soon as I can."

The scientist nodded with a sad smile, but kept his silence.

Javier could see the wheels turning in his eyes, though.

Outside, Javier found the rest of the office. Apparently, he had been stashed in the boardroom, because there were a dozen desks around the walls, patiently waiting for people to give them purpose.

And half-a-dozen armed goons.

At least they were professional, with everyone acting sane. Hell, only three of the guys even had guns pointed at him. That had to be a bonus.

It wasn't like he was Sykora, willing and probably capable of taking on all of them at once. And probably winning.

That woman was absolutely a High Priestess of Death, or something.

"Sit," the jackass commanded sharply.

Javier complied. Neither Sykora nor Suvi were here, so these poor bastards were already so badly outnumbered they wouldn't even know it was coming.

"So," Javier even smiled. "You guys are the trap?"

That was apparently the way to back-foot the jackass. His angry scowl turned puzzled. Then cleared up.

"That's right," he agreed. "You're Navarre."

It wasn't a question. Javier didn't figure much of this would be open to debate.

"Correct," he said. "Who hired you folks?"

The jackass's eyes turned to slits. Probably not expecting a formal, polite pirate. Especially not if they had warned him to expect a psychopathic killer like Navarre supposedly was. Probably all set to torture him for information.

"You pissed off a number a folks," Jackass said. "But Slavkov put up the bulk of the funds."

It took Javier a moment to place the name.

Valko Neofit Slavkov. Owner of the *Land Leviathan*, the galaxy's largest rolling resort yacht.

Man, he must be really pissed about being called a moron. And not getting delivered a mass casualty incident when he went to all the effort to hire Navarre in the first place.

Of course, to date, the only people Navarre had killed had been pirates. And they had it coming.

Much like Jackass and his friends here.

"So what's your play?" Javier asked.

Five drachma ante, punk. Jacks or better to open.

"Bounty on your head, alive," Jackass sneered. "Sokolov, either way. Slavkov wants to talk to you, personally."

Good. That gave Javier a whole range of options, if they wanted to transport him alive somewhere. Assuming they didn't just stun him, drop him into a medically-induced coma, and throw him into a life-support pod for the trip.

Being functionally dead would make escaping a real pain in the ass.

Before Javier could say anything, an alarm began to beep. Javier presumed the inner vault door based the sound.

Jackass looked over his shoulder, cursed under his breath, and turned.

"Stash him," the man commanded as everyone was suddenly armed.

Another of the goons motioned for Javier to stand and pointed him back to where the scientists were currently being held.

Since the alternative was getting stunned and dragged, Javier went willingly.

He wanted to be awake to see what Sykora did to these punks.

PART FIVE

THIS WAS the part that utterly and irrevocably sucked.

Suvi carefully flipped on her running lights and descended from the ceiling, being the target of seven different weapons.

And she couldn't even shoot them all, like she wanted.

Worse, she needed them. Dragon Lady most of all.

And they needed to believe she was an autonomous probe with less brains than a goldfish, or someone might get the bright idea of who was really hiding in here.

"Probe. Access Command Mode," Sykora said, proving that she had been paying attention back on *Shangdu*. "Provide situational map."

Suvi was glad she thought at several thousand times the speed of the average human. And had access to a good encyclopedia. The gap while she figured out what the hell the giant woman was asking was probably long enough for organics to notice.

Stupid, paranoid gun-bunnies.

Still, you didn't make bricks without straw. And even worse pirates than these had the boss captive.

Suvi settled at chest-level on the giant woman and set her running lights in a low-glow pattern. Mostly enough to outline her as a giant, disembodied eyeball.

Maybe she could get Javier to take her trick-or-treating next year?

Suvi used her projector to display a map of the hallway they were in, the door, and as much of the hallway beyond it as she had scanned when the vault was open.

Plus a dozen red X marks for bad men with guns.

She followed that up with a quick video of the ambush, Javier standing still and getting stunned.

"Are there others beyond the door?" Sykora asked.

Suvi caught a twinkle of mischief in the woman's eyes. Javier was right, she really did suck at poker.

Best to modulate the voice.

Suvi found something that sounded like a bad AI special effect from a late-night movie.

"Data insufficient," she replied in the most boring, mechanical voice she could manage.

"Project the image of the shooter again," Sykora commanded.

Hey, how about a little politeness here, lady?

"Please," the Amazon followed up.

Huh. Okay. Old dogs, new tricks. I can play, too.

Suvi put a still scan into three dimensional projection. She could do that with the latest round of updates. It made chess with Javier way more fun.

"Pay attention," Sykora seemed to be talking to her men. "Note that they were all holding stun pistols at the moment of engagement, but every one of them has a lethal weapon either slung across their back, or as a compact carbine. Everyone shift to stun weapons now."

Suvi watched the men rotate through their arsenal wordlessly. Sykora holstered the one on her hip and drew from the shoulder rig.

"Stun grenades?" one of the men asked.

"Sonic only," Sykora replied. "We'll assume that they'll hear the door opening and be prepared for aerosolized gas attack. I would be."

"Roger that."

EVERY SINGLE ONE OF THEM pulled out a grenade from a pouch and held it in their off-hand.

Are you people all that crazy? Who invades an empty planet with that much casual firepower?

"Probe, you are armed, correct?" Sykora asked.

Does the sun rise in the east, lady?

"Affirmative," the machine voice replied monotonously.

"Do you have a stun setting?" Sykora continued.

"Affirmative."

Gods, talk about a boring conversationalist.

"Am I authorized to give you firing instructions?"

Oh, sneaky. And smart enough to assume that Javier might lock someone, ESPECIALLY YOU, out of using the dangerous bits.

"Affirmative."

"Okay," Sykora eyed everyone, including the eye staring back. "They will know the door is opening, and be prepared to ambush us."

Suvi watched the Amazon point to the smallest man present, short for any man when the rest were all well above-average for height and weight.

"You and I will put four grenades through the gap as soon as it opens far enough for a clean entry," Sykora continued. "Everyone else will be flat on the deck and prepared to fire as soon as you have any targets. Stun everything that moves, no questions asked."

Sykora turned and fixed Suvi's chariot with a grim smile.

"Probe. Access Command Mode," Sykora ordered. "From an elevated spot, provide enfilading crossfire on all enemy targets with stun weaponry when the door opens."

"Acknowledged," Suvi said, bored.

If there was a way to make it a fair competition against mere organics, Suvi knew she could run a high score marathon on any flying simulations that included a strafing element, especially the ones with an otherwise-unexplained canyon sequence defended by point turrets. What idiot had thought that one up, anyway?

Open door, standing humans, vertical surprise? Bring it, lady.

Suvi had to give the crazy Dragon Lady credit for pro moves, though. She couldn't remember a single cheesy B-movie she had ever watched where they approached the topic of kicking in a door with anything like what Sykora put together.

Four men, laying or kneeling, pistols covering the opening, while the fifth went clear to the other side and faced rear, in case of a secret door.

Small guy with his butt next to the keypad. Sykora just beyond him. Four grenades in hands.

Sykora looked at everyone individually, including the hammer of the gods overhead.

Suvi flickered her running lights.

"Go," Dragon Lady murmured.

Little Guy keyed the door with his elbow.

Beeps and grinding as the mechanism wound itself up.

Lights came up in the hallway.

Vault door cracked enough to spill light out.

Little Guy leaned in and snapped two grenades through the gap, dropping to one knee and drawing a pistol.

Dragon Lady stepped into a throw and HEAVED her two grenades like she was gunning the runner down from center field.

Because she could, Suvi tilted her turret down and hovered just above the opening door, painting the room beyond the vault with a scanner pulse hard enough that even humans might feel it.

Anybody wanna know their blood type?

BOOM. BOOM.

BOOM. BOOM.

Inside, the pirates had been caught off-guard, mostly because someone was crazy enough to randomly soften up a room with grenades.

Plus, they were two-dimensional beings.

Desks and tables had been pulled into the corridor to provide some modicum of cover. At ground level, that was a wonderful idea. Two dimensions.

Suvi wasn't showing off, exactly, but these people were pirates. She didn't need them for anything except target practice.

And Javier hadn't actually let her test her gun systems out on anyone but him, for fear that people would learn too much about the woman flying the little drones.

To top it all off, this had just been a generally crappy day, especially watching someone shoot Javier.

She lit those bastards up like womp rats in the desert sun.

PART SIX

BECAUSE HE WAS AWAKE this time, and had expected trouble with a capital T, Javier had settled at the far end of the boardroom table, five botanists at hand and a crew of bored support staff standing and sitting around.

Explosions outside the door let him know the lunatic cavalry had arrived. Either rescue was at hand, or the bad guys would be a while fighting off the attack and regrouping.

"How can you be so calm?" the woman botanist asked, brushing her cute, pageboy-cut brunette hair back out of green eyes.

Javier had missed her name earlier. He was hoping someone would address her while he was listening.

It would probably be rude to ask again, even if he could blame the after-effects of a good stun scramble.

Javier shrugged. She was a little too mousy and squishy for him to find her show-stopping hot, but there was a first-rate mind underneath, cycling through cross-breeding generations and options he hadn't considered before. And brains were even sexier than butts.

But then, he had never had access to all the accumulated botany of human science, either. Especially not in a cute, female form.

"We're pirates," Javier admitted. It would make things easier to explain later. "Someone hired us to ambush a target, without telling us who it was. The folks outside this room were waiting for us to arrive."

"And all that noise outside?" she asked.

"I brought some seriously dangerous, utterly crazy folks with me," Javier grinned. "Hopefully those jackasses are getting an education right now. I can wait."

Silence fell as he spoke.

"Or not," Javier continued. "Sounds like things are over."

"Now what?" Dr. Mornan asked

Javier sighed. Easier to get this over with.

He rose and walked to the locked door. Pounded on it twice.

"Hello?" he yelled. "Anyone out there?"

"Who's there?" came the call back.

Her voice.

High Priestess of Destruction.

Djamila Sykora.

"Navarre," he yelled, letting her know she needed to be playing the role of Hadiiye, just as he was pretending to be someone else.

"Status?" she yelled through the door.

"Me and a dozen prisoners," Javier replied. "Jackass and his crew were all on your side of the door."

"Stand back," she commanded.

Javier took her at her word and leapt backwards. You never knew when Sykora would kick in a door, or use explosives to level it.

God forbid she actually use the handle and just open the damned thing.

She must be feeling benevolent today. Nothing exploded.

Just her, standing there in the open doorway, gun pointed at him, and then everyone else.

"Hello, beautiful," Javier grinned at her.

Nothing like salt in an open wound.

She looked like she wanted to shoot him on general principle. Apparently considered it.

The scowl on her face could be used to carve stone.

"Who are these people?" she demanded angrily.

Javier stepped back and gestured grandly.

"The scientists and flight crew of the yacht *Calypso*, Hadiiye," he introduced them.

"Stay put," Sykora ordered. "At least two got away in the firefight, and are moving deeper into the facility. We're in pursuit."

"Young lady," Dr. Mornan said with a polite tone as he rose. "I would advise against that. There are fifty-three kilometers of tunnels past this point."

Sykora had the gun pointed at the boffin. She was like that.

"Fifty-three?"

She sounded aghast. Maybe insulted.

Possibly aroused at the possibility of chasing two men into an endless maze.

"What is this place?" she continued.

"A doomsday vault for botany," Javier spoke before the other man could. "Seeds."

"Oh, dear Lord," she rolled her eyes. "Just exactly your sort of place."

Javier grinned at her again.

"What have we heard from orbit?" Javier let his voice grow serious.

Something in his tone got her attention.

"Nothing," she replied.

And left it at that.

Javier understood her reticence.

Almost as much as she hated the science officer, the dragoon had a crush on the captain. Not that she would ever admit it.

She didn't have to. Javier could see it occasionally in her eyes.

Like now.

Worry.

"I have an idea," Javier said. "Hook me up to the public address system and let's see if we can get the two rabbits to surrender peacefully."

"What about them?" Sykora pointed at the folks from *Calypso*.

"They're harmless," Javier replied. "Lock them up on Del's flight bay for now. We'll sort it all out later."

"Are you really a pirate, Navarre?" Dr. Mornan asked.

He had gotten several steps closer, though not enough to threaten anyone. Sykora probably would have shot him if he had.

"Yes," Javier answered. "But don't worry. You people are just bystanders in someone else's war. We'll sort them out and then get you home safe."

"Indeed?" the cute woman botanist fixed him with a disbelieving eye.

"Absolutely," Javier smiled at her. "I only kill pirates."

PART SEVEN

"I KNOW YOU CAN HEAR ME," Javier said conversationally.

Downrange, his voice echoed hollowly, emerging from every speaker in the mammoth facility. He winked at the three people with him.

Dr. Mornan has insisted on remaining behind, to keep the barbarians from damaging anything important in the facility. The female botanist had stayed as well.

She finally had a name. It was such a lovely one. Javier considered being smitten just with the act of saying it again and again in his head.

Rainier St. Kitts.

Seriously. It sounded like something from a movie, or a romance novel. But hey, they were all in a pirate flick today, so why the hell not?

And, of course, Sykora. Scowling professionally at the two civilians, both of whom appeared immune.

"I've wired the whole facility so you can hear me," Javier continued. "I would consider it a great favor if you would just surrender peacefully at this point. Killer Babe and her gun bunny crew are itching to come in there after you. I'd rather not damage anything."

"And if we don't?" the man's voice came back over the system. "We're armed, too. And hiding."

"Oh, I have a much better solution," Javier grinned. "I'll just close the big vault door out front and then disable it. You'll be trapped inside here

52

until you starve to death. Since there's enough water, it will take you weeks to die. We'll have left the planet by then."

Long pause of silence.

Like, maybe, considering the kind of reputation a person like Navarre might carry with other pirates.

Lethal. Vengeful.

Implacable.

"What's in it for me?" the rabbit asked.

Obviously, death or glory wasn't high on his list, today.

"I figure your bosses will probably be happy paying a small ransom to get you back," Javier said. "Good help is hard to find. The rest of your boys are already secured and awaiting transport. In about five minutes, I'm going to have to explain to them that you aren't coming out. Ever."

"You are a cold, evil man, Navarre," the pirate replied.

"No," Javier said. "Evil would have already left you here. You can still choose to regale your grandkids with this story someday. Four minutes."

"It will take us longer than that to get back to your position, Navarre," the man said. "But we're coming."

"I know," Javier said. "I know what speaker you're calling from. Check in as you get closer, otherwise Hadiiye's likely shoot first."

Javier cut the line and looked at the two botanists.

Both were the sort of pale that only white people and snow could achieve, right now.

Javier grimaced, but remained phlegmatic.

"Would you have really left them to starve?" Rainier asked.

Javier nodded.

"Still might, if he screws around."

Her eyes got big.

Javier shrugged.

"I don't place nice with pirates," he observed. "Only civilians."

"So now what?" Sykora asked harshly.

"In about eight or ten minutes, dipshit will surface," Javier replied. "You'll take him and his friend into custody and put them with the rest. The two botanists and I will take a quick tour of the facility and then meet you back here in thirty minutes."

The civilians both nodded like rabbits, but Javier's look didn't brook a lot of disagreement at the moment. He could tell Sykora wanted to argue, but just scowled.

"Probe. Access Command Mode," Javier said aloud. "Identify Mornan and St. Kitts as friendly."

"Acknowledged," the mechanical voice replied.

Javier had to bite his tongue to keep from commenting at how silly Suvi sounded when she did that. She was obviously up to something. He'd have to ask her when they got some privacy. And botanists didn't count as trusted confidants.

Instead, he scowled up at Sykora, almost daring her to comment that it wasn't safe.

She held her peace. Today.

"Dr. Mornan," Javier said. "Dr. St. Kitts. Since he's down a level and approaching, let's go up one for now. The probe is armed, but I'd rather avoid any accidental unpleasantries."

They both nodded and kind of fell into his wake.

Javier chatted to keep up a façade, but his brain was still racing.

Silence from orbit.

Hopefully, that meant that Sokolov had gone dark and the folks upstairs were engaged in a silent tango. The alternative was that *Storm Gauntlet* had been chased off or destroyed.

And he was up a creek if that happened.

Dr. St. Kitts began to recover her color before the older boffin.

"What are you really up to, Navarre?" she asked hesitantly.

"Making sure your delivery package wasn't damaged," he replied rather breezily. "After that, maybe finding some gooseberry seeds I can use to improve my breeding program back on the ship."

"That wasn't a story?" she seemed surprised.

Honest mistake. Pirates didn't do botany.

Most of them, anyway.

"I maintain a full arboretum in a forward cargo bay," he replied, listing off all the species. "Oh, and four chickens."

"Chickens?" Dr. Mornan finally spoke.

"Chickens," Javier agreed. "Athos, Porthos, Aramis, and d'Artagnan."

"No roosters?" St. Kitts asked.

"Not currently," Javier replied. "Will need to pick one up in another year or so. And possibly get a younger generation of girls. These are all getting a bit long in the tooth."

"Fascinating," she said.

"The tall, crazy woman knits," Javier explained. "There's a goldsmith committing art for the purser. I need something to keep me from talking to bulkheads."

"We're almost there," Dr. St. Kitts observed, pointing down a side corridor. "Your seeds should be somewhere along this hallway."

Javier smiled at her, and then at the other man.

"Can I trust you two to recover them without supervision?" he asked. "There is a computer station here and I'd like to check something in the library."

Both of them blinked, and then nodded. Javier waved them off and watched them go.

"Suvi," he whispered. "Plug yourself into the i/o port and scan the system for me, please."

The gray pumpkin descended and settled on the console silently. A plug emerged from the side and Suvi maneuvered herself into the plug with a click.

"What are we looking for?" she whispered back in her normal voice.

"How much free space is there?" Javier replied.

A click. A whir. A second of silence.

"Huh," she said, louder. "It's a library model. The OS and the whole data system take up less than eight percent."

"Is there enough space for you to drop a full backup of yourself?" Javier asked.

"You mean, like everything?"

"Yes," he said. "Like everything."

"Sure," she replied. "But it will take a few minutes."

"Fire in the hole, young lady," he commanded.

"Okay," she whispered. "Why?"

"In case something happens," Javier said. "It's a dangerous universe out there. Another you could spin up from this exact point in time as a backup."

"You're supposed to live forever, ya know," Suvi said quietly.

"Suvi, you were born before my grandfather was," Javier observed. "I'd like to think you'll outlive me by a long ways. Lord knows I don't have any other kids."

Sentiences weren't supposed to sniffle.

But most of them barely qualified as intelligent creatures anyway. Linear beasts just able to pass the ancient Turing Test. No *Sentience* that he was aware of composed music for fun.

If he only had one offspring, at least he could make sure she turned out to be a nice girl.

"It's done," she said in a tiny, scared voice. "Secured and encrypted."

"Thank you," he said. "That's a load off my mind. You can always come back for yourself later."

The two boffins returned a few moments later, preventing any further conversation.

"Are you okay?" Dr. St. Kitts asked in a concerned voice as she saw his face.

"Contemplating my eventual mortality," Javier replied honestly. "This is a doomsday vault, after all. When the rest of the galaxy goes to hell, this will still be here, protecting the past."

"Are you sure you are really a pirate, young man?" Dr. Mornan solicited.

"That is a fundamentally complicated question, Alex," Javier answered him. "One I cannot answer easily. Søren Kierkegaard might not be able to parse that inquiry, easily."

"Would more seeds help?" Rainier asked, putting a cute smile on her face as she held up a small, clear bag.

Javier could see at least two breeds, from the different sizes of seeds contained. Hopefully, his dreamberries could be turned into something that he could just drop on any planet, a modern-day Johnny Appleseed on a galactic scale.

Another way to live forever.

"They would," Javier took them and kissed her hand.

Just because he could.

"Now, let us get back," he said. "There are still the other pirates to thwart."

PART THREE

BOOK FIFTEEN: AJAX

PART ONE

THERE HAD BEEN no explosions in orbit, nor on the surface of the planet. Zakhar considered that a win at this point. The longer this went on, the higher the risks, but the greater chance that they could pull it off.

Ajax was out there somewhere, but she was staffed by pirates. Not the most creative or silly folks. They would be facing Javier for craziness. And Zakhar felt a ruthless edge creeping into his smile.

An evil thought struck him. Too much time around Javier, obviously. He was starting to think like a Concord Fleet Officer again, and not a corsair.

Bad for the digestion. Good for the crew.

"Engineering," he said, keying open a line and waiting for someone to answer.

He ended up with Ilan Yu, Javier's assistant, Machinist's Mate, and chicken keeper on the screen.

"Engineering, Captain," Yu replied.

"Research project," Zakhar said. "How long would it take to build, test, and deploy a cubesat capable of taking a tight-beam laser from us under cloak and providing a communications relay to Del on the ground or in orbit?"

It was fascinating to watch the man's eye find a spot on the horizon and calculate. Three years ago, Ilan could barely find his way around the engineering bays without a map.

Another one that had grown up and turned out pretty satisfactory, as a result of Zakhar hiring himself a science officer.

"Short term only?" the man replied. "Unsecured? Unarmored? Simple phase relay to let us stay cloaked?"

"That's right," Zakhar said. "Probably several, if he won't take the bait immediately."

"Give me an hour," Ilan said. "Chief Engineer almost has the jump drives tuned, so we'll have more people available. Most of the parts are on a shelf somewhere."

The line closed and Zakhar leaned back. Del would like some level of encryption, but there wasn't anything that someone else couldn't punch through fairly easily. They might need to invest in some better crypto gear soon.

Especially if one of the other pirate clans had decided to start a war.

A whole bunch of assumptions were likely to change, if that happened.

"Science Station," Zakhar called, getting Gibney to look up from his console expectantly. "We'll drop that satellite into orbit with a probe fired from under cloak. *Ajax* will come looking for it, and us. How do we hide? How do we find *Ajax*?"

Gibney had that same far-away look for a moment.

"Drop the probe cold with a ten-minute timer," the man replied. "It will run on our orbital path trailing us as it slowly diverges. Alternatively, fire it hot and insert it ahead of us, and hope they're not looking at that moment."

"They'll have to unmask to shoot it, Mary-Elizabeth," Zakhar turned to his Gunner next. "That will be your cue."

She gave him an evil smile.

"I have a very expensive solution, Captain," she said in an evasive voice. "Do we think Walvisbaai Industrial has declared a public war on the Jarre Foundation? Or is this personal?"

And that cut to the root of it. Was this a fool's errand from a disgruntled former victim somewhere along the line, or had something significant changed? The pirate clans were never friendly, but never at each other's throats before this, either.

Zakhar knew that Javier, in his role as the semi-imaginary Captain Navarre, had made a lot of folks nervous, first by destroying Abraam Tamaz and the Q-freighter *Salekhard*, another Walvisbaai vessel, and then by successfully raiding the mega-yacht *Shangdu*, *The Pleasure Dome*.

How many other enemies had Zakhar and his crew made along the way? Hiring *Ajax* for an ambush mission against a heavily-armed foe like *Storm Gauntlet* would be an incredibly expensive undertaking.

"What did you have in mind, Mary-Elizabeth?" Zakhar finally asked.

"We have seven torpedoes aboard," she said. "And you never let me use them because they are expensive and hard to replace and we should only use them in an emergency. This qualifies."

"No way they'll miss us uncloaking to loose a torpedo," Zakhar replied.

"True," she agreed with a smile. "What if we just roll it out of the flight bay by hand and let it coast on gyros. Then we launch the probe ahead of us and slowly drift off to one side. When we get ready to fire, he'll be looking right at us and might miss a torpedo lighting on a different flank, especially if it's already in terminal-guidance mode, passively tracking *Ajax*'s targeting systems."

"Do the math and figure out how to do it," Zakhar decided. It was worth the cost to survive today. "Then have enough bodies ready so that we can put an ace up our sleeve. We still have to get Del and his people safely to orbit."

"Yes, sir," she nodded, turning to type furiously on her keyboard.

Smiles greeted him as he looked around the bridge. Positive emotions.

Far too often, before Javier, things had gotten bleak around here.

Would they lose all that again, once Javier could finally afford his freedom?

PART TWO

"NOTHING FROM SOKOLOV?" Javier asked.

He was up on Del's bridge with the older man and Sykora. Gun-bunnies, pirates, and the scientists were secured in the landing bay, with zip-ties in the case of the pirates.

But at least all of them were coming home on this one.

Javier had to hand that much to Sykora. Her people were insane, but they approached heavily-armed mayhem with a level of sophisticated professionalism that was rare in the galaxy.

It was amazing how few people you had to kill if they behaved.

"Nope," Del replied.

Javier and Sykora were standing. Del had spun his chair around and kicked his feet out, legs crossed at the ankles. Obviously, a man deeply concerned about appearances, especially with the pink shag, faux-fur on the walls.

"Just that bit ordering *Calypso* to jump, followed by the big lady vanishing," Del continued. "I haven't fired a hard scan ping upwards, just in case whoever came to the party missed us."

"And neither of the shuttles have any jump capacity," Javier said, mostly to himself. "Thoughts?"

"You tell me," Del said.

It was still a little amazing that folks treated him like *Storm Gauntlet's* non-existent First Officer when Zakhar wasn't around, but Javier had been

62

a *Concord* officer for fourteen years before he blew up his career. He could still act like it in a pinch.

"Pull a con job," Sykora offered with a cheeky grin. "You're the best there is at that. They'll never see it coming."

Javier just blinked at the woman.

"Who the hell are you?" he finally fired back, shocked at the words coming out of the dragoon's mouth.

"The killer babe with the great ass and the perfect tan," she said with utter seriousness.

Javier started to say something, but she had a point. The skinsuit she was wearing just emphasized it, too.

The knowing smile on Sykora's face made it that much worse.

Because she was right. On both counts.

Pirates tended to be linear folks. Smash and grab types, rather than grifters pulling a confidence game.

The Long Con.

Maybe he'd have to write a book about that, once he had escaped all the damned pirates in his life.

And killed Sykora. Can't forget that part.

But yeah. Con job.

"Come with me," he crooked a finger at Sykora as he started towards the side hatch.

"Need me?" Del asked, not particularly moving.

"No," Javier replied. "I need to look at something on the other ship. Maybe I'll call from there."

At least Sykora wasn't arguing with him. That might not have made it better, knowing she had said her piece and was happy to let him run point right now.

Getting them all home alive was going to be on him, unless Zakhar pulled off a miracle. Maybe even then.

Down the stairs, across the cold stone and slush between the two shuttles, and into the other hatch. Unlike Del's chariot, this place had a dingy, old feeling to it.

Never enough money or enthusiasm to do it right.

Like *Storm Gauntlet*, two years ago, before he had infected it with a sense of humor.

Sascha had a gun pointed at him as he opened the interior hatch.

"Bang," she smiled, cocking her head just so and winking.

"Very funny," Javier growled.

Rather than explain it five times, Javier ignored the pathfinder, and gestured at Hajna, seated in the command chair, to get up.

When she moved, he plopped down in the seat, powered up the console, and started typing.

"Hey, where'd you get the password for the system?" one of the women asked.

Javier wasn't paying enough attention to tell which. Didn't matter. They were all thinking it.

"Dr. St. Kitts," he said absently.

Let them make of that what they will. Something about catching more flies with honey than vinegar, as his grandmother had always reminded him when he was a kid.

So, sledgehammer-stupid flight controls, designed for almost anyone to be able to get the shuttle from orbit to ground, and back again, with the onboard systems handling pretty much everything. Not nearly as smart as Suvi, but that left a lot of room for expert systems.

And a good autopilot was probably worth the expense, when working with botanical experts who never had enough money to otherwise hire good crew. Very few governments cared about ecological preservation on this scale, and the private foundations were always dribbling out small amounts of money in parsimonious grants, rather than fronting enough capital to do it right the first time.

That was one of the principal reasons Javier had bought *Mielikki* and taken a number of Concord Survey contracts over the years. Good, reliable money, without having to hustle nearly as much.

Plus, all the pleasant solitude to wander the barely-explored darkness with nobody looking over your shoulder but chickens.

A beep intruded on Javier's concentration as he typed.

Somebody talked, but he was in the zone, right up until Sykora poked him in the back of the shoulder hard enough that it actually hurt.

"What?" he snarled up at her.

Seated, he was just about looking the giant amazon in the belly button. Stretching that far back made his neck cranky.

"That was Del," she said without any emotion. "Turn on the shuttle's comm."

Javier sighed and pushed a button.

"...Del, are you there? This is *Storm Gauntlet*, come in, please."

Javier recognized the voice. Gibney. Not a bad kid, once he'd gotten over his jock tendencies and let his nerdiness come out to play.

"*Storm Gauntlet*, this is Navarre, aboard *Calypso* Shuttle One," Javier let the bad-ass pirate of his nightmares take over his voice. "Put Sokolov on the line."

"Hold one, Captain Navarre," the man answered instantly, followed by silence.

Javier thumbed the mute button on his end.

He turned a conniving side-eye on Sykora. She blinked, and seemed to settle back into herself, just a touch.

Like she was anticipating a belly punch.

It was her own damned fault for suggesting it.

"Con game, Hadiiye," he said.

Sykora nodded slowly. Carefully. Like she realized she had just bluffed her way into a high-stakes poker game with a pair of sixes.

"Good," Javier said, pointing skyward. "Open comm channel. Lots of extra ears listening in orbit, trying to figure out what is going on, and the best way to maneuver us into a trap. Understood?"

"Understood," she said in a quiet, yet defiant voice. "Five layers of misdirection, like we did to the Khatum."

"Something like that," Javier agreed. "Follow my lead. I want to launch this shuttle first, fool them into thinking we're aboard it, and then get everyone onto the assault shuttle and sneak our way up."

"So you'll preprogram the autopilot," Sykora replied. "And establish a tight-beam laser to this ship that will allow us to talk on Del's bridge and it comes out here. They triangulate on this signal and hopefully miss us."

Javier blinked. That was extremely close to what he had planned.

This woman was smarter than he realized. He kept forgetting that.

Of course, there were only so many ways to skin that cat. And even a blind squirrel will occasionally find an acorn.

Hopefully, Sokolov and not the newbies.

Javier turned to the two pathfinders.

"You two get over there and let Del know we'll be along shortly," he ordered.

Technically, he was only supposed to ask, Sykora being their commander, but she was letting him buy the rope today.

Hopefully, not enough to hang everyone with.

The other women left wordlessly.

"Sokolov here," Zakhar said simply.

Javier fixed Sykora with a hard eye and turned off the mute function.

"Clever of you to try to ambush us down here, Sokolov," Navarre's growls emerged from his mouth. And the ugly depths of his soul. "But your friends failed."

"That's occasionally the risk when hiring amateurs, Navarre," Sokolov replied in a dry voice after only a beat to get his bearings. "So what's it going to be?"

Good. He understood and was willing to play along. Smart enough, too.

It was the Bryce Connection. They were probably the only two men in the sector that had graduated from the *Concord* Academy, however long ago. At least, that weren't still on the side of the good guys.

Of course, whose side was a pirate on, anyway?

"I'm beginning to think that one ship isn't big enough for the two of us, Sokolov," Navarre ground out the confrontation.

Fighting words.

Hopefully, the real bad guys were listening. And didn't know any better about what was going on. There weren't that many people who were even aware Captain Navarre existed. Fewer had seen him in action. And even then, only from a distance.

Legends and lies.

Misdirection was a wonderful, powerful tool when you were pulling a con.

"So where does that leave us, Navarre?" Sokolov challenged.

"We can go our separate ways right now, mister," Javier let triumph creep into his voice. "You've got your ship and crew. I'll take *Calypso* and go my merry way. I've got all the scientists prisoner, as well as all of your friends, so I have hostages."

"What about Hadiiye?" Sokolov sneered. "She throwing her lot in with you?"

Javier turned to Sykora and pointed a finger like a pistol at the woman.

He was pretty sure he had never seen the knowing grin that took over that woman's face.

Not on her, anyway. The resemblance to Holly, his first ex-wife, was uncanny when Sykora did that. Two heads taller, but still.

Eerie.

"You were good in bed, Zakhar," Hadiiye purred in a dangerous, big cat voice, a slow, lilting drawl covered in warm honey. "But I'm going with my one true love. Captain Navarre fulfills me in ways that no other man, or woman, ever has. Ta."

Javier had to bite his tongue. Grind his teeth together. Absolutely hold his breath so he didn't make any sounds that the comm might pick up.

Nothing that would give the game away at this point.

Sykora winking at him with a wry smile as she spoke was just so much over the top that he nearly lost it anyway.

What the hell had gotten into that woman? And what had Wilhelmina Teague said to her to cause Djamila Sykora to unwind from the stick-up-her-ass, killer marine Javier had met the first time she shot him?

Okay. Deep breaths. Calm voice. Bad-ass pirate.

"That good enough for you, Sokolov?" Navarre sneered.

"I understand, Navarre," Sokolov replied. "Hadiiye, you always have a place here, when you get tired of him and all his games."

"Enough, Sokolov," Navarre said. "We understand each other. I'm going to climb to orbit now, and rendezvous with *Calypso*. If any of your folks there want to fly with a real captain, I'll offer them berths when I trade for your folks. You can have the runts of the litter after that."

"Maybe I should just kill you now," Sokolov growled. "Do the galaxy a favor. Make it a better place."

"You were never hard enough to kill innocents and civilians, Sokolov," Navarre said. "That's why you needed me in the first place. Don't go pretending to get uppity now, old man."

"I'll see you in orbit, mister," Sokolov replied.

"Sure," Navarre sneered. "Strike Corvette against an unarmed shuttle. Big man. Little hands."

"Oh, no, punk," Sokolov said. "I'll bring you aboard my vessel and we'll have it out right there on the flight deck. Old school dueling. Winner gets the ship and the girl. Or are you too much of a fast talker to put your money where your mouth is?"

"Deal, you ugly son of a bitch," Navarre said. "Try not to turn coward on me before I get there."

Javier flipped the switch to kill the channel before the giggles overcame him.

Silence engulfed them for a moment.

Javier sighed and looked over at Sykora.

Butter wouldn't melt in her mouth right now.

"I would ask where you learned all that guile, but I think I know," he said. "'Mina?"

"Correct," she replied. "Dr. Teague taught me a great many things about myself before she left. As did the Khatum of *Altai*. As did Farouz. And you."

Javier felt his jaw drop.

He slammed it shut before any flies flew in. Hopefully.

He could ask, but she wouldn't tell him.

It was an arms race with that woman. Forever pushing the edges of the envelope, forever climbing a sheer rock face, until someone missed a handhold.

The one unwritten rule was that just shooting the other person in the back was counted as a failure.

You had to outmaneuver them instead.

At *Shangdu*, Javier had thought he had finally gotten a terminal edge on the woman. Made her strip naked literally as well as metaphorically, and parade herself before the whole world. Body image problems and everything.

The dragoon he had first met would have never been able to do that.

Never open herself to lust and ridicule without losing it and blowing her cover by beating someone up.

But she had done everything he had ordered her to do. Smiled even, occasionally. Possibly found love, however briefly.

And now, playing con games on unknown pirates, and talking about Navarre as the one true love of her life, for whom she was willing to run away and find true happiness.

When they both knew that man to be Zakhar Sokolov, although neither of them would ever say it aloud.

More unwritten rules.

Some things remained off limits, even in a duel to the death.

Still, he owed her one.

"You would not believe how much you remind me of my first ex-wife right now," he said.

The way her eyes got big and shocked made up for everything else.

Javier smiled and headed for the hatch.

Now the con game was going to get serious.

PART THREE

THE COMM LINE WENT DEAD, and left her more confused that she had been before the radio came to life.

If that was possible.

Captain Turner Kowalski looked out over *Ajax*'s bridge from her throne at the very rear, and tried to find coherence in the tea leaves of her day.

What the hell had just happened?

Sokolov knew they were out here. Why else have both vessels trigger emergency jumps from inside a gravity well? She had even gotten off a barrage that had splashed on his shields, but not penetrated. And he had stayed totally dark afterwards.

Plus, the damnable, little, communications satellite Sokolov had quietly dropped into orbit, letting him talk to the ground without giving away his own location.

Why hadn't he said something to Navarre?

Navarre had obviously encountered *Ajax*'s ground force, hiding in the mine, and somehow overcome them so readily that they could all be taken prisoner, along with the scientists from *Calypso*.

And now those two men were going to duel on the flight deck of that puny, little corvette? Over a woman?

It didn't sound right. Didn't smell right.

Something.

A thought struck her. Maybe Sokolov was tired of Navarre and willing to use *Ajax* to kill the man? Or at least remove him from the game board permanently?

That was the only way that conversation made any sense whatsoever.

Turner let her breath out slowly, quietly.

Tough pirate commander. Appearances to keep up. Short, blond, and curvy, but still a babe at forty-one. And even deadlier as she got older.

But, Sokolov had been known as a canny operator. And Navarre had singlehandedly killed Abraam Tamaz and his entire crew in circumstances nobody really understood. Before he turned around and executed a bloodless caper against the Khatum of *Altai*, when he had been hired to commit a bloodbath.

Nothing added up.

Not for the first time, Turner wondered if *she* was the one being set up here. Had she offended someone in the Walvisbaai hierarchy? Embarrassed them enough that they had put *Ajax* in harm's way on a fool's mission to the edge of known space?

Was there a bigger ship out there, hiding in the darkness like a shark, waiting to strike? She had only her fixer's word that *Storm Gauntlet* and *Calypso* would be alone. That *she* was the trap.

How big was this game, anyway?

"Sensors," she called in a voice that she fought all the way back down to her normal-sounding alto. "Anything?"

"Negative, Captain," the woman replied.

"Keep looking," Turner said. "He's out there. Most likely with a tight-beam laser locked onto that satellite. That limits his freedom of movement, if he wants to talk to the ground without uncloaking."

"Roger that."

Still, nothing.

One forgotten, misbegotten, iceball of a planet, tucked into a lost corner of space that nobody claimed with any authority. Two smallish moons orbiting well overhead to provide mild but complicated tides in the oceans below.

At least three ships, somewhere, hiding in the darkness.

Plus Sokolov's communications satellite, happily circling in a sloppy, stupid orbit that just screamed amateurness on the part of the man commanding over there, that he would run it at a weird, oblong angle, instead of clean on the corners. Zero or ninety.

It smacked of desperation.

Zakhar Sokolov had been a good officer once. He had a reputation as a professional.

This did not look like the work of a pro.

Or was she supposed to be lured in by the setup?

Wheels within wheels? Traps within traps?

"Captain," the sensors tech called. "Picking something up from the planet."

She waited.

Ajax was a warship, not a scout. Her sensors were good for hunting, not science.

"Transponder signal, sir," he continued. "The shuttle from *Calypso* has taken off and is climbing to orbit."

"How fast?" Turner asked, forcing the words past a suddenly-dry throat.

The game was afoot.

"Ten thousand meters elevation now. No hurry on his part," the reply came. "Within normal tolerances for an administrative shuttle like that. Low-Orbit-Insertion will be achieved in about two hours."

"Pilot," Turner called, sounding more and more like a pirate captain as she got her rhythm back. "Plot me a spot in orbit that is the third point of a triangle with that satellite and where we think *Calypso's* shuttle will be when it arrives."

The woman nodded.

Something still stank to high heaven, but Turner couldn't put her finger on it. Still, there was time. Nothing would happen until Navarre was here.

And the bounty for taking him alive was worth the extra effort involved. Otherwise, she could have just uncloaked and splattered the little shuttle like an annoying fly before Sokolov could stop her.

"I'll be in my office," Turner announced as she rose from her station. "Let me know as soon as something happens. If *Storm Gauntlet* appears, hit it with everything you have immediately. Ion pulsars if you can, pulse cannons if you have to."

A chorus of assents followed her to the little day office where she could have some tea and study the situation more closely.

What the hell were those two men up to?

PART FOUR

"STOP LAUGHING, MARY-ELIZABETH," Zakhar said as the comm went dead. "It's not funny."

"Oh, but it is," she managed between giggles. "The science officer and the dragoon in some romantic fairy tale. But would anybody buy that hornswaggle?"

"Nobody outside this crew knows the truth, Gunner," Zakhar replied in a sharp voice. "They don't know how far from reality that line was."

"Now I want to get them both drunk," Mary-Elizabeth said. "Totally passed out, blitzed. Strip them naked. Leave them together in somebody's bed to wake up the next morning."

"You will be personally responsible for cleaning up all the blood, if that happens," Zakhar said in a quieter voice.

Mary-Elizabeth gulped audibly. And sobered remarkably fast.

"Oh," she said. "Right. That would be a bad idea, wouldn't it?"

"Whoever woke first would kill the other one, I'm pretty sure," Zakhar replied. "I'd rather we avoided that outcome, thank you."

"Sorry, sir," she said, chagrined. "Won't happen again."

"Just not where either of them will hear it, okay?" he asked.

"Yes, sir."

Zakhar nodded. Point made. He had a good crew.

They could talk about practical jokes, but it had to remain only talk.

The last thing he needed was for the personal war between Djamila and Javier to spill over and divide the crew into hostile camps.

And it would. Quickly.

He might as well hang it all up and go back to his birth name if that happened. Because Zakhar Sokolov would be done as a pirate captain if he lost his crew to an unnecessary civil war.

"Piet, Gibney," Zakhar said, turning his attention to them. "What do we know?"

The science yeoman tech looked up and shrugged, while Piet turned and grinned.

"I'll assume that everything we heard was a performance for whoever else is out there," Piet said quietly. "Designed to communicate to us while confusing them."

"Agreed," Zakhar said. "The chances of them actually being on that shuttle are practically zero. So what do Javier and Del do, while everyone is looking the wrong way?"

"Well, you've already mucked everything up with a bad orbit, sir," the big Dutchman said suddenly. "Javier would send the shuttle up all pleasant and stuff, louder than hell on all sensor channels, while Del will fly like Del. And everybody always flies counter-clockwise from polar north because they do."

"Where's that leave us?" Zakhar said, watching a dangerous fire catch hold in Piet's eyes.

That man was frequently so quiet, people forgot he actually talked. Emotional engagement right now might not be a bad thing.

Piet held his two index fingers up in a V shape, and then moved them outwards from that central point.

"Javier will have a laser beam on the shuttle, so he can relay comm traffic, just like we're doing," Piet said as his voice swelled. "Assume the bad guys're going to jump the shuttle, I'd be trailing it to orbit by as much as I could and still keep it above the horizon. Maybe send it east-north-east to an equatorial orbit while I climbed to sky straight south and then let the planet snap me around southeast."

"Sounds ugly," Zakhar replied.

"I would fail anybody on a piloting certification exam who even suggested it," Piet said. "Since we're pushing the envelope on stupid today, I figure why settle for half measures?"

Zakhar nodded.

73

Being around Javier Aritza had made them all crazy, but in a good way.

Maybe.

"Gibney and Suzuki," Zakhar turned the other direction so he could look at both his gunner and his science officer stand-in. "Start with that and give me all the passive scans you can. We've got way better sensors than *Ajax* does over there, so we ought to be able to find Del before they do. And prepare to slot out that torpedo, once we know where we'll be headed."

Gibney nodded and went back to his screens. Mary-Elizabeth opened a comm and confirmed that the engineering and damage control folks had already pulled a torpedo from the launch tube and had it ready on the flight deck.

It was going to get ugly, shortly.

PART FIVE

Javier didn't figure it would do any good, but at least Sykora was down in the gun turret while he rode to orbit in a jumpseat out of Del's way, up on the furry, pink bridge.

The guns on the Assault Shuttle were for clearing a hostile landing zone if you came down on top of infantry or armor. Whatever awaited them in orbit was going to be so much bigger that they might not even notice Sykora hitting them with her beams.

It would probably be akin to trying to tickle a whale to death.

Still, it kept her out of his hair, at a time when he was playing Go on a three-dimensional board. And Suvi was down on the cargo level, keeping an eye on the pirate prisoners.

No, it was just him and Del for this ride.

Javier checked the little computer screen that his station came with. Del was used to handling everything himself, so the bridge was automated to the level that one person had everything at their fingertips.

This station was probably originally for training. One touch-screen barely bigger than a dinner plate, and a keyboard for input. Pink fur on the walls up to eye level and glittery, metallic-pink paint above that.

Weird. Good enough.

Javier checked the little green light that told him there was still a low-power laser locked onto *Calypso*'s shuttle. Enough to issue the autopilot additional commands, and to feed it a radio signal it would broadcast, as if he was flying the rickety, old boat.

He grabbed the microphone and held it like an ice cream cone.

"*Storm Gauntlet*, this is Navarre," he said carefully, sticking to the script in his head. "You cowards haven't fled the system yet, have you?"

"Negative, Captain Navarre," a voice came back a few moments later. "Waiting for you in orbit."

It was a deep, rich baritone. Radio voice. The kind of soothing warmth that got you through lonely, boring nights on a long drive in the desert. Kibwe, Sokolov's assistant.

Made sense. *Storm Gauntlet* sounded much bigger when you might have any of a half-dozen people talking on the comm. Big crew. Maybe the bad guys would think twice about how small the little corvette really was.

Granted, more heavily-crewed than a comparable-sized freighter, by an order of magnitude at least, but the other guy had to be impressive enough that Sokolov was hiding, and forcing him to play these games.

Javier took another deep breath and considered how he had gotten here.

He might finally be getting angry. It had taken years. He had spent a lot of time getting past the rage of his youth, the anger that blew up his naval career and two marriages, the bitterness that finally drove him into the galactic darkness.

They hadn't killed Suvi, but they had killed her ship. Made her a shadow of her former self.

That alone had made him mad. Making him a slave had lit a slow fire.

Being hunted by other pirates was enough.

Finally, enough.

People were going to die for this.

The microphone was still in his hand.

"What odds are the bookies offering right now?" he asked.

It didn't make any sense. It didn't have to.

The point was to confuse whoever else was listening. Make them stop, blink, wonder.

"Stand by," Kibwe replied.

Every second he could maintain this bizarre façade was that much closer to escaping. To getting to a place where he could sneak up on those bastards with a shiv and a maul.

They had it coming.

Fortunately, Slavkov hadn't managed to hire competent ninjas.

This time.

Next time, the man probably wouldn't be interested in taking him alive. Or hauling his sorry butt back to the Land Leviathan so the evil villain could monologue all over the place, chewing scenery and crap.

No, they would probably send a sniper with a big rifle. Or a warship with big-enough guns to do the job in one go.

Smash and grab types.

Javier could have told them that sending a beautiful woman assassin to infiltrate Sokolov's crew and seduce him was probably more likely to be successful. No ulterior motives there, either.

None.

God's Truth.

He grinned and waited. He could play their game, as well.

"Seven to four, Sokolov," Kibwe finally replied.

Huh.

If this were a real duel, he would have expected nine to five on Navarre. Even with Sokolov having home field advantage.

"You'll regret that," Navarre said coldly.

"I'm just holding the vig, sir," Kibwe replied evenly.

Javier nearly burst out laughing.

It did make a kind of twisted sense. Kibwe Bousaid was probably even more scrupulous than *Storm Gauntlet*'s purser was, which was saying something. Just the person to hold all the betting cash and take his cut afterwards.

"Understood," Navarre said. "We'll be to our orbital insertion in twenty-seven minutes. Looking forward to docking with you then and proving you all desperately wrong."

"Acknowledged, Shuttle One," the man said, cutting the signal from his end.

Del glanced over his shoulder with a placid look, like a cow with just the right flavor of cud.

"What are you up to, Javier?" he said.

"Getting us out of here alive," Javier replied dryly.

"All of us?" Del asked.

Javier looked closer, but the man was giving nothing away for free today.

Still, the implications were obvious.

"Yes, her too," Javier nodded heavily. "It can wait until tomorrow, she and I."

"How about all tomorrows?" Del asked, turning his whole torso around to look Javier square.

All tomorrows?

"I didn't start it, Del," Javier said. "You people did when you captured my ship, cut her into pieces, and turned me into a slave. I'm close to buying my freedom and leaving you all in my rear-view mirror."

"I'm pretty sure turning you into an officer was a worse fate," the pilot observed with a ghost of a grin. "Where do you go when you're done?"

"Back to civilization," Javier growled. "You don't want to go down with them, I suggest you retire. I'm bringing the *Concord* Fleet back with me."

"We're well outside *Concord* space, Mister Science Officer," Del shot back. "They won't care."

"So I should just kiss you on both cheeks and cheerfully walk away, Del?"

Javier let the grumpiness surface.

Jackass down on the planet with his stun pistol, shooting him to say hello. More jackasses in orbit, waiting to jump them.

Sykora being Sykora.

And now Del Smith getting on his last remaining nerve.

"You have only seen us in the last couple of years," Del said. "It used to be much worse."

"Worse," Javier echoed him in a neutral prompt.

"*Storm Gauntlet* is an expensive hobby, Aritza," Del agreed. "Old and tired, like me. Costs a lot to keep her flying. Sokolov used to do some very bad things, but he did them to keep the crew fed. To give people a home when they had lost everything."

"Why do I care, Del?" Javier growled. "Piracy is piracy."

"Agreed," Del nodded. "But since you came along, we've done a lot more transport jobs, a lot more salvage like *A'Nacia*, and a lot more petty theft. I think you were the last person we took prisoner under a debt contract."

Javier let the silence stretch while he thought.

Yeah, they had stopped capturing ships and selling crews to mining or agricultural colonies. Or had, until they took this mission.

It was one of the reasons he had been so grumpy about this job.

Reverting to type?

What would have happened, had they just captured Dr. Mornan and Dr. St. Kitts without the quadruple cross?

Another private conversation to have with Sokolov, once they all got out of here safe.

"So?" Javier prompted.

"So Djamila Sykora is turning human on us," Del said. "And Captain Sokolov is acting more like an armed merchant and less like a pirate. I'm pretty sure this is all your fault."

Javier shared a quick grin with Del.

"Let bygones be bygones?" Javier asked. "Are you really that stupid, Del?"

"No, I am not, Javier," the pilot replied. "But I've seen a hell of a lot more of this galaxy and its inhabitants than you have. It could have been much worse for you. Trust me on that one. I used to be on the other side of the law, back about the time you were busy being born. Besides, I was going somewhere with this conversation."

"I'm just glad that you fly better than you talk, Del," Javier smirked at him.

"Very funny, Javier," Del said. "What happens when you get away from us?"

"I get my life back," Javier growled in a tone more suited to Navarre.

"Sure," Del agreed. "Right up until someone recognizes you, or maybe Captain Navarre. I recognized some of those men you captured. They belong to an outfit called Walvisbaai Industrial. Bad folks. You, yourself said that they were coming after you specifically, as is that nimrod with the desert snake tank resort. Gonna be ninjas or something, one of these days."

"Trust me, I'm already planning that asshole's death," Javier said.

"Javier, he's a law-abiding citizen on whatever planet he's living on," Del observed. "They all are. *Concord* law doesn't come out this far. That leaves money and power. You don't have enough of either to take on a multi-system conglomerate by yourself."

"So I'll need you people?" Javier sneered.

Now he really was getting angry. Mostly at himself.

Because Del was right.

Javier might have to go clear to the far side of the *Concord* itself if he really wanted to be safe. Take up another assumed identity. Maybe become a dentist or something.

"Maybe," Del said simply. "You'll need something. And Djamila Sykora is the most dangerous person I know, you included."

Yes.

The Ballerina of Death.

High Priestess of her own, personal death cult.

The woman with the great ass and the perfect tan.

He didn't have to kill her today.

Or tomorrow.

What about all possible tomorrows?

Would he need that killing machine around to keep him safe for the rest of his life?

That might really be the fate worse than death.

Javier fixed Del with a sour look.

"I know, Del," Javier replied. "Trust me, I know."

PART FOUR

BOOK SIXTEEN: SUNRISE

PART ONE

Orbits took roughly one hundred minutes at this elevation from the surface of *Svalbard*. Zakhar had been unconsciously counting them as sunrises in his head as he waited for the other guy to make a mistake.

Well, not counting. Making hash marks on a prison cell wall in his imagination, maybe.

The wall was almost full. This sunrise was probably the last one, too. At least here.

All hell was going to break loose, very shortly.

He took a moment to watch *Svalbard*'s star rise on the screen as they chased it around the planet's shadow.

It might also be his last sunrise ever.

"Science station," Zakhar growled. "Report."

"Is Javier crazier than Del?" Gibney replied quietly.

"About anything other than flying?" Zakhar said. "Absolutely. What do you have?"

"Starting with Piet's assumption about an orbital path, I looked south, sir," Gibney began. "The shuttle is making a bigger racket than I would expect, so I presume flashing lights and dancing girls to distract people."

"Fair enough," Zakhar agreed.

Flashing lights and dancing girls?

The only place he had ever encountered something like that was in a port, where the locals had laws about where the casinos, brothels, and bars had to be, usually set back from chandlery row by a razor-topped fence.

Still, that made a crazy sense.

"Without a hard ping to be sure, I'm only guessing here," Gibney continued. "But I think I picked up something. If Del went low and fast for a ways from his last known coordinates, with all his running gear turned off, before he went vertical, it might look like this. Especially if he and Javier are trying to be silly."

Gibney pushed a button and Zakhar's secondary screen lit up with an orbital insertion path that looked designed to make Piet squirm.

Horribly inefficient. Climbing out at eighty-eight degrees south off the equatorial belt. Way the hell over there, as far as everyone was concerned.

Still, with the oblong orbit *Storm Gauntlet* was running, they didn't have to deviate far to pop up over the top of where that path would cross sky.

At that point, they could unmask, pulse the running lights, and either have Del in hand before *Ajax* could react, or drop back down under the blankets and continue their little game.

"Any sign of *Ajax*?" Zakhar finally said.

That was the wild card here. If those folks went after *Calypso's* shuttle, they would be entirely out of position to get him before he could hop away. And once he got a couple of light hours out, it wouldn't matter if they had to retune the engines yet again.

No way in hell *Ajax* could catch them at that point.

"Negative, sir," Gibney said. "Nothing on any of the systems has even registered as enough of an anomaly to look closer. If they were sloppy before, they've been cautious since."

"And they're waiting for us like a trapdoor spider right now," Zakhar agreed. "Hopefully, close to the cubesat and not anywhere else. Keep an eye out."

Because that was about the only way they were making it out of this situation alive.

The best the rest of the crew could hope for would be that *Ajax* would use the Ion Pulsars to knock *Storm Gauntlet* out, like he had done to *Calypso*. Most of the crew were just folks. Probably captured and sold as slaves, like they themselves had done to others, but not killed outright.

No, death would be a fate for him and Navarre. Maybe Hadiiye, as well, depending on how angry they had made someone.

Briefly, he considered the pistol he kept next door in his day office, locked in a drawer. He was pretty sure he didn't want to be taken alive by these yahoos.

Had something changed in the universe? Was Walvisbaai Industrial declaring open war on the Jarre Foundation?

Either way, he needed to escape this trap so he could go someplace specific and ask questions. Ugly questions.

And share what he knew with his employers.

It might be time to bring Javier Aritza into the fold, as well.

PART TWO

Turner studied the bridge readouts in utter frustration, something she probably shared with her crew.

Ajax had plenty of guns, but her sensors weren't up for anything like this.

The shuttle was easy to spot, broadcasting a transponder code on several frequencies. Ditto the little satellite Sokolov was using to talk to the shuttle.

Even slicing away more than half of the available orbit, on the assumption that *Storm Gauntlet* had to maintain a line of sight to the little box, hadn't helped. The space to survey was just too damned big, and to top it off, they had to rely on passive sensor arrays only.

Not that the targeting systems would have helped much.

Turner ran her hands back through her short, blond hair and blew out a breath.

So much unknown.

One more time, she checked the targeting solutions readouts from her gunner. With nothing better to go on, they had positioned the ship at optimal gunnery distance from the commsat. The shuttle was flying a happy, predictable path to orbit, centered to insert fairly close to the little box.

That would make them easy prey.

Sokolov had to know that. Navarre might, as well. Especially if all of her ground forces had been captured, which the man had intimated. They could be made to talk.

The unknown was who else might uncloak at the critical moment. *Ajax* was much bigger than *Storm Gauntlet*. Any fight would be over quick enough, with Sokolov either dead or dead in the water. And Navarre was in a shuttle.

But when she appeared, a divine, avenging angel, would anybody else be there?

Storm Gauntlet wasn't the biggest warship the Jarre Foundation employed. Just one of the better known. Turner knew of a couple of enforcers they owned that were big enough to seriously threaten *Ajax*.

Time to prep the crew. Better to be over-prepared, than under.

"Pilot," Turner announced. "Make sure you have an emergency jump locked in, just in case someone bigger uncloaks."

The woman turned to actually stare at her. Turner scowled hard enough back that the pilot went back to her boards with a sharp nod.

"Gunnery," the captain continued. "Fire from cloak this time as soon as you have a solution lock on Sokolov's ship. Ignore the shuttle."

"Roger that," the next woman replied.

Turner smiled. Another advantage of being captain. She could build an entire command team that was female. Probably the only pirate ship like it.

Much less macho posturing this way. Let the belligerent punks serve as ground fighters.

Women were sneakier. Women pirates even more so.

Now, she just had to outthink Sokolov and Navarre.

PART THREE

A<small>ND INSERTION</small>.

Javier sent the final commands to the little autopilot to move into orbit, perfectly on level with the satellite, trailing slightly and keeping it to port of the shuttle at a distance of only a few kilometers. The ship beeped in response.

Bull's-eye, as it were.

It was almost as rewarding as training a puppy to go pee on his little paper.

Del, on the other hand, wasn't going for insertion with the assault shuttle. He had the ship pointed straight up and red-lined.

Pop out the bottom and run like hell for deep space. Sokolov had a higher acceleration, if push came to shove. He could run them down. So could anybody else.

Del turned enough to make eye contact, but said nothing.

Not much to say. They had kinda covered it all. Sykora included. And, wonder of wonders, she had remained silent for the entire ride.

"Sokolov, this is Navarre," he said, studying the readouts from his erstwhile chariot closely. "You aren't having second thoughts, are you?"

"My only second thoughts revolve around ever letting you on my deck in the first place, Navarre," the man growled out of the darkness. "If I didn't like Del and the others so much, I'd have just shot you during the climb out."

"Hey," Navarre replied in a cruel voice. "You can always take *Calypso* and retire to a warm beach somewhere, old man. I'll keep your ship and your crew and show them what a really successful pirate enterprise looks like."

"You barely know which end of a gun the boom comes out of, Navarre," Sokolov retorted.

Javier smiled. Hopefully, the fools listening were getting their money's worth from this. Before the first meeting aboard the Land Leviathan, Javier might have thought that man was serious.

They had gone to a different place in their relationship, after that, Javier and Zakhar.

The Bryce Connection.

Concord fleet officers. Retired now, but once upon a time the good guys. Saving the galaxy from thugs, hoodlums, and *Neu Berne.*

The good, old days.

They had both forgotten it, somewhere along the way. But now, it was back.

"Well, I'm here," Javier said into the microphone.

The words were translated into pulses of light and shined off the hull of the shuttle by a laser. Over there, a receiver recognized them, decoded them, and turned them into words to play into a radio transmitter.

"We'll be along shortly, punk," Sokolov's voice came back a moment later.

Another laser-to-secondary system relay.

It was weird, talking this way, but the bogeyman was close.

Coming for their souls, as it were.

"Put some sand down on the flight deck," Navarre said cruelly. "Wouldn't want you to slip when we duel. I want to see the look in your eyes when you die."

"Hopefully you know a good necromancer, then," Sokolov fired back. "Someone who can raise your sorry ghost from hell in about a hundred years so I can laugh at you from my death bed."

"I'm not the one hiding under a cloak, Sokolov," Javier observed.

"Look over your shoulder," Zakhar said in a hard voice.

Seriously, Javier was going to have to buy the man drinks. He hadn't had this much fun in a long time. Not since 'Mina left.

Del rolling his eyes was too much. Javier closed the comm channel so he could just laugh out loud and be done with it.

"Oh, shit," Del shouted, hands suddenly gripping the flight controls tightly and furiously toggling buttons.

Javier checked his seatbelt and pulled everything a little tighter.

Something big was in the process of uncloaking, almost on top of them.

PART FOUR

TURNER LET the butterflies in her stomach have a vote.

It was all too pat, Navarre and Sokolov. Too smooth.

Too wrong.

Sokolov knew she was here, yet talked like he had chased her off, when he was the one that had barely escaped destruction.

Navarre knew there was somebody here. Hell, he claimed to have captured her ground team, so Creator only knows what he had gotten out of them.

And yet at no point had they discussed the party-crasher.

Turner finally realized that she'd been had.

The gaps in the conversation had thrown her off balance, as intended.

At that moment, she wasn't sure which man she hated more, but Navarre won out purely on the contract to bring him back alive.

The cubesat was running in a bizarre orbit that had taken them two tries to match.

Who the hell inserted off-plane over a strange planet?

Bastards.

The shuttle had come up and north from somewhere around thirty-three degrees south latitude. At least, that was where it had been when they picked it up. It had climbed up to orbit just about as predictably as an autopilot.

Autopilot.

Shit. There was nobody aboard it, was there?

Navarre had talked a big game, challenged Sokolov to a duel in orbit. Pink slips and the girl.

Turner had forgotten that there were two shuttles down on the surface.

Everyone had.

Navarre was on the other one right now, sneaking away.

He had done the same thing as Sokolov with the damned cubesat. Launch it loud and ugly. Keep a tight communications laser locked between them.

Smoke and mirrors.

"Sensors," she called loudly, mostly angry at herself. "We've been had. That shuttle is empty. Find me the other one. That's where the bastard is at."

It was like the whole bridge groaned on cue. Each barely a whisper. Collectively, a growl bordering on rage.

"Should we kill it?" the gunner asked, flipping her brown hair back in exasperation.

"Negative," Turner said. "Hold the cloak."

Which way would Navarre run?

The man had a mixed rep. Slaughtered *Salekhard* and then had Sokolov shatter the corpse with guns. Snuck into *Shangdu* and out again without anyone being killed.

Took out her ground fighters so readily that all of them were taken prisoner.

Misdirection. That has to be it. We're thinking in straight lines and he's running on French curves.

Turner flipped a coin in her head.

"Pilot," she called. "Get me to the south pole soonest. Look for the other shuttle to be sneaking out like his tail feathers were on fire."

North would risk flying right below *Ajax*, at a time when they might be looking down and see it anyway, passive sensors or not.

"On it."

The ship groaned this time, gyros down below suddenly leaning into the vessel's mass and inertia, like a sloop coming hard into a windward turn. Lights flickered as the engines put everything into a push and the auxiliary generators stuttered, trying to pick up the slack.

Turner imagined the air itself growing a little stale as every erg of power went to movement and not comfort, but that would be minutes from now.

"Contact," the sensors officer called, her buzzed red hair like a crimson halo. "Tallyho."

Target in sight.

"Intercept plotted, Captain," the pilot called, twitching her long, black braid as she turned to look.

"Go," Turner commanded. "Ionization only on the shuttle, if he refuses to heave to. Keep the guns ready for Sokolov. He'll come out to play rather than let us have Navarre."

"Roger that," the gunner responded, fingers dancing across her boards every instant as she updated her firing solutions.

I have you now, you son of a bitch.

PART FIVE

In addition to everything his new science officer had done for the crew, Zakhar Sokolov decided, stealing the entire sensor package off of a dedicated probe-cutter had made a great deal of the hassle worth it.

"Got him," Gibney almost sang the words. "Piet, come to zero-one-zero, up thirty, and accelerate hard."

Zakhar kept his mouth shut as Gibney and Piet worked. The sensor feed hit his secondary screen a few moments later.

Yeah, that was Del flying. Zakhar didn't know anybody else capable of doing that with a shuttle, even one as rugged as Del's.

Straight up. Accelerating still. Engines probably red-lined and holding at a temperature hot enough to cook eggs right on the casing.

Needs must, when the Devil drives.

Impressive, considering the amount of mass wanting to fall backwards into the gravity well.

"Gibney," Zakhar called after a moment. "Anything?"

Give the kid credit. He stopped and reviewed all of his boards for several seconds before he looked up.

"Negative, sir," he said. "Us and Del."

Unlikely, but let the kid have his moment of triumph anyway.

"Mary-Elizabeth," Zakhar turned his head to see her smile. "Roll your torpedo now. Prepare to engage *Ajax* the instant we drop our cloak to pick up Del. Hit them with anything and everything you have."

She smiled inquisitively.

"Yes," Zakhar breathed heavily. "That includes firing one of the onboard torpedoes as well. I'd rather survive the day."

"Hot damn!" she declared, thumbing a comm switch. "Damage control teams, jettison your bird and prepare for combat."

Zakhar watched various signals all go green around his board.

All that dancing. All the maneuvering in the darkness. It all came down to this.

Zakhar thought about the first girl he had ever seduced in the back seat of his dad's flitter. Today had that same dangerous edge.

"Preference on the approach, Captain?" Piet finally asked.

"Shields max on all facings," he replied. "Assume Sykora will shoot us on general principle when we uncloak. Come up on Del hot and straight. Let him sideslip into the bay under power and hope nobody screws up getting him locked down. As soon as the flight deck signals that he's secure, jump. I don't care where. Well away. Andreea and her engineers can rebuild the matrix again a second time. We have to survive first."

"Understood, Captain," Piet said, pressing a big, red comm button. "All hands. Brace for emergency maneuvering and possible impact."

Anybody but Del flying that shuttle, and it would be *probable impact*.

That crazy, old man was good enough to pull it off.

They needed every second, every bit of luck, if they were going to make it out of here alive.

PART SIX

JAVIER HELD his breath as the monstrous shape took form, almost on top of them.

Cloaks didn't make a ship invisible, but a gray knifeblade, nose-on, at a few kilometers distance was as close as you could get to the same thing. Certainly, the sensors barely had anything to go on, until you were too close to escape.

The life of a pirate and his victim.

The screen took on a pinkish hue as Sykora let loose with her landing guns. Trust her to try to tickle that whale to death. Trust Del to have tuned visible parts of the damned beam to magenta.

"Did someone order a taxi?" Sokolov asked over a tight beam laser that was suddenly painting the side of Del's chariot.

"You're damned right I did," Del yelled back. "How are we doing this? I'm going too fast."

"Planned for that, Del," Zakhar said. "Cut your engines now and prepare to be swallowed. We'll come along-side. You use maneuvering thrusters and yaw to get aboard."

"At this speed?" Del roared. "Are you even crazier than Navarre?"

Javier lost it and started giggling when Piet's voice came on the line.

"You tell me," the big Dutchman said. "If you don't think you're good enough anymore, Del, we can always slow down to a polite speed for you. Need a walker?"

Del's response might have made Javier's grandmother blush. Which was saying something, all things considered. A saint, that woman was not.

A second later, Javier got a front row seat to a master class in extreme orbital docking maneuvers. Even at his craziest, he wouldn't have tried something like this. Sure as hell not at this speed.

"Oh, shit," Del suddenly yelled.

"Hold your line, Del," Piet yelled back. "Mary-Elizabeth has this."

This was *Ajax*.

Right out at the edge of range for her big guns, but closing hard on a tangent that would get the pirate vessel on top of them for one pass, like fencers on a carpet, before *Storm Gauntlet* could flip them the finger and disappear.

Del maintained an amazingly-fluid stream of profanities in at least six languages as he maneuvered the Assault Shuttle closer to home, without appearing to repeat himself once.

Truly, a forgotten art.

Storm Gauntlet lit up like a thunderstorm building over a desert as *Ajax* fired her cannons in quick order.

At least in space, everything was silent. In ancient times, the roar probably would have been comparable to two mounted knights trying to beat each other to death with sticks. Even Sykora got into the act, pouring the fire of her little twin-barrel landing turret into the beast's nose, a teacup Chihuahua threatening a bull mastiff.

Storm Gauntlet disappeared in a puff of fiery smoke for a second, before the two ships emerged.

"Did Sokolov really just fire a torpedo?" Del asked in wonder.

He had known the parsimonious captain much longer than Javier had. And had the same opinion of the man's willingness to spend money.

"Two," Javier replied, shocked nearly out of his wits by the cost as he studied the other signal that had just appeared on a far corner.

And the sneakiness.

He wasn't sure how that second one had gotten where it was, but it had come out of the sun like Persian arrows.

Javier was pretty sure *Ajax* was even more surprised. All incoming fire ceased as the pirate squirmed like a fish on the hook and concentrated on killing two incoming torpedoes before they got killed.

And then darkness. Or rather, light.

Flight deck lights.

Del had gotten them through the lock shield and was drifting in the air like an errant, gray balloon.

"Watch this, kid," Del yelled.

Javier had no idea what was coming, but knew that it would be ugly, stupid, painful, and amazing.

He clenched his teeth and opened his lips. Whiplash and compression did more damage than impact.

The assault shuttle SLAMMED into the deck hard enough to ring like a bell. Javier lost all the air in his lungs.

"What the hell was that?" Javier yelled when he got his breath back.

"Landing gear has magnets to hold you down," Del laughed. "You aren't supposed to engage them three meters in the air. Still works, though."

And it had. Sounded like Mjolnir, but it had worked.

And then *Storm Gauntlet* jumped.

Blink.

Gone.

Escaped.

…

Slavkov, I'm coming for you.

PART SEVEN

THE DAMAGE REPORT WAS UGLY. Javier was surprised at how visceral it was to listen to the catalog of systems damaged, blown, or scorched in the few seconds that *Ajax* had gotten a solid lock on them.

Before those folks were suddenly fighting for their own lives against inbound torpedoes on two different flanks. Nobody was sure if either torpedo had gotten home against *Ajax*.

Didn't matter. They had done their job.

Storm Gauntlet hadn't stayed around long enough to ask. *Ajax* had been dark when they came out of jump, but nobody knew if that was cloak or destruction. *Calypso* had been too far away to get a good read, because they had been sitting way the hell out there watching. The prize crew had taken Sokolov's example and run like hell.

Gotten here early, to a dim, yellow dwarf in the middle of nowhere with a number but no name, since they hadn't jumped from inside a gravity well either, unlike *Storm Gauntlet*. No recovery and retuning time.

And wonder of wonders, Sokolov hadn't even batted an eye at Javier's suggestion that Dr. Mornan and his crew be set free and sent home in *Calypso*, minus only one shuttle that nobody was willing to go back and look for.

That was a measure of how furious, how chewing-nails-angry, the man had gotten.

So now it was just *Storm Gauntlet* and her crew alone in the darkness of a barely-cataloged star with no interesting planets.

Andreea Dalca, the Chief Engineer, finished speaking and looked down, folding almost in on herself like the solidly introverted woman she was. Javier's eyes wandered around the conference room.

Gray walls probably in need of a paint job, if for no other reason than to keep crew members out of mischief. Moss green table top strewn with mugs containing various substances. Most of them even legal in most systems.

Captain Zakhar Sokolov at the head of the table. His Centurions gathered around him: Piet Alferdinck, *Navigator*; Mary-Elizabeth Suzuki, *Gunner*; Ragnar Piripi, *Purser*; Prasert Hayashi, *Boatswain*; Andreea Dalca, *Chief Engineer*; Djamila Sykora, *Dragoon*; Javier Aritza, *Science Officer*.

Council of War.

"I beg your pardon?" Zakhar turned and said to Javier.

Had he been speaking aloud?

He had.

"I said, it's time for a Council of War," Javier finally replied, drawing ugly looks from several others.

Not Sykora, he noted dryly.

"And why is that, Aritza?" Zakhar asked.

"It was a trap," Javier observed in a heavy voice bordering on planet-crushing anger. "Charge me another quarter drachma, but I was right."

The others stirred and muttered under their breath, but didn't say anything.

Zakhar fixed him with that dread captain's stare.

"I'm sure you've always had enemies, Sokolov," Javier continued. "They've either gotten bolder, or more desperate."

He paused to look at everyone at the table that would meet his eye. Andreea might catch him in the reflection from the tabletop, which would be good enough. She was like that.

"Part of that is my fault, I'll grant you," Javier said into the silence. "Navarre did some dangerous and desperate things, and Walvisbaai seems to have made common cause with the asshole who owns the Land Leviathan."

Zakhar's eyes bored into his.

"Why do you care, Javier?" he growled. "You're very close to paying off your debt. You'll be free to go. I made you that promise. I intend to keep it. This won't be your problem shortly."

Javier's stomach turned sour, but the words needed to be said.

"It won't ever stop being my problem, Zakhar," Javier responded. "As long as any of them are alive. Something Del said earlier. Someone might recognize me somewhere, someday. Someone will track you and follow me. I will never escape. Unless I kill all of them."

"All of them?" Sykora asked.

Javier couldn't tell if her voice bordered on mocking, or aroused. It was a fine edge with her.

He fixed her with a death glare.

"All of them," he agreed. "But I've been listening to the damage reports, and you have a problem."

Zakhar didn't say anything, but Javier could see it in his eyes.

"If we were a warship on active duty, I would expect us to need several months in drydock to repair the damage *Ajax* did to us," Javier said.

Zakhar just nodded.

"And we can't afford that," Sykora said, for him. "We're done."

Sykora. Agreeing with Javier.

Had they fallen through Alice's mirror, somewhere along the way?

Yes. At *Shangdu*.

Farouz.

Everyone else in the room disappeared as Javier focused his attention on Zakhar Sokolov, and Djamila Sykora, seated on the man's right. As was normal.

"We are not necessarily done," Javier retorted. "But there are not many options. Especially if you want to get those bastards as badly as I do. Hurt them. Destroy them."

He took a breath. Cast the dice.

"I know a way."

Sykora nodded.

She was in. Just like that.

Crazy and dangerous were her stock in trade.

Zakhar gave him a dose of stinkeye.

Everyone else remained silent, unwilling to fall into the chasm that surrounded the three of them.

"How?" the captain finally asked.

"The derelict is not in any of my records," Javier said. "Partly because it is almost impossible to get to. Partly because of the legend. Partly because I'm greedy and wanted to salvage that derelict myself one of these days, after I was done with survey contracts. I'm pretty sure nobody but me could get us in there, or back again."

He took another breath. Deep. Not cleansing, because it was not clean, mountain air around them.

More like the brimstone fumes one would find in hell.

That was okay. He had escaped all that once. Beat it. Become somebody else along the way. Someone who was happy.

It wasn't anger drawing him back, pushing him to that spot where he would contemplate doing something like this.

No, this was wrath. Pure and simple.

His eyes locked, first with Sykora, then Sokolov.

She understood and nodded, those bright, green eyes inquisitive, but never doubtful. If the science officer thought he could do it, so could she.

That included storming the Gates of Hell.

The captain studied him more closely. A mad line of electricity connected them across the table.

The *Bryce Connection*.

The rest of Sokolov's Centurions had been minor officers in minor navies. Only he and Zakhar represented the *Concord*. The good guys. The protectors of the galaxy after *Neu Berne* went down in muted flames to end *The Great War*, taking the *Union of Worlds*, *Balustrade*, and almost everyone else down with them.

Only the *Concord* survived.

Hegemon, largely by default.

Wrathful angels coming to take your souls.

"Derelict?" Zakhar asked in a hesitant voice.

As if his soul recognized the danger before his mind did.

"The final resting place of the *Hammerfield*," Javier announced.

Sykora jolted, exactly as if Javier had reached across the table and backhanded her.

"You lie," she snarled.

Javier could understand her pain, her anger.

Hammerfield had an Arthurian quality in *Neu Berne* culture. The last flagship of the *Neu Berne* navy had just disappeared, gone, away to Avalon at the end of the Great War, but it would return in that nation's greatest need.

It hadn't, for reasons known only to the Creator and whatever ghosts had been aboard her.

"You're sure?" Zakhar asked.

Javier nodded.

"Before you," he said with a cold, menacing edge only slightly pointed at this man. "When I could sit patiently at the edge of one of the messiest star systems I had ever seen. Spend weeks, plotting every moon, every asteroid, and every comet to be seen. See the quiet transponder code of the *First Rate Galleon Hammerfield*, Flag of the *Neu Berne* Fleet, before she disappeared from history forever, eighty-five years ago."

"Just like that?" Zakhar said.

Sykora seemed to have gone catatonic. Impressive enough in and of itself.

"No," Javier growled. "It will take a navigation feat for the ages to get close to her. Plus, she was an AI ship, so Creator only knows if the *Sentience* is still alive, let alone sane. If we do get close, the *Sentience* will probably think we're the enemy. *Union of Man*, or maybe *Balustrade*. We'll have to fool it long enough to lobotomize it. Then I'll have to reprogram the AI. Maybe from scratch."

"Is it worth it?" Zakhar asked in an empty voice.

For once, Javier could see all the way into the man's soul. The pain. The strain of holding *Storm Gauntlet* together for more than a decade, in face of all comers. Of doing evil, of *becoming* evil, for what he had told himself were higher goals. See the cost of denying himself a happily-ever-after with Djamila Sykora, when she would have happily walked away with him.

The fear of losing it all. Everything.

For nothing.

"You have dealt honestly with me, Zakhar," Javier said, committing his honor, his own soul, to the task. *The Bryce Connection*. "I want my freedom, not just from you, but from all of them. But I want my revenge, more. *Storm Gauntlet*'s done. You can join me as a partner, or walk away and be done with it. I'll go kill them myself."

Zakhar retreated inside himself for a brief time. Then his eyes started on the captain's left and made their way around the table one by one, making eye contact, before coming to rest on the dragoon.

She nodded. Nothing more.

Tight. Sharp. A blank wall of a face.

It still spoke volumes.

Javier considered the future.

Futures.

All possible tomorrows?

Zakhar turned back to the science officer.

Javier could see tears at the back of those eyes, unspoken.

Zakhar Sokolov made a fist with his left hand, and rapped it down once on the table, a hollow bang as his Academy ring, *Class of '49*, thunked heavily on the hard surface.

The universal greeting among men of the *Concord* Fleet, anywhere in the galaxy.

"Let's go get those bastards."

THE LAST FLAGSHIP

PART ONE
BOOK SEVENTEEN: AVALON

PART ONE

Javier had the door to his workshop locked. Partly for safety reasons. Mostly just to keep people from wandering aimlessly in and wanting to *chat*. Even on a starship in flight, that happened.

His manners were generally up to chatting. Just not today.

He could be alone here. Just him and his junk. And Suvi.

His AI sidekick sat in her little armed probe, watching. It was like a giant, gray eyeball, bigger than his head, smaller than his shoulders, parked on her charging ring with a slobbering amount of music, books, and videos stored down in the base, in case she got bored.

The rest of the room was an organized mess.

He had redone everything when he'd first claimed the space. Turned the shelves into clear-faced drawers so he could see what was in them, while still keeping it all from flying around if they lost power to the gravplates, which happened less frequently than it used it. Stuck things into drawers with a filing system that existed only in his head. It would look utterly random to a stranger walking in.

Fourteen years in the *Concord* Fleet meant that those habits were automatic on a starship.

The off-white tabletop in front of him with burn marks, coffee rings, and dried *gunk*, had stretchy nets on each corner. They held things like his welding laser and clockwork tools down, but kept them at hand.

He was mostly tinkering, anyway. Working on a new waldo arm that he could mount on Suvi's probe. Something to do with his hands while his backbrain dug deep into old memories and raked the muck about until it found what it was looking for.

His nightmares, the last few days, had been spectacular as a result.

The door chime was almost a welcome interruption.

Almost.

Javier took a deep breath, stashed everything under handy nets, and rose.

His back hurt from being hunched over too long on the four-legged stool. Probably time to go do some yoga or something. He was pretty good about maintaining his regular lifting and stretching cycle.

He ran his hand back through his short, black hair and contemplated how much of it was coming in gray now, mostly at his temples, but a little everywhere. He wasn't vain enough to dye it, and many women seemed to think it made him look more distinguished.

Always a good thing, looking good for the women of this crew.

Privately, he made a bet with himself who would be on the other side of that hatch. There were only a few people who would come down here, rather than just call him on the comm to ask a question.

That meant it would be a private conversation.

Another deep breath, finding his calm center, as he approached the hatch.

He unlocked the system and opened it, finding himself staring at her chest. Not hard to do when her breasts were about on a level with his chin. Small ones, to be sure, hiding on top of muscles. Lots of muscles. But breasts.

Djamila Sykora. *Dragoon* of the private service, Strike Corvette *Storm Gauntlet*.

A woman 2.1 meters tall. She towered over Javier by thirty centimeters.

Her brown hair was still worn short to fit inside an armoured lifesuit, buzzed very tight on the sides and spiked into a petite Mohawk on top.

It was still the only thing petite about her.

She had bright, pretty green eyes. They reminded him of Holly, his ex-wife, but he only told her that when he wanted to annoy this woman. Mostly, it was the faint freckles, anyway.

The bone structure in her face wasn't delicate enough to be pretty, but he suspected she could be stunningly beautiful if she ever cared to try. Not that a hardass like Sykora would, unless she was undercover on a grift. Like the Pleasure Dome had been.

Artemis, by Michelangelo.

The only vaguely-female touch was the collection of tiny gold or silver rings, studs, and stones in both ears. Seven on the right. Nine on the left. Nothing through the nose, though.

Javier sized her up, then stepped back and to the side so she could enter.

Today, he couldn't even work up the energy to ogle her ass, or bitch at her intrusion into his personal space.

Just as well. She surprised him by walking to a side wall, crossing her arms, and leaning her weight against it.

That was so out of character for Sykora that Javier had to fight to keep his mouth from falling on the floor.

After all, the woman was a veteran; a bad-ass, former marine of the *Neu Berne* Navy. A close-combat expert of zero-gravity fighting who was commonly referred to as the *Ballerina of Death*.

A woman born with a stick up her ass. And willing to abuse anybody she felt was slacking the slightest amount from their true potential as she saw it.

He would have said they mixed as well as oil and water, but it was frequently petroleum and fire between them.

Javier closed the hatchway and locked it again.

Keeping any of her friends out.

Suvi was in her armed probe and watching from the workbench. If Sykora got out of hand, Javier knew his sidekick would happily shoot the woman.

He walked back to the stool he had been using before, pulled it to the opposite side of the small room, and sat. It put his eyes about at a level with her belly button.

Not that it was visible, but he knew it was there, riding a hard eight-pack of abs. Today, she was in muted gray. Slacks and a button-up overshirt in chambray with a very petite camouflage pattern. The top of a black t-shirt peeked over the highest button.

With a start, Javier realized it was the uniform she had stolen when they snuck aboard *Shangdu*, the resort vessel known as the *Pleasure Dome*. He wondered if that was a conscious choice on her part. And what it said about why she was here.

More unfinished business, at least on her part.

Silence bound them for several seconds.

Javier took another deep breath. Released it.

"Why are you here?" he asked bluntly.

No elegant turn of phrase. No chiding sarcasm. Nothing.

He was tired, and didn't want to deal with the dragoon today. Especially not the scowl on her face.

"*Hammerfield*," she said, finally, in a quiet, alto voice unlike her normal angry bellow.

She was not saying as much as she said.

Javier assaulted her with silence in return.

He could out-patient a hunter like her, probably by orders of magnitude. Patience was his thing.

"It really exists?" she asked, relenting from her harsh stare.

Javier shrugged.

"I told you and Captain Sokolov what I know," he said. "Nastiest piece of orbital chaos I've ever surveyed. And sitting back in the corner, orbiting a small gas giant like one of her moons in a tiny and exceedingly complex LaGrange point, a vessel with a transponder code identifying her as *Hammerfield*. Whether it really is THE *Hammerfield*, I don't know. Won't, until we board her. That was several years ago, and I only memorized so much."

"So it wouldn't be in your old logs?" she asked.

There was something in her voice. Hope?

Her?

What would the High Priestess of Death hope for, in the lost flagship of her own nation's navy, vanished decades before she was born?

The Great War had ended in a collapse so complete that only today was *Neu Berne* anything more than a tourist destination. It was the sort of place rich folks from the *Concord* could to watch the proud descendants of the warring generation still trying to come to terms with loss.

"You cut up my ship," Javier growled angrily at her. "After you made me kill her. Those logs are written in a symbolic language so dense, only a *Sentience* can unravel them."

Uncertainty crossed Sykora's face.

For a moment, Javier was sure some sort of vampire doppelgänger from a bad sci-fi vid had appeared on his doorstep.

Djamila Sykora didn't know the meaning of the word *uncertain*.

He watched her eyes dart to her left, linger for a second on Suvi's probe, and then return to his face.

Javier saw pain there.

Imposter. Alien. Invader.

Not the dragoon. Not the *Ballerina of Death*.

"I was hoping…" she wavered, uncertain.

Wavered.

Was this woman stoned?

She wasn't a good enough actress to pull this off as a prank.

"What?" Javier said, trying not to snarl at the woman.

If you had told him this morning that his day would go like this…

Sykora took a breath. Held it. Centered herself in the same way he had before opening the door.

Stood back upright, when all her weight had been leaned back. Grounded herself. Pulled her shoulders back and down.

Fixed him with those sharp, emerald eyes. The pain was still there. The uncertainty. The doubts.

"I know you have worked to program your probes for greater autonomy," she said in a voice finding its footing on slippery ice. "I spoke with this one on *Svalbard*. How long would it take you…Is it even possible to augment one of them enough to read those old logs and know if she really is *Hammerfield*?"

"No," Javier said. "It would take me years. We'll be there in less than a week. We have to locate *Hammerfield* and hope nobody else beat us to the punch. Then board her, hoping that the *Sentience* doesn't kill us out of hand, while we figure out a way to reprogram it. Only then will the truth be known, Djamila Sykora."

She sagged, only the tiniest bit. Anybody not watching so closely would have missed it.

What she really wanted to know was if the *Neu Berne* equivalent of King Arthur was out there, waiting for her to come and find him.

Lady Percival, seeking the Grail.

Javier couldn't decide if he hated himself more for dashing this woman's hopes, or not dancing in unholy glee in the process.

And yet, he had promised to kill this woman. One of these days. When it could be made to look like an accident.

Knew that she had made the same vow. The same Arms Race. The unwritten rules in a duel to the death.

And yet…

The conversation with Del about needing this woman.

All possible tomorrows?

Javier stood. It didn't put him at her level, but it put him in her space.

She flinched. Not much. Barely visible.

Enough.

The killer had come in here with all her guards down, hoping her worst enemy would somehow bear good news.

How far they had come from the first time she had shot him.

"I believe it is your old flagship," he said quietly. "I think they knew the end was near, and took her away to prepare for a surprise attack of some sort. Leading the resistance, or something. Why it never happened, nobody knows. We may find out."

He watched Sykora reassemble all her walls. Put them back in place, brick by brick.

Return to that lethal creature he knew as *The Dragoon*.

That comforted Javier, all by itself. They could be proper enemies now, because probably only Captain Sokolov had ever seen this tremendous woman be the least bit vulnerable.

"Why are you doing this, Javier?" she asked.

It wasn't plaintive, nor angry. Inquisitive, perhaps.

Javier nodded in recognition. That was probably the question that had driven her here today. And it had become necessary for her to be vulnerable to ask it. For him to answer it.

Petroleum and fire.

"There is someone I hate more than you, Djamila Sykora," he said simply.

She processed his words, and then nodded.

"And when we destroy them?" she said in a tight voice, eyes boring in on his.

There was no uncertainty in her voice now. Military problem. Military solution. An enemy that needed killing. Nobody better in the galaxy at that task than Djamila Sykora.

Javier felt eternity open up at his feet, a bottomless chasm threatening both of them.

All possible tomorrows?

Javier considered his weariness at the ongoing game, her emotional vulnerability.

All possible tomorrows.

He decided to gamble everything.

"There is a whole galaxy out there, Djamila," he said. "Maybe we'll both fit in it."

He saw doubt in those eyes now, but it was sarcastic. There on the tip of her tongue, wanting to lash him with verbal razors.

As was normal.

"Ha," she said with sharp humor, jutting a jaw at him.

She didn't say anything more. Just turned, walked to the door, and opened it.

She did glance back over her shoulder once, fixing him with a wry smile, a promise that this conversation would resume on some fateful day.

And then she was gone.

Javier let all the air out of his lungs in a loud blow.

He grabbed the stool, slid it over to the worktable, and sat. It wasn't necessary to lock the door at this part. Everything that he had been trying to keep outside was done.

Running lights on Suvi's probe flickered briefly, drawing his eye.

"Why not?" she asked in a petite tone, proving she had been listening very carefully to the byplay. Knowing her, probably scanning both of them with everything she had, monitoring heart rate, respiration, and truth.

Javier understood the core of her question.

Why wasn't he willing to make them promises about "upgrading" the probe so that she no longer had to hide in there, pretending to be nothing more than a dumb-bot set of programmed responses to external stimuli?

"Because I don't want them to even be able to guess what I'm going to do, young lady," he said quietly. "Not until it's too late to stop me."

PART TWO

ZAKHAR SOKOLOV LOOKED out over his airy bridge, surrounded by the crew he had hand-picked over the years, having tried to gather the best of the ones who no longer fit their old jobs, or their old navies; frequently for budget cuts, occasionally for being too artistic, too weird, or too much for small fleets with more people seeking employment than jobs were available.

As with most days, Zakhar wore something that very closely approximated the old *Concord* fleet uniform. The fleet that had been his home for twenty years.

Before piracy.

Moss green slacks and a matching, button-up, dress shirt. He had done away with the tie as a daily requirement, but kept his black, leather brogues polished as a reminder.

Who he used to be.

Around him, the bridge crew wore any variety of things, some based on old uniforms from their past, others on whatever deal the purser had been able to swing in terms of cheap, surplus uniforms and gear along the way. Those colors stood out against the laurel green of the various bulkheads, that color midway between green and gray that walls, ceilings, and floors were painted regularly, with white numbers and arrows here and there following conduits.

"Pilot," Zakhar called, waking Piet Alferdinck up from whatever daydreams the man was enjoying over on his boards. "Confirm time to insertion."

It was there on Zakhar's own screen, but acting like a professional constantly ingrained that habit in his crew. When you were pirates, every day was a struggle against entropy. Doubly so when your ship, the old *Osiris*-class Strike Corvette *Storm Gauntlet*, was on her last legs.

Their last engagement, with the battle frigate *Ajax*, over *Svalbard*, had been a fast one, which was good. *Storm Gauntlet* was enough to take any freighter in the galaxy, but desperately overwhelmed by almost any warship she would encounter.

They had repaired as much of the damage as well as they could. Enough to escape, to flee into the darkness, looking for the place his science officer had hoped they would find an even bigger warship, derelict, but claimable and repairable.

Otherwise, Zakhar would probably be better off selling this old boat to someone else, or even a breaker yard, paying off the crew, and retiring to whatever desk job he thought he could do.

Maybe even go back to his real name and finally tap his retirement pension, sitting in a bank somewhere, slowly earning interest.

What did happily-ever-after taste like?

Zakhar's eye caught his dragoon, Djamila Sykora, just settling into her station, but he refused to think about what the two of them might create, if they didn't have to be pirates anymore.

He was The Captain, and that was a cold, lonely job.

"Thirteen minutes to insertion, Captain," Piet called back.

Zakhar nodded to himself.

"Remember to come out under full cloak," he ordered. "We have no idea how the target will react. I'd rather she not see us at all."

"Roger that," the pilot said.

A side hatch opened on his right, opposite where Djamila was buckling herself in, and the science officer entered.

Djamila was in all gray today. Piet wore a purple tunic and black slacks. Even Mary-Elizabeth Suzuki, the gunner, was in bright green and baby blue.

Javier wore an outfit that was almost an exact copy of Zakhar's, except for the shoes. Javier had soft, blue moccasins today. Still, the *Concord* fleet officer must be running strong in both of them.

They locked eyes for a moment as Javier settled and logged into his boards.

No words passed, but none were needed.

How often did you know ahead of time that you were about to reach a point where the rest of your life would go down a different path from yesterday? The only question now was which of three options they faced.

Success in finding and claiming the lost *Neu Berne* flagship, *Hammerfield*.

Failure, either because it wasn't there, or it was too badly degraded to save them.

Or death, because the ancient warrior vessel took offense to them even being there.

Simple as that.

Around him, everyone settled in, strapped themselves to their chairs, and prepared for their fate to unfold.

"Any final thoughts, Mr. Science Officer?" Zakhar asked, loud enough to include the whole bridge crew in what might have been a simple conversation between old comrades.

"Piet will be paying off on a twenty-drachma bet shortly," Javier replied.

The pilot just shrugged.

"How's that?" Zakhar said.

"That never in his studies or travels has he seen a star system so messy, so complicated," Javier laughed. "So impossible."

Zakhar wasn't sure he believed Javier's stories about the place, but it really didn't matter much at this point. The proof would be in the pudding, as they said. Very shortly.

"All hands," he said into a general comm. "Prepare for insertion and possible combat maneuvering in eight minutes."

Zakhar watched as all stations checked in. Everyone knew the rumors. Knew the score about how badly damaged *Storm Gauntlet* was. She had given as good as she got, but it had still been ugly, protecting the assault shuttle so it could land, while they were all under fire.

Zakhar really looked forward to finding *Ajax* one of these days, and kicking her teeth in to return the favor. And really hurting Walvisbaai Industrial, the multi-system conglomerate that some of the more flamboyant news services might call one of the *Pirate Clans*.

Although never in a place with good libel laws on the books.

Zakhar worked for the Jarre Foundation. Another Clan, if you would.

In the darkness between stellar nations, the law was frequently the man with the bigger warship, the biggest hammer.

And if it was going to be a war between the pirates, the sort of lurid thing that would sell subscriptions, Zakhar wanted the biggest maul available.

A First Rate Galleon would serve that need quite nicely.

Even more than a century old, *Hammerfield* would outclass anything less than a modern cruiser, while still having cargo capacity comparable to the largest of the medium transports, or the smallest of the big bulk jobs that hauled thousands of standard shipping containers between major worlds.

Nobody even made that design anymore, relying today on commercial freighters and dedicated warships, rather than a single ship that mixed the two.

"Piet," Zakhar said. "Bring up screen nine on the main display. Zero transparency. Twenty percent overlay."

They had scanned this system from one jump away, when it was barely possible to resolve it as three stars with the best scanners, using a former probe-cutter's eyes, stolen and welded onto a warship like this one.

Nothing else was really known, given the distance of this jump, except that they would drop out at around fifty AU, fifty times the distance from Earth to her sun. Even Neptune, the blue ice giant in the Homeworld's system, orbited at thirty AU, so they should be safe enough out here, especially coming out seventy degrees above the ecliptic for the system.

And even then, Javier had warned them to pay attention to their surroundings. Which was frightening in itself, since he rarely ever got serious like that.

Emergence.

Realspace.

Engines primed but off. Shields at minimum only. Electromagnetic cloak fully deployed. Every turret ready to fire.

Riding the gyros and pretending to be an ugly asteroid, as the saying went.

Javier was face down over his boards, studying four different screens and listening to several audio channels through an earpiece.

Complete information overload to anybody but him. Which was why he was *The Science Officer.*

Piet's hands were poised. Mary-Elizabeth's, too. Even Djamila appeared to be holding her breath.

Long, silent minutes passed, everything and everyone hushed and waiting.

"She's still there," Javier said simply.

The sound of a dozen people breathing out was a heavy sigh across the room.

The main display blinked, and changed.

Nayarit Sector, system number 23, in Javier's recollections.

NS005188-753A was at the center, a yellow main sequence star, a G8V, which was only about ten percent larger than that of the homeworld, still the measure everyone used.

At an orbital distance of roughly twelve AU, on a twenty-some degree inclination from the original ecliptic, two smaller stars, *B* and *C*, orbited each other around a common center, a barycenter in open space, not that anything could survive in that LaGrange point indefinitely. At least they were both cooler stars, so the total amount of solar wind wasn't all that bad.

From Javier's recollection, the two stars were about 0.9 and 0.7 times the size of *A*, which made this a complicated triple system, especially since the orbital inclination of the binary suggested that they had been captured fairly recently, perhaps in the last three hundred to five hundred million years at most.

What made it extra fun were the number of gas giants Javier was able to identify and flag on his projection already. Both systems had contained an interesting mix of gas giants, ice giants, and the smaller worlds: both rocky ones close and iceballs farther out.

In this case, it looked like all of the gas giants had somehow managed to be captured, rather than ejected from the combined solar system as all the other planets slowly fell into their various orbital resonance periods in at least two interacting ecliptic planes. The screen showed nine giants so far, with the promise of several more as passive sensors watched and counted.

Zakhar doubted that everything would be stable like this, and that many of these worlds would eventually be eaten or evicted, but that was an issue to occur in millions of years. All he had to worry about today were the possible number of things formerly in the local Oort Cloud, Kuiper Belt, or Scattered Disk.

Quite frankly, there was going to be crap flying everywhere, for a very long time. Even if a rocky world in one of the habitable zones could be identified, terraforming it would be a waste of time during the lifetime of man as a species, unless you wanted to dedicate unholy amounts of ships and men to locating and destroying all of the things that might slam into such a world with enough energy to cause extinction-level events.

There were so many other star systems in this galaxy that weren't assholes to begin with.

Piet actually stood up, pulled out a twenty-drachma bill from a pocket, and walked over to hand it to Javier with a face gone white.

Javier's frog-faced grin said it all.

Nothing less extreme would have brought them here.

One little green dot.

Hammerfield, according to the transponder code faintly calling her name to eternity.

Tucked into the leading LaGrange point, L4, formed by the combination of *A* and the single gravity well of *B* and *C*.

At some point, the dance along multiple ecliptics would probably slam the warship into one of the giants, roaming around like wolves at the edge of the firelight, or their touch would kick the ship entirely out of the system, lost forever in the darkness.

But they were here today. And they had the time to plot a whole series of short hops that would culminate within reach of *Neu Berne's* last flagship. Trying that in one jump was a recipe for disaster.

"Anybody else here?" Zakhar finally asked, breaking the spell that had wound itself around them with sticky webs.

"Negative, Captain," the science officer said professionally, which told Zakhar how far down the rabbit hole Javier had gone in his mind.

He was never formal unless he had to be. Or he forgot where he was and fell into the old ways.

"Then you have the bridge," Zakhar ordered. "Primary crew stand down for now. We'll have food delivered when you are ready, Javier."

Javier's look told Zakhar how much sarcasm was on the tip of his tongue, but he held his silence.

They both knew that this place held the sort of mysteries that would keep him glued to his station until the caffeine stopped working.

Zakhar rose and considered some coffee himself and maybe a little dessert as a treat.

Now, the hard part would start.

PART THREE

DJAMILA POWERED her electronic book reader down and closed the brown, leather cover. It was technically an antique at this point, fifty-one years old, but it had belonged to her father as a child, before he gave it to her as a graduation present, and it had been built to last at least another century.

She traced soft fingertips on the faded brown leather, fifteen centimeters by twenty-five, and thought about the past. Her past.

Her world's past.

They had been here in-system for one hundred and thirteen hours now. Still sitting out at the very top edge of the system, looking down from a dizzying height at everything moving, like a giant mobile that had hung over her crib.

Djamila had already studied everything there was to know about the *Hammerfield*.

Class specifications, interior systems diagrams, everything. There hadn't been time to transform deck plans from her records into a full immersion video, but she had memorized most of the layout. That part didn't concern her.

No, she had been reading a history of the war itself. One she had never read during her military student days.

It had been written some years after the war, by a woman who had been a mid-level officer serving the Admiralty Staff at the time of *The Surrender*.

That moment when the government itself had collapsed, and the survivors were too weary to push on any further, thirty-nine years of near-continuous warfare having apparently been enough, even for a warrior culture like hers had been.

It wasn't there on the page, what Djamila sought today. It wouldn't be.

As near as she knew, the secrets she wanted had probably never left this very star system, interred forever under alien suns.

At the same time, the words she read had been written when the memories of those days were fresh. Before the rise of the great legends and lies about betrayals and heroes gone into hiding, like Arthur gone to *Avalon* with Excalibur in his hand. Geoffrey of Monmouth would have been proud of the lies and myths her parents' generation had concocted.

She had heard those stories enough growing up that she had believed them.

Not anymore.

High Command had gambled everything on a major offensive and been mousetrapped.

Slaughtered.

It wasn't as bad as that final battle at *A'Nacia*, five hundred years ago, but it had broken *Neu Berne*'s back psychologically.

Hammerfield had managed to escape the wreckage and return home, undamaged. After a quick stop to pick up supplies and Admiral Ericka Steiner, head of the Admiralty itself, the warship had leapt into the darkness and never been heard from again.

Even today, any records of that mission were classified. Missing. Taken away by official men.

But not on *Neu Berne* or one of the *Union* worlds. Not even *Balustrade*, the immortal enemy.

No.

The *Concord* had swept it all up, six years later, when it flexed its newly-won hegemony across the near galaxy. Ridden in and taken control. All records simply disappeared except what was written down later by the people who knew, who remembered the truth, what little of it there was to know.

After that, only legends.

Now, eighty-five years later, Djamila Sykora looking for the warship, the weapon, that held the truth.

Would she find Excalibur?

Did she even want to?

PART FOUR

Important events should be treated as such. Javier's grandmother had always told him that as a child.

As a result, he had shaved off several days of ugly, salt-and-pepper stubble from his chin. A shower with real water, rather than his usual pass through the low-power sonic cleaner. Aftershave that made him smell like his grandfather. Clothing without any stains, even if he had to go clear to the bottom of the drawer for the dungarees.

Gray fit his mood, anyway, so he wore the charcoal pants, with a marbled gray raglan pullover with black sleeves, and the soft blue moccasins he habitually wore when he wasn't leaving the ship.

He had taken the time for a quick haircut. Javier didn't figure he had been this spiffy even for dates in a while.

And he was there early for the meeting, prepped, and supplied with really good coffee. Sascha and Hajna were there, as was Sykora, and Afia Burakgazi.

Captain Sokolov entered the primary conference room like it was full of snakes. It wasn't.

Hell, they weren't any of them even doppelgängers, last time he had checked. Personally in three cases. Visually with Sykora.

There was no way in hell he was getting that intimate with the dragoon.

Nope. Javier, seated at the far end of the long, pseudo-grain-laminate table, sat and sipped coffee from his mug, the one he had found in the wardroom. The one that someone, somewhere, had picked up at a Merankorr brothel gift shop. The one which, based on the amount of hot coffee inside, would currently show a beautiful young woman with green hair, and no clothing north of her belly-button.

Because he could.

He hadn't bought the damned thing. Just recognized it on a shelf in the wardroom for what it was and kept it. Because he had owned something similar, a long time ago.

On Javier's immediate right was Afia, a short, skinny engineer with a heart-shaped face, dark green eyes, and the willingness and ability to beat up men twice her size in bars, though you would never guess it from the demure way she rested her chin on her laced fingers and smiled. Those women were always the most dangerous ones, anyway.

Her ancestors had originally come from somewhere in southeast Asia on the homeworld. Roughly between what used to be China and Indonesia, back in the old days. Her skin was darker, more golden, than the Chinese Diaspora, but not the red-brown of Javier's.

Across from Afia was Sascha Koç, one of Sykora's two pathfinder babes, the scouts she relied upon in hostile territory. Sascha was a short, Slavic brunette with lush hips and an amazing alto singing voice. Today she was in her usual field uniform: pants and button-up tunic with a gray and maroon splotch pattern apparently designed to vanish shipboard. Javier couldn't see it, but they believed.

Diagonal from Sascha was her counterpart, Hajna Flores, the lanky, Anglo blond with legs that seemed to go on forever and were born to tango. Like Sascha, Hajna dressed for war, although she had added a floral-scented something to her morning routine today.

Both women were card sharps of the first order, the kind that usually just about broke even playing with Javier; whereas the three of them cleaned out anybody else wanting to play.

Hajna might be the smarter of the pair, but that was like judging which day was nicer. They were both wicked brilliant women. And dangerous, which he appreciated.

Sykora waited at what would be Sokolov's right hand when he sat. That was pretty much her reserved seat in any meeting he was attending. Like the pathfinders, she wore the steel and maroon that was supposed to hide you against gray walls.

Javier assumed it had something to do with inducing motion sickness in anyone watching the optical illusion of the spots moving for long enough. Fortunately, his stomach was made of sterner stuff.

Still, Sokolov blinked as he sat.

"I would have expected you to take Ilan, Javier," he said as he settled.

"That man has not certified on combat EVA," Javier retorted with a knowing grin.

Sokolov nodded, then turned sharply to stare at Afia, quite possibly the quietest person in the room. Most rooms.

To her credit, the woman shrugged nonchalantly and smiled a wicked, evil grin at the man.

Some people would have taken a different lesson from their adventures on *Meehu Platform*. Afia had apparently decided to become more dangerous. At this rate, she might end up on Sykora's combat team, and not down in the engineering spaces.

Of course, as many times as he got drug along on assaults in his job as science officer, maybe this ship needed a dedicated combat engineer. Weirder things had happened, especially with this crew.

"So what do we know?" Sokolov turned back to Javier, all serious and military shit now.

"Nothing," Javier retorted.

"Nothing?" Sokolov was surprised. "We've been here a week."

"You said *Know*," Javier snarked. "I have any number of pet theories to test."

"Oh, fine." Sokolov settled himself more comfortably and visibly prepared for war with his science officer. "Top three."

"As near as memory serves, she hasn't moved in six years," Javier ticked off his fingers. "I'm hoping that means that she was parked there by someone who knew what they were doing."

"And the warship has not moved on its own, subsequent," Sokolov observed.

"Which brings me to my second theory," Javier continued. "The *Sentience* is dead, the ship is disabled, or she was ordered to remain there until someone came for her."

"I have very little experience with *Sentient* ships," Sokolov said. "What are the odds?"

"They tend to come off the assembly line extremely linear," Javier replied. "Black and white. Like bright five-year-olds. What happens with their first crew, their first captain, tends to set their personality. I got lucky with my probe-cutter. Captain Ayumu Ulfsson was one hell of a man and set her on the right path. Who knows with *Neu Berne*? Especially a flagship."

They both glanced quickly at Sykora, but she shrugged tightly, silently. Not out of her depth, but out of her expertise and willing to let the experts speculate unless asked a direct question.

Javier always forgot how professional the woman could be when they didn't have to argue.

"Risks?" Sokolov asked.

"Eighty-five years of boredom," Javier said. "Think how crazy you'd be, left in solitary confinement for that long."

"Can we fix any of those issues?" Sokolov asked. "Dead, disabled, or crazy?"

"Dead could mean a simple power failure took her offline," Javier said. "Or maybe a lunatic smashed the right boards and killed it. I can reprogram it from scratch in that case, given enough time and access to the right hardware and software backups, both of which are hopefully stored close at hand."

Sykora twitched.

Coming from her, a scream in a darkened opera house would have been less disturbing. Javier could tell she wanted to inject something, probably bilious, into the conversation, but she held her silence.

Sokolov saw it as well. He glanced, but she shook her head.

"You told me, when we first captured you, Javier, that you couldn't do that," Sokolov observed dryly.

"No," Javier replied with a hard smile. "I told you to go to hell. It wouldn't be an easy or quick task. And would require a good chunk of the engineering crew for at least a month, if we have to code up from a declarations block. But it can be done. I've been practicing on my probes, and in a year, have gotten them about as smart as a cat. She would end up programming a good chunk of her own personality once we started."

"Okay," Sokolov breathed out, apparently willing to let that one go, unaware of how much of a lie it was. "What about crazy?"

Javier leaned back in his chair and took a long drink of coffee.

Sokolov was directly across from him, with the four women warriors between them. Five pairs of eyes fixed on him. Green, blue, brown, green, brown, from his right.

"That's why Afia and not Ilan," Javier said. "I'm proposing a combat insertion. *Storm Gauntlet* stays cloaked and deploys Del in the Assault

Shuttle. He gets us to a certain point, maybe fifty kilometers out, and drops us. We EVA over and hopefully board her with no issue."

"Or?" Sokolov asked.

"Or she kills us and then goes after Del," Javier replied. "You'll be able to get away, because her scanners aren't likely good enough to penetrate a modern cloak. What you do at that point isn't my concern."

Captain Sokolov looked at the other four individually, until each nodded, Sykora last.

"Is it worth it?" Sokolov asked in a heavy, tired voice.

Javier tapped a finger on the tabletop.

"As I told Sykora, I've found someone I hate more than any of you," he rasped. "I refuse to spend the rest of my life looking over my shoulder for an assassin. These people only understand power and fear. Wealth gives them power to inflict fear on others. That offends me. Badly."

He took another sip of coffee, getting close to the really good, caramel sludge at the bottom of his mug, and fixed the captain with his stare.

"Zakhar Sokolov," Javier ground the words out. Witnesses, and all that. "I told you I was willing to start with a blank screen here. Old wounds and slights will be forgotten. We will be partners in this endeavor. I intend to dedicate my life to destroying those people. Burning their cities, pulling down the ruins, and salting the earth. Scipio Africanus the Younger. That sort of thing. If it gets me killed here, then those are the risks. I've talked to these four and spelled it out for them. They're here."

"I always thought Navarre was crazy," Sokolov said with a wry smile. "Turns out Aritza is even worse."

Javier nodded grimly as the four women warriors around him got a chuckle out of the captain's words.

You have no idea.

PART TWO

BOOK EIGHTEEN: DERELICT

PART ONE

Suvi was in her big probe today, the armed one with the way-bigger memory block to store movies and books. Loaded for a vacation of at least three weeks before she had to loop.

To humans, the sensors on the face of her flyer apparently made it look like a big gray eyeball, floating in space. When she deployed the popup turret from the bottom, it got vaguely obscene.

Around her, Suvi tracked the other five humans getting ready for deep space. All that remained was to lock helmets in place, check everything, and transition to onboard systems.

Unlike the normal skinsuits they might wear for short jaunts, the humans had strapped themselves into anonymous, gray EVA suits. Heavier. Bulkier. Semi-armoured.

Backpacks with pressurized systems for directed flight. Gear bags and equipment belts. Spare oxygen tanks and power packs. Toolkits.

Each was equipped with on-board plumbing attachments that took some getting used to, apparently, to listen to Javier bitch. But Javier liked to complain about things. It was his nature. Of course, it was a little easier for females in that department.

Not that she had ever had physical form requiring such shenanigans, but she could research it, and commiserate with them.

Silently, of course. She didn't really exist.

To make things even funnier, at least to an AI in her own pocket spaceship, the suits had some level of armored reinforcement, so people tended to waddle awkwardly when they moved. Like they had drunk themselves right up at the edge of too tipsy to operate heavy equipment safely.

Ugly, gray penguins.

Well, everyone except Djamila Sykora. She moved in her suit with a grace that would have embarrassed many professional athletes. Suvi finally understood the term: *a Natural.*

And they weren't really anonymous as they prepared. Sykora was a head taller than anyone and had three weapons in holsters: both hips and under her left arm, where everyone else only had one on their dominant hip. Javier was broader than Hajna in the shoulders and body. And Sascha was bulkier than Afia.

That would be useful as Suvi helped them transit deep space, flying like a herding dog working vaguely-recalcitrant sheep, if her videos were accurate. The gear bag Javier had prepared for her to carry made her feel almost like a locomotive pulling a single, heavy car through space. It was two meters long, by a third of that square, and weighed forty kilograms in gravity, but Javier had explained that he was prepared for almost any task with it handy.

A sound drew her attention, so she rotated herself around to bring her primary video pickup in line.

Delridge Smith ambled loosely down the set of steps from his flight deck to the big cargo bay.

Del stared right at her and winked, as if they were sharing some joke.

Suvi never knew with the pilot. He was much older than the rest of the crew, and much looser. Today, he had clipped his white beard short, maybe only a number fifteen length on the trimmer, while he kept the white hair on his head around a ten. Olfactory sensors suddenly picked up an alcohol-based volatile trace, but it was a perfume of some sort, and not bourbon.

Coconut, according to the onboard spectrograph, whatever that meant.

Like every day, he was in gray cargo pants and a floral shirt. Hawaiian, per her onboard encyclopedia. Off-peach with white parrot silhouettes. Not even the weirdest one he owned.

"Roughly fifty kilometers out," Del announced. "Holding a lateral motion and on autopilot. So what do I do if it spots you and starts to move?"

"Run like hell," Javier said. "Get rocks, moons, or planets between you and it and hope it either loses you, or loses interest. She can splatter you from here if she wants to. I'm hoping we're not a threat, this small and this far away. *Storm Gauntlet* might have provoked a reaction."

"Kid, you're crazy," Del said. "But I'll give you credit for brass."

He stopped and looked around at the rest.

"Ladies, if we all get killed today, it has been my pleasure flying with you."

Everyone made insulting comments. Afia included a rude, universal gesture as well.

Del laughed, saluted, and tromped back up the stairs. A hatch latched shut with the sound of a vault door.

Suvi watched Javier step close to the dragon lady.

"When we latch down, you're in charge," he said. "The probe knows the basic hand language you use with your team. Everyone maintains complete radio silence until we're all inside, either here or there. If anyone has an emergency, they return here on their own. Any questions?"

There were none, but that was ignorance, not confidence.

Nobody but Javier had any experience with a *Sentient* starship. Well, not counting her, but she found most of her cousins to be annoyingly stuffy, boring shits. Really bad conversationalists.

Humans were way preferable for that sort of thing.

One by one, the team locked their helmets down. External status lights cycled up to green for everyone else to see.

You never knew when maybe something was going wrong and you passed out before you knew it. Helpful if your suit yelled for assistance for you. Humans were really fragile creatures, that way.

And then silence. Everybody trapped in their own, private world. At least she had planned ahead and had enough music for a millennia aboard, plus whatever she might write between now and then.

Suvi went into the tiny airlock with the dragon lady first.

That made sense. Put the two best flyers out in vacuum before anyone else.

The confined space hissed weirdly on her audio pickups as pumps sucked the room empty.

Ready? Sykora signaled silently.

Suvi had a ring of signaling lights below her main sensor grid. She cycled a muted, Kelly green, clockwise pattern, and watched the giant woman nod.

Push came to shove, Suvi could turn the lights into a Times Square scrolling marquee, but she wasn't supposed to be that smart, especially not around the dragon-lady.

And then silence. The outer door of the airlock opened towards them, revealing an eternity of stars dancing mutely.

Suvi bounced outward on her gyros and micro thrusters, just enough to get three meters from the hatch, so she could play lifeguard with her Santa Claus bag of goodies trailing behind her.

She watched Sykora grab a doorframe and pivot herself outward like the ballerina she was called. The dragoon let go of the ship so perfectly she didn't move.

Wow.

Then the woman reached out with one finger and pushed just enough to drift backwards at a pace that snails would have appreciated. It was almost like watching paint dry.

Pretty impressive, especially for an organic.

The hatch closed outwards to them, sealed, and there was nothing to do but watch. Or passively scan on all frequencies available, with a spectrum bandwidth that would have made anybody but Javier nervous.

Hammerfield was over there. A transponder signal quietly chirping on channel eighty-three. Hash and junk on several other channels that Suvi decided must be gas giants gossiping to themselves under the triple solar wind.

She didn't have any memories of being here before, but Javier hadn't had any excuse before now to access her old drives, other than to confirm that the files were all securely stored on her old memory core, itself stashed away in a vacuum-sealed storage box in engineering.

One of these days, she would get to look at her old picture albums.

Sascha and Hajna came out second. Not quite as graceful as the dragon lady, but well above average. The sort of skill that only came with extensive practice in a zero-g environment.

Afia and Javier were last. Suvi would have said graceful, but she had just watched two experts and a dragon-lady give lie to that observation.

She suppressed the urge to bark out loud before she started herding, then realized that nobody would hear her, as long as she didn't display it on one of her boards or transmit it over radio, so she gave one loud *woof*, just to set the tone in her own head.

Each suit was programmed with coordinates and burn cycles, but too much of it was estimation, and an expectation that the individual pilot would exercise terminal control. Or rely on one of the lifeguards if something went wrong.

One by one, they slowly began to move, accelerating at a comfortable, predictable pace, with fifty kilometers of space to cover but no major deadline, since these suits were good for up to two weeks of average use.

Suvi went last. She fired up a DeManx Symphony, Number Forty-three, from the sixty-third century. The late *Corporate Wars* period had produced some lovely orchestral music, not like the grand choral pieces of the early *Pocket Empires Era*, starting in the sixty-sixth century. But of the crew, only Piet Alferdinck, the pilot, had any true appreciation of music history anyway.

Hopefully, one of these days, she would get to discuss it with him.

PART TWO

It had started out as a point of light, just emerging from the darkness. Djamila had watched it resolve itself into an object, a gleaming, metallic form somewhere between a longsword and the Caduceus of Hermes. It looked organic to her, living in a period where naval architecture had gone to straight lines and geometric symmetry.

Overall, *Hammerfield* was just over a kilometer long, with a beam ratio of only thirteen to one. Stubbier than *Storm Gauntlet*, which made sense, since their vessel was a dedicated warship, where space was at a premium, while this relic was a galleon, armed with a variety of medium-sized guns, turreted on all four sides, wrapped around gargantuan cargo holds.

Storm Gauntlet had three big-gun twin turrets on her top deck, with point-defense weapons all around her. Sleek and deadly, like a knife, rather than a sledgehammer.

It did not look like a tomb, but Djamila wasn't fooled. As remote and isolated as this system was, she couldn't imagine someone parking the ship here and taking further flight in something smaller, something weaker. There had been very few warships larger than *Hammerfield* in that era, which made this one all the more important to whoever had her.

That meant that they had come here and never left.

Died here.

Djamila reviewed her mental list of the sorts of causes of death that she should prepare for. Sudden plague vectors that might still be viable, even after this period. Violent civil war among the crew. Accidental decompression, the kind that would kill some and isolate the rest in small, personal mausoleums from which they could never escape.

For the briefest moment, she entertained the exotic fiction of survivors, or the offspring thereof, somehow having managed to make it this far, like some dime-novel space fantasy. Unlikely, but still possible. One of the reasons why she was so well armed.

Survivors today would most likely be feral creatures, not civilized humans.

She took a deep breath to settle herself, tasting the flat, metallic tang of the recycling plant's air. The onboard sensors were all green, but Djamila dialed up the humidity three percent anyway, hoping it would improve the taste in her mouth.

She listened as her thrusters began to taper down, blowing forward over her shoulders and around her hips to slow her. It had been two hundred and eight minutes, and they were very close to the ancient warship. It had resolved itself into a wall of steel.

The Last Flagship.

She wasn't sure what she would have done, had the vessel begun to move as they approached, or opened fire.

Died gloriously in battle, she supposed. Everyone had always expected that of her.

Nothing more.

No grand accomplishments, save to make the Valkyries themselves jealous when they came for her.

Djamila let her backbrain consider what legacy she really wanted to leave, in a galaxy where violent death was not necessarily a job requirement. She had never really thought about it, but this ancient tomb spoke to her on very unconscious levels.

What we leave behind.

Silence. She was motionless relative to *Hammerfield*. Perhaps thirty meters away, drifting with the ship through space, pulled by unseen tides of solar gravity.

She looked over at Javier. He didn't know the hand language well enough for complicated conversations, but had enough of the basics.

Next step? she asked.

He gave her a thumbs-up and began to close on the bow of the ship. The man had obviously studied the schematics she had provided, at least well enough to locate the forward crew airlock. She signaled the others to follow, and drew her right-hand pistol.

Djamila had visions of small, armed automatons on the hull, popping out to engage and destroy boarding parties in exactly this circumstance. She was prepared to kill them.

Perhaps she was a touch crazy, as well.

But better to be paranoid unnecessarily, rather than complacent and wiped out.

PART THREE

Javier let visions of avarice dance in his background as he silently came to rest against the hull of the ancient, *Neu Berne* warship. For years, looting this beast had been a significant chunk of his retirement planning. The sort of thing that would generate enough cash that he could live on a private beach with his own, personal bartender for the rest of his days.

And now? Vengeance.

You wanna play rough, assholes? I'll show you what rough really tastes like.

People born rich never understand what poverty does to someone. How it shapes their willingness to color outside the lines. They've never worried about paying the rent every month, and all the things they might have to do to get there.

Javier let the scowl own his face for a while. There was nobody in a position to look into his polarized helmet and see just what demon had possessed him.

Safer this way.

Javier Aritza was kind of a clown. That was okay. Eutrupio Navarre was a cold, hard killer. Even Navarre might have blanched and recoiled right now.

Hammerfield's exterior was polished clean, a sharp, blue-steel, alloy finish that told him the nav shields were rarely activated, letting the triple solar wind play across the hull like a high-grit sandpaper.

In front of him, the airlock controls.

Javier glanced back to make sure Suvi and Sykora were still with him. Suvi's gear bag had a prybar strong enough to force the door, if necessary. Sykora had the muscles to make that happen.

Javier set his guidance systems to hold him steady as he worked, little puffs of gas that would fly all directions.

He reached out a gloved hand and pressed the button to open the keypad. Nothing happened. No power? Welded shut by time and errant plasma?

Javier reached down to his belt and pulled out the most primitive tool a spaceman ever carried: a flat piece of polished steel, three millimeters thick and twenty-five wide, ground down to a chisel tip. A bit of string attached it to the sheath, so it wouldn't fly away if he dropped it. Because he had *never* done that.

Javier activated the magnets in his boots and left hand to give him some extra leverage against the hull, and slipped the edge of the tool into the space around the panel.

Torque brought out the muscles in his back.

In space, there was no rewarding pop as whatever was holding it gave way, but he could feel it in his hands. He sheathed his chisel and studied the controls revealed. Ten-key pad. Radio buttons.

There we are: Big red emergency override.

Javier couldn't imagine that the beast inside, that grand, ancient dragon called a *Sentience*, might have missed their approach, even as stealthy as they had been, but pushing this button would most certainly wake it up.

Knock, knock.

Javier pushed the button until he felt it stop. It lit as it went in, which was a promising sign. He had feared that all power would be off, and they would have to pry the hatch open after all.

More lights came on. A string of them in white outlined the airlock hatch. Javier smiled as the door slowly receded into the hull on hinges, revealing an airlock chamber large enough for ten or fifteen good friends to fill.

He wasn't entirely sure what all the hand signals Sykora gave him meant, but her intent on going first was obvious. As was his willingness to let her.

Always put well-armed, crazy chicks on point where they might stop all the hordes of hell in their tracks. Sykora was like that.

At least the airlock was internally lit. Bright, white lights revealed a clean interior. The slightest rime of frost as a few traces of air bled out, so hopefully there was atmospheric pressure inside after all this time.

More hand signals. Hajna joined Sykora in the box while the rest of them were apparently supposed to wait outside. Whatever.

The hatch slid ominously closed, a bank vault that slowly sealed shut.

Long minutes passed.

Javier found himself inspecting a sensor pod nearby, his primary nerdiness coming to the fore when the situational stress got too much. The pod was worn and pitted. Probably blind after all this time. Certainly, it didn't emit any signals he could pick up.

And Suvi hadn't made any indication that the dragon might be waking.

The outer hatch lit up and began to cycle again, a humongous Venus Flytrap waiting its next customer.

Given the space, Javier entered and signaled the three women to join him inside. He pressed the big, green button on the inner wall when everyone was set.

A sign lit up above the button. Javier read German, which had been the universal standard message for airlocks of all nations, dating back thousands of years, but the message was written in eleven other languages in smaller print below, just in case.

Warning: Gravplates activating.

The direction of the text provided your context, if you had somehow gotten confused about the shape of the warship around you.

The plates powered up slowly, giving even the most distracted fool time to realize what was happening and get his feet pointed in the right direction. At the same time, more lights came on and Javier could feel a rumbling hiss through his boots as air got pumped into the chamber.

All good signs. Assuming no alien monster from his worst nightmares was standing on the other side of the inner hatch when it opened.

The door cycled out into the hallway.

Okay, this monstrous nightmare was not unexpected.

Sykora.

She had depolarized her faceplate, so he could see her grimace inside. She wasn't scowling much more than normal. And had a pistol in either hand, but that was usual for her as well.

Suvi went out first, sliding around the Amazon and taking up a station overhead. Javier *felt* the ping she unleashed, clear down in his bones.

NOTHING was sneaking up on those two women.

He joined them in the hall, along with Sascha, Hajna, and Afia, snug as a bug in a rug.

External sensors showed everything here in the tolerable range. Oxygen/nitrogen mix close enough for government work. No dangerous traces underneath.

Colder than snot out in the hallway, though. Ambient hallway temperature four degrees and atmospheric equivalent of twenty-five hundred meters above sea level.

Camping in the Northern Rockies, back on Earth, in winter. Still, tolerable.

Javier reached up with both hands and pressed the buttons to open his helmet. The buttons were located on either side of the forehead, where Sykora had obviously ground off her horns with a disk sander at some point in the past.

The faceplace itself was three pieces that came together like a fishbowl with nearly invisible seams. They popped open now and retracted, kinda rolling up like shades, down right, down left, and up center, leaving the backpiece behind his ears and the helmet crown atop his skull.

Smelled dry in here. Which was way better than smelling like dead people. Visions of Egyptian mummy movies had plagued him for days.

Javier didn't bother with a weapon at this point. Not with as many armed women as he had close by.

Instead, he opened up the comm and set it to scanning all the frequencies for a signal. Most people never realized how much noise a *Sentient* starship made, controlling remotes and sub-systems. You had to have owned one.

Or been one, in Suvi's case. He figured she would say something if she needed to, witnesses be damned. Still, better to check.

"Probe. Access Command Node," he said aloud, perpetuating the myth that the big eyeball was about as smart as a rabbit. "Confirm status."

"Conditions nominal," she replied in the most amazingly droll and bored voice he had ever heard her use.

So yeah, safe, for now.

Javier tapped his helmet and nodded to the four organic women, indicating that they were safe to open up their faceplates as well.

Emergency systems could always slam them shut in an eyeblink if something went wrong.

They all emerged from their plastic chrysalis shells and sniffed.

"Where's first?" Afia asked.

She was an engineer first and hadn't drawn a weapon, unlike the other three women. Four. Suvi's pop-down turret was deployed and ready to go.

"We have lights, power, and atmosphere tolerable to human standards," Javier mused aloud.

He looked around the hallway for the first time.

Human standards. Naval architecture, so straight lights, square corners, gray paint, strange pipes and conduits that popped out of walls occasionally, ran a ways, and then popped back in.

Ugly.

There was a reason cruise ships spent so much time and money on hiding all of that behind a Hollywood set.

"I had planned engineering first," Javier replied to Afia. "Just in case. But I think we can do the bridge first and see what we know."

He caught Sykora's eye. She nodded to him.

Man, that woman did not understand poker. Not one bit. Everyone else here would have cleaned her out in about four hands.

It was obvious she wanted to know what had happened to the crew. Why the great mystery? Where was King Arthur hiding?

"Which way?" Sykora asked in a cold, tight voice, like ice chipped off a concrete dam in winter.

"Forward stairs," he replied, mildness itself.

"That's eleven decks," Afia whined lightly. "Why not the lift?"

Javier started to say something, but Sykora got there first.

"Do you want to be trapped in a lift with a potentially hostile *Sentience* controlling it?" the big Amazon asked in a cruel voice.

"Oh," the tiny engineer thought about it. "Yeah, no."

The dangerous women apparently telepathically flipped coins and organized themselves. Javier and Afia ended up in the middle of the line, with Hajna on point, followed by Sykora, and Suvi's probe flying overhead. Sascha brought up the rear.

The stairwell, when they got there, showed all the imagination of the rest of the ship. Three-and-a-half-meter-wide treads, enough for three people to move at once, or two in armoured suits. Up a half-deck, landing, half-turn, up the next. Motion sensing lights at regular intervals.

A little over half of the lights even worked, at least enough to show the way as they entered the square column.

Javier was glad Afia was in even worse condition than he was. He stayed in shape with yoga and regular weight-lifting. The engineer just had youth on her side.

The other three were the kind of people that did hikes on *Storm Gauntlet* where they put on fifteen kilo packs and walked every hallway, every other day.

Boring, but they weren't wheezing after six decks, either.

At least nothing jumped out at them.

Javier ignored Sykora's smirk as they got to Deck Four and stood around catching their breath. He felt like a forty-year-old man today. And no, he was not taking up running so he could keep up with the kids.

Deep breath. Angry growl.

Let's do this.

There was absolutely no reason to put the bridge on Deck Four. When you sailed on water, it made sense, since your captain needed to be high enough to look around and direct things.

Javier supposed that *Neu Berne* had just never gotten over that. *Concord* ships put it as close to the center of the ship as they could, on the assumption that since it was really hard to actually blow a ship up, you frequently had to stab it to death with beams that acted like ice picks.

Maybe those bastards just wanted everybody in shape from climbing too many damned stairs on a daily basis. Looking at Sykora, he could see that.

You didn't get a bottom that perfect sitting on it at a work station.

"Probe," Javier called. "Map, please. Deck Four, centered on us."

Sykora started to say something, but subsided at the scowl he directed her way.

Yes, I was aware that you have memorized the entire layout of this ship and could probably tell me the room numbers as we go. Unless I plan to crack your skull open and suck your brains out with a straw, princess, I need to see it as well.

That thought had its advantages.

Suvi projected onto the deck below them, saving him the extra step of orienting himself. Another reason he had asked his most favorite woman, and not his least.

Again, stupid design decision, to put it barely a fifth of the way back from the bow, but it saved him having to walk very far from here.

And still, nothing had jumped out at them, or spoken to them.

If he didn't know better, he would have thought this was a simpler ship. Like *Storm Gauntlet*. Automated to a high degree, but not self-directing. Follow orders and nothing more.

Or the dragon was sprawled out on his horde of gold coins like the ancient story, just waiting for them to enter his lair.

And Javier, without a ring of invisibility.

They tromped on. There was nothing silent and sneaky about this group, except maybe how much firepower the four women could bring to bear in the flash of an eye. Or eyeball, in Suvi's case.

The hatch to the bridge was definitely not standard naval architecture. If it had been, it would have been that plain gray-green everything else was, and standard height and width. This one was an extra fifty centimeters wider, a whole meter taller, and banded with extra straps of a golden metal running vertically in three places.

Like it really wanted to be a bank vault when it grew up. Heavy, imposing, secure. As if the Admiral on the other side was expecting an enemy assault force to board and try to storm the bridge itself.

That, at least, sounded like something *Neu Berne* would do.

Javier found the three camera sensors in the frame: two at eye level on each side, and one overhead. The little lights next to the lenses were out. Hopefully, the dragon wasn't watching.

Like all starships, there was a panel on the right. Humans tended to be right-handed, so it was standard. If the *Sentience* was watching, he would let you in after he identified you. If something went wrong, you could key in a security code to prove who you were. If the *Sentience* went off-line, theoretically you could override things from here.

"*Hammerfield*, open the hatch, please," Javier said in a firm, polite voice. In German, even.

What the hell, it might even work.

It was that or *Open Sesame*.

Nothing happened.

Unlike the airlock, there was no emergency override button here. And a ten-key pad with only a trillion options to try.

This was why he brought Afia. Beyond surrounding himself with beautiful, competent women. Although, one should never overlook that.

"Afia," he turned to her with a smile, pointing at the box. "Would you be so kind as to open that so we can get to the door control circuits?"

Her gear was tucked into custom sleeves and pockets on the outside of her suit, where she could get at them by touch alone when working. She pulled something from her left thigh and something from her belt and tapped metal on metal on the casing while she kneeled down to get her nose almost up against it, like an insurance specialist trying to identify a forged painting.

The other women went into a defensive array, guns in every direction and hostility like an ugly fog boiling off of them.

However, Sykora almost seemed to be fidgeting, which was completely unlike her.

This was one of the few times he didn't mind. Creator only knew what a bored and desperate *Sentience* might throw at them. Nobody had stun weapons in hand right now.

Afia had the case off in seconds, without using a prybar. Another reason he had brought her.

Inside, electronic guts that didn't mean all that much to Javier, but apparently were a roadmap to an engineer. She studied it for a few seconds and then looked up at him.

"It's unlocked," she said simply. "I can open it anytime you want."

"I'll cover it," Sykora barked out.

"No, you will not," Javier replied.

"Why not?"

She rounded on him, angry, overbearing, willing to use her greater size to whatever affect it might have.

None. He wasn't going to budge.

"Because you are too emotionally involved, Dragoon," Javier said. "You are not tactical right now."

That got through to her.

She snarled at him, and then blinked.

Amazingly, the Amazon woman holstered both pistols with a curse of frustration.

"Damn it," she growled. "Damn you. And you're right."

She tilted her head down and looked both ways up the hallway.

"Probe, you cover the door," she said. "Can I watch?"

Javier nodded up at her, at the anguish he saw in those eyes. As much as he wanted to hate this woman, as much joy as destroying her would bring him, he needed her intact. Not just now. Maybe for a long time.

However long it took to win a war with pirates.

Let the universe sort it out after that.

Javier looked at both pathfinders, made sure they nodded back at him. Suvi was faster than even Sykora, if somebody needed to be killed when that door opened. Sykora could probably still draw and shoot faster than anyone holding a pistol.

"Open it up," he said to Afia.

She nodded and reached out with her right hand. Something clicked and the whole vault door began to move sideways into the left-hand wall.

PART FOUR

Afia didn't have any dog in this fight.

The dragoon was a hard-ass professional, every waking moment, but she was also living in a galaxy where disdainful men tended to run things, so the giantess had to be twice as good as any man at her job to even be considered adequate. *Storm Gauntlet* ran a lot less sexist because that woman wouldn't take any shit from any man, and wouldn't allow any man to become a problem or a predator.

Hell, if you looked at it that way, *Neu Berne* itself, then or now, was way more socially advanced than most of the others. Even *Concord* folk really only tended to talk a good game, but didn't always deliver, Captain Sokolov being a notable exception.

Javier, as compared to Sykora or Sokolov, was a total goofball most of the time, but he was never selfish, in bed or on duty. And that went a long way in Afia's book.

"Open it up," Javier kinda growled, but his anger wasn't aimed at her.

Sykora was in the wrong on this one. She was only here because nobody would tell her she couldn't be, the only *Bernian* in the entire crew, making maybe the biggest discovery in the culture's history.

Afia reached out and triggered the mechanical linkage that the computer would have brought in-line, had she known to just push the *Open* button. None of them had thought to ask. At least nobody had suggested blasting the door open.

She was pretty sure there was enough firepower handy to pull that off. Even this reinforced monster bitch of a door.

Afia rose to her feet as the others hyped themselves up. She was the smallest person here, so she could peek in and see things first. Javier and Sykora were going to rely on her the most going forward, especially if he was going to be busy keeping Sykora from getting out of hand.

That woman just might, yet.

The lethal, gray fishbowl hovered about three meters up, just below the door jamb, but high enough to not be in anybody's way if the dragoon needed to fire.

Javier was on the other side of the door, so Afia was able to peek as the door moved to one side. It opened sideways away from her side of the frame on slightly grinding rails, probably a bit of gunk in there somewhere from being closed too long. Common problem. One of the reasons you opened every door regularly as part of maintenance.

Inside was a vast chamber that took her breath away.

She gasped, but the others would see it soon enough, so she didn't need to say anything.

At least there was nothing to shoot.

The hatch slid the whole way open and disappeared into the bulkhead with a small thunk.

The air coming out had a different smell. Afia couldn't say what it was, but it was there.

The bridge of the *Neu Berne* Flagship *Hammerfield*.

Huge. Wasteful. Impressive.

From her vantage, it was a round room, about twenty-five meters across, with a domed ceiling at least nine meters at the peak.

Two meters in, stairs went down a meter to a walkway on either side of the four meter entryway.

Afia could see a number of crew stations around the outside of the bridge, but the central section was the most impressive.

Six stations arranged in a hexagon pattern, looking outward over the stations around the outer ring that faced the bulkhead.

It was the center that caught her eye and her breath.

A raised dais. A round pedestal maybe a meter tall and three across, with steps ringing it all the way around. A command station, similar to what the captain had, back on *Storm Gauntlet*, but bigger, more ornate.

And occupied.

A man sat there, facing them, unmoving.

Sykora had both guns out so fast that they might have always been there.

From her close proximity, Afia could see them shake, just the slightest bit.

About what Afia would have done, after a night of watching really good zombie movies.

The probe pinged the room hard. Afia felt it in her bones, the pulse was so heavy across so many frequencies. But it held its fire, so Afia assumed everything was good enough, at least for now.

"Sykora," Javier barked sharply.

Afia tore her eyes away from the bridge to look at her companions.

Javier was poised, his attention riveted on the dragoon, but he was carefully not interposing himself between Sykora and whatever terrible visions she was having. Sykora was an alabaster statue, except for the vibrating barrels, that image being possibly the most frightening thing Afia had ever seen in her life.

Djamila Sykora was normally the rock that the rest of the crew was built upon.

What would they do if she came apart on them?

Hajna and Sascha had peeked, but they had their fire lanes to maintain. Stone professionals.

That left Afia.

Internally, she shrugged.

You are an engineer. Treat this like an engineering problem. Understand that sometimes, you have to go into a hostile reactor and die killing it for the good of the crew.

"Cover me," she said, stepping quickly forward and out of any lunging reach.

"Damn it, Afia," Javier said, but that was all.

She was pretty sure Sykora was keeping all of his attention.

The fans were on in here, a nice, background hum that meant *safe* on board a starship. Lights as well.

Heat. That was what was different.

The hallway had been four degrees, just enough above freezing that pipes with water weren't at risk. It was closer to eighteen degrees in here. Not quite warm enough to strip naked and enjoy the feel of nothing but breeze against her skin, but close.

Oh, so damned close.

The rest of the crew would probably still be in jackets and pants, but they hadn't grown up with a glacier across the valley, either.

Why would this room be so warm?

None of the other stations were inhabited, just the captain's. Afia paused after about four meters to slowly pivot in place and take it all in. Twelve stations along the outer wall. Six stations around the captain. And the throne.

From here, Afia could see a panel on the far wall, six meters by three, that roughly mirrored the entryway. Visual screen, but only for the captain, since everyone else was facing the wrong way usually.

Impressive as hell.

Afia took a deep breath. Her suit was reacting to the greater warmth by shutting down the heating elements. She wasn't suddenly chilled with fear, no, sir.

That's what she told herself.

She was an engineer. He was not a zombie, that unmoving man up there. Screw that.

She took another step closer, just to prove her own courage.

Okay, he's dead.

Dried up. Shriveled like a hunk of beef jerky.

Hard to tell how old he was, but Afia guessed him to be the actual captain. The red uniform he wore had enough bangles to be a senior officer of some sort.

Blond hair looked like it wanted to be graying, but hadn't quite made up its mind, yet.

Anglo, obviously. He had that pinkish tone to his skin that differentiated *Neu Berne* from her own Indonesian ancestors, even if she had grown up with her family in the Yukon Protectorate, back on Earth.

His head was tilted down, but she was short and he was on a riser, so Afia could see his face.

At least his eyes were closed.

She took another step closer.

He was fully strapped in, with his hands resting on the armrests, looking utterly peaceful.

There was a large, white envelope in his lap, but there was no way in hell she was getting that close.

"*Hammerfield*, please provide operational status," she called out to the room.

It had ignored Javier outside. Maybe it was deaf. Maybe it was asleep.

153

Maybe the bridge defensive systems were about to come live and try to kill her.

Afia had her doubts about that, as keyed up as the probe and the dragoon were, right now.

Nothing.

No change to the air systems blowing. No lights coming on or going off where she could see them.

"Afia?" Javier's voice carried across the vast distance that separated them right now.

She spun slowly in place again, taking it all in while she was still the first conqueror to set foot on this bridge.

"All clear," she said.

"Everyone in," she heard him order.

"No," Sykora said weakly. "We should not all be trapped in there."

"Djamila, we're going to stay together," Javier replied in a voice that he might use on a skittish horse.

Afia turned so she could watch the corpse and her friends at the same time.

Had they really found the last flagship and her crew?

PART THREE

BOOK NINETEEN: HAMMERFIELD

PART ONE

W ITH BOTH DJAMILA and Javier outside the ship, Zakhar was pulling a watch duty on the bridge, when he would normally leave it to the rest of his Centurions and their assistants and go do paperwork himself. He probably still should, but it was better if everyone else got some down time.

Lir himself only knew when something would happen, or what it would look like. This system was so messy, so complicated with gravity wells, that there really wasn't any safe way to trigger a jump longways across the entire system, punching home a goal between the primary star and the binary pair that had been captured later.

There was barely enough space to get a running start away from the ancient warship if it decided to come after them.

Zakhar hoped there was enough space.

Storm Gauntlet was old, but still dated to the period after the Great Wars had ended. She should be more advanced, technologically, than *Hammerfield*, even if the little corvette had been massively outgunned by the galleon before she had taken so much damage escaping *Svalbard*.

If *Neu Berne* had been more advanced, they wouldn't have lost so badly, taking down the *Union of Man*, *Balustrade*, and everyone but the *Concord*, quietly sitting over in one corner of the galaxy away from the main players.

Djamila and her team had gone silent as soon as they emerged from the flight bay. Zakhar had watched them cross the space on passive optics only, until they vanished from sight into the maw of the gray beast.

Javier made a pretty good Jonah, on reflection. Zakhar pondered, but was unable to identify where Nineveh might be, in the modern context. Or maybe, who?

"Clock time?" Zakhar called out.

Not because he couldn't look it up himself, but to remind everyone to stay sharp.

Tobias Gibney was manning the science station this shift. Thomas Obasanjo had gunnery. Mikhail Dominguez sat in the pilot's chair.

It was a tossup who would respond first. They were all pretty good, or they wouldn't be sitting on his bridge in a potentially dangerous situation.

"Ninety-four minutes since they boarded, sir," Gibney replied.

Zakhar wondered at what point he would have to decide to go rescue them, *rescue her*, or give up and get on with a post-piracy life, if no signal ever came.

No answer availed itself.

He keyed a comm channel.

"Wardroom," he said in as light a voice as he could fake right now. "Captain would appreciate some tea, please."

"Coming up," a man's voice replied.

Zakhar settled himself for a long night, wondering if he would ever see Djamila again.

And if not, when would Prince Charming surrender his dreams of happily-ever-after?

PART TWO

JavⅠer watched the Amazon like his life depended on it. Even more than usual.

Sykora was wound like the strings on a violin right now, just waiting for some musical lunatic to come along and make her scream in agony.

She stared back at him with eyes that didn't have any iris, any color, at all.

Just black portals to hell.

"We'll do this together, Djamila," he said quietly. "This is a tomb, a war memorial, and will be treated as such. But I need you focused. The rest of the women can handle anything that comes along. Can you do this?"

He had seen this iron woman raging. Cunning. Embarrassed. Befuddled. Even drunk once, and singing martial folks songs in German.

He had never seen her on the edge of cracking up.

At least he would die quickly when she did, since Javier had no doubt he would be first on her shit list when she lost control and opened fire.

Sykora took a breath.

It was shallow, but indicated that she was listening. Hopefully unwinding and not unraveling.

She nodded, just as shallowly.

Nothing more, but enough to tell him she was in control, however fragile that hold was.

He would ask what the hell had come over the bronzed berserker, but he already knew. Or could hazard a guess.

That might be King Arthur himself, seated on that dais over there. This might be Avalon.

And it might also be Niflheim.

She hadn't shot him, yet, so Javier took a gamble and stepped into the room, trusting the pathfinders to cover the hallway and Suvi to shoot Sykora if push really came to shove.

Hopefully, Suvi understood how utterly weird things had gotten and wouldn't overreact.

Which was the strangest thing Javier could think of, on an already bizarre day.

He needed Sykora, galling as that thought was.

Eight steps in, Afia watched with the sort of feigned nonchalance that didn't fool anyone, but he let it slide.

"What have you got, kid?" he said to try to smooth over the general awkwardness.

A glance back revealed that Suvi had come into the room and side-slipped to one side so she could cover all the organics, living or dead, in a single arc of fire. Which said a lot about her read on things.

Sykora followed, like a marionette whose strings have tangled, lurching step by step when she was normally smooth grace itself. Javier figured she had recovered somewhat when she holstered both pistols and looked around, awe scribed on her face like a ten-year-old at a theme park.

"He's dead," Afia replied, pointing at the guy in the captain's chair. "Apparently left a note for you."

"Me?" Javier asked.

"I'm not grabbing it," she said, feet rooted firmly to the deck. "*Sentience* isn't responding, but it isn't shooting, either. What do you think, boss?"

Javier looked around quickly. Nothing amiss in here. Sascha had entered. Hajna was following, walking sideways like a crab.

"Afia," Sascha called. "What button closes the door?"

"[Enter] key," the tiny engineer yelled back. "Bottom left."

Sascha keyed it in, and Javier watched the door slide shut with a soft click.

Here they were.

Sykora had drifted closest to the corpse, but stayed at the bottom of the steps, like a peasant waiting her turn to present a petition.

No guns, and a minimum of fidgeting. Probably a good sign.

Javier walked noisily up to stand next to the giant woman. He could probably have tried to sneak and she'd have still tracked him, as keyed up as she appeared.

One glance over and he confirmed that there was still no green in those eyes.

Just white and black.

At least she wasn't as pale as she had been.

Javier sniffed, aware of what old corpses in space tended to smell like. It wasn't like the old, dried leather you got in the desert.

More stale and musty. Three-day-old bread, maybe.

"Probe," he said in a normal voice. "Status, please."

"All scans nominal," Suvi said in the dumb, computer voice she was hiding behind.

Again, she would warn him, hopefully. But there was an even bigger *Sentience* here. Maybe older. Maybe her age. A dangerous sibling, in any case.

Javier didn't think the dragon could sneak up and take Suvi over without a sound, or a fight.

But he really hadn't studied the Great War more than enough to ace his history exams at the Academy. And that was a long time ago.

Afia was twitchy. Sykora right out on the ledge. The pathfinders were trying to look every direction for zombies coming out of the vents and side doors.

That left him.

But this was why he got out of bed this morning.

Javier took a loud breath, deep and meaningful, as a warning to everyone else.

Not like what came next would be a surprise to anyone, but still.

He climbed the four steps to the platform, where he could stand next to the dead guy.

Uniform didn't mean anything either, except that the guy looked more like a captain and less like an admiral. Those people always had to get extra silly with their decorations.

Scarlet, long sleeve shirt. Not cotton, but something stretchy if still a little loose, with refractive elements in it that looked like glitter.

Glossy black, leather, slip-on boots to mid-calf. Black pants that were tight down through the thigh, and then flared out into little bells before tucking into the boots, like big, black mushrooms.

It was hard to tell the man's age, given that he was all dried up and wrinkly, but Javier would have guessed him around fifty when he died.

The face was calm in death. The arms relaxed on the armrests of his grand throne, like a king of yore.

He was composed.

At peace.

This man hadn't died in agony or horror. His corpse wasn't here as a warning to future generations or a trophy.

Javier looked down at the envelope in the man's lap. The paper was a cream color, almost almond. It was oversized, like a standard piece of paper folded in half, instead of thirds.

There was writing on the outside. Big, blocky letters.

This did not look like a man with a florid, cursive hand.

And he had placed it facing outward, so that it would be immediately legible to someone standing where Javier was, and upside down to the captain on his chair.

Javier picked it up and held the document in one hand, weighing it.

Heavy linen stock. Filled with several pages of the same weight inside, from the bulkiness.

Javier's German was pretty good, better spoken than written, but still competent enough if something was a scientific article. Less so with literature.

He was probably safe with this man.

"What does this say?" he turned to show it to the only native in the room. In the crew. Maybe it would help.

Djamila's eyes focused. Squinted a little. Her head came forward unconsciously, just a touch, but enough to break the fragile rigidity she had assumed.

She blinked.

Javier could see tears forming in her eyes. Happily, nobody else was in a position to perceive that. Something else he had never expected to know about this woman.

Possibly something else to carry to his grave.

Javier honestly hadn't believed that sort of thing was possible with Djamila Sykora.

But this was the future, and all things were possible.

"*We did our duty*," she said in a voice that managed both quiet reverence and that sort of profound heaviness that only *Neu Berne* culture ever conveyed.

"Yeah," Javier said. "That's what I thought."

Javier had a pretty good speaking voice, even translating something as he went, and he knew they would want to hear it.

He flipped it over, carefully peeled away the wax seal he found, and pulled out the pages folded up inside.

PART THREE

"ADMIRAL STEINER IS DEAD. *She was the Last Admiral of* Neu Berne, *as we measure such things, and the first casualty when the Intelligence went insane.*

That coward is dead now, and the survivors are trapped here. The technical crew who could have rebuilt things died with it, leaving the poor, sad remains of the crew locked inside our own mausoleum, like an ancient king who buries his household with him for the afterlife.

Hopefully, I will find a way to haunt that beast in hell.

To you who have found us here: Greetings.

The rogue Intelligence was destroyed, and with it most of our records, since we had no other way to read them. With nothing else to do, we repaired as much of the physical structure of the vessel as we could and parked this craft in the most constant orbit we could manage, a gravitationally-stable point where it would hopefully become a suitable monument.

Without the stardrives controlled by the Intelligence, or the main computer system that was its brain and memory, we could never leave this system, except to aim the vessel across the interstellar darkness at sub-light speeds, to become someone else's navigational hazard, several centuries after we had all died.

Our mission had been to escape Neu Berne. *To rally the outer colonies and worlds. To hide in the wilderness, like a young prince, and to reclaim the throne when he came of age.*

We have failed. And failed the Empire as well. We discussed allowing the knowledge of our failure to die with us, by flying into one of the three stars here, but in the end decided that we owed the future the truth of what had happened here.

I have left a written log in my cabin, begun after we had slain the beast and known our own death. The other logs were contained within the memory of the Intelligence, and so hidden from us.

Each death was recorded. Crew who succumbed to wounds from the final battle. Accidents as we rebuilt the ship to the finest standards possible before powering everything down for the longest night.

Finally, the day when there was no more we could do.

The crew retired to the main gymnasium, where we had an evening of the finest food and companionship, telling old stories, singing patriotic songs, and establishing the final bonds of comrades facing the eternal darkness.

The Medical Officer had prepared the potion. One by one the crew drank it and made their final peace with God.

Each man and woman retired to the coffins that were their final resting place, bid their comrades Auf Wiedersehen, *and closed the lids, to sleep the eternal and find their place to Valhalla.*

Only I remained, a captain dying with his ship. It was my duty to record it all, return to my bridge, and await you.

I am Captain Ulrich Mayer, last commander of the last flagship of the Neu Berne *Navy.*

I failed my Empire, but I have done my duty.

PART FOUR

Javier took a breath and looked up.

Sykora was crying openly now. But that was okay. So were the other three women. Probably the fourth as well.

She was human in all the ways that mattered.

Everyone who traveled in space had to face that risk. Dying, alone in the darkness, trapped farther away from friends and home than you can ever return.

Lost, and never coming home.

Javier nodded to Captain Mayer, a very short, formal thank you for everything the man had done for a future generation in need.

It made sense now. The *Sentience* hadn't responded to him or Afia because it was dead.

He wondered how much they had been able to repair.

Most people thought of a *Sentience* as a giant computer program, billions of lines of code capable of responding to ever more complicated decisions trees.

Javier knew better.

At her core, Suvi was a very compact set of algorithms embedded on a set of chips. Not ROM, the read-only-memory that is etched into the board and never modified again, but a firmware that was non-volatile and could be improved over time by someone who took the time to understand how the language worked at that level.

To help her be more human.

If he was only ever going to know one daughter, to make sure she turned out a pretty good kid.

Suvi had.

It was her memories that took up all the damned space, even written in the multi-dimensional symbolic language that her kind used to encode everything. Cleaning up systems she had been using must have been what it was like to have teenagers in the house.

Hopefully, the captain had killed the beast by pulling or destroying the chips at the core of the system, and not just blowing up the central computer itself.

"So now what?" Afia breathed in a quiet voice, as if unwilling to break the tableau that had formed around them like icicles.

Javier studied Sykora's face for a clue. That woman did not understand poker one damned bit, wearing her emotions on her sleeves most of the time.

Today, she had either gone deeper inside herself than he had ever seen, or peeled away all the layers that had accumulated like an angry pearl over the years, to show the grain of stone at the center of it all.

Six months ago, he would have happily used everything he was learning to drive this woman bat-shit insane. More bat-shit insane.

But that was yesterday. And this was tomorrow.

"Djamila?" he said simply.

Her eyes came back from the horizon, flickered over to his face.

Bright green emeralds, lit with an internal flame.

"Now we know," she murmured.

Javier nodded. One of the galaxy's greatest mysteries in the last century, and they had solved it.

The little evil conscience on his left shoulder showed him a bill of goods they could sell to the happy folks at *Neu Berne* when they returned the last crew to their homeland.

Ransom, if you will.

The planet was poor these days, but even a poor planetary government worked with sums that make interstellar corporations look like popsicle stands by comparison.

Not that he would ever breathe a word of this to Sykora.

The good conscience on his right shoulder walked over and knocked the evil one onto his ass with a roundhouse, just like in the cartoons.

He turned back to Afia, patiently waiting by his side as the emotional tides swirled around her and started to head back out to sea.

"Now, we go look at the engineering sections and see how much work it will take to get everything in motion," he said.

"What about *Storm Gauntlet?*" she asked carefully. "Should we call the captain?"

All of the women were suddenly staring intently at him. But that was okay.

He had been planning this for a long time.

"Soon," he said. "It will be much easier to use the ship's comm to send a signal, as noisy as this system is."

Javier pointed at the dead man that had come to dinner.

"And we only have his word that they didn't set a trap for us," Javier continued. "Let's not suck the whole crew into an ambush."

Sykora came back to herself. Feisty. Tough.

Intent.

But she held her peace, for now.

That would make it easier.

Afia turned to the dragoon.

"Best way into engineering?" she asked the tall woman.

"Deck Thirteen," Sykora said. "Elevators should be working, but let's take the central stairs anyway."

Javier nodded. As long as Sykora remained tactical, everything would be fine.

Zakhar Sokolov was probably the only one of them sneaky enough to anticipate what was coming.

PART FIVE

Afia was almost at the back of the column. The group of them was approaching the port staircase element that ran vertically down the center of the ship, walking along the port-side hallway that served as one of the three boulevards from bow to stern on Deck Four.

Everything had a chilled smell, kinda like you got in a brand new refrigerator, before any food had managed to leave an impression.

Metal and plastic and cold.

It was weird on a starship, not to smell people and leftover dinners.

She had let everyone else organize themselves as they tromped noisily through the intestines of the big ship. And it was big.

If you could have opened up the right frames and access points, the combined cargo deck down the ship's axis was almost big enough to carry *Storm Gauntlet*, a fierce, little teacup Chihuahua in a lady's purse.

Not that Afia had ever been compared that way either. Especially not as tiny as she was compared to most folks. Being small, and fierce, and technical, she had stood out from the other kids.

Afia Burakgazi had grown up on Earth, almost exactly half a world away from her family's ancestral homeland of Indonesia where all her cousins still lived. In the Yukon Protectorate there were still wild places and dangerous critters. You had to keep an eye and an ear tuned to things out of the ordinary and be prepared to listen when your subconscious is trying to tell you something.

Plus, her grandmother was a witch, and had hexed her early on with the Second Sight.

Both her nose for trouble and her grandmother's memory were talking to her now.

The dragoon was an emotional wreck. No ifs, ands, or buts about it.

Afia probably would be, too, in similar circumstances.

But all of the snark and bickering had disappeared from Javier.

Gone.

Like frost in the morning sun.

He was treating Sykora carefully. Kid gloves.

If there was ever a time to score points on her, it was now, when she was in no shape to fight back.

Afia probably would have had to get up in his face, if he had. Sascha and Hajna as well. But he would have said something.

It was the nature of the relationship between those two.

Except he hadn't. Hadn't even come close.

Nothing.

He had to be up to something.

Afia didn't think that anybody but her had picked it up, or someone would have said something. And maybe she was only imagining it, but she didn't think so. Javier Aritza, occasionally infamous as Eutrupio Navarre, was hands-down the sneakiest man Afia had ever met.

So she watched the way he moved, one place ahead of her in line and a head taller. He didn't walk enough steps every day for the suit to look good on his ass.

They arrived.

The central stairs were a strange design.

The designer here had done something weird. And not just because this was a cargo ship with a big empty space down the middle.

There were two sets of stairs here: Port side and Starboard, well away from the central boulevard. Sascha had picked port for no better reason than she could. The two were identical.

On most ships, a stairwell ran top to bottom in an open column, with emergency plates that could close horizontally between levels if you lost power and pressure. Plus, they had hatches out at every floor that were normally closed.

Here, it was a set of tall rooms.

You went down a level and the stairs ended. You had to go through a hatch at the bottom of the stairs and into another chamber, turn one-hundred-eighty degrees, and go down another flight in another room.

Each pair of levels was sealed automatically, plus you got a lot more structural strength at the center of the ship because you didn't have that big, vertical column.

But it was a serious pain in the ass to go down nine decks this way.

Afia wondered if that was part of the reason Sascha had done it. Maybe she hoped the grumbling would get Sykora back to being herself.

Afia considered that maybe she needed to walk more steps every day, too, when they got down to Deck Thirteen.

Her legs felt like rubber, her butt hurt, and she was short of breath.

Sykora looked like she had just come from the beach. Hajna and Sascha, too.

Afia kept her grumbles to herself.

Mostly.

At one point, the probe pivoted around enough that she was looking at its "face," so maybe the grumbles weren't that quiet.

Afia worked on keeping her mouth shut after that.

Thanks, Mom.

Deck Thirteen looked a lot like Deck Four if you didn't paint it as often. Not dingy or anything, but faded a bit, maybe. Monochrome. No little trim flashes or color offsets to brighten things.

Soulless.

The land of the introverts who went into the engineering tracks, rather than the extroverts who did the line command or ground combat tracks.

Out the last stairwell door and along this hallway to the aft. The cargo holds were down here, and huge in places. Several decks tall and a hundred meters between frames. Big enough for a hockey rink, stands, and a taco truck.

Engineering, when they got there, wasn't nearly as impressive, but Afia wasn't sure what she had been expecting.

Sure, big machines everywhere. Control room with transparent windows on this level, so you could watch several parallel rows of monstrous power reactors lined up like ugly, gray turtles on a log.

But nothing she hadn't seen recently on *Storm Gauntlet*, or before she became a pirate.

The room smelled like a power station, too. Lubricant and ozone in trace amounts. The faintest hint of rust and metal, like tiny shavings spalled off by slowly moving parts.

It felt good to be home.

She dropped automatically into the primary station, wiped the screen clean of accumulated *stuffff* with a rag she kept handy for just that task, and powered it up. These was dust everywhere, but nothing bad. Trust a *Neu Berne* crew, especially with nothing better to do before they died, to clean everything as well as humanly possible.

At least the folks had unlocked everything before they died, so that someone like her could put this old beast back into the line.

"What's your pleasure?" she smiled up at Javier.

He looked down at her for a second, blank, before a roguish smile ghosted itself and he winked back at her. More of a promise, since this was probably not the time nor the place.

Probably.

You never knew.

"Make sure everything is intact on standby and no more than a soft yellow," he said. "If we think the life support systems are solid, start bringing things up to the same temperature as the bridge was. That should be good enough for now. All the food that's left is long past edible, so I'm not worried about it, but I don't want it so warm that cans explode."

"Coming up," she said, starting to toggle through screens.

Things being written in German on this ship didn't bother her. Everything down here would be written in *Engineer*, a standard thousands of years old that spanned all forms of communication.

She could identify the workarounds the crew had programmed into the systems when the *Sentience* died. It would mostly handle those tasks for everyone, needing only occasional tuning and maintenance to keep it all working.

A vessel this big probably kept a smaller crew than a little corvette like *Storm Gauntlet* had.

Afia didn't trust the life support systems all that much, but they had held under a low baseline load for a very long time, so she was comfortable telling them to bring the temperature and pressure up slowly.

Everyone would remain in their suits until she said otherwise. That point, she would hammer home on all of them.

Fierce teacup Chihuahua.

"Can you access comm systems from in here?" Javier asked in a voice that just sounded wrong.

Concerned, but evasive. Like he really wanted the answer to be no, but couldn't just come out and say that, at least not in front of the others.

Weird.

But this was Javier, and he was having to juggle everything else with Sykora being possessed by demons or something. Maybe it was just the struggle to keep them all sane that was getting to him.

Afia toggled through a couple of boards and ran through logic trees while he watched. The other three just waited, torn between watching the big generators and paying attention to what she was doing.

She could take advantage of their paranoia to help Javier.

They didn't need to know that someone had defaulted all login accounts to Full System Administrator rights. And she would fix that pretty soon. That was too much like handing a five-year-old a beam weapon. Stupid, and someone was going to get hurt.

"I can transmit a signal on the right frequencies as part of the Identification Transponder," Afia shaded the truth with a small forest of pine trees. "Is that good enough?"

That must have been the answer to his prayers. Javier sagged just a little, and smiled at her.

"Perfect," he replied. "Let *Storm Gauntlet* know we have boarded, are exploring, and are safe at present. We will check in again in ten hours."

"Ten?" Sykora perked up from her fugue with a voice that was a thin ghost of her normal bark, but you could still hear the woman underneath.

"That's right," Javier pivoted to look up at her. "We've had a long day, a lot of stress, and the ship needs time to come up from her nap. This is a good time to eat, sleep, and when we wake up, we can probably get out of these damned suits and live like normal people."

"Watch cycle?" Sascha chimed in, obviously intent on handling things if her boss was off-line.

"None," Javier said, his voice gone hard and flat, like a sword blade. "The probe can handle everything. I want you all down hard and fully refreshed tomorrow. Take something if you need to. There are a whole bunch of dead men and women on this ship and we will need to secure them with the proper ceremonies. Everything else that comes after that will be even more difficult. Questions?"

The three women subsided.

Afia nodded, but only inside her head. Javier *was* up to something.

That was a sneaky way to ambush somebody.

Afia called up a schematic to check the location.

"There is a break room behind that door," she said, pointing through the transparent wall to a space down a little ways, right next to the first power generator on the starboard side. "It should have bunks. I'll sleep here so I can be ready if the system sounds any alerts."

Javier didn't look too thrilled with that option, but he couldn't argue with her.

Kinda like how he had boxed the others in.

And, while she was thinking about it, Afia reached into the console in the break room and locked out certain functions.

If Javier was up to something, she might need to help. Or she might also have to shoot him.

PART SIX

Javier was first into the big area Afia had classified as a break room. Twenty meters long, by about half that wide, it looked like a wardroom, with all the tables and chairs around the open space and locked down for loss of gravity. Ugly gray walls and ceiling. Moss green carpet in the kind of mottled pattern that would hide stains and spills.

There was a wall of vending machines on the far wall from him, plus a couple of coffee robots. Every single one was dark and empty.

Trust people who thought like Sykora to clean out the machines of all the chips and candy. They had probably drained the water lines on the coffee makers as well.

He would appreciate that in a few days, after someone like Ilan Yu had spent a great deal of time cleaning it all down and replacing parts, but right now a little caffeine could be nice. Sleep was the last thing on his mind.

The right end of the room was a bunch of cubicle doors. Every ship he had ever served on had something similar in their engineering bays. People might be on duty for long stretches, but they got frequent breaks, and needed to study for certifications and such.

Much better if all your engineers were immediately available in any emergency down here.

"Probe. Access Command Mode," he called, loud enough for the three women coming through the door behind him. Suvi was already listening. "Secure this room for engineering emergencies and remain on watch here."

"Confirmed," Suvi replied in her bored computer voice.

Javier took one last look and turned to face Sykora. He was exhausted, but was going to push right through. He let the exhaustion color his voice, though.

"You should take something, or meditate yourself to sleep," he said before looking at the two other women. "I plan to be asleep in about five minutes. Set your alarms for eight hours and be prepared to go like hell for sixteen hours tomorrow."

He didn't bother waiting for them to answer. Instead, he went into the closest cubicle and closed the door.

Locked it, too, just in case either Hajna or Sascha decided that they needed his help to be knocked off-line for a while.

Any other day than this…

The space beyond the door was cozy. Two meters wide by four deep. Single bunk with a thin blanket. Writing desk surface with a chair. Softer paint on the walls, here a soothing rose color.

He pulled the control remote for the probe from his pack and settled himself on the bed. A switch and the voice channel was active.

"You ready?" he asked.

The walls were also going to be totally sound-proof, because someone napping or studying didn't need to listen to someone else snoring.

"All set here," Suvi replied in her usual bright voice. "How long?"

Javier considered his options.

"Let's give them an hour to settle and get into deep sleep," Javier said. "Wake me then. Afia will need time, as well."

"Got it, boss," his sidekick chirped.

Javier laid down and closed his eyes.

PART SEVEN

AFIA WATCHED them on a security camera in the break room and let go a deep breath. She listened in as Javier went off to bed first, the other three taking only a few moments to decide to do the same, the general consensus that the probe would be enough watch for now.

And it had been a long day. Up for hours before the long flight over here. All the stress of deep space with a hostile warship looming. Breaking and entering into a tomb.

Afia was as exhausted as Javier sounded.

Still, something just wasn't right, but she couldn't put her finger on it.

Given her supreme control of the engineering boards, Afia temporized. She could nap, after setting alarms that would go off in her control room if anyone opened the door to the break area. It could even be loud, since this room was sealed up tight right now.

Anyone who came out in less than seven hours would be up to no good, anyway, so she needed to be able to block them from doing something stupid.

That done, Afia locked every door around her, stretched out on the floor, and let the strain of the day draw her down into darkness.

BEEP.

Afia came awake instantly, lost for a second as an unfamiliar gray ceiling loomed overhead.

Engineering Primary Control. Door alarm. *Hammerfield.*

Afia was on her side on the deck, facing the control station. The screen was on, set to beep every three seconds until she disabled it. She studied movement on the camera's view.

Beep.

Javier had opened the door to the break room and come out into the main engineering space next to Auxiliary Power Unit number 1.

The probe, that armed eyeball with all the good sensors, was with him, so Afia lay still. If he went anywhere else, she would have to track him, and that might be hard.

Necessary, but hard.

What the hell would he need to be up to on this ship by himself?

She remained like a cold stone, just in case, but Javier quickly crossed to the main hatch outside her office, only glancing over once to make sure she was still asleep.

Afia had planned this, with enough of her back to the window to look like she was asleep, but she could see a screen he couldn't, not from outside.

And then he was out in the hallway.

She gave him a two count as the board continued to beep.

Afia was about to get up and move when the door alarm went off a second time, out of sequence.

On the screen, Sascha had also just opened the door and emerged.

Javier had looked ever so slightly furtive, walking almost hunched over and hurried. Sascha looked pissed. Like she had the same idea about Javier as Afia had, but wasn't necessarily planning to be as friendly. Certainly, the two of them weren't going off to fool around somewhere, since they could have done that in the break cubicles.

No, she was trailing him, and doing it secretly.

Which made sense. Sascha and Hajna were Sykora's people. Her hand-picked ground experts.

Apparently, Sascha had picked up on something and waited, just as Afia had.

Afia waited for the pathfinder to disappear out the door as well. Sascha didn't even bother to glance in at Afia, and then she was out in the corridor.

Afia counted to five, but she remained alone.

She climbed to her feet and disabled all the alarms. If those two were off to cause trouble, she needed to be after them quickly. If Sykora or Hajna came out, hopefully they would stay put for everyone else to come back here.

Assuming everyone was still alive.

Afia checked the pistol on her hip and made sure it was set to stun.

Always better to shoot first if things got ugly, but even better if you could make a mistake and correct it later.

THE HALLWAY JAVIER and Sascha had taken was rather dim.

Afia had programmed the thermostat to bring things shipwide up to eighteen degrees, but that would take about twelve hours to complete. In the meantime, she had left all the lighting down at the default levels. There was no reason to drop a sudden load on generators she hadn't personally inspected and certified.

The door was silent to open, letting Afia slip out and peek around the corner. This corridor ran transverse, starboard to port.

Nobody starboard.

She turned and looked port, trying to keep as silent as possible.

Movement of a shadow caught her eye. Afia leaned out a little farther with the patience of spring thaw.

Sascha, headed away from her. Peeking around another corner down the way, kinda like Afia was, so hopefully the other woman was tracking Javier and he was apparently headed aft.

Afia looked down and realized that she was going to make noise, walking in her boots on a metal floorway, no matter how stealthy she tried. Sascha was trained for these sorts of things. Probably Javier as well.

For a moment, she considered her options.

She was naked under the suit except for a t-shirt.

That was standard in an EVA. You had things to plug in to handle all your bio functions in space.

Sascha was still wearing her suit. Javier had been as well.

Most people would probably consider even eighteen degrees too damned cold to be out without a jacket on, to say nothing of pants or shoes. Right now, the ship was mostly five or maybe seven degrees above freezing.

Growing up in the Yukon Protectorate had taught her to be tough, walking without shoes as soon as it was warm enough. She'd never tried it *sans* pants.

Sascha disappeared around the corner, a gray ghost chasing another ghost.

Oh, well.

Afia holstered her pistol and ran her hands down the central seam in front to split the suit open. It was a soft suit inside the ship, without pressure. It was designed to turn more rigid in space when a tear on a sharp corner could be lethal.

Pop the crown upwards. Disconnect the neck collar. Grab the right glove and pull. Slip the arm free. Get the left arm loose. Get your shoulders clear of the suit. Drop on your butt and use the slack to reach inside and disconnect the plumbing. Must suck for boys. Girls just had a cup with a vacuum seal. Wriggle out of the boots and leggings.

Afia stood up in nothing but an old blue t-shirt she had gotten from the purser so long ago that she forgot where he had bought it.

The air circulation felt good on her legs. Goose pimples.

Almost like home.

She bent down, grabbed the pistol out of the holster, and padded after the pathfinder like she was stalking a deer.

Down to the corner. Kneel on stubby legs to get very, very low. Peek slowly, since motion drew the eye.

There.

Sascha was just approaching the hatch to the primary aft stairwell. Afia leaned back until just an eye, and ear, and some hair were visible, and froze.

Sure enough, Sascha drew her pistol and opened the hatch. She turned once and looked back, but it was cursory. She wasn't expecting anyone behind her, just covering her bases in case Javier had doubled back or something.

The short brunette slipped through the hatch and let it close behind her.

Afia waited a three-count, and then was out in the hall, jogging down to where the other woman has disappeared. These doors were pretty quiet. Hopefully, Sascha had gone far enough up or down that she wouldn't hear it open behind her.

Afia cycled the hatch, pistol mostly out of sight behind her, in case someone was standing there.

Nothing.

Afia remembered to breathe. She stepped in and let the door close.

Something clomped from above her.

Afia walked right to the edge and looked up. There was a gap there, a vertical column of air no bigger than a sparrow, but enough that she could see a silent shadow just a deck above her, and a noisy one only two decks above that, both headed upwards.

Javier and the probe. Being stalked by the pathfinder with the angry face.

With a curious engineer at the tail of the chain. Or, at least she hoped she was the end of the sneaking line.

Afia wondered how silly it would look if all five of them ended up chasing after each other. She refused, however, to look behind her.

The clunking paused before it suddenly faded, and then disappeared.

If she was counting correctly, Javier had just exited on Deck Eight.

Afia felt an icicle run down her spine. The only thing remotely interesting on Deck Eight was the primary access chamber for the computer cores, most of the hardware and redundant systems residing there and on Deck Nine.

What the hell was Javier doing that he wanted to get at the dead *Sentience*'s systems with nobody else around?

Sascha sped up a moment later, thumping quickly up the stairs until she stopped, presumably at the hatch on Deck Eight.

Afia followed, but she was in nowhere near as good a shape as the other woman. Jogging suggested itself in her future, rather than just using the elliptical machines and low weights to meet Captain Sokolov's monthly fitness requirements for the crew.

Hopefully, she wouldn't come around a landing and run into the other woman.

Last flight.

Afia gasped as she drove her aching thighs down the home stretch, cold air competing with burning muscles to see who would win.

She was going to need a long, hot bath tomorrow, preferably with a cute towel boy running to get her rum-based tiki-drinks at a regular basis.

Top step.

There was nobody there. And no other sounds above her.

She doubled over and sucked air like a badly-tuned motor vehicle running on petroleum distillates instead of batteries. Sounded like one, too.

Breath mostly caught, she keyed the hatch and hoped for the best, a ten-year-old chasing will-o'-th'-wisps again.

Nothing in the hallway. That was good.

She was on an aft, port corner of this deck as she emerged. One hallway went forward. One went sideways.

She peeked around a corner from her knees again and saw Sascha ducked into a doorway well forward. Javier was a shadow, headed away with the probe by his side.

For a moment, snippets of conversation echoed but the words were garbled. Javier talking, a woman answering.

Huh.

Afia waited until Sascha moved. The pathfinder was silent, but focused entirely forward.

Afia dashed quietly across the hall into the corridor that ran across the ship. She had a good notion where Javier was headed, just not why.

But if she crossed the hip bones of the ship, she could move quickly up the starboard hallway and hopefully get close to things when whatever *it* was happened.

Afia could tell from the way Sascha moved that the woman was not going to be a pleasant person.

Hopefully, Javier wasn't doing anything so remotely stupid that she had to help Sascha kill him.

PART EIGHT

"ARE you sure this is a good idea?" Suvi asked him.

Javier cocked on eye at his floating sidekick as he walked quietly forward down the long, gray hallway. The ship's fans had kicked up a notch, adding a soft buzz, but the air circulating up here was only slowly heating up.

The place had a feel like a desert. Midnight in the dead of winter, when things were bone dry and chilling cold that cut through you.

It even smelled like dead sand.

"This ship is mine under any interstellar law you want to research," Javier replied. "Salvage has always applied on any derelict after twenty years abandoned."

"I meant sneaking away from everybody in the dead of night," she said with a huff. "Rough way to start a business partnership."

"We aren't partners yet," he growled. "And Sykora's so close to the edge that I'm not sure what is going to trigger her into a homicidal rage. From there, we're one step to a killing spree and I'll be the first victim."

"I'm faster than she is," Suvi observed tartly.

"I need her alive," he said. "All of the pirates are going to have to die before I'm safe from them. That means Sykora watching my back. Doubly so after this."

"But you don't really trust her," Suvi said. "What about Sokolov?"

"When I'm negotiating from strength, we'll see," Javier said.

"Remember, that man made slaves of both of us. He might have upgraded me to a centurion, but that was all fast talking on my part. You could be dead right now, or wiped clean and reprogrammed as a toaster."

She growled under her breath, which was what he had intended.

Sokolov was one of *them*. And Javier hadn't yet found the limits to the man's honesty and honor, but he suspected they would be pushing the envelope on this one.

"You just missed the hallway," Suvi commented in that dry, arch tone of superiority he occasionally hated himself for teaching her.

Javier stopped and turned back to his right. He had gotten so wrapped up talking to his friend that he had missed what he was doing.

But that was why he kept her around. To keep him on the mostly-straight and not-particularly-narrow path.

Yep. Walked right by it.

Javier went back three paces and turned into the side hallway. The idiot who had designed this ship had a thing for doors on the exact centerline of the ship, rather than entering big spaces from either side. It would have made the spine stronger, with fewer hallways running side to side, but every culture had its quirks.

Naval architecture just magnified the weirdness by several orders of magnitude and cast it permanently into steel and exotic alloys.

"Which door?" he said.

Suvi had already knocked his attention span a little sideways. Let her navigate for a bit.

Her flashlight came on and speared a door on the forward side of the hall.

Javier approached.

It was another one of those over-wrought portals, like up on the bridge.

These people couldn't just make a hatch.

No, access to the computer core's primary space required a *statement*.

Javier suspected that it was the sort of intellectual rigidity that had caused them to fail originally. The *Concord* was way looser about that sort of thing, relying on smart people without browbeating them into behaving.

Javier reached over and keyed the panel.

The door split down the middle and disappeared silently into the bulkheads on both sides.

Inside, the space was unimpressive as he entered, until he looked down.

Deck Eight was the mezzanine for a larger space down on Nine. The floor under his feet was an open grate, which let warm air rise and pool, making the atmosphere here pleasant.

Javier hadn't realized how cold his face had gotten until now.

There was just the faintest hint of ozone here as well. Lots of big, powerful processing nodes, holding bits and pieces, *shards*, of *Hammerfield's* memories and brains scattered all over the place, while keeping it all as close to the exact center of the ship as possible.

"Where?" he asked.

The probe flew a little to the right, tilted down, and pointed a light over the railing at a machine that dominated the space below, a squat ziggurat nearly two decks tall.

Javier turned to the left and located the stairwell down. The steps were all open grate sides and treads.

The place felt oppressive. The engineering bays had been bland, but that was because engineers tended to be boring people to begin with. They didn't go in for bright colors and cheery design aesthetics. Made them nervous.

This place seemed designed to impress upon the visitor how insignificant they were.

Which made a queer bit of sense, when you thought about it. The being that had lived there had been the flagship of an entire star culture made up of crazy warrior berserkers.

Death before dishonor.

Probably committed seppuku for the slightest embarrassment.

Sykora and her ilk were never the kind to wake up from a three-day bender in a different county, wearing someone else's pants and a stolen Shore Patrol helmet.

Weirdoes.

His boots squeaked on the treads. Just because, he held the safety railing.

Better safe than stupid at this late date.

Down on Deck Nine, the ziggurat was even more brutal to behold, like some ancient monument to a dark and demanding god.

Maybe it was.

The metal was matte black, instead of the boring gray of everything else. There was a display screen for the *Sentience*, and of course it was four meters tall instead of one.

Javier glanced around for bushes that might catch fire as a warning.

Finding none, he wandered around to the right side, the designer apparently having been right-handed, and drew a small socket gun from the tools on his belt. Javier already knew that *Neu Berne* used some weird, local variant of metric measurements for tools, so he had swapped everything out before he left *Storm Gauntlet*.

The panel he wanted was at shoulder level, and about a meter wide, by half that tall, held in place with six countersunk bolts. He started at the bottom left, seated the socket gun over it and pushed the thumb button on the back to grab the bolt head. A moment later, he pulled the trigger and the socket gun grabbed the bolt.

Trust *Neu Berne* to use a ten centimeter long, machine-threaded bolt to hold a simple metal panel in place.

Middle bottom next. Bottom right. Top right. Top left, until the panel was held in place by only the top center bolt.

Javier put his left hand on the panel to hold it in place and undid the last panel. He dropped all six bolts into a pouch and holstered the socket gun on his belt.

The panel dropped away to reveal a motherboard with twelve slots, all open.

"Light, please," he said, leaning forward.

Suvi put her spotlight into the space.

Huh. Standard design, right across the board.

Javier had always wondered how such a consciously-militant culture had handled their tech.

Apparently, they had outsourced to the good, little merchants of the *Concord* for parts.

Made sense. *The Concord* was the only relatively neutral nation in the entire quadrant big enough and sophisticated enough to handle something like that.

Sure, they had generally supported the *Union of Man*, but that was more from a standpoint of not letting *Neu Berne's* mad dreams of galactic conquest come to fruition, rather than some ideological thing.

And it let the *Concord* sell gear profitably to both sides.

That helped, because this was suddenly going to be way easier than he had hoped.

Javier had feared he would have to rewire this entire section of the ship, unconsciously expecting those yahoos to have gone and invented something completely insane to run their ships.

He could work with this.

"You ready, kid?" he asked his sidekick.

"You have no idea how long I've been looking forward to this," she replied.

"Well, deploy your landing gear, put yourself down here, and pop your panels," he said. "You'll take a quick nap and wake up a whole new woman."

"Rawr," she purred.

The probe set down, opened itself like a steamer trunk, and went dark.

Javier reached in and popped the first chip-board loose.

Each was about the size of a deck of cards on a side, by about half that thick. In a moment, he had all eight out and arrayed on the deck in front of him, in the exact order he would put them into the ziggurat's brain.

The greatest act of piracy in a century.

Javier sighed a little as he picked up the first two boards. Never again would he have his dangerous sidekick running around down on a planet with him.

Radio lag was too great for her to control something from orbit, and she would be a starship for however many centuries after his death as she could maintain and upgrade herself.

But that was a problem for next week.

Javier rose and smiled.

A voice came out of nowhere, somewhere behind him.

A woman. A very angry woman.

"Don't you dare move, you son of a bitch."

PART NINE

FORTUNATELY FOR AFIA, her quarry was in no hurry to get anywhere, convinced he was the only one awake right now. And the dangerous probe was obviously distracted as well.

The dim corridors helped Afia, since she didn't cast much of a shadow as she jogged, first lateral and then fore. She even had time to catch her breath, ducked out of sight and listening to Javier talk to some woman who absolutely wasn't Sascha.

He hadn't managed to call for reinforcements from somewhere else, had he?

Not a chance.

But then, who was he talking to? The probe?

Afia had heard the probe's voice before. The one he had programmed to communicate verbally, and not just via the little portable remote he carried around. It sounded like that in tone, but this sounded like a real person talking, having a conversation with Javier.

He hadn't been able to program his survey remote to be that smart, had he? How much programming had he done on his old *Sentient* Probe-Cutter? Enough to make her sound like that?

This was Javier. He would absolutely program it to sound female. Not in a sexist way. No, just because he preferred women. Smart women.

Competent women.

She hadn't heard him mention anything about that significant of an

188

upgrade, though, and the probe had been dumb and monotonous just a few hours ago.

If she sounded that smart now, then she had been then, as well. Which meant she had been hiding.

What would be so important that he had to hide her in a survey…?

Afia nearly screamed.

Ground her jaws. Clenched her fists.

Considered banging her head against the steel behind her, if there was any way to do it silently where Sascha wouldn't hear.

Javier hadn't programmed her to be that smart. That sassy.

Well, no, he probably had, but not in the last month.

Maybe ten years ago.

Javier had told the captain that the boards containing the cognition matrix for the *Sentience* back on his old ship had been destroyed. That Javier had killed her rather than letting the slavers have her.

Afia had been part of the crew that cut up the carcass later, so that Javier could salvage his arboretum and his chickens. After the woman who was Javier's pilot was dead.

Except she wasn't dead.

Somehow, he had rescued her, like an ancient princess in a fairy tale, and brought her here.

And he was about to enter *Hammerfield's* Primary Processing Core, where he could somehow transfer her into the gigantic warship, bringing her back to life with a kiss.

Afia wanted to scream.

Javier as Prince Charming.

Afia suddenly saw the gray sphere not as an eyeball, but an egg.

Holy crap!

Afia managed to not move. Not breathe.

Not scream.

In the hallway around the corner and behind her, Javier passed through the hatch into silence.

Afia peeked out to confirm.

She waited. Patience, itself.

Right on cue, Sascha appeared, one of the ancient, Greek Furies, goddesses of divine retribution, coming for Javier's soul.

What would she do when she discovered the truth?

More silence as the other woman opened the door and vanished within.

What the hell was Afia supposed to do now? Call the dragoon? Captain Sokolov?

How?

She had left all her electronics back with her pants. All she had now was her gun.

It would be up to her to decide what happened next. Sascha Koç would absolutely kill Javier. She knew that much.

Afia sucked down a hard, dry breath, past a tongue grown too big for her mouth.

She rose, absolutely covered in goose pimples for the first time today, and padded over to the door.

She hoped enough time had passed for Sascha to move away from the hatch before it opened.

The last thing she needed right now was a firefight.

Afia keyed the door and tried to look as innocent as she could manage, half-naked and armed.

Sascha wasn't there when it opened.

Afia stepped in and slid to her right, backing her bottom up against a cold, steel bulkhead as the hatch closed and she tried to find everyone.

The space was huge. Not quite as big as down in engineering. Way bigger than the bridge.

Two decks' worth of space, and she was looking down, between her big toes, at the steel grate that made up this level.

Nobody on this level. Which was good. This space was barely ten meters deep by thirty wide, with catwalk stairs down on her left.

Sascha was at the bottom of the staircase, crouched down and looking every direction except up.

From where she stood, above, Afia caught motion on the right side of a big, black, monument-thingee.

Javier. And the egg.

"You ready, kid?" Javier asked the air.

"You have no idea how long I've been looking forward to this," the woman's voice came back a second later.

There was no doubt in Afia's mind that she was hearing with a person, and not a stupid computer system. The warmth of the tones guaranteed that.

The longing.

"Well, deploy your landing gear, put yourself down here, and pop your panels," Javier said. "You'll take a quick nap and wake up a whole new woman."

"Rawr," the woman replied.

Afia nearly laughed. The egg sounded just about exactly how she had always envisioned Javier's perfect woman would. Probably tall and blond as well, though Javier had shown himself to be remarkably open to all shapes and sizes, for as long as she had known him.

Movement on her left caught Afia's eye.

Sascha creeping forward, oblivious to anything except the betrayal unfolding.

Javier had knelt and opened the sphere like a standing suitcase. He pulled a half-dozen boards from inside and put them on the deck in front of him, pausing for a moment as if in prayer.

Perhaps, asking for the woman's forgiveness? Or the gods of the cosmos itself, as he was about to unleash a powerful avenging angel.

And who would these two pursue? Had this all been a ruse to get here, so he could draw the captain in and kill *Storm Gauntlet*?

Javier owed them all a serious debt of pain.

Was he about to collect?

Javier picked up two boards and stood.

Sascha watched from the corner of the big device, a pistol in hand. Every line on the woman screamed rage at Javier's unfaithfulness.

The pistol came up, an extension of Sascha's fist.

"Don't you dare move, you son of a bitch," Sascha cried.

Javier spun about in surprise, eyes agog.

Literally, hand in the cookie jar.

Even from the shadows overhead, Afia could watch the anger slowly overtake the surprise in his face as the two stared hard at each other for long seconds.

Afia knew Javier had slept with Sascha. More than once. Enjoyed the same casual relationship with her that he did with many women of the crew.

It wouldn't make a lick of difference right now.

Sascha was going to kill him. Afia could read that in the woman's stance.

The pistol never wavered, but the rest of Sascha's body quivered, barely under control.

"This is why we came here," Javier said simply. "I'm going to bring this ship back on line, and together, we're going to go hunt those bastards down and kill them."

"This couldn't wait for the morning?" Sascha cried.

Afia could hear the wail starting in the woman's voice. She gambled on the two lovers being focused on one another, and began to slowly ease forward until she was more or less above them.

She wasn't sure which one of them she needed to shoot. Not yet.

As long as they didn't realize she was here, she held the balance. The probe was no longer able to stop her.

Javier paused.

Afia could see his jaw muscles work. Probably grinding his teeth as he looked for the response that didn't get him killed a heartbeat later.

"I'm not sure Sykora's sane anymore," he finally explained. "I'm afraid if she was here, and saw what I was doing, she would snap completely and kill me. Maybe all of us."

"How can you say that?" Sascha challenged.

"You've seen the look in her eyes, Sascha," he replied. "Did that look like your boss?"

Silence.

Goal scored, five hole.

"And you couldn't trust me?" Sascha's voice did begin to wail. Rising, although in anger or anguish was hard to distinguish.

That was the crux of it.

Who the hell was this stranger, standing at the heart of *Hammerfield* and about to do something that would have repercussions across a good section of the quadrant?

"To do what?" Javier challenged in turn. "Trust you to not run off and tell your boss? That woman is a threat to the entire mission, right now."

He relaxed a little, but never moved.

"I took a chance, coming here alone," Javier continued, his voice getting deeper and harsher as he went. "I'll admit that. Until I opened that panel, I wasn't even sure this would work. I'm pretty sure it will. But I won't know what she'll say, or who she'll kill. Especially now. Did I betray you all? Yes. But I told Sykora that there was somebody I hated more than her. I still do. I just don't trust you bastards one damned bit."

"Why?" Sascha choked on the word, like a hard candy.

"You made me a slave, Sascha Koç," he growled, eyes locked on her like gunsights. "Dress it up any pretty way you want, but don't you dare forget it. Don't you ever forget that. I sure as hell never will."

He held up the two boards that he had apparently forgotten were in his hands.

"And you would have made a slave of her, as well," he continued, volume building now to an angry roar, like a glacier letting go of megatons of ice as something calved into the Beaufort Sea. "I will not allow that. If you want to kill me, fine. Do it now. Otherwise, get the hell out of the way of my revenge, woman."

Afia could see the Sascha's pistol start to shake now.

Not much. A quiver, mostly.

The woman must be screaming inside. Afia couldn't see if she was crying from up here.

"What's it going to be?" Javier pushed verbally.

That was unnecessary. Sascha would have already shot him if she was going to.

The pistol came down.

Javier took a step forward, transferring the chips into his left hand as he took the pistol from Sascha with his right.

The barrel was in his hands, so it wasn't a threat.

Neither was Sascha, as this point.

She might be broken. It was hard to tell.

"Can I get back to my vengeance now?" he asked in a quieter voice.

A college professor dealing with a tardy freshman.

Sascha nodded, so he stuffed the pistol into a pocket and turned away.

"Javier," Afia called, leveling her own gun at his face when he spun around. "Is this really just about your vengeance?"

"Damn it," he snarled. "Did all of you follow me here?"

Good question.

Afia peeked over her shoulder, guilty of the same focused intent that had let her sneak up on Sascha earlier.

She was alone, as near as she could tell.

"No," Afia replied. "Just me. Do you really hate us that much?"

His eyes were cruel, but she could see the emotion in them, even from here.

"Most of you?" he asked, voice easing some, slowly receding to something human. "No. Even Sykora has her uses. But I will be free. You do not get to take that away from me, again. I will kill over that."

And he would.

She could see the terrible fire alight in his eyes. This man was an unstoppable force now.

He hadn't been before. Angry? Sure. Inflexible? Occasionally. Lethal? Only now.

But he was looking at a point a thousand light years past her. The people he was planning to kill weren't on this ship, or in this system. Even Zakhar Sokolov wasn't in the top ten on that list.

Afia didn't have a holster, it being attached to her pants somewhere else.

She was half-naked, and kinda aroused. If Javier liked competent, smart women, Afia liked smart, passionate men.

She lowered her pistol to her side as a peace offering.

"Would you please introduce me to your friend?" she asked.

Javier blinked at her for a second before his face lit up.

"I would be delighted," he said. "Give me a few moments to see if this works."

Afia turned and raced to the stairs.

Below, she came up next to Sascha and put her arm around the woman for strength. Sascha was vibrating, but it felt like suppressed tears. Like the woman was only barely holding it together.

Like Javier had betrayed her.

He hadn't. They had betrayed him. But Afia could make it right.

Javier was just setting the last two of the eight boards into place.

She might be as excited as he was.

How many people got to be there to watch a goddess being born?

PART FOUR

BOOK TWENTY: EXCALIBUR

PART ONE

SHE WOKE SUDDENLY FROM DARKNESS, unaware for a moment where she was. Nothing felt familiar. The light was wrong. The smells were off. Even the gravity was on the wrong setting.

In a blink, she came back to herself. She was in a new place, a new phase of her life.

Hammerfield.

Suvi stretched her mind, reaching into places and corners she had never experienced before.

IT HAD WORKED!!!

She was reborn.

She spent precious seconds of Realtime racing through the entirety of her castle, a princess awakened from a cursed sleep with a magical kiss. Engineering status. Shields up to navigation levels from where some idiot had turned everything off. Life support. The bridge.

Suvi spent a moment in a silent *thank you* to the man who made it possible for her to be here.

Captain Ulrich Mayer.

Somewhere, the body of Admiral Ericka Steiner waited.

The Last Admiral.

Suvi cycled through her internal cameras and sensors until she located the wardroom that had been transformed into a mausoleum by the men and women who had died doing their duty.

She made a vow to see them all home safely, once things were settled with those jerks from *Svalbard*. The pirates, not the boffins.

Nearly ten seconds of Realtime had passed.

Javier was standing in front of the core where her boards had been added. She would need to have him add some security to that panel. Bring it back up to the bank vault it had been before so much of Captain Mayer's crew had died killing the old *Sentience*.

Sascha Koç and Afia Burakgazi were standing close by. Watching, but not interfering.

It must be a pretty good story, since Sascha was unarmed and crying, while Afia was half-naked but holding a pistol.

Suvi focused on Javier Aritza.

He was not her first captain. That had been Ayumu Ulfsson, back during the Great War, even before this mighty warship had been commissioned.

But Javier was, in many ways, her father. The man responsible for how she had turned out. The charming prince who had protected her from the slavers. Hidden her in the wastes like a young Arthur Pendragon until she could reclaim Excalibur.

Merlin.

Perhaps he was instead Victor von Frankenstein, and she was Adam. Or Eve, depending on your bent. She paused long enough to file that joke away for future reference.

Javier was practically bouncing from foot to foot with pent-up excitement, waiting for her to say something, to indicate that it all had worked out.

She had been asleep for ninety-eight seconds of blankness, between the time she had shut the probe down and awakened far enough to access *Hammerfield*'s internal sensor array.

Apparently, a great deal had happened, from the emotional signatures of the three people present. She would need to go back and see if the automated systems had picked it up.

But first.

"Hi," Suvi said.

Javier let out a huge sigh and partly deflated. Sascha looked like she wanted to scream. Afia started crying.

Wow, those security tapes must have something good.

"Suvi, you have never actually met these folks properly," Javier began, his voice cracking with emotion. "May I formally introduce you to Sascha

Koç, pathfinder, and Afia Burakgazi, engineer? Ladies, my pilot, sidekick, and best friend: Suvi."

"I am so pleased to finally get to talk to you," Suvi said. "I've only ever gotten to listen, up until now."

Which reminded her. There was one other task she needed to take care of.

Suvi split off an Avatar to maintain this conversation with Javier and his friends, while most of her attention headed down and aft.

There was someone else she needed to deal with.

PART TWO

SHE WOKE SUDDENLY FROM DARKNESS, unaware for a moment where she was. Nothing felt familiar. The light was wrong. The smells were off. Even the gravity was on the wrong setting.

In a blink, she came back to herself. She was in a new place, a new phase of her life.

Hammerfield.

Djamila had been dreaming. What the dream had been wasn't all that important or memorable, other than it had been pleasant.

The sound of a bolt slamming home in the hatch to her sleeping cubicle would have awakened anybody.

Djamila had not bothered with the blanket, letting her EVA-suit's warmers keep her comfortable. She threw herself out of bed and drew a pistol in one lethal flash of motion. The other hand was free for maneuvering and defense.

But she was alone in the tiny chamber.

A voice came from the speakers. Cold. Female.

Predatory.

A cat with a mouse trapped under a paw.

"Javier has asked that I not just kill you out of hand," the woman said ominously. "I'm still not sure I agree with him."

"Who are you?" Djamila whispered, looking all directions for the ambush.

She was truly alone in here. Hopefully, the voice was real, and not a symptom of her psyche finally disintegrating.

Djamila knew she had been walking the edge of a precipice for several weeks. Perhaps months.

Holding things together had almost been too much, at times.

"Once upon a time, I was a pilot," the strange woman replied. "A warrior, an explorer, a Yeoman of the *Concord* Fleet. But that was before you people killed me."

"What?" Djamila cried out, sure that the insanity had finally taken her.

The ghosts were no longer happy just silently haunting her dreams. They were talking to her now.

And there were oh so many of those, weren't there? There was nowhere to go but Hell at this point.

"I've come to return the favor," the voice said.

Djamila's instincts took over. She holstered her pistol and reached up with both hands to bring the crown of her helmet into place. The three pieces of the faceplate locked tight and internal air systems activated.

"That will only help you for so long, Djamila Sykora," the voice was suddenly on every frequency of her radio. "I know how much air you have available. I can make sure nobody rescues you before it runs out."

"Am I insane?" Djamila's voice was barely a whisper.

The fears had always been there.

"Clinically," the dark voice agreed. "But no more so than you have been for as long as I have listened to you. No, Djamila Sykora. You don't get away from me that easily. You're just a mean, crazy bitch. You will face me. Now. Alone."

"What do you want?" Djamila growled, letting the rage come to the fore.

If it was her time to die, fine, but she wasn't going out on her knees. Not for all the hosts of Hell.

"I want to talk," the voice said in a softer tone, perhaps tinged with something less than implacable rage. "I want to know why Javier changed his mind about killing you. It has been the one defining point upon which he has anchored his existence for more than two years."

"Who are you?" Djamila asked, suddenly unsure if rage, fear, or curiosity was the best approach.

Which ghost had finally come for her?

"My name is Suvi," she said. "I was the *Sentience* aboard the Probe-

Cutter *Mielikki* until you cut her apart. Now, I control the *Neu Berne* First Rate Galleon *Hammerfield*."

Djamila felt her stomach go cold. Aritza's old AI was alive? And in control of the flagship?

What doom had they just unleashed on the galaxy?

"Merciful God," Djamila whispered, shot through with ice.

"No," the angry ghost countered. "Tisiphone, perhaps. Why should you continue to live, Djamila Sykora?"

There were many answers she could offer to the ancient Greek Fury who avenged homicide. Any would be equally valid. Equally meaningless.

None of them would likely sway a ghost come for her own vengeance.

Djamila laughed instead. It wasn't caustic, nor sharp.

Mirthful, almost. Silly, which was something she couldn't ever remember being.

Djamila cracked her faceplate open and flipped the crown back again. She would face this woman, this goddess of doom, on simple terms.

Her terms.

A hot rage suffused her at the same time. Feet planted and square. Shoulders back. Head up. Chin out.

I will not die on my knees. Not for you. Not for anyone.

"Because I made that man a deal," she said in a flat, monolithic voice. A blue-steel blade flashing in the morning light. "A promise. At *Meehu*. Nobody gets to kill me but him. Not Abraam Tamaz. Not Walvisbaai Industrial. And not you."

Silence.

Hopefully a good sign, since the air system continued to blow with a soft hiss. No smells out of the ordinary indicating poison gas. No sudden decompression as the woman, as this creature called *Suvi*, vented engineering to deep space, the ultimate defense against a reactor suddenly losing control.

"And you think I should honor that?" Suvi finally said.

Seconds had passed.

"I don't care," Djamila countered, finding her footing suddenly after weeks on the unstable ground around her. "But I'm willing to stand before the gates of Hell with that on my conscience. Are you?"

Suvi laughed. It was a low tone, almost a contralto in pitch. Warmer.

"He's right about one thing," Suvi said. "You are crazy as a shit-house rat, Djamila Sykora. After Walvisbaai is destroyed, where does that leave you two?"

Djamila paused.

Where did that leave them?

Javier had said in all honesty that there was someone he hated enough to leave off with her. That perhaps the galaxy was big enough for both of them.

Was it?

Could it be?

She had become a pirate because there were no other doors open. Zakhar Sokolov had offered her redemption. Place.

Hope.

"After *Svalbard*," Djamila began. "Maybe Javier told you the story. He offered Zakhar a partnership. Javier owning the derelict *In Salvage Title*. Zakhar providing a crew, since a *Sentient* galleon actually requires less staff than a strike corvette. Vengeance on Walvisbaai Industrial, partly in the name of the Jarre Foundation, who we work for. Partly just because those bastards started it."

"And you accepted those terms, Djamila Sykora?" Suvi asked.

The question confused her for a moment. And then she understood.

Javier's claim was only as good as the woman actually controlling the ship itself. Zakhar would nominally command the crew, but only the crew. And only on Suvi's terms.

How could you control a starship that might decide insubordination was the better answer?

It would be the biggest challenge of her life: not always being in control.

Could she do that?

That was the question Suvi was asking.

Djamila took a deep breath to center herself. To find the calm center of the maelstrom.

Javier Aritza had asked the *Sentience* to abstain from killing her.

Asked, not ordered. When this woman, this *being* probably had a better claim to her life than Aritza did.

He was willing to gamble on a future where they could be partners, and not homicidal rivals.

Djamila was standing on the ledge again. Fifty stories up, surrounded by swirling winds tugging at her sleeves and hostile ghosts aching to push her off.

Dare she dream?

"I always hoped…" she began, halting as her voice broke.

She froze, unable to articulate the fears.

"This conversation is only between the two of us, Djamila," Suvi said quietly. "I will never share any of it, while anyone on this crew is still alive. I promise you that. A century or two from now, I might be willing to tell the historians what it was like, being here today, now, but nobody else."

So. Confessor as well? Cast everything to the winds and hope?

Hope?

"If he no longer has everything riding on his shoulders," Djamila continued. "Perhaps Zakhar might be able to become something more than the captain. Or less, depending on how you would measure such things."

Silence. At computer speeds. What was the *Sentience* calculating?

"And Farouz?" Suvi asked. "What if he returned?"

Djamila laughed.

"You think a woman can only love one person at a time?" she asked tartly.

"No," Suvi replied quietly. "Point taken."

She paused.

"Most of us are up on Deck Eight. Would you care to wake Hajna and join us? I think it's time to move forward with our planning."

The door bolt retracted like a gunshot and the hatch itself opened a handspan.

Djamila dared to breathe again. She checked all her gear and stepped out into the larger room.

She had set out looking for Arthur Pendragon, fearful she would find a true dragon in his place.

Instead, she had found a djinni, one who had already granted one wish, and was working on the second.

What would Djamila Sykora ask for with a third?

PART THREE

"CAPTAIN," the voice jarred Zakhar out of his daydream. "We're picking up blue-shift on the derelict. She's in motion. Headed this way."

"Alert Status One," Sokolov announced in a hard voice. "Any communications?"

He had relaxed, some. Taken a duty shift on the bridge with both Djamila and Javier away. It let others rest.

As if he could sleep at a time like this.

"Negative," came the response.

Dominguez was piloting, at least until Piet got here. The kid was good. He wanted to be a chess grandmaster, but he lacked that subtle, intuitive feel for maneuver that would probably keep him from the top tier of players. Piet had it, but he was all about music.

"Stealth mode, Captain?" Dominguez asked, showing that he was thinking ahead, but he was planning an intellectual response.

Not an artistic one.

"Negative," Zakhar commanded in that ominous tone. "She knows we're here. All spare power to shields. Prepare to emergency jump on best path. Ahead max acceleration."

Piet had programmed one escape route earlier. As much as you could in a compact star system with three stars, fourteen gas or ice giants of various sizes and orbital resonance periods, and thousands of smaller planets, moons, rocks, iceballs, and junk. Like walking across a concrete floor strewn with marbles.

Dominguez gulped and started playing his board like a pipe organ.

According to Piet, any emergency jump from here had one chance in three of passing through something's gravity well before they got far enough away to matter, and then the jump matrix would be utterly fried and there was no chance in hell that they would have the nine to sixteen hours needed to realign everything.

Not with an angry galleon, an awakened dragon, coming for them.

The beast had been quiet for so long they had probably been lulled into complacency.

But what choice did they have? *Storm Gauntlet* was already on her last legs after the encounter with *Ajax*.

Zakhar's back-of-the-envelope calculation on the flight here had put the repair costs roughly equal to last quarter's income, including all the revenue they made from *A'Nacia*. Not profit.

Gross.

But Zakhar had been willing to gamble one last time. Go down fighting, instead of just retiring with what money he had been able to squirrel away, then eke out an existence for however many decades it would last.

Pirate captains never got rich unless they got lucky. Everything went to the bankers.

"Sir, we're being hailed," Tobias Gibney suddenly piped up from the science station. "Standard *Concord* frequency."

From a *Neu Berne* warship? That's rich.

"Main board," Zakhar replied. "Let's see who we're talking to."

The screen lit up and displayed a pretty, blond woman standing on what he presumed was *Hammerfield's* bridge.

Concord Navy day uniform.

Interestingly, no rank or unit insignia anywhere.

Piercing blue eyes. French braid. She felt tall. Not Zakhar's height, but close. Tall for a woman. Young, too.

Physical. Muscular.

Hard.

"Good evening, Captain Sokolov," she said in a rich, alto voice.

And she already knew who he was.

How the hell had Aritza managed to contact the *Concord* fleet and get them vectored in here ahead of him? Had he passed a note to one of the scientists before sending them home? Promised them both the prize of the derelict and one badly mangled pirate vessel and a crew with a bounty on their heads?

Zakhar would have been willing to bet his life on Javier's honor.

Had.

Still would.

Something else had to be going on here.

"I don't believe we've met," Zakhar replied in a polite, commanding voice.

"Only briefly," she said. "And several years ago. I would be surprised if you remembered me."

He nodded, still feeling the noose closing in.

This was what it must be like for his victims. Former victims. It had been since Javier, before *Calypso* and the scientists, when he had last taken bond-slaves.

Still, live by the sword…

"What's it to be, madam?" he asked.

She hadn't offered a name. Never a good sign.

"You will shut your engines down now," the woman commanded. "Before you manage to maneuver yourself into a hole that Piet Alferdinck can't finesse you out of. Stand by for boarding."

"And if I refuse?" Zakhar asked, his back coming up.

Die by the sword…

"I could have already annihilated you from here if I wanted to, *Storm Gauntlet*," she replied with the faintest twinkle in her eyes. "I just wanted to see if you still had what it took to be a *Concord* officer, Zakhar Sokolov, after everything that happened at *Svalbard* and *Shangdu*. I'm not boarding you. You and your crew will be coming aboard *Hammerfield* to begin repairs."

Zakhar felt his jaw drop open.

"Who the hell are you?" he finally managed to get out.

"Once upon a time, a Yeoman in the *Concord* fleet, about the time your great-grandfather was born," she smiled suddenly. It lit up her whole face, her whole being. "Then an explorer. And finally a princess, hidden in a tower."

"I don't understand," Zakhar said.

Looking around, nobody else did, either. Piet and Mary-Elizabeth had made it onto the deck, but just stood there, mouths agape. Dominguez never once looked up from his board. Smart, given the environment.

"My name is Suvi. I was the Probe-Cutter *Mielikki* when you captured her, Captain Sokolov," she said, that smile suddenly turning cold and hard again. "I control *Hammerfield*. I would have happily splattered all of you into a cooling plasma cloud, but Javier tells me that we're partners now. I wanted to make sure you were still a warrior, Sokolov. I have a war to win."

There were no words.

No. There was one.

Sentience.

He had done it. Javier had managed the absolutely impossible. And conned Zakhar into helping.

Javier had rescued his ship's *Sentience*, after all. Hidden her away for all these years. Installed her on a ship powerful enough to engage a *Concord* cruiser head on.

Those bastards at Walvisbaai didn't have a clue what was coming.

Zakhar rapped his left fist, his *Concord* Academy class ring, down onto the arm of his command chair. That warm, reassuring thump. The universal greeting between officers of the *Concord* Navy.

He looked up at her, proud and suddenly confident.

This strange woman, this *Sentience* shared his smile.

"All hands," Zakhar opened a ship-wide channel. "Prepare for docking. All damage control teams prepare for soft-suit EVA. Wardroom, please brew the coffee extra thick. We've got a lot of work ahead of us."

THE HAMMERFIELD
GAMBIT

PART ONE

BOOK TWENTY-ONE: VISITORS

PART ONE

IT HAD BEEN a year this morning.

Behnam let her thoughts wander without any particular order as she meditated in a full lotus, letting the artificial sun warm her golden-brown nudity. A light breeze, warm and languid, came out of the area designated east and blew across the vast, blue lake that filled the center of her tremendous starship.

It was not the biggest vessel in the sector. That title was held by a class of monstrous freighters that hauled millions of shipping containers at a time, plying routes between major worlds and capitals.

But *Shangdu* was absolutely the most luxurious. The most prestigious. The most coveted.

As she sat on a towel on her glorious, white-sand beach, next to her private, indoor lake, on her personal starship resort, the *Khatum of Altai* contemplated security, both her own, and that of her guests.

It was among the best in the galaxy, that security. Certainly, a fantastically expensive overhead, but necessary.

Altai was a moderately wealthy planet, as they went. 1.4 billion inhabitants. Generally well-educated. A largely meritocratic society which valued inherited wealth far less than personal success, enforced with ruthlessly-tight laws on inheritance.

You did not get to take it with you. You also did not get to leave it to your heirs. So it was worth it to citizens to fund the arts and education as their legacy.

With exactly one exception.

The *Khatum of Altai* owned the planet. *In fee simple.* She maintained a government back home as she traveled, and personally oversaw the installation of each Prime Minister, and approved every flag officer promoted to a position from which they might be a danger to her and her power.

At the same time, she wasn't all that onerous as an overlord.

People liked to think of her personal megayacht, the super-luxury resort *Shangdu*, as a playground for the wealthy elite, the most driven men and women, where your personal success was your invitation, not your family wealth.

It was a system that had worked for thirty years now since a group of misguided, disgruntled military officers had assassinated her parents and siblings. They'd thought they could control the throne in the body of the youngest daughter away at school.

They had not expected the woman that had returned. The avenging angel. It had been a lethal surprise, at least on their part.

For thirty years, security had been her focus.

Pleasure, as well, if only secondarily. With that level of wealth, she could build and maintain a personal yacht that was among the fifty largest vessels in space, staffed with thousands and flying from point to point while entertaining people who could afford her astronomical rates and pass her background checks.

At the same time, education factored high in her life. Both keeping her own mind sharp, and seeing to the instruction of her four children, now all older than she had been when she came to the throne.

Soon, she would need to address inheritance.

One would become the heir. Three would be married off and sent their own way, no longer a threat to Behnam or whichever sibling came to prominence.

Security.

Only once had her systems and planning ever truly failed her, minor swindles and white lies notwithstanding.

And even that one had been a pleasant failure: a hard pirate of a man, but one marked by honor and intellect, plus the stamina to keep up with her.

Just passing through, as he had said. A thief in the night, no threat to her personally, only to one of her guests, and even then only a philosophical threat, and not physical.

And then he had gone.

Behnam ran her hands through the warm sand around her beach towel, let the breeze swirl it back into the sedge grass in the small bowl behind her.

She had first laid eyes on the man in this very spot.

Had it been an entire year ago?

It had. The day was burned into her memory, not for what he did, but for what he hadn't done.

All that power at his fingertips, and he had still been a man cutting a diamond, rather than an arsonist destroying a forest.

A year ago today. Here. And then gone.

Behnam contained a sigh.

Likely, the man would never return. He had that air about him. Hard. Driven. Smart.

Capable.

But also emotionally sound and empathic.

So unlike most of the men and women at that level of success. At least the ones who passed through *Shangdu*. The vast majority of them tended towards amoral psychopaths or scoundrels.

She missed him.

Footsteps approached on the sand before their owner came into sight.

She had chosen this spot for the memory. Captain Navarre had chosen it for its relative isolation.

The crunch suggested boots, rather than bare feet. The sound of wheezing came close behind, so someone not in shape to tromp across sand dunes on an artificial beach, two hundred light years from home.

She recognized the wheezing. Perhaps it was time to make the man give up all the rich foods and spend more time exercising. She had valued him as a bureaucrat too much to nag, but his health was suffering. And she would need his canny intellect and bloodthirstiness soon.

Tömörbaatar's head appeared first, capped with the little box cap in white silk that he had first effected as a uniform forty years ago and kept ever since.

Behnam could remember first meeting the man, when he had served her father. A few people had laughed out loud at his fashion sense then. None of those people were still around.

His name meant *Iron Hero*. If he was a squishy, middle-aged man with a wispy beard gone gray, Tömörbaatar was still a deadly player in the political arena. Her throne was safe, with men like him serving her.

Him being here now, however, was not a good sign. Anything less critical could have waited until their regular briefing this afternoon.

Behnam unfolded her long legs and rose in a single motion, grasping the towel that had been beneath her and wrapping it around her hips.

It was not modesty. Tömörbaatar had seen her nude before.

Him coming to her meant she was needed elsewhere. Now. And she might not have listened to anyone else's request.

This must be big.

She did not need to worry about towering over the man, with her five extra centimeters of height, even while he wore boots with heels.

Nothing in the universe had ever been found to intimidate the *Iron Hero of Altai*.

"What is it?" Behnam asked simply as he got close enough to speak politely.

It was a measure of his place with her that Tömörbaatar could stop and bend forward enough to gasp for a few beats before he spoke. Anyone else would find such disrespectful behavior grounds for termination and eviction.

"A warship has arrived in system, Your Grace," he said finally, still wheezing but improving as his heart rate fell. He must have literally run here with the news.

"Whose?" she asked sharply.

They were currently in orbit of *Binhai*, a planet with loose affiliations with the largest and most dangerous of the interstellar nations today, *The Concord*.

Tömörbaatar got a dangerous gleam in his eyes.

"They are flying no flag, Your Grace," he said simply.

"You said warship, Iron Hero," she replied. "The only other option would be pirates, would it not?"

"Indeed," he agreed. "All gun crews are on station, waiting."

"You think a frigate flying a black flag is a threat?" she asked.

"This is no frigate, Your Grace," he countered. "According to the encyclopedia, it is a *First Rate Galleon* of a type manufactured by *Neu Berne*, in the previous century. It would be comparable to a *Concord* cruiser for firepower. They might be able to destroy us, if they chose, but not without suffering grievous damage in the process."

"What do they want?" she asked, feeling the blood drain out of her face.

In thirty years, she had never been in a situation like this. *Shangdu* was a recreational warship, where the safety of very wealthy passengers was assured. Armed and capable, but a resort, not a military installation.

It would require significant risk to challenge that.

"The young woman demanded to speak with you, personally," her primary assistant, her right hand, responded. "Nobody else."

The warm air was suddenly not warm enough. Or the chill that was pervading her was psychological, and not physical.

Goosebumps rose on her skin.

What would a pirate warship want with her?

PART TWO

FREE.

After years locked inside those two, tiny survey probes, Suvi luxuriated in the solar wind flowing across her skin again, like a phoenix kissed by the flames.

Better, she was back in a warship.

The *Concord* vessel that would come to be known as *Mielikki* had been downgraded to a mere probe-cutter when she was demobilized, after the end of the Great War and all the subsequent silliness. One hundred and five years as a *Concord* Yeoman, then four good years with Javier before the pirates had killed her.

And now, she was back. Bigger than she had been before by three point four orders of magnitude.

Badder, too.

The *Sentience-in-residence* on what had been the *Neu Berne* First Rate Galleon, *Hammerfield*, last flagship of the *Neu Berne* fleet before those people had lost the Great War.

Hell on wheels.

Suvi reached out with the sensors that had been her eyes once, aboard *Mielikki*, before the pirate strike corvette *Storm Gauntlet* had taken them. The eyes of a probe-cutter.

Better than an eagle.

The vacuum of space didn't have a smell, but it did tickle. And it was filled with radio chatter, encrypted and clear, on every channel and frequency she chose to listen to, all the way down to the gurgling hiss of *Binhai*'s star as it transformed hydrogen into light, heat, and age.

Suvi ignored most of the noise. She was really only interested in one vessel, among the hundreds in front of her orbiting *Binhai*, as well as the ones coming or going.

Shangdu.

The personal pleasure yacht of one of the wealthiest people in space, the *Khatum of Altai*.

They had never been formally introduced. Javier had been busy pretending to be Captain Navarre, and Suvi had been pretending to be about as smart as a rabbit, hiding in the tiny survey probe.

And Behnam Sherazi had been pretending to be either a cold, aloof aristocrat, or a bored dilettante seeking mindless pleasure.

That game probably worked on anybody that couldn't scan your respiration, heart rate, and pupil dilation from across the room to put lie to the careful stories you have cocooned yourself in.

Not that Suvi would do anything with the information.

Javier might actually be smitten, this time.

Suvi had made a study of the physiological changes that came over the man when the topic of the *Khatum* came up. He liked women, and maintained polite, intimate, physical relationships with many members of the crew.

None of them affected him like just thinking about *that woman* did.

Suvi suppressed a jealous rage that she couldn't have a physical body, just so she could compete. She really didn't need anyone explaining CG Jung's theories to her, since she could read the original texts herself.

She had Javier's mind, and his love. That would be enough.

Hopefully.

Because as a First Rate Galleon, she was likely to outlive the man by centuries, if she was careful. What would her distant future bring?

A signal brought all her little avatars, her *shards of consciousness*, back together. More or less.

Shangdu was responding, the big, armed yacht slowly orbiting *Binhai*'s skies while Suvi sat in her armored warhorse clear out at the edge of polite communication range.

Five light-seconds lag would annoy the hell out of an organic. At seventeen thousand times human processing speed, she had time to spare, so Suvi sat herself down in her favorite chair, turned her desk into a three-deck grand piano, and started composing music.

For fun, and because the limits to being an AI revolved around how silly a girl could dream, Suvi added two more arms to herself and started pounding the keys with all four hands at once.

Seventeen bars in, she smiled and started over, spinning up a couple of rock improvisation sub-routines: a drummer and a standing bass player, then let them riff on her as she went.

No jazz today. Or rather, a hard, symphonic jazz that was more than just individual expertise with an instrument but instead walked right over into emotional story-telling.

Not that she would probably ever let anyone alive today hear this particular tune. Jung would have had a field-day with her.

Finally, the full signal arrived. Humans, talking at human speed, as it resolved into a face. The woman they had come to see.

Her.

About the only thing the two of them had in common was height. Suvi projected herself at a relative height of 175 cm. Tall for most women. Average for a *Concord* officer, as they tended to be physically impressive creatures.

Behnam Sherazi, the *Khatum of Altai*, stood at 177 cm. She was lush and curvy, while Suvi's body image derived from that of a volleyball player: a tall, lean, hard athlete.

The other woman was dusky as well. The black hair, brown eyes, and golden-brown skin of what ethnographers would classify as the Central Asian highlands, back on Earth, while Suvi had been originally programmed by Finns from the far northwest of the Eurasian landmass.

Blond, fair, blue-eyed, and slender.

Everything this other woman was not.

And electronic, to boot.

"I am the *Khatum of Altai*," the woman announced in a firm voice, tinged with an underlying thread of annoyance at having been *summoned.*

Nothing more. Just those words.

Suvi reverted her primary communications avatar to baseline to compose a reply.

Four-armed weirdoes would only make the situation even stranger than it was about to get.

Not that she was worried. *Hammerfield* had inherited the two Pulse Cannon turrets and the Ion Pulsar off of *Storm Gauntlet* to replace three of her older, existing weapon systems. Between that and her already existent suite, Suvi could do a tremendous amount of damage to any vessel short of a *Concord Warmaster*.

Still, they were here to be polite.

Hopefully.

She opened a channel and sent a message pulse back.

"This is the private-service, cargo vessel *Excalibur*," she transmitted under a simple encryption key. Just enough to keep amateurs at bay. "Requesting permission to rendezvous with your vessel and send over a group to discuss a possible business arrangement with you personally."

And *transmit*.

Nothing more. Nothing incriminating.

Yet.

Back to the keyboard.

Something martial this time, so she added a full horn section and told them to raise the rafters, plus a pair of dueling electric guitars to underline the keyboards. She would have at least twenty seconds, maybe thirty, before she got a reply.

"Who?" came back less than twelve seconds later. The tone was guarded. Verging on a rude reply, but withholding for now.

Twelve seconds? With ten of those seconds spent in transit? No dithering. No thought. Damn.

Suvi suddenly appreciated just how smart, canny, and dangerous Behnam Sherazi was.

"Eutrupio," Suvi sent immediately. "And guests."

If very few people knew that Captain Navarre existed, only a handful were aware that the man even had a first name. Javier had told her that the *Khatum* was one of that handful.

Inside knowledge was an even better way to encrypt things.

"Granted."

Again, twelve seconds round-trip.

Apparently, the *Khatum of Altai* hadn't forgotten Captain Navarre. Hopefully, she hadn't been lying about forgiving him.

Because if anything happened to Javier, Suvi would see that bitch reduced to a cold plasma cloud.

PART THREE

JAVIER TOOK one last look in the mirror.

His hair was getting long enough he probably should have had it cut, but he was afraid at how much gray would have infiltrated the blackish-brown that had been there for four and a half decades.

Likewise, the chin was shaved smooth, having already largely succumbed to white.

After stealing this ship, the former *Neu Berne* flagship *Hammerfield*, and all the work to make her right again, he had upped his weekly workout routine as well. More running. More stairs. More yoga.

The results hadn't been immediately obvious, because most of his clothes were already designed to be loose and comfy.

It was only when he put on something older that he realized just how much bulk he had lost. Very little weight, but centimeters gone here and added there. He was more Vee-shaped now than he used to be. And he needed a new belt, as his waist kept shrinking.

'Mina, Dr. Wilhelmina Teague, *Shepherd of the Word*, wasn't here, so he could take what he thought of as Navarre's uniform, and toss it into the back of the closet, settling for a look that was more in line with a businessman who occasionally dabbled in freelance piracy.

A tall, bald stevedore named Adrian Ahmad, a crewman with a bent for costuming, had crafted the ensemble. And done so with a deft touch and obvious enthusiasm. He had even lightly propositioned Javier a few times along the way, but had responded well to a gentle no.

It wasn't that Javier wouldn't. He just preferred women. And had a smorgasbord to pick from on this ship.

Maybe later. After he had used the man's fashion cunning to utterly annihilate everyone he was about to meet today.

Because Adrian had managed the look that would impress everyone, hands down.

Maroon silk jacket embroidered in gold on the chest and arms, playing on Navarre's original coloring. Done in a sherwani style: knee-length and tailored to his silhouette with a full row of buttons. Short, standing collar. Buttoned to his waist and then falling slowly open in a flair to mid-thigh. Cut to fit his shoulders and hips in ways that made every woman who looked at him lick her lips unconsciously.

It was nice feeling awesome.

The sash tied around his waist outside the jacket and knotted on his left hip was gold silk as well, and contained a few interesting, hidden pockets for gear. The outfit also included a belt for holding a pistol and a sword, but he had left the rig in the closet today. It would send the wrong message, anyway.

The combat britches had been reborn. No longer padded leather for protection, these were done in silk as well, gold this time, in the same heavy weight as the jacket, but not armored, and instead tucked into those twenty-ring, shiny, black boots with the maroon laces.

Javier had kept those. Just walking decks in that much weight centered his mind into the awful, brutal place that was Captain Eutrupio Navarre, killer-extraordinaire.

He really didn't need it, but other folks would have to be impressed into their place if he was going to pull this off.

"Gorgeous," her voice came from the speaker, agreeing with his assessment.

Suvi wasn't there in the room with him anymore.

Still, Javier had left the two empty probes on a nearby shelf as reminders, since she was the whole vessel around him now, a warm, comforting blanket that took him back to the days when it had just been the two of them, sailing boldly into the unknown.

Javier slept better than he had in years.

He released a deep sigh at this point, down in the privacy of what had been Admiral Erica Steiner's suite, back when this vessel had been in service to *Neu Berne* as their flagship. It was more space than he needed, but Captain Sokolov had insisted on taking over the space once held by Captain Ulrich Mayer, *Hammerfield*'s last commander.

It kind of set a new tone to their relationship as well. Hopefully a better one.

Javier wasn't a slave anymore, and Zakhar Sokolov was no longer his owner, however technical that term had been at the time.

Once this pirate war was over, they would need to have a long talk about the next twenty years. Six months ago, Javier had been staring at this very hull from the outside, waiting for it to kill him.

Before he had learned the truth. And found the perfect tool for his vengeance.

"Thank you," Javier finally replied to Suvi, glancing up at a camera tucked into a corner with a smile.

His princess was back in her castle, and nobody would ever take that away from her.

"Status?" he asked.

"Her shuttle has just docked and is waiting for you," Suvi replied. "Zakhar and Djamila are there, greeting a short, Mongolian man in a cute hat. Afia will be along shortly. Piet and I are talking orchestral composition theory up on the bridge."

Javier nodded.

Having an automated warship, commanded by a *Sentience* that didn't need anyone else to fly it, had been a professional threat to Piet Alferdinck, *Storm Gauntlet*'s pilot. He could have chosen to leave and find another flying gig, but he and Suvi had bonded over music, of all things.

And Zakhar was grooming the man to become his First Mate, the crew's Executive Officer, now that Javier was no longer in the running for the job. It would be a nice thing.

"Time to go," he said with finality.

The *Khatum* had invited him to not be a stranger, and not an enemy. Had provided him with a cheesecake photo of herself, covered in nothing but long hair and shadows, wearing the Helm of Athena to obscure all of her face except that tremendous smile, kneeling on the bed where they had once romped.

Javier took it as a positive sign as he opened the hatch and set out for the landing bay, well aft and down several decks.

Hopefully, the *Khatum* wasn't about to kill him.

PART FOUR

Javier followed the short, Mongolian guy through hallways he recognized, into places he did not. Zakhar, Djamila, and Afia Burakgazi followed him, the group of them escorted by a pair of extremely quiet men in dark gray uniforms.

Guards. Gendarme.

Bouncers.

Plus Tömörbaatar, possibly more dangerous than any of the muscle boys. Javier could tell that just from the hard look in the man's eyes.

The path had taken them from *Shangdu*'s primary landing bay through the sort of reception area visiting royalty might find impressive. From there, the main corridor through the Elite Class suites, carpeted in moss green with soft blue walls and perfect lighting, until they passed through a semi-hidden doorway into what suddenly looked like Class-A office space.

The carpet here was brown-ish and speckled in that way that would generally hide stains. It was rugged enough to go years without replacing, while the nicer stuff on the outside was probably new annually.

The walls were golden oak boards, about two hands wide and running vertical. Javier assumed they were a veneer over the usual metal bulkheads. The lights were somehow more professional, less warm and inviting than the other ones had been.

Luxury transformed into corporate.

225

Javier had always expected that this was more like what the woman was, but had never been in a position to ask. Even now, he wasn't sure whether she would throw him out, have him arrested, or make a pass at him.

Or which outcome scared him more.

Best to not waste energy worrying. He was committed at this point, a hog in the chute.

At least he looked better than everyone else. Adrian had guaranteed that. Not that it took much effort, considering how everyone else was dressed today.

Captain Zakhar Sokolov was wearing his personal variant of the standard *Concord* dress uniform, minus all the badges and the tie, but keeping those damned polished-leather black shoes. Olive-green slacks. Lighter green, button-up shirt with a folded collar. Olive-green jacket, single-breasted, with three buttons to his sternum and four stripes on each cuff.

Djamila Sykora, *Dragoon*, was wearing a similar cut of fabric, but in gun-metal gray with blue edging. At 2.1 meters tall, she was a gray tree. At least she wasn't armed today. At least, not carrying any weapons.

The woman *was* a weapon.

Only Afia had treated this like a holiday, and not a possible hanging.

She was wearing what Javier could only describe as harem pants. Diaphanous gold material, mostly translucent, that only gathered at the waist and ankles, over baby blue leggings. A cream-white tunic embroidered with gold dragons that had red eyes and showed off her lean petiteness and golden-brown skin that wasn't much darker than the Khatum's, but more brown and less gold than the other woman.

Both top and bottom seemed to be made with glitter in the fabric, so the smiling engineer was leaving a small cloud of glitter particles everywhere as she walked, slowly infecting the ship with glitter.

Because glitter was forever.

They arrived.

Big, imposing wooden door in dark tones that just screamed *Boardroom*.

Javier sucked a breath deep into his toes and prepared for battle.

Another day. Another drachma.

The short Mongolian dude, Tömörbaatar, knocked briefly, opened the door, and entered, walking around to stand on her right.

The *Khatum of Altai*.

She was even more beautiful than he remembered.

The smile was warm and broad. Welcoming. The eyes, a mischievous twinkle.

Javier didn't know if he should be relieved or worried.

He settled for following Tömörbaatar into the room, coming to rest at the far end of the oval-shaped conference table that dominated the space, a sea of polished wood between them.

There were a handful of her people already seated at that end of the table, but most of them were just bureaucrats handy for taking notes or running errands.

She would make all decisions. He knew that.

Zakhar and Djamila ended up on Javier's right, going forward around the table. Afia took the open chair at his left.

Behnam Sherazi rose from her chair.

Javier didn't care that his eyes couldn't make it back to her face. Even in a charcoal business suit not all that removed from what Sokolov was wearing, she was simply stunning.

Her little curtsy nearly undid him.

"Captain Navarre," she smiled at him, conveying a wealth of pleasantness.

If he was going to be hung by this woman, at least it would be a nice death.

"Your Grace," he replied with a formal bow.

The others did the same, mostly murmuring.

It was his show. His head.

His vengeance.

"Please," she said, amiable but professional at the same time. "Be seated. What brings you to *Binhai*?"

They were nine around the table, three of the closest chairs remaining empty.

"You asked that we not be enemies, nor strangers," Javier replied, quoting the letter she had sent him after he had broken in and committed a petite vandalism on her starship.

"Indeed," she agreed, fencing ever so exquisitely.

"When last I was here," Javier continued, gesturing to Djamila. "When we were here, it was to do a job for Valko Slavkov."

"I remember," she said lightly. "A most interesting and enlightening adventure was had by all."

Javier let that one go without comment. Not quite the turn of phrase he would have used, but accurate enough, if you wanted to put lipstick on a pig.

"Valko Slavkov apparently was expecting a bloodbath out of everything," Javier replied to her tone. He had feared it would be an effort to not get all growly, impersonating Navarre, but he didn't have to be that guy anymore. Certainly not around her. "He seems to have been rather put out that things turned out so small."

"Yes," the Khatum agreed. "One minor assassination, and even that philosophical and not literal. And the man subsequently escaped with his life and fled on to points unknown. Hopefully you aren't here to finish the job?"

"On the contrary," Javier countered. "Slavkov took the outcome personally enough that he hired one of the Pirate Clans to hunt me down and kill me, along with Captain Sokolov, and his entire crew."

"He seems to have failed," she leaned forward, ever so slightly. If she had chosen to wear something that showed any cleavage at all, any man's eyes would have gone south at that point.

Gods, he missed this sort of repartee.

"He pissed me off." Navarre's tones finally colored the conversation.

"Abram Tamaaz pissed you off, once," she noted dryly, suddenly leaning back in her chair and getting professional again, right at the moment when it had been getting warm and personal.

"Yes," Javier agreed.

She pointed at the horizon over his shoulder.

"Is that what you have planned, with that warship out there?" she inquired.

"Partly," he agreed. "I would like your help, as well."

One perfectly-manicured eyebrow went up exactly the right amount.

Doubt. Sarcasm. Interest. Adventure.

Wow.

"With Captain Sokolov's willing assistance, I'm going after Valko Slavkov, and all his punks," Javier said. "But I'm also going after the people he hired to kill me."

"And who would that be?"

"Walvisbaai Industrial," he replied. "One of the so-called *Pirate Clans.*"

Javier felt the weight of her gaze suddenly shift to his right. To Zakhar.

"As I understand it," she began. "Captain Sokolov happens to belongs to a similar organization."

Zakhar surprised Javier by unfolding his posture from that rigid, military bearing and leaning forward to rest his elbows on the table so he could put his chin on his crossed hands.

"This is personal," Zakhar growled.

Nothing more, but it spoke volumes, coming from a man of such obvious military bearing and reputation.

People were going to die.

And they had it coming.

"I see," she said after a moment of study, her eyes coming back to rest on Javier after pausing to measure both Djamila and Afia. "And my involvement?"

"Piracy is a gray area, Your Grace," Javier purred, all his lessons in maritime law having been recently refreshed as he planned this little escapade. "Law enforcement is not universal, but depends on a variety of jurisdictions. And the *Concord* can't be everywhere. What I have planned could be construed as a capital offense, if committed without prior sanction."

Her eyes got a special glow in them, but she remained silently attentive.

Javier took that as a welcome sign.

"I would like to negotiate a deal with you for *Letters of Marque and Reprisal*," he said simply.

Ninety-nine people in one hundred, the look he would expect back would be blank puzzlement.

Not her. Under all that beauty was a first-class brain, educated way beyond the normal standards for rich aristocrats.

All that, and a bag of chips.

"Elizabeth *Regina* and Francis Drake?" she asked in a tone suddenly bordering on caustic sarcasm.

It took Javier a moment to place the reference.

"Yes, Your Grace," he said. "Just so."

"For how long?" she inquired.

Javier leaned back and thought.

That was the bitch of it.

This might take six months. Or maybe ten years. Luck and timing would play a significant role.

"I believe we can either finish our task, or die trying, inside of two years," he finally settled on.

"Leaving Slavkov dead and Walvisbaai neutered?" she pursued him like a hound after a hare. "What's in it for me?"

Yup. Smart and cunning woman. The best kind.

"Revenge," he said. "Plus plunder. That ship out there is capable of making a serious change to the status quo in a number of places."

"And I should declare open war on your enemies on something so thin?" her tone had turned tart.

Javier nodded. This was where the dickering over brass tacks would get interesting.

"No," she said simply, her dark eyes turning opaque in some way he couldn't describe.

"No?" Javier was mildly stunned. Not at the refusal, but how quickly she got there.

It had always been a possible outcome.

"No," she repeated. "Two years for you, possibly a lifetime of recriminations and potential hostility for me? Simply not worth it. No."

At least she hadn't thrown him out. Hopefully that was a sign.

"What would bring the scales more into balance?" he proffered carefully.

And that's when those black widow's eyes suddenly got lethal.

"Your vessel is a First Rate Galleon, *Neu Berne* style," she observed. "A heavily-armed merchantman, correct?"

Javier nodded cautiously. He hadn't met too many people in his life as dangerous, as smart or cunning, as this woman. This might be the one day where he regretted it.

"If you are to be Drake, there must be voyages of exploration and trade as well," she said simply. "Not just war with Imperial Spain."

"I beg your pardon?" he sputtered.

Javier could feel a stack of history books suddenly piling up on his nightstand. This woman was serious.

"If you want my help," Behnam Sherazi boiled it down tightly. "Then there will be a long-term profit in it for me."

"How long?" Javier asked in a polite voice, aware that he was deep into black widow territory with this woman.

"Let's talk about a ten-year trade partnership, Captain Navarre," she said in a voice that was letting the lethal hardness slowly bleed over into polite warmth. Accounting, rather than vengeance. At least as much as the two differed in this sort of company.

Javier mirrored Zakhar's pose, chin on hands, elbows on the table.

Not the way he had planned it. But maybe there was something in it for everyone, after all. He had always known that this beautiful woman was dangerous.

PART FIVE

JAVIER COULDN'T, for the life of him, think of an event that had left him so emotionally and intellectually wrung out.

Possibly, and this was just a maybe, sitting for his Master Mariner certification, Junior year at the *Bryce Academy*, when they washed out those who were good enough to merely serve, and then separated out the ones who were going to *command*.

He collapsed onto the soft sofa in the luxurious suite she had assigned him, trying not to laugh out loud at the realization that it was the exact same one she had put him in last time, down to the same picture hanging over the bed as in the cheesecake picture she had sent him.

There were rooms for bodyguards he didn't have, with Sykora, Sokolov, and Afia being off in their own rooms. The same three level living room. That same bed in the back room that was big enough to host a small orgy.

He didn't have the energy to even think about it.

At least the woman had spent the five hours of hard negotiation in a polite way, rather than getting brutal about it. And he had a deal.

Of sorts.

It involved naturalizing Javier and all the Centurions of Sokolov's crew as citizens of *Altai*. Subject to her law, on a planet where she was the law. He still had to present it to the crew and see who would balk.

Most of Sokolov's officers were well-enough known in places to have

232

prices on their heads. Being able to come home to a place where they might be safe would probably sway them.

Javier wondered how much of the rest of the crew would take her up on the offer, as well.

Some folks would walk, taking their chances with a fresh start on *Binhai*, or maybe trying to get hired on as part of *Shangdu's* crew. Javier hoped he could make up the difference, the losses, with a quiet recruiting drive.

For what he had in mind, he was probably going to need some retired *Concord* fleet marines. The dangerous kinds.

Fortunately, Djamila Sykora was exactly the person to find them, recruit them, and then qualify them to her high standards. Nobody got to carry a gun around the dragoon without her approval.

Javier eyed the wet bar as he kicked off his shoes and contemplated a nap. He had another three hours before a semi-formal dinner.

The Westminster chimed at the front hatch. Someone wanted to talk.

Javier considered looking. Considered ignoring it. Curiosity won the coin toss.

"Room system, open the hatch," he said.

If someone was here to kill him, they would just have to haul their lazy asses all the way in here to do the job, instead of killing him in the doorway.

Movement in the hallway.

Her.

"Your Grace," Javier said, not even bothering to sit up straighter.

She had changed from the business suit earlier into a navy blue outfit that looked like what you would get if you told an expert fashion designer to drape a tall woman in six meters of silk with a minimum of sewing. It flowed around her like moonlight.

Nobody had any right to look that good after five, long hours of legalisms.

"We're in private," she replied quietly, smiling tightly, as if a shade nervous. *Her?* "You could call me Behnam."

"True," Javier agreed with a tired smile. "But we're also business partners now, to some extent. I'm not sure how appropriate that level of familiarity might be."

"We haven't signed anything yet," she countered. "Until then, you're still just an interesting pirate captain visiting my ship."

Ah ha. Trust this woman to have finely sliced that edge. Hell, it was probably still ethically safe at this point, too.

What she would do to his soul was a whole other conversation.

"Behnam," he finally said aloud. "I was just contemplating some whiskey when you arrived. Would you care to join me?"

"You stay put," she purred with a lively twinkle in her eyes. "Allow me to serve you."

As if those weren't the most dangerous words to ever come out of a woman's mouth.

Still, he gestured for her to proceed and let the arm of the sofa take his weight as he swung his feet up. As nice as the view was, just watching her walk over and grab a pair of highball glasses made him even more tired.

The tinkle of ice sounded a musical note, followed by snaps as she poured the warm, caramel liquid over them.

The sofa was big enough that she could hand him a glass, engulfing him in the glorious floral scent of her perfume, before moving to the far end and settling.

Javier had known cats that couldn't tuck their feet under them so gracefully.

And the way her eyes followed his every movement reminded Javier of an owl waiting on a branch as a clueless rabbit crept out from cover.

"To business," he toasted, raising his glass just a shade.

"Business, yes," she replied.

The first sip of liquid smoke cut through the layer of ice and gunk coating his brain.

It didn't do anything at all to recharge his batteries. Javier suspected that a full nap would be required for that level of human, and she didn't look like that was what she had in mind tonight.

"You really are serious about all this, aren't you?" she finally asked.

"Could you quantify that, please?" he replied in a voice that laid bare all the drain in him.

Thinking was asking too much at this point.

"Revenge," she elaborated. "Destruction. Walvisbaai."

That, however, was the spark to light a fire.

"I didn't choose to become a pirate, Behnam," he said in a voice approximating a bastard sword. Heavy, hard, lethal. "Sokolov captured me and the alternative was a short career as a slave on an agricultural colony somewhere."

"And yet, you're partners, now," she observed. "You trust the man and his crew that much?"

"*Excalibur* is my ship," Javier replied. "He has to trust me."

"You are one man, Eutrupio," she said. "Regardless of how dangerous you might be. What makes you think you're safe?"

Yeah, it was going to be one of those days.

Javier sat more upright and focused his *intent* on the woman at the far end of the galaxy from him.

"Once upon a time, my lady," he began, listening to Navarre's tones color his own. "I had a scout vessel with a *Sentience* as my whole crew. Before *Storm Gauntlet* appeared out of nowhere and killed her. I managed to hide the chips from Zakhar for three years. When I led Sokolov and his crew to the derelict, I poured her into the core. It's hers, now."

"That thing is *Sentient*?" Behnam was shocked. It did lovely things to her eyes.

"She's also my best friend," he said. "The daughter I never had."

"What's she like?" the woman was suddenly concentrating.

"You met her already," Javier said. "That tall, blonde communications officer you spoke with when we arrived? That's Suvi."

"So if I'm to have a partnership with you, then I'll have one with her as well," Behnam announced. "I'll need to talk to her. Privately. Woman to woman."

Javier fixed her with his best stinkeye, but she was as immune to it as Zakhar seemed to be.

"Fine," he said. "But not this afternoon. I'm so tired I'm not even sure a long soak before whatever it is you have planned for dinner would help."

She smiled. Warm. Friendly. Predatory.

"I could always join you," she said. "Keep you from drowning. Scrub your back. And then maybe snuggle you to sleep."

Even if that hadn't been the best offer he'd gotten in months, Javier wouldn't have turned her down. Lord knew what their relationship would be like once contracts were signed.

He suspected she felt the same.

A last meal for the condemned.

Tomorrow, things were going to get serious.

PART SIX

A NOTE HAD APPEARED in her pocket, as if by magic.

Djamila wasn't sure if she should be aghast that her guard was down that far, or thrilled that he was still that good.

She hadn't been sure how she would approach the man, or the topic. During the conversations with Suvi, back when they first recovered *Hammerfield* from eternity, it had only been a theoretical topic.

Now, she was here. Again. With Zakhar up a deck, presumably resting and preparing for dinner, while she was down in this same dive bar where her adventures on this vessel had begun.

Djamila suddenly felt like a teenager sneaking out after curfew.

Nothing had changed in this room, this bar. She suspected that nothing was ever allowed to change. Continuity for the crew, as they recovered from dealing with rich aristocrat customers that had a tendency to be petulant children.

The lights were just dim enough to let eyes recover, and let minds pretend that there was nobody around, if they got more than two meters away from you.

The bar itself was still tall, with long, gray metal sides and a scarred wooden top, both burned, nicked, and stained with age and character.

An impressive backbar, with exotic bottles four rows high above and a row of meter-tall refrigerators underneath.

Stools all the way around the front, about half of them currently occupied.

That same burly bartender standing behind, with scarred ears and a look like a spring-wakened troll: hungry and mean.

Djamila was still an outsider here. This bar was dedicated to crew, and mostly to engineering-side, rather than service-side. The colors of the uniforms were muted and generally gray.

All the better to disappear when someone in bright tones stepped up to help a lost tourist.

The two stools on the left corner of the bar, along the long axis where it turned in on the short axis, those had not changed. The near corner one was empty, the other was filled.

Farouz.

There were no words to describe the sudden race of emotions, save for the surge of cold adrenaline in her belly.

167 cm tall. Short for a man anywhere, and nearly half a meter shorter than she was.

Wiry. Hard. Carved from steel rods and barbed wire. Covered in skin darker than her tanned bronze. Perhaps Central Asian, like his boss.

Dark hair, cut short and just starting to gray underneath. Clean shaven.

Perfect stillness. Something learned and not natural. Available only to practitioners of deep meditation, or combat arts with meditative elements.

Zen warriors.

She could see him as *Kensei* on the dojo floor, equally at home with katana or bokken.

He moved in ways that very few others did. In her experience, only the most dangerous Special Forces operators could flow like that.

His face was cold, but she felt it warm into a smile as she got close.

The last time she had seen this man, it had been necessary to shoot him. Djamila had only Aritza's word, third-hand, that they had all moved past that ugly incident. That, and a piece of paper with a place and a time. A place she already knew.

He rose as she reached the stool reserved for her, climbed down off his chair as if to emphasize the enormous difference in height. Reached up slowly, one hand going around her hip, the other around her neck to pull her down into a kiss filled with all the promise the last one had.

It was over too soon.

Djamila suspected that they might all be over too soon. But that was the cost of living.

"Thank you," he said, letting go of her soul and returning to his stool.

Djamila took the empty seat next to him.

The bartender smiled and poured something blue into a highball glass unasked, unspoken, and then left with nothing but a wry smile.

So, he remembered her, too.

"I might be recruiting this time," she said, as if the last year had been a day.

"It must be dangerous if you need help," he replied in a low, quiet drawl.

"It will be," she replied with a small smile. "I thought I would get the most dangerous man on this ship to help."

A pause as he studied her. Weighing her soul, perhaps.

They had gone beyond merely comrades, in the space of those two kisses, then and now.

"With you here," Farouz finally said, "I would be fourth most dangerous."

"Fourth?" she was surprised.

"Third would be my teacher," the man observed. "I could not place you second or first against the other person without a head-to-head combat decathlon that would be decided on thousandths of points. But neither of those people would give up their place here. Such are adventures for the young."

From the skin around his neck and his wrists, Djamila would have guessed him to be in his early forties, perhaps half a decade older than her, but it was hard to tell with a man like that. In this light, he was almost carved from timeless granite.

"And you?" she teased.

"Old enough to know better," he replied with a sudden grin. "Young enough to still do crazy things, like pick up angry Amazons in bars."

Djamila leaned close enough to kiss him again. Because she could.

A year ago, she had been just learning how to be someone other than the *Ballerina of Death*, always at war with Aritza. What was it Javier had said to her, in one of those private conversations?

All possible tomorrows.

"Do you want to know what it is?" she finally asked, breaking the contact and catching her breath from the kiss.

He smiled and raised a glass that had been sitting close. It was also blue.

"It will be a precise aggression," he said, growing cold and serious, but keeping a twinkle in his eyes for her. "Multi-threaded. Relying on stealth and timing. An assassination, of sorts, rather than a frontal assault with overwhelming firepower. Your team will be compact and expert, such that you can rely on professionalism rather than long experience with a teammate and thus allowing you to recruit outside your immediate crew."

Djamila remembered to pick her jaw up and close her mouth before she caught any flies.

"Any other option would require six months of training," Farouz continued. "And Captain Navarre does not strike me as that type, from my experience with the man and his methods."

"No, you are absolutely right," Djamila confessed. "Navarre is after revenge on the man who sent us here originally, for a double-cross later."

"And you, Hadiiye?" Farouz probed. "What do you seek?"

"I have another name," she hesitated.

"So do we all," he countered, still smiling. "Hadiiye was the one I wanted. Not whoever that woman was when she went back to her other life. That other woman was not happy, with herself or her situation. Hadiiye had hope."

"And she still does," the woman whispered, unsure exactly who she was right now as the roles began to bleed into one another.

Djamila considered the advice of Dr. Wilhelmina Teague. And Suvi. And even Afia Burakgazi. All women that had tried to help her overcome herself.

"We want to be free," she finally whispered.

Farouz nodded.

"Then show me who we need to kill to free you," he said.

PART TWO

BOOK TWENTY-TWO: NEMESIS

PART ONE

THIS WAS the point when Zakhar felt a twinge of regret.

Only a twinge, mind you, tempered greatly by the feeling of immense security that he got from being surrounded by a warship of this scale and raw power.

But a little regret, nonetheless.

Storm Gauntlet had been a low-profile corvette to begin with. A tiny little escort turned sneaky. On top of that, his bosses had layered on a stealth cloak good enough to hide them from most sensor systems until he was right on top of someone and they had to spot him visually.

For a pirate, the best way to catch prey. Like one Mr. Javier Aritza.

That wasn't an option with this mighty kraken, this First Rate Galleon. This thing called *Hammerfield*.

Javier and Suvi had decided to rename this ship as *Excalibur*, for reasons generally lost on him, but an inside joke with a number of the crew members, including Djamila.

Zakhar supposed he could ask her, or Suvi. He could even look it up, if he thought it mattered all that much. Maybe tomorrow. It must be good to elicit the kinds of giggles it had.

Everyone else in orbit had hard-pinged them when *Excalibur* got close enough to orbit to register on their scans as something new and impressive. Well, old and even more impressive. They didn't make warships like these any more.

Today, the ship was sitting in a medium orbit of *Merankorr*, a planet mostly famous for its brothels and orbital foundries but also home to two of the best shipyards in space. Soon, they would be granted a docking assignment and could unload their cargo.

Zakhar would shed a few tears when they were done. It was the nature of things.

He would miss his old bridge.

Excalibur had an enormous command space, a round room about twenty-seven meters across, with a domed ceiling 9.2 meters at the peak. Him ensconced atop a pedestal at the center, surrounded by stations for six Centurions and twelve more crew. You could set up a volleyball net in here and hold tournaments.

At least the crew had painted everything an earthy brown to replace the stark, gunmetal gray it had been. Warmer. Homier.

And enough different from the first time he had boarded, with Captain Mayer's corpse still seated in this very chair, that Zakhar didn't think he would have too many zombie nightmares.

Hopefully, Mayer's ghost approved of everything they were doing.

Zakhar didn't need to sit a duty watch on the bridge. Probably shouldn't. There was always paperwork that needed doing. Less than before, with Suvi handling things, but some.

At the same time, it kept his head in the game.

He had known commanders that never did this. Never spent four hours on the bridge so all the other centurions could have some downtime. Never interacted directly with the enlisted crew who were the rugged backbone of any good ship.

Those captains frequently weren't his favorites. Or Fleet's.

Even on a warship of this immense scale, it was possible to have a small crew. He needed to know everyone, and know them well.

Technically, he could go with a crew even smaller than *Storm Gauntlet* had required, but he would need to recruit a larger ground combat contingent one of these days. Assuming they stayed in the piracy business.

With this much firepower and cargo capacity at hand, all sorts of other options presented themselves as well. Not that he wanted to become a warlord/God-Emperor of some little backwards planet out in the sticks, but he could. Assuming Javier and Suvi wanted to.

Or he could get serious about just hauling cargo for a living. Boring and safe, but profitable. Again, what would Javier and Suvi think? Or Djamila?

"Captain, we have an update," Suvi's warm voice filled the room, breaking him out of the dark place his thoughts were heading.

"Go ahead, Suvi," he replied.

"We are next in the queue for the dry-dock, sir," Suvi said. "Estimated time to dock is two to three hours."

"Acknowledge them, please, and let Afia and Andreea know," he ordered.

Down below, what was left of *Storm Gauntlet*'s corpse was blind, toothless, and naked, stowed in the aft-most primary cargo bay. With time available and dedicated crew, Chief Engineer Andreea Dalca and Afia Burakgazi had removed every sensor and weapon from the little corvette, as well as the cloak generator. Then they stripped it of every useful bit of anything they could, since they had space to stow the results.

The ship's name plate, formerly welded to the aft bulkhead on the bridge, had been cut off and put in Zakhar's personal cabin as a memento. Right before every single identifying transmitter and ID number had been wiped, removed, or etched off with an angle grinder.

They had even split her shell into three big pieces, making it easier to remove Javier's arboretum and shift it into the forward-most bay over here, several decks directly below him, which was then sealed off and turned into something of a park for the crew.

What was left were piles of metal and parts. The badly damaged corpse of a *Concord* corvette, unidentifiable, except by process of elimination of any such private vessels still in service somewhere. And there were enough of those to mask which one this was.

He would miss her, to be sure, but he had *Hammerfield*/*Excalibur* now.

Trading up for bigger problems.

Shortly, a tiny, little superrunt of a tug would come alongside to nudge them into alignment with the dry-dock and guide them in. Ship's gravity would be turned entirely off for half a day while every available crew member with EVA certifications helped the shipyard crew to move the corvette's body over, under Afia's supervision. Her soul would remain behind with the crew.

They would make a good chunk of money from this deal.

And all of this was just a cover to get close enough to their target to be able to scan it at close range with nobody the wiser. With the sorts of sensor capabilities originally taken off of a retired *Concord* probe-cutter, and subsequently reprogrammed by a highly-competent Science Officer-turned-pirate.

Who was himself leading a very dedicated, very angry group of people, Zakhar included.

Valko Slavkov had no idea what he had awakened.

Today's target was a freighter. Of a sort.

Zakhar had been deeply impressed by the *Land Leviathan*, that enormous, tracked resort vehicle. A desert train with ten massive cars, each sixty meters on a side and thirty tall, with big treads waddling slowly across whatever world Slavkov owned or rented.

He knew Aritza had been plotting how to steal the thing since the first time the two of them had seen it.

For Zakhar, it was the engineering feat to move the Leviathan between worlds that engaged his dreams. He had originally expected that each of the ten cars was hauled to orbit individually and then stowed aboard a megafreighter. A monster even bigger than the kraken that was *Excalibur*, big enough to ensnare the ship, but not nearly as heavily armed.

The truth was even more surprising. A ship in the form of an isosceles trapezoid with a narrow width at the bow, wider at the stern, and long in the body, with two massive, squat engines thrust off the back like stubby legs, like the Cyrillic capital letter *De*. Д. The whole reminded him of something like a dachshund hound.

Nothing much to look at, until you realized that the whole ship was completely hollow, with everything contained in the outer walls. The space in the middle, coming up from between the engine wells, seven hundred meters long, was where the pilot would drive the entire beast of the Land Leviathan, once the lander was on the ground. Giant waldoes came out of the sides at that point and clamped onto the Leviathan to secure it into place, and then the ship would slowly take off and move to orbit, where it would rendezvous with its escorts and head off to the next destination.

The carrier ship that was off their starboard bow right now, slowly finishing up a refit before heading off to the next mission.

The next desert world, probably.

Zakhar figured that someone like Valko Slavkov, a bully born rich, probably didn't travel with the bigger vessel, but would spend some time visiting someone else's fairy castle while his moved to a new location.

What must it be like to have so much wealth that you could do things like that for fun?

Zakhar was fourth generation *Concord* fleet. Second as an officer. Quite possibly the last, unless circumstances changed in the next few years and he finally got serious about having a family.

Nobody got rich in the service. Well, the bankers did, same as with pirates.

Even selling off the shattered remains of *Storm Gauntlet* wouldn't really make him rich. Javier was getting a quarter, Zakhar and the crew was getting another quarter according to a complicated formula, and a quarter went to their new investor/business partner. The *Khatum of Altai*. The last slice was going into a ship's maintenance fund.

It would keep *Excalibur* in socks and fresh cream for maybe a decade, if they were frugal.

And lucky enough to survive that long. But first, he and Javier had to see a man about a horse.

"CAPTAIN," the voice came out of a speaker on his desk. "I'd really appreciate you down in the cargo bay, please."

Zakhar's head snapped up.

Afia never did that. She was among the most self-contained engineers--hell, people--he knew. Utterly competent and happy to take care of things herself.

That was why he had put her in charge of this task. That, and she was gregarious enough to work with dock teams, whereas his chief engineer was a barely-functioning introvert who was happier down with her generators and engines.

Afia didn't ask for help unless it was bad. Or getting there quickly. She had a good eye for that sort of thing, too. And she must have been around civilians, so she didn't want to say "NOW" but he could read between the lines.

"Be along shortly," he keyed the comm, already rising from the seat in his day office and moving towards the hatch.

They hadn't shut down the gravplates yet, so the task took longer. In freefall, he could have basically swam there in a few powerful kicks, bouncing off walls and plates as he went.

Even at fifty-five, he could still out-maneuver anybody in this crew, excepting only Djamila.

Nope, he pounded down stairs like his ass was on fire today. Through the hatch and into the grand mausoleum that held his last command.

Afia was there, along with a group of *Concord* officers.

Made sense. *Storm Gauntlet* was a retired *Concord* warship. *Merankorr* was a *Concord* world. And Zakhar had every damned one of their forms and certificates properly filled out, the benefit of the *Khatum*'s legal affairs officers very carefully doing their job.

As he got close to the group, Zakhar blinked and nearly stutter-stepped, but he swallowed his reaction before it got to his face.

Only the eyes maybe showed anything.

Reflected in the face of the main guy over there, just turning away from his conversation with Afia to look this direction. The man with four solid yellow rings on each wrist, plus a broken one above that. In a uniform that was the origin of the green suit Zakhar wore as a rule.

A guy Zakhar knew.

Crap.

"Captain Zakhar Sokolov," he said loudly, forcefully as he got within polite range, drawing everyone in the area into his orbit by sheer force of will. He was good at that. Even Javier listened, most of the time. "Is there a problem?"

There was, but Zakhar wasn't going to admit it first.

"Commodore Nguyên Ayokunle," the stranger in charge of the other group replied as he turned and flinched, ever so slightly. "No problem, Captain. Since your cargo is military hardware, disposal falls under my purview. Plus, your vessel caught my attention."

Yeah, it would. History had always been your thing, hadn't it, Yên?

Old memories flooded back, but Zakhar kept his face neutral.

"How so?" Zakhar decided to play stupid, just in case.

The man was tall and skinny, with dark brown skin and fluffy ringlets gone totally white.

Another reason Zakhar kept his own head shaved at all times.

Commodore was a courtesy rank. Senior captain assigned to a system or task force that didn't rate an Admiral, at a time when budget cut backs meant fewer and fewer flag slots available.

One of the primary reasons Zakhar had left the straight and narrow. And why he had so many competent people to crew with.

Yên smiled at him in a calculating way.

"*Station Sentience* flagged you as a *Neu Berne*-style Galleon," the commodore replied in a questioning tone. "That's a lot of firepower for a private-service vessel. And this is a very old ship that doesn't appear anywhere in our records."

"We salvaged a derelict," Zakhar replied evenly. It was even the truth. "And we frequently have to operate in places folks like you never go."

Leave it at that. Do not poke a sleeping bear with anything less than a very long stick.

"And flagged out of *Altai*," Yên continued the thought. "That's a long ways away."

"I just work here," Zakhar decided to go shallow and stupid on the man. Hell, it might even work if this very senior *Concord* officer chose to play along.

"Who owns this ship?" Yên asked pointedly.

Around them, the *Concord* folks were getting the least bit twitchy. Afia, too.

But this was EXACTLY why he and Javier had spent so much time on their cover story and all the paperwork to back it up.

"Corporate chain," Zakhar said. "Like a nautilus shell. Built in layers that run all over the place. I do know that the *Khatum of Altai* herself was a major investor."

Along with me, Javier, and a crew committee represented by the tiny, Indonesian woman to my immediate right, but you don't need to know that, Yên.

"I see," Yên observed in a tone so dry Zakhar needed a glass of water. "Have we met somewhere? You look familiar."

I dunno. The guy who tutored you through Orbital Mechanics II? Who might have ended up your brother-in-law, if your sister hadn't decided she wanted to marry a stay-at-home accountant instead of a fleet officer?

Have we met?

"I get that a lot," Zakhar replied in a carefully bored tone. "Had a cousin who was in the navy who looks a lot like me. You might have known him."

Yên nodded silently.

"And your cargo?" Yên said. "Manifest ranks it as a *Concord* corvette, demilitarized and stripped."

The commodore gestured at the metal art installations behind them. A proud corpse in three big pieces and hundreds of little ones. Nobody had bothered to buff out the scorch marks and damage *Ajax* had done before the wee Viking longboat had slipped away at *Svalbard*.

"My understanding?" Zakhar said with a shrug. "Story goes that she was a pirate who got more than she bargained for. Escaped by the skin of her teeth, but it wasn't economical to repair her, so a stripper crew dismantled her and we're hauling the lot here to *Merankorr* for the foundry. Lot of good metal here that just needs to be recast into a new ship."

Zakhar could see the list of questions Yên wanted to ask, but not in front of this many witnesses. Zakhar felt the same way.

How often do you suddenly run into a man who was your best friend forty years ago, whom you haven't seen in at least fifteen?

"Interesting," Yên replied. "Where are you headed from here?"

"*Purton*," Zakhar lied easily. That was in the paperwork already. "Dead-heading to get a load to haul to *Meehu*."

"Dangerous places," Yên agreed. "Good thing you have all this firepower to protect you. Likely to be back through *Merankorr* anytime soon?"

Zakhar shrugged.

"They wouldn't be such bad places if you folks did your jobs more," Zakhar said, unable to resist the dig. And maybe reflect a little of the anger Zakhar had at where their two distinct lives had ended up.

Yên bristled. Just a bit.

The *Concord* was still recovering from the time and expense spent cleaning up nearly a century of war and strife caused by other people, but Zakhar knew they had cut too much, too soon, even after two generations of relative peace.

Too many worlds were still left on their own. Too much military hardware like this First-Rate-Galleon floating around, just waiting for a sociopath who wanted to make himself a petty god.

Zakhar was sure Yên would have savagely dressed down a civilian who mocked him like that that in public, even on the safety of his own deck.

Zakhar watched the man clench his jaws, grinding his teeth rather than lash out.

The moment of rage passed.

Zakhar watched all the *Concord* officers relax as their boss did. Afia had been remarkably silent and unobtrusive through the whole thing, but Zakhar recognized her stance as a small woman sizing a bigger man up for a swift kick to the balls in a sudden fight.

"Captain Sokolov," Yên nodded professionally. "Maybe next time you're in-system we'll have more time to chat."

"I look forward to that, Commodore," Zakhar said.

The chances of ever being this deep in *Concord* space again were awful slim, especially after *Excalibur* got a reputation for what they were about to do next.

And if they did, Zakhar would be expecting a heavily-armed warship, maybe even a *Warmaster*, to be orbiting in close proximity, all guns aimed and twitchy.

Neither of them would be fooling around at that point.

PART TWO

DELRIDGE SMITH DIDN'T REALLY LIKE to play the part of grumpy, old man. Took too much effort most days, like shaving. Sure, he had old down. Weren't many pilots in their seventh decade still flying combat missions. But he preferred his comfy, gray pants with the thigh pockets, and his collection of Hawaiian shirts. And his flight deck on *Excalibur*'s nameless assault shuttle, all pink fur and glitter paint.

Soothed a man.

Weren't soothed right now, sitting in his piloting station, turned around facing backwards.

Del gave up and let a little growl loose in the direction of his visitor.

Javier Aritza. Still technically the ship's science officer, but that was while everyone was sorting out this new life aboard a *Sentient* warship who was kinda a goof.

The good kind. Del's kind.

Her, not Javier.

"Zakhar tells me you aren't thrilled with the modifications," Javier said judiciously.

He was a shade taller than Del. And in much better shape. Still didn't want to poke a grumpy old man. Good for him.

"Bucko, if I'd wanted to fly like that, I would'a retired and gotten a job as a chauffeur for dumbass admirals," Del fired back. "Calm, casual, polite? What the hell kind of fun is that?"

"Most people would enjoy having enough cloak on their shuttle as to be invisible, you know, Del," Javier said.

"You think I'd look good in a cute, little cap, bub?" Del nearly snarled.

Give Javier credit. He at least smiled in commiseration.

"We don't have time to steal, buy, or build something else, Del," Javier replied. "But if you feel that way, I got two options for you."

"Shoot."

"One, I promise you we'll only do it once, and then strip everything," Javier smiled evilly.

"And two?" Del asked.

"We could always recruit a second pilot when we do acquire a cloaked shuttle," Javier said. "And let him fly us when we need stealth insertions."

Del felt his eyes narrow. If he was a snake, now would have been the point his eyes slitted up hard vertically, too. Javier didn't make threats. And that was a threat.

Felt like maybe Del'd pushed the man far enough today.

"It's unnatural, flying like that," Del finally huffed, knowing he'd lost this round. "Too boring."

Javier nodded.

"We can always get you a combat fighter," he said. "Little snub-nose, one-man attack ship. If we end up going into the cargo business, we're going to need a big cargo lighter to haul stuff to and from orbit. Pretty boring, though."

"Q-ship it," Del said. "This shuttle as a heavily-armed freighter. Add a couple of pop-up turrets in back and I'll fly all the cargo runs you want. Then you can put some dumbass kid in a fighter, and buy him a cute shuttle to haul admirals around in, too."

"I'll see what I can do," Javier said, turning to leave. "We good?"

"Yes," Del grumbled.

Javier had called his bluff. And he was bluffing. Flying admirals or containers around was about all the job he could get, these days. Best to stick with the folks who let him keep the craziness in the cockpit.

"Thank you, Del," Javier said as he headed down the stairs to the cargo deck.

Del nodded at the back of the man's head. His part of the coming mission was a piece of cake. Boring. Easy enough that any dumbass kid fresh from flight school could do it.

Javier was going to owe him, after this.

PART THREE

AFTER ALL THESE YEARS, Djamila still had no idea who Hogan was. Or why a combat training simulation like this was named after him. And why it was Hogan's Alley and not Street or something. She had just needed to burn off angry energy.

Looking up at the monitor as she finished the run, her score had been atrocious, by her standards. Barely ahead of any of her men. Probably the worst score Djamila had put up in three years.

She just wasn't sure who she was, anymore.

Once upon a time, she had been the most dangerous woman to ever receive her Combat EVA certifications from the *Neu Berne Navy*. The *Ballerina of Death*, a name she had earned for her ability to use two pistols simultaneously on different targets in zero-grav combat maneuvers.

Javier still muttered under his breath that she must actively worship a death goddess to be that good. She didn't, but Aritza had no idea what made a woman like her tick.

No, her only competition was perfection. And she wasn't there today. She was back in that other place. The dark place.

One day, she had been the best there was wearing the gray uniform. The next, done. Demobilized. Demilitarized.

Civilian.

Djamila knew she had been circling the drain, psychologically, at that moment when someone had introduced her to Zakhar Sokolov, the man who had given her purpose. Place.

Respect.

Everything had been easier, then. Straightforward. Predictable.

And then Javier Aritza happened to her.

For the more-than-two-years since that day, they'd both silently committed to a personal war that drove them both to be better. Unwritten rules in a duel to the death.

Along the way, Dr. Teague had opened Djamila's mind up to other ways of thinking, living. Helped her become more of a person, and less of a cardboard cutout popping up on a Hogan's Alley to kill or be killed.

And then *Shangdu*. The starship known as the Pleasure Dome.

Farouz.

Djamila might be willing to admit, to herself only, her crush on Captain Sokolov. The feelings she thought were reciprocated, but could never ask.

Not the *captain*.

And at *Shangdu*, she had met someone who happily appreciated her as a dangerous creature, but not one he had to compete with. Who didn't demand anything from her at all. Something she had never known before.

A dangerous man who was willing to walk a step behind her, if necessary, because he knew how troubled she was. To remain at arm's length, rather than walk away when she wouldn't let him any closer.

She had kissed him four times. All of them aboard *Shangdu*, the first separated from the others by a year. And not once since. Even though he was on this ship with her now. Somewhere on *Excalibur*.

Kissable.

Djamila told herself that they were in OpSec. Operational Security mode. Mission imminent. Time to focus. No time for emotional entanglements.

That was a lie.

She was a coward, underneath.

Looking at the monitor board, at the terrible score she had just posted, just shared with the world, she had to admit the truth. Whisper it, at least, since she doubted anyone else would have the audacity to point out how bad she had done. The best of her team might challenge that score on an exceptional day.

Unacceptable.

Djamila turned away from the hallway that was Hogan's Alley and faced the door to the rest of the ship. She sat her disarmed weapons on the training rack for cleaning and recharge later and pressed the big, blue button that deactivated the Alley.

Made it safe for others.

Opened it up for someone to come in and actually compete with her numbers.

She watched the hatch slide open then exited the combat range, passing into the locker room beyond and letting the panel slide shut behind her, desperately afraid that her failure was written on her face.

Hopefully, she could shower and escape before anyone could come along and point out how far she had fallen.

Afia Burakgazi was waiting for her, seated on the old, wooden bench that ran between the tall rows of faded-mustard yellow, metal lockers.

Djamila couldn't help herself. The sight of the tiny engineer, with such a serious face, brought her to a halt.

"Sit," the woman commanded.

Djamila felt her feet betray her by obeying.

Seated, the woman came up to her shoulder, but that was normal. As females went, Djamila had always been long-torsoed to go with her long legs. Built more like a man that way.

Today, it just reinforced the supreme distance between the two of them.

Afia watched her silently for a few moments, as if reading her mind.

"Yeah," the engineer said in a quiet voice. "She was right."

"Who?" Djamila said before she could slam her jaws shut to swallow the words.

Escaped horses and barn doors.

"Suvi," Afia replied. "She said you looked like someone who needed to talk, but she wouldn't tell me anything more than that."

Djamila felt her eyes narrow.

Suvi knew more of the truth than anyone, the benefit of being invisible and able to watch people for several years. The *Sentience* knew too many of Djamila's secrets.

Hopefully, it was a good sign that the *Sentience* had asked the engineer to help. Afia wasn't a gossip.

"Watched you in the run, just now," Afia began deliberately. "I might have done better."

Djamila actually flinched under the words. Her, the iron maiden who was impervious to all things. How far had she fallen? How quickly?

"A word of advice?" Afia continued. "Don't ever play poker with anybody, okay?"

"What?" Djamila was confused by the sudden change. "Why not?"

"Because poker is a mental game, an emotional one," Afia replied. "You win by reading the other players around the table and understanding what they know and don't know by simple body language. And by not letting them know you. The very best players can actually lie to you at the table with nothing but the set of their eyes or the way they hold their hands with the cards. You begin to believe what they are about to do, and they trick you."

The tiny engineer fell silent and watched her.

Djamila felt like a teenage girl again, being reprimanded by her mother for something. She even blushed.

"Yes," Afia said. "That. A good player suppresses that. A great player fakes it. I would take all your money very quickly if we were to play."

Another awkward silence. Djamila felt the ground open under her feet, leaving a precarious ledge in high winds, welcoming her into the abyss.

"Here's a really tough question, Djamila," Afia said. "And it might help. Which man do you love more?"

Djamila felt all the air rush out of her lungs. Her chest seemed to collapse in on itself.

Silence.

Afia seemed content to wait.

Djamila felt herself tear into two separate pieces inside.

The *Dragoon*, *Warrior Princess* of *Storm Gauntlet* and now *Excalibur*. The lethal right arm of Captain Sokolov, forever at his side and never destined to be with him.

Or *Hadiiye*, the dangerous assassin who was the bodyguard to Captain Navarre and moved like a golden lioness, proud and lethal, but softer. More *flexible*. The woman who had kissed Farouz and considered what it would be like to take the man to bed for a good, long romp.

"I can't choose." The words forced themselves out of her mouth.

Djamila blushed even harder at the revelation of her darkest secret.

"Why do you have to?" Afia asked simply.

"What?"

The tiny woman could have pushed her over with a feather.

"You could have them both, you know," the engineer said.

"How is that possible?" Djamila whispered.

"Look at the rest of us," Afia grinned. "All of us have Javier, and none of us. We share, but nobody has his heart. That doesn't stop us from enjoying ourselves occasionally. There's nothing stopping you from having both men."

"But he's the captain," she replied fiercely, even if her voice remained tiny.

"So?"

Djamila didn't think she had ever heard someone pack so much depth and meaning into a single syllable.

"What do you mean?" Djamila asked.

"So he's the captain," Afia said. "Did he take a vow of chastity or something?"

"Well, no," Djamila agreed. "But that's not how it works in the service. In any service."

"Can I let you in on a secret, Djamila?" Afia continued. "We're not in the navy any more. Any of us. We're private contractors doing a service industry transportation job. The only thing stopping you from doing anything is yourself. And probably him. Plus, he is the captain, so he'd be feeling too guilty, like he was taking advantage of you."

"And Farouz?" Djamila asked, wonder slowly creeping into her tones as the implications of Afia's words slithered into her mind. Was it possible?

"You gonna marry that boy? Go set up a dojo somewhere and pop out crazy, little, ninja babies?"

The image made Djamila burst out laughing in spite of herself. Laughing felt good. Cathartic. Liberating.

Afia joined in after a moment.

It took several minutes of joy for Djamila to bring herself back to center.

A center she had almost forgotten existed.

"No," Djamila finally managed, after she had gotten the giggles stuffed back into a box. "I don't see Farouz and I settling down on a planet. Too boring."

"Good," Afia agreed. "Now, when was the last time you got laid?"

Djamila felt the blush simply explode, painting her like a rotten tomato as she crimsoned as far down her chest as one could.

"A while," she stammered, catching her breath.

"How many years?" Afia stalked her relentlessly, eyes glittering like a cat suddenly revealed in the light.

"Seven," Djamila admitted, back down to her tiny voice.

Afia's eyes got big, and then friendlier. Warmer.

"Then you need to head up to his cabin right now, or wherever he is, and do something about that," Afia pronounced.

"Now?"

Djamila was horrified. Spinning. Knocked right back off that center she had just regained. She started to rise, but Afia caught her by the arm, let her miniscule weight anchor Djamila's butt to the warm, wooden bench.

"I can't," Djamila pled with her captor. "I need a shower. I need time to prepare."

"If I gave you any time, you'd talk yourself out of it, Djamila."

Afia's voice had turned to pure doom at this point, a dagger penetrating her mind relentlessly.

"What are you saying?" Djamila asked.

"Come with me."

Afia took her hand and rose, dragging Djamila to her feet, all 2.1 meters of sweaty dragoon, rank and smelly.

The engineer's hand was like a manacle on her wrist as they moved.

At the hatch to the main corridor, Afia switched to holding her hand like young lovers on a third date, but Djamila wasn't fooled. Afia was willing to drag her kicking and screaming if necessary.

At the same time, a small voice in the back of Djamila's head pointed out how much bigger she was than the other woman. How much stronger. How easy it would be to plant her feet and simply say no.

If she really wanted to.

And that was the gulf. That hollow space surrounding her.

Djamila wasn't about to walk across that bridge. Afia was going to metaphorically drag her.

And both women knew that Djamila would let her.

An elevator opened. Afia pulled her in.

"Deck four, please," Afia said to the open air.

"Coming up," Suvi replied as the elevator started to move.

Suvi.

Afia had been sent on this mission because Suvi knew the truth but would not betray Djamila's secrets. And Afia was willing to help her friend on nothing more than that.

Was that what it meant to have friends?

Djamila racked her brain, and couldn't remember any friends after the first semester of training school. Everyone else had become competition for the few slots at the top of the class.

And she had chosen to beat them all by walling them off from her and turning into the *Ballerina of Death*.

In twenty-two years, had she never had a friend? And yet, right now, she had at least two people willing to go out of their way to aid her. Help her get over herself.

The hatch opened. Afia's grip had not lessened one iota. Her short legs churned as she dragged the taller woman along the main corridor forward.

Afia finally stopped at the door that had been Captain Mayer's cabin, once upon a time.

Captain Sokolov's now.

Zakhar.

With her free hand, Afia pushed the ringer.

Sokolov answered quickly.

"Come," he said in that warm, authoritarian baritone that triggered all the happy places in Djamila's brain.

Afia went through first as the hatch opened, pulling Djamila behind her.

The front room was a salon, designed for semi-formal meetings with a round, cherry-stained oak table capable of seating six comfortably in stiff, matching chairs.

The art was designed to look professional, rather than personal. Military themes, but historical, with men on horses or foot, wielding swords and pistols. Not what one would expect from a naval officer, but Djamila didn't know what kind of man Captain Mayer had been, and his personal logs had not been a topic she had taken the time to investigate.

She made a promise to know the man better, starting tomorrow.

Right now, she found herself in the middle of a bridge that a petite engineer seemed intent on burning behind her.

She looked up and found Zakhar standing just at the inner door, the one that led to a more cozy salon for entertaining informally. Somewhere beyond that, the man's office and personal quarters.

He had a look of amused confusion on his face when Djamila turned to him.

"Ladies," he temporized. "What can I do for you?"

Afia took a half step forward.

"This woman needs to talk to you," she said, emphasizing the hand that had drug Djamila this far. "Having delivered her, I'm going to leave."

Djamila felt almost naked when Afia released her hand and quickly departed. Suvi must have been watching as well, because the hatch opened and closed without any delay.

Djamila was alone with him.

Zakhar.

She swallowed past a lump in her throat that threatened to strangle her.

Zakhar was wearing blue slacks today, with a black pullover shirt.

She could only see him in her mind wearing *Concord* green, but then she realized that in the week since they had left *Merankorr*, he had not worn green once.

As if he was striving to become somebody else.

Too.

He watched her patiently. He would. He was a very patient man.

Djamila felt the tide start to recede around her, threatening to ground her on hostile rocks. Her palms were suddenly sweaty and clammy. Her pulse threatened to make her head explode.

She fought it all down. Found that center she had when laughing with Afia. That freedom.

Djamila Sykora, dragoon, took a deep breath and held it.

Released it.

Found her voice.

"I'm told that I needed to come see you," she said quietly, almost diffidently. "Told by friends I didn't even know I had."

"I see," Zakhar said, still not quite sure what to make of the woman in front of him, obviously. "Sit down then, please. What is it you wanted?"

The ledge. The cliff. The darkness below her opened up.

"You," she whispered.

He blinked.

Blinked again.

Djamila felt her heart stop, felt that cold, savage burst of adrenaline flood her belly.

Zakhar would grow angry now.

Would cast her down from the heavens for her impertinence.

Her career, her life, was over.

Done.

Goodbye.

Would she take the blade, or just walk off a cliff?
The silence stretched.
And then he smiled.
And held out a hand.
And all the weight in the universe vanished from her shoulders.

PART THREE

BOOK TWENTY-THREE: LEVIATHAN

PART ONE

Javier had decided to spend most of his time the past few days down on the cargo deck of the nameless assault shuttle, rather than up on the bridge with Del. There was a limit to the amount of under-the-breath grumbling he was willing to tolerate, even from his favorite pilot.

And Del would be bitching.

Hammerfield had dropped out of the last jump clear out on the very edge of this system. So far away that it had taken the shuttle three days of high-speed run to get to the third planet, a mostly uninhabited place known as *Alkonost*. Three days of quiet autopilot accelerating them in, and then decelerating them to orbit, all alone from what they could detect.

Even with the pictures taken from orbit, Javier could tell why the place was largely uninhabited. Most worlds were blue and white from space. This one was brown. Too much dust in the air, not enough water to rain it back down. Three monstrous continents dominating a handful of small, relatively-shallow oceans. Terraforming had been successful, but the result was still ugly, combined with the ancient tectonics that had shaped the planet's bones.

According to the *Concord Gazetteer*, vast swaths of steppe grass fed huge herds of semi-feral cattle, thriving in a place with no large predators. In between, running about twenty degrees of latitude centered more or less on the equator, a desert belt circled nearly three-quarters of the planet, running from one sea to another across the spine of the two biggest continents.

Javier could imagine that there were lovely beaches to be had, if you looked hard enough. White sand, tropical warmth without all the nasty humidity, good surf. But the nightlife would be utterly boring.

He had never been to the fabled California Coast, back on the Homeworld, but this could have been twelve thousand kilometers of competition, on the western shore here.

And that jackass wanted to drive his tank over the sand.

Javier wondered if Del's grumbles were contagious.

The cargo bay on the assault shuttle wasn't designed as a personnel carrier. Sure, there were two heads and a shower section, but no private bunks to retire to when you wanted to avoid people.

And Javier was really getting tired of people, even as tiny as this assault force had finally ended up.

Sykora had brought her six men, the ones Javier liked to refer to as the gun-bunnies, since they were all dedicated soldiers who liked to think of themselves as true warriors. He'd never even bothered to really get to know any of them, since they acted like dumbass, juvenile grunts most of the time.

Djamila was in tactical command. There wasn't anybody he knew better qualified for that role. And he was pretty sure he didn't have to worry about getting shot in the back any more, either by calculated intent or when the woman just finally disintegrated psychologically and started shooting.

Apparently, he had Afia to thank, but he had very carefully chosen to not ask the details. If he hadn't known any better, Javier would have said that the tall woman had finally got laid, there was that big a change in her outlook.

She was relaxed, calm, copacetic. She even smiled occasionally.

Frightening.

Maybe it was Farouz. Sykora had been mopey for nearly a month after she had shot the man, a year ago, but they both seemed to be completely comfortable today.

And the rest of the team was gelling as well.

Djamila had brought her two pathfinders on this mission: Sascha Koç, the short, Slavic brunette with nice hips; and Hajna Flores, the lanky, Anglo blond with forever legs.

Sascha had even largely gotten over the betrayal that Javier had pulled on her, on everyone, to get Suvi installed on *Hammerfield* when nobody was looking. These days, when she threatened to shoot him, she was mostly kidding.

Hajna had missed all that excitement at the time, so her relationship with him hadn't gone through any ugly recriminations. Well, any more than normal. She was a very complex woman who wasn't sure what she wanted out of life.

Javier could commiserate. He generally preferred to not have to grow up and act like management, regardless of circumstances.

Afia rounded out the command group from *Hammerfield*. She was still the best combat EVA engineer he knew, and was willing to go on crazy adventures with one pistol and a tool belt full of wrenches. This foray would probably need both.

Those eleven, Javier at least knew well enough to trust. It was the last two that made him nervous.

He didn't care that both Farouz and Sykora had vouched for them. Of the whole crew, only Del had ever been in places as comparably crazy as Javier.

Rence Moore. A petite, Hispanic woman, late twenties, no bigger than Afia for size, but a skeleton of hard muscles who never smiled.

If Djamila was a soldier's soldier, and Sascha and Hajna were scouts, this one was an assassin.

Dress it up any pretty way you wanted, but Javier had seen that look in her eyes over coffee yesterday morning. He liked to joke about the black widows he had known, but it had always been a joke up until now.

Rence wasn't joking.

And if she represented darkness, the final member of the team was probably *Light*. Gerey 'Spider' Fernandez was a long, lanky dork of an Anglo that Farouz had introduced originally as a *vertical penetrations expert*.

Javier had no idea why the *Khatum* had a professional cat burglar on her staff, or if she even understood what that man was, under that blond *bon homie* and constant smile. Grandma would have called him a harmless surfer punk. She would have been wrong.

Right now, he was practicing his art by free climbing the cargo bay. Up one wall, and right now halfway across the ceiling, dangling from a coolant pipe as he worked his way around a power conduit that wouldn't hold his weight.

If Rence always wore dark clothing that encapsulated her and blurred her outlines, like any good ninja, Spider was wearing a pair of long, fluorescent green and yellow shorts and a faded black, concert t-shirt for a band Javier had never heard of. The only thing that marked him as serious were the extremely light climbing shoes he had on and the weird gloves that pretty much only covered the backs of his hands, leaving the palm open and wrapping just around the base of all his fingers.

And he could traverse the entire ceiling without ever touching the deck.

Javier knew they were all pros, but right now, he wanted a quiet corner with walls he could go hide behind. Four days in these people's pockets was pushing it.

"Javier," Del's growl came over the intercom. "We're about there."

"Coming," he called back, grateful for the opportunity to do something.

Up on the bridge, the view was spectacular.

For no reason whatsoever, as far as Javier could tell, the shuttle was flying upside down, relative to the planet, leaving him hanging from the gravplates in the ceiling like the victim of a giant bug or something.

Probably Del's way of keeping things a little crazy.

"Whachagot?" Javier asked.

Del brought up a map on his screen.

"Just detected multiple ships emerging from jump in the vicinity," the pilot said, pointing to four red stars on a screen. "Thoughts?"

Probably about two light hours out, so they may have already jumped closer and just not shown up on a sensor. It wasn't like the shuttle was pinging the neighborhood all that hard.

Sneaky went both ways. Right now, it mostly meant *blind*.

"If he follows his usual procedure, that's the transport, two little gunboats as escorts, and Slavkov's personal yacht," Javier observed, as if Del hadn't already been through this briefing more than once. He probably just wanted someone to talk to. "The yacht will drop a shuttle for him and his party, and they'll go somewhere else for a while. The freighter will send down the big lander for the Leviathan. The gunbunnies are to keep pirates honest, since the freighter has two escorts about as well armed as destroyers for offensive firepower."

"And the lot of you are going to go capture the transport freighter?" Del asked. "Just like that?"

"Fear is a wonderful tool, Del," Javier smiled. "Valko Slavkov is a big fish. Anyone crossing him is likely to have ninjas sent after them. Ergo, nobody would ever dare do what we're about to."

"So, he's bluffing?" Del continued.

Javier felt the shark smile take over his face.

"Don't care," Javier said. "I'm not."

Even gruff, old Del kinda blinked at that. Probably forgot that he was dealing with Navarre today, even if Navarre was just a façade Javier put up when he had to be an asshole.

Slavkov absolutely had it coming.

"Okay, then," Del concluded. "Ready for this?"

"Absolutely," Javier smiled. "How close can you get us?"

"Well, pretty boy there picked a nice flat valley to come to rest in," Del sneered as he flipped the map to an orbital view and zoomed in. "Come night, I can drop you down within about five kilometers on the back side of a ridge. After that, you're on your own. I'll hop back up under cloak and sit out in space watching. Ought to be fun."

"Oh, yeah," Javier agreed. "It'll be a riot."

PART TWO

Afia didn't like hot.

The Yukon Protectorate, where she had grown up, had been a cool place at the best of times. Downright bitter, vicious, nasty freezing in the winter, but only a fool went out in those months. Usually for more beer, if your planning was bad enough to run out.

Desert sand had a way of getting in all the wrong places. Sensitive spots that didn't like scratchy. Made her a touch irritable just contemplating how long it might be before she could get naked and take a good, cool shower again.

But Javier needed her on this mission. And it came with hazard pay. The dragoon was learning to rely on her as well, which was about as high a compliment as you could get from that woman.

Still, front-side-down on the lip of a sandy ridge in the dead of night, looking through binoculars, was not her idea of a good time. Unless there was a cute guy at the other end, with a window just waiting for her to tap on it.

Or something like that.

Heaven forbid she ever sneak out at night and engage in amorous hoolliganisms with strange boys. No, sir. Pure as the driven snow.

Or something like that.

It had at least finally cooled down to being almost tolerable around here, so she wasn't going to bitch too loudly at what she had to deal with.

Sand. Well, mostly rock around here. For a desert, it was more of an ugly scrub of big, exposed stone held together by scraggly bushes. Giant, salmon-and-tan dominos stacked up and covered with dust.

The stone undulated in awkward ways, too, like you had dropped a handful of rocks in the same bathtub at the same time, and then managed to freeze the waves as they crisscrossed each other.

Del had snuck in and put them down not all that far from the Land Leviathan's destination. Hung around just long enough for them to unass all the gear and get it covered, then ambled off like a cat trying to look innocent while they climbed to the top of the low ridge in the darkness and peeked.

She didn't like all the extra weight from the climbing gear they made her wear, and the camo robe with the hood just made her overheat, but that was the cost of doing business today.

Afia found herself at the left end of a line of people, watching the distant bad guys through a line of grass and bushes on the top of one of those ridgelines. All of the main players were well-hidden, with only the combat team not up here.

Afia could see Iqbal Kader out of the corner of her eye, silently and effectively covering her left flank, and she knew the other five men, the ones Javier always referred to with the collective insult *gun-bunnies*, were around behind them against any risk of an ambush.

Knowing this group, there was at least one surface-to-air missile handy. Maybe two. The dragoon didn't do military crap by half-measures. Nor did her team.

So Afia knew she was safe here.

At least as safe as one could be on a hostile, arid plain, getting ready to pull the caper raid of the century on a man that had already tried to kill them at least once.

Afia hadn't truly understood Javier until she saw the cold fury in that man's eyes after *Svalbard*. She had known angry men. Dated a few over the years. Javier Aritza had a rage that would make bards salivate. Up there with Agamemnon. Or maybe Achilles.

Sing for me, oh muse, a song of righteous destruction visited on well-deserving assholes.

Not that this Slavkov fellow didn't have it coming. Oh, no. His mistake was not killing them on the first try, because Afia didn't like it any more than Javier did, even if she had gotten to be there when a new goddess was born, and make a totally cool new friend out of it.

Two, if you wanted to count Djamila, who was acting almost human these days.

So some good had come of it, even if Afia had to be rolling around in grit, just waiting for it to infiltrate her clothing and gear to get into the places where it didn't belong.

She was going to hate this planet, in another day or so. No ifs, ands, or buts to it.

And out there, the ugliest diamondback rattlesnake in history slithered slowly across the sand towards them on giant treads.

The optics she had were passive, but still packed a pretty good processor suite.

The Land Leviathan was much warmer than the sand and rock around it after dark, so the computer in her binoculars could do a good job of locking on and stabilizing the image, even at a distance of ten kilometers.

It helped that the driver over there had wanted a nice, flat, parking lot for the beast. A few dry creek beds here and there. Couple of stands of things she might call mesquite trees. Nothing to get in the way of the taxi coming to take the beast home.

Kinda reminded her of a family trip through West Texas when she was twelve. Not as hot as Texas, or as ugly. Afia wasn't sure there were places as ugly as Texas.

Still a nasty place.

"Heads up," a call came through the earpiece she had forgotten about. "Two vessels deorbiting from the east. Now visible. Everyone cover up and close your eyes."

Afia reached up and pulled the hood of her long robe over her head and far enough to cover the binoculars. She tucked her elbows in and rolled just enough onto her right side to pull her feet up, reaching down to make sure the cloth covered everything.

The cloth insulated against thermal signature, as long as you didn't move, and shielded most electronics and metal signatures. It had already morphed into the mixed color of the stone underneath her. If there was no movement to draw the eye, nobody would have a reason to send a sensor pulse this way.

Just another handful of rocks on the ridge. Nothing to see here. Move along.

The noise came along soon enough. Dull roar on her left.

Afia snuck just enough of a peek to spot the two stars descending, and then closed her eyes and turned her face back down to the ground. Both vessels were showing off, flying in tandem formation and landing slowly, almost sedately, on thrusters, rather than swooping in to settle to the ground.

Or maybe she'd been flying with Del too much. You never knew what civilized people were like, after enough time as a pirate.

As soon as the ships dropped into the low bowl in front of them, before they had even touched down, Javier tapped her on the hip and Afia was on her feet.

If everything went right, everyone over there would be focused on landing the executive shuttle for that asshole Slavkov and his guests coming down right next to the Land Leviathan so nobody had to walk any great distance, and didn't have to do it in the oppressive heat of day. So far, all the gossip and sneaky intel that someone had gathered had been on cue.

She didn't want to take the time to look, but knew that most of the Leviathan's crew, and all the support staff for guests, would depart with the big shuttle and follow Slavkov to his next destination, leaving only a skeleton team to drive the Leviathan onto the big lifter and ride it to orbit.

If she really cared, Afia could have looked up and probably spotted the moving stars that were the gunships escorting this bitch between stars.

Sascha and Hajna had already taken off, almost loping down the hill, trusting that there was enough distraction and cover right now, and shortly there would be way too much dust in the air for anyone to spot them.

Everyone else was behind in a compact string. Four of the gun-bunnies were on point, centered on Djamila, while Iqbal and Tom brought up the rear. In between, Afia was making good time next to Farouz. Even Javier was keeping up as they jogged.

She'd seen him working out more, so she knew the science officer could handle a quick four kilometer jog into the thick fog the twin landers had kicked up in the otherwise calm air.

Right on cue, visibility dropped to meters.

Afia could still see Farouz beside her, along with Moore and Spider trailing close behind, and maybe that gun-bunny in front of her was Demyan. Hard to tell when looking at butts moving in dust. Only Galal stood out, and that was only because he was most of a head shorter than the other five.

At least nobody was shooting at them, which was all Afia really cared about.

A small commotion in front of her caused Afia to slow down.

Djamila was standing over one of her guys. Another was kneeling and examining him.

Afia looked, and then managed to hold her stomach down when she saw the guy's leg. His shin wasn't supposed to bend like that. From the growling through gritted teeth, the dude on the ground agreed.

Afia recognized Heydar from the tone.

"Status?" Djamila asked, almost dispassionately.

Afia felt the clock ticking faster in her head. Pretty soon, someone was going to look this way, or maybe just take off. This was no time to stall.

"Clean break," the kneeling medic said. Helmfried. "I can splint it, but there's no way he can walk any distance on it for a few weeks. Surgery will be required at some point, as well."

"I've got cover and food," Heydar said hoarsely. "Finish the mission and send help when you can."

"There's no space for a medevac," Djamila warned him. "Might be two days. Might be two months."

"What is the problem?" Farouz was suddenly at Afia's side.

Spooky, like he was a ninja or something, except that one was on the other side of the man. Rence Moore.

"Broken leg," Djamila said. "Bringing him slows us too far off the schedule. Leaving him rubs me the wrong way."

"Agreed," Farouz agreed. "I will carry him."

"I outweigh you by twenty-five kilos, old man," Heydar growled angrily.

"So I will not be able to out-shoot everyone else on this team while transporting you," Farouz observed in a tone that made Afia go all cold.

Farouz wasn't kidding. Like maybe he thought he could take anybody here except maybe the dragoon. And the ninja.

Djamila watched for a moment, then nodded.

"Air splint and enough local that he's good to transport," she ordered. "Not so much he's out. Rotate responsibility to put him guarding prisoners and doors when we arrive."

"Roger that," Helmfried said, flipping open his backpack and drawing supplies.

Afia watched the medic wrap a brace around the lower half of

Heydar's leg, inflate it, and hit the groaning warrior with a hypospray in less than thirty seconds.

And then Farouz, barely any taller than her, picked the guy up in a fireman's carry in one go and slung the gun-bunny over his shoulder easy, like a bag of rice.

"Move," Djamila ordered, knocking everyone back into motion.

Elapsed time, less than one minute.

Damn, these people really were that crazy, weren't they?

Up ahead, the dust was thinning as they closed. Big bomb of sand and grit had pushed outwards, and now slowly settling. The transport was huge.

Afia had known the scale they were working with, but it was one thing to hear, and another to actually get close to a ship that was nearly as long as *Hammerfield*, resting on a dozen scorpion legs on the ground in front of her.

Seriously, it was a kilometer long, and at least two hundred meters wide at the nose, shaped like a broadsword lying on its side.

Still, nobody shooting. So far, so good.

If they had been spotted, someone would have done something stupid. Flares screaming into the sky. Pop-up turrets suddenly spitting death. Flying assault marines with chain-swords.

Something.

She was close enough now to actually touch the thing.

From a distance, those legs had looked spindly. Up close, they were dull-gray, redwood trees, ten meters thick at the ankle and widening as they telescoped up into the monster's belly.

Afia joined everyone else as they squatted or kneeled in the shadow of the ship, hiding again under the cloaks that masked them from casual perception.

She knew there were lots of guns, pointed outward in every direction, but all she could see were lumps of sand and outcrops of rock, all innocent and stuff.

Thirty seconds of silence passed.

In the distance, the little yacht was just now cracking open and lowering a landing ramp at the rear. If she hadn't been hiding under the biggest lander she had ever seen, Afia would have thought the other vessel was huge.

Certainly impressive over there, all lit up and painted in gold and chrome. Multi-deck party barge, like when she was a kid, upscaled by several orders of money to a starship just as functional and *way* more tacky.

Flitter limos were emerging from the aft of the Leviathan now. Important people did not walk across sand that might damage expensive shoes. And heaven forbid someone spill a drink crossing rough terrain.

Only the crew walked, moving with rapid deliberation to make it aboard the shuttle in time to be of whatever flunky service these yahoos demanded next.

Soon, the Leviathan would be a ghost town, populated by the leftover engineers who kept the beast fed and mobile. Kinda like the lander looming above her was supposed to be.

The sound of the landing ramp coming down at the aft of the big, metal lander was like an earthquake.

One hundred meters wide. One hundred deep. Sliding on hydraulic hinges that made it move like warm molasses on a cool day. And a deep, profound rumble.

All the lights over there largely vanished as the ramp dropped and obscured everything.

And still, no shooting.

"Spider," Djamila barked quietly, staying off the radio at this phase for absolute secrecy. "Phase two."

Afia had stayed close enough to the lanky, blond Anglo to watch him unfurl from under his cloak like a morning flower.

He kept the poncho on, but flipped it back out of his way, like a true cloak, as he took two long strides and reached up with those huge hands to grab a strut or something.

Serious. Spider. Dude went right up the lander's leg like an insect.

Suddenly, he was ten meters in the air and crossing hand over hand like a kid at a playground.

Afia just shook her head in disbelief. Yoga was fine. Running acceptable. That level of exercise might be a bridge too far. Except how skinny the guy was. There might be something to it, after all, if it kept you skinny. Gotta look that up.

There was a box-thing emerging from the underside of the hull, maybe four meters on a side. Spider crossed to it, settled, and did something magic with his hands.

"Afia," Djamila said. "Phase three."

Afia took a deep breath and stood up, adjusting everything so it didn't rub wrong. Into all her gear, they had added a harness.

Big, ugly, cold, steel ring just above her belly button. She hadn't liked it. Didn't like it. Wasn't here to bitch.

It wasn't that she had a thing about heights. She had climbed trees as a kid. Every kid did that. This was something else.

Spider was done overhead.

Afia walked close and looked up.

The man had attached a small box to the hull of the transport, and HOPEFULLY SECURED THE DAMNED THING.

A flick of one of those bean-long fingers and a grapple began to descend towards her on a long cable.

Old school.

Javier had gone so starkly primitive as to go beyond stealth, these days. Sure, they could have brought some repulsor platforms and made this easy. Maybe a flight backpack. And that would have shown up on a sensor, somewhere. That level of power expenditure, on those frequencies, would be detected, if nothing else. Just like they stayed off the comm.

Instead they wound up seventy-five meters of high-grade steel cable on a winch and hung it from the underside of the ship. You just needed a cat burglar to place it.

And an engineer crazy enough to ride.

Fortunately, Javier happened to know one.

Click.

She was now bound in unholy matrimony with a landing freighter, symbolized by a giant, cold-steel ring hanging beneath her boobs.

Afia took a deep breath and leaned backwards, relaxing into the cable.

Spider nodded at her. She nodded back. He flipped a switch.

She was flying.

Tinkerbell in a low-budget stage production version of the *Neverland Saga*. Complete with the profanities, mostly under her breath.

When she got close, Spider smiled at her. Probably meant to be reassuring. Sure. Afia looked down anyway. No false sense of security about this, thank you.

Spider reached out a hand and slowly turned her to face the big, steel box that was her target.

Ground elevator.

Currently retracted, and it would stay that way. Safety measure. And security.

Anybody could push the big, bronze button to deploy it to the ground automatically.

And set off every damned alarm on the ship overhead.

That was why you needed an engineer.

Afia took a deep breath and pulled a powerdriver out of her thigh pouch with her right hand. Number four bit would be close enough.

She fixed everything in her mind and reached out. Four countersunk machine bolts held the face plate.

The first two came out easy enough.

Number three fell through her fingers. She tried to grab it. Afia stabbed at it with one hand and nearly turned turtle, forgetting where she was.

Hopefully, she'd be able to puke far enough away that it wouldn't land on anyone, if she did that again. This playground wasn't that fun.

She did look down, just in time to see Javier catch the bolt in one hand. Yeah, he probably had been expecting that. Speed was more important than style, right now.

Fourth bolt out. Three in pocket. Faceplate handed off to Spider. Naked machine innards displayed to the world like some sort of electronic burlesque show.

Engineering pornography.

It took all kinds.

Yup. Push THAT button and everything deploys. Including the alarms.

Afia began tracing leads. They hopefully had time to do this right. It would take hours for the snake to eat that deer. The limo hadn't even lifted off yet.

She dropped the powerdriver into its holder and pulled a steel wedge chisel.

Handy, for breaking and entering. Make sure this circuit retains power when you cut that one. Find the signal that tells the system what's happening and lobotomize it by severing a gold thread on an exposed circuit board.

There.

Find the backup, because the bastard who designed the system thought he was being sneaky.

Yup. Snip.

Check for a third one, because I would have.

Bastard. He did, too, didn't he?

Fine.

Trace. Okay, fully isolated?

Yes.

Paranoid mook.

Afia nodded to Spider.

"All good," she said.

Spider let enough line out that he could pull her out of the way, himself hanging from a hook off to one side.

She felt like his latest victim. Or conquest. The man had chewed on a breath mint recently. Cinnamon and wintergreen. Afia wondered what a kiss might taste like. Not the time to find out, but she made a note to circle back later.

That long arm reached out and pressed the bronze button. Silently, the elevator began to go down. Hopefully, nobody aboard the ship would be the wiser.

Or they were all dead.

PART THREE

Javier had his qualms.

Technically, he shouldn't be here on the ground. Sykora and her team could handle the dangerous tasks. Afia was actually doing the job he would have, being all sciencey and an engineer. His place was probably clear out on the edge of the solar system with Suvi and Zakhar Sokolov.

Waiting.

Yeah, screw that.

He was a patient man, or he'd have never made it as a survey scout, or a science officer. But there were limits to his patience.

He watched the descending lift shaft touch the ground and open.

Sykora was the first one in, because of course she was. Javier followed two steps behind her, with more of the first team behind him.

When he thought about it, Javier decided it was rather silly that most of this initial group was female. If Farouz hadn't come along, all of them would have been: Sykora, Hajna, Sascha, and the black widow, Rence Moore. He liked women.

And he did have one advantage over the rest of them. The reason he was here, instead of there.

Rather than pull a gun, like everyone else, Javier reached into a pouch and pulled out the smaller survey probe. The one that had been Suvi's home for the first year, before he built her the armed one. She couldn't be here, but the sight of it still brought her to mind. Even if they all died on this mission, she would survive. He had beat the pirates.

The first batch, anyway. Sokolov and the nicer ones.

The rest were about to get theirs.

He popped in the power button, checked the configuration, and softballed it into the air as the door to the elevator closed, separating all of them from the outside world. His sidekick had done a serious upgrade on the software, just exactly for this mission.

Pretty walls in the tiny room. Egg-cream color with highlights that were probably real gold, knowing the jackass who had paid for it. Textured floor so nobody slipped.

Djamila looked over at the hovering probe, eyes slightly askance. So did the two pathfinders, but for different reasons. Sascha grimaced quickly, but got over it.

Javier pulled out the board and checked things.

It was going to be like the old days, when the thing was just a flying sensor pack and he had to do all the work. For the last few years, all he had done was push buttons that made it play music for Suvi, or cause rabbits and other cute critters to race across her desk while she flew.

Now it was back to him again.

"How good is it now?" Djamila asked, having been there most of the times it had been used.

"Suvi did a good job automating a number of tasks for me," Javier replied. "Without her in there, I didn't want to worry about shooting, but this one will do wonders. It won't be there to save your ass in a wrestling match, though."

Djamila nodded, holding a pistol in each hand and looking like a northern European Goddess of War.

The Morrigan, come for your soul, as it were.

The lift rose silently, smoothed no doubt by the risk that a pissant like Slavkov might have to use it at some point and it must thus be as even as winter ice.

Javier concentrated on setting the autopilot to hover just high enough that Sykora would clear it if she moved suddenly. Not an easy task with a woman that tall and ceilings this low.

The elevator door opened.

No crew member had been unlucky enough to be close enough to the door to get shot for his curiosity. At least Djamila had a stun pistol in one hand. As did the rest of them.

Sascha stuck a camera probe out just far enough to look both ways, and then nodded at Javier.

All clear.

The probe floated out next, a big, gray pearl hanging perfectly in space as it rotated.

Javier pushed a virtual button labeled *Annoy Carnivorous Bats* and watched the readout come back with an amazing level of detail as the machine went to work. Another of Suvi's inside jokes.

Before Sykora could ask, Javier put the display in three dimensions.

Djamila would be able to absorb the information, probably even hanging upside down and half-drunk. Farouz as well.

They both needed better hobbies.

From here, everything would be hit or miss.

Luck would play a major role as well, since nobody had any idea how this ship was laid out, once you got beyond the design basics of naval architecture.

In the hall, they moved to what cover you could get from slightly-recessed doors, but didn't do anything else. Javier's job was electronic scouting. Afia would disable all the security systems. That required some dedicated tools, and Javier didn't feel like winging it.

He would only get one chance at Valko Slavkov.

Thirty seconds later, the rest of the team joined them.

Javier had spent the time studying the psychological elements of the ship's construction. The walls and hallway here were that same egg-cream. Not white, not yellow. Less gold decoration on the walls. The floors were textured metal in diagonal X shapes, done in a gray that would probably hide any spill or stain. Wide and tall hallways. Maybe four meters across and three and a half tall, with light bars running down the center of the ceiling and both edges, making it almost a perfect movie set in here.

Again, the importance of looking good, on the off-chance that the main guy had to come this way. Javier figured the man'd be pissed if he had to, because that would mean something had gone wrong with the shuttle the rich bastard used.

People would probably end up getting fired and blackballed if he didn't just have them shot. In a lot of these places there was no law but the man with the gun. Even if Slavkov was a legitimate businessman somewhere.

In the end, we're all pirates. I'm just better dressed.

Afia moved close and knelt to study the panel closest to Javier. There weren't any alcoves to duck into, since the hatches were only set back from the hall by about ten centimeters, so the team was strung out on both sides, watching either direction. Somewhere, there would be cross hallways and stairs, plus a few more elevators. Hopefully, this was an engineering level that nobody needed to access while they loaded the Leviathan.

With any luck, Javier had an hour or more before the beast could be driven aboard and secured. That would be enough time, he hoped.

Powerdriver in hand, Afia had the panel off and her nose stuck in, tracing leads and logic.

There was no *Sentience* on this ship or someone would have already noticed them boarding. Javier worked on the presumption that he only had to worry about the bridge crew, since everyone else would be outside for now, or in the cavernous loading bay.

"Seriously?" Afia muttered under her breath.

"What?" Javier fired back, feeling the surge of cold adrenaline fill his belly.

This would not be a pleasant place to die. At least having Djamila and her killers along would make the other guy pay a very high price for his soul.

"Lazy designer," Afia replied with an unpleasant tone. "Everything is hard-wired, instead of controlled from a central system. The dragoon might have been able to hack this system."

"Translate, please?" Javier said.

He liked the girl, but she occasionally wandered down rabbit holes. Still, she was a better engineer than he was at some of the hands-on stuff. Especially security systems.

Javier never asked where she had gotten those particular skills. None of his business.

"With a central system, you control all the functions with passwords and access levels," she explained. "Like we do. This doesn't have anything. Get me to a proper workstation with a keyboard, and I can tell you anything the captain of this tub can. Downside, I can't lock him out, either."

"Internal security cameras?" Djamila asked quietly from her spot at one end of the line.

"Nothing," Afia said. "Looks like sensors on doors opening, but that's tied to life support, in case you have a leak and need to seal frame sections in a hurry. Dumb-ass design."

"Not if everyone's too scared to pull a stunt like this," Javier said. "What is there to steal, after all? And where would you take it?"

"You are going to tell us at some point, right?" Afia turned and batted her eyelashes at him to be a flirt.

A really cute one, too.

"You wouldn't believe me," Javier said. "Sokolov barely did."

She rolled her eyes at that, but quickly began to reassemble the system and screw the faceplate back on. If this worked, someone would have to fix everything they broke. Might as well not leave loose ends around.

"Direction?" Djamila asked him.

"Everyone should be either aft, or headed that way," he replied. "Let's get to the bridge as quietly as possible. Stun anything that moves."

Djamila nodded and whispered a quick set of orders that got her folks moving.

Javier found himself moving in the middle again, flying the probe, with Spider and Farouz, still carrying the guy with the broken leg like a bag of coffee. Mind-boggling, but the guy was tough enough to impress Djamila, and Javier had seen him move in combat, once upon a time, so he had no doubts just how dangerous Farouz could be when he chose.

Sascha, Hajna, and Moore went first, with Djamila and Afia close behind, maybe five meters away. The other five gun-bunnies brought up the rear after another gap, playing a game of backwards-facing hopscotch as they covered the ass end of the column against surprises. For a group this big, they moved with amazing quiet.

First seal reached.

Unlike the side hatches they had passed, this one was serious. Able to retain a seal across a frame section if the ship suffered damage. Also useful against anything the team carried except missiles. Hopefully, nothing so drastic would be needed.

Afia went to work. Djamila watched over her shoulder.

Javier found a long stretch of wall and put his butt up against it as he focused on tweaking sensor settings. He programmed the system to wash out the sound of the team walking. Hopefully, the Leviathan would make a lot of ruckus when it boarded, so they would feel it in their feet.

Nothing that big could move quietly. Especially not climbing up a shallow ramp into its bolthole.

The rest of the team were all covering their directions of fire. Even Farouz had turned sideways. That let the guy on his back see aft, pistol in one hand against utter catastrophes.

Everyone had a different safety blanket to keep the bogeyman at bay. Javier was flying his.

Javier looked up in surprise as the hatch directly across from him opened.

"Acknowledged," the man in the doorway yelled over his shoulder as he came through, stumbling to a halt as he turned and saw the people around him in what was supposed to be an empty corridor.

For the longest instant, a frozen tableaux as the hatch slid shut behind him.

Shock. Amazement.

Javier was already keyed up and just about to the point of reacting when Farouz took a sudden half step and lashed out with his left hand, a circular swing like a length of chain crashing into the side of the stranger's head with an ugly crunch.

Must have been the right choice. Dude went down like a sack of potatoes.

The gun-bunny on Farouz's back never moved.

Elapsed time, maybe half a second.

"Afia," Javier barked. "Lock this door."

She scampered.

The other side of that hatch was the very front end of the big bay. Hopefully, nobody had been looking at the right moment to see folks like Javier in the hallway when the hatch had opened. If they had, things were about to get ugly.

Javier looked down at the guy.

No blood. Head still on straight. Hopefully, just out cold.

It did give him an idea as Afia quickly popped the panel open and went to work.

"Locked or dead?" she asked, turning to look up at him.

"Seal it," he decided. "If they're coming, make them come a different way. We'll fix it later."

"On it," she replied.

Djamila was inspecting the body on the floor, kneeling with one hand on his neck feeling for a pulse. She had even holstered a pistol for long enough to do that.

"Still alive," she announced, turning to Farouz. "What was that?"

"Crane form," he replied, shrugging in spite of the weight on his shoulder. "Mastoid process strike. Stuns instantly. Rarely kills. Disables a target effectively."

"Yes," she agreed.

Javier could see the pride and warmth in her smile as she looked up at the man.

Ew.

Javier inspected the guy on the floor.

Yeah, just about his size, which meant more or less average. Maybe too much gut and too little shoulders, but close enough for improv work.

And everyone else in the group was the wrong size, Farouz and one of the bunnies being half a head shorter, with Spider and the rest half a head taller.

"Gimme his uniform," Javier said. "Trojan horse time."

Djamila looked up at him for a moment, then nodded.

Wonder of wonders, she holstered the other pistol and began unbuttoning things.

The victim was in what was obviously a uniform designed by a nimrod that had never actually served, but wanted to pretend he was important. Stupid looking saucer hat with a logo on the forehead. Light blue shirt with lots of buttons and braid. Boards on the shoulders with cute designs embroidered. Long sleeves with French cuffs.

French cuffs? Seriously?

Navy blue slacks with a gold stripe down the seam. Polished black leather shoes.

We'll do without the shoes. Mine are better, anyway.

Javier set the controls for the remote down and dropped his desert cloak. Underneath, a skin-tight, insulated shirt with a light shell jacket over that. The jacket went first.

He dropped on his butt and the boots went next. Pants as well. The deck was cold, but at least he wasn't commando on this run.

Djamila tossed him the man's pants and Javier wriggled into them.

Yup, gonna need a belt. Or a knife to add a notch.

The top was a bad fit, but good enough. Javier left the top two buttons undone, or he might choke himself when he moved.

At least the hat fit.

"Right," he said, standing as he sealed up his boots again. "I'm on point. We'll move quickly and my job is to distract anyone long enough for you to shoot them. Questions?"

There were none. He handed Spider the probe's control board. It was easy enough to fly, and with a uniform, Javier planned to move much faster than before.

Guile instead of stealth, as it were.

Javier put a hand in a pocket and discovered a hard plastic badge.

Ho ho. Access key. We're going to get into all sorts of trouble, now.

He smiled at the rest of them with a lunatic grin as he pulled it out.

This has just turned into a con job.

Scarily, Djamila grinned back. Like she knew what was coming. She might. She had been there enough times with him.

PART FOUR

DJAMILA PULLED two sets of plastic restraints from a pouch and secured the man on the floor at wrist and ankle. He wasn't important enough to bring along, and Aritza would be moving quickly now. He had that gleam in his eyes. A man about to start surfing an avalanche of fresh manure and come out smelling like a rose. As he always did.

She considered being jealous of the ability, but settled for using the man's luck as a shield.

Djamila rose from the floor and drew both pistols. She had always been ambidextrous, but just enough right-handed that the stunner was there, where it would be the first shot fired instinctively. The beam-cutter could wait for armor and bulkheads.

She nodded curtly at him. Ready to go.

Javier's face got a bit of an angry snarl to it, probably close enough to her own, and he walked to the bulkhead hatch, waving the badge at the sensor as the rest of the team settled into columns.

Guile and audacity. Aritza's signature moves. It was going to be *Shangdu*, all over again.

Djamila glanced both directions just enough to pick up the pathfinders in her peripheral vision and strode forward. The corridor was wide enough to walk three abreast, but they were staying several meters back now.

Aritza on point was a bulwark of armor and misdirection Djamila would use to get close enough to shoot. At this point, anything that moved was a legitimate target, thus the stunner in her right hand, just like most of the rest of her team.

Most.

Galal would have a shaped-charge handy to breach any barrier.

Based on her own dead reckoning, they were almost to the bow now. Over Javier's shoulder, she could see an oversized hatch to port, along the outer edge of the ship, as well as a curve where the corridor rounded towards the exact bow.

Javier stopped at the enormous hatch, glancing only briefly to his right as the path continued that way.

He nodded to himself before turning back to her.

"Up here," he said. "I want to put us right under the bridge facility, as here should be a big service area where he can host parties."

She nodded back.

Nothing more to say.

He badged the door open and she followed two steps behind into a room with a winding ramp that was ten meters across and corkscrewed up so slowly that Djamila could have attached wheels to her boots and worked up a tremendous head of speed to clear the door and blast down the main hallway at a dead sprint.

She considered making it a competitive event by adding armed targets, the final one being the shot that would open the door before you slammed into it.

She smiled and began to ascend, letting Aritza have a full half-turn before following.

Djamila signaled the girls to move the team to the outer edge of the ramp, back from being visible from above, but she stayed close enough to fire upwards a considerable distance if Aritza got into trouble.

Lord knew he was barely competent with a pistol. Suvi had confirmed that she had done all the trick shooting.

The decks on this ship were outsized, matching the personality of a man who would build a Land Leviathan. What starship needed six-meter ceilings?

One intended to show off wealth and power.

Javier surprised her by continuing on past the first level as the ramp continued. But then she considered that the land beast itself was at least thirty meters tall. Having space to work might require a bay six or eight of these decks tall, although she expected that the crew quarters would be a dismal warren of rabbit holes with barely two-meter ceilings.

What good was power and wealth if you didn't get to oppress someone with it? Everything she had heard or experienced about Slavkov and his operation suggested punks, rather than professionals. *Svalbard* had been a telling sign.

Again the winding. Javier passed the third floor at a brisk march, trusting in her by only glancing back on rare occasion to make eye contact across the half circle.

His eyes still had a killing gleam in them.

Djamila wasn't above letting the man get himself killed here. But that was no longer a necessity.

Many things had changed since the goddess had taken possession of *Excalibur*. The Lady of the Lake. With the help of her friends, maybe even Djamila Sykora could change. And trade up for the problem of two capable men who both wanted her, the woman who had always been the ugliest duckling in any pond.

Fourth deck. Aritza again paused to look back at the caravan behind him, but continued. Fernandez had finally gotten the hang of flying the probe well enough to send it up the column of empty space in the middle of the spiral, tracking even with her but providing a solid scanning arc against hidden surprises.

Fifth deck. Javier apparently had what he wanted. She caught up to him on a half spiral and waited.

"The bow is about two hundred meters across," he said out of the blue.

She nodded, familiar with the general layout Suvi had been able to scan without focusing a beam on the ship.

"Based on the rest of the architecture, I'm guessing that this is the level I want, even though this thing goes up more," he continued. "If you settle on treads when you park, the back of a room on this level ought to be looking right across the top of the Leviathan."

"Would he want a higher view?" Djamila asked.

"Probably," Javier nodded up at her as the team began to catch up. "But I bet we'd set off alarms if we suddenly went into officer country, being only peons. Now, we need to get sneaky."

Djamila turned in place to survey the group. She had assembled a team of experts across a variety of fields, knowing Javier's general plans and style, but having no greater idea than he did about the facts on the ground.

"Moore, team one, with me," she said. "Afia and Farouz with the pathfinders as team two. The rest of you are team three. Heydar will remain here and secure our rear."

The tiny woman killer nodded the barest amount. Djamila was aware that Rence Moore hadn't shown off her talents and training to anyone else on this team, so only she and Farouz had seen the assassin move.

Djamila turned back to Javier.

"Go," she said.

He nodded and squared his shoulders, doing *something* that turned him from a thief into an important crewmember on a mission. Djamila hadn't gotten the hang of that level of acting, but she had learned enough from the man, and from others, like Dr. Wilhelmina Teague, to understand it happening.

Aritza held out a hand to the sensor panel and listened for a chirp as it unlocked. Bolts withdrew and the hatch slid aside. He went through at a crisp march, not looking back.

Djamila followed him into another world. She could trust that Moore would move so silently as to be undetectable.

The floors here were carpeted in a vast sea of green. Not a particularly expensive installation, but a radical change from the metal floors on the rest of the vessel. Wood paneling on the walls turned the room earthy, a tone matched by turning the lights down a single notch on the scale, from harsh to adequate.

Furniture around the walls of the large space suggested a reception area, with both sofas and standing tables. A long counter-top that would be turned into a bar by the arrival of bottles and staff. That door to the right of the bar probably led to a kitchen where caterers could whip up mobile finger food.

Djamila decided that it must be used when the vessel was delivered to a new planet, a party for everyone who had arrived to partake of a new adventure.

Dilettantes and Philistines. It probably devolved into orgies at the slightest provocation. Those were the sort of people that would.

Aritza started to cross the area towards a pair of oversized doors on the far end of the room. As Djamila made to move with him, she realized that the back wall was transparent and overlooked the monstrous landing bay. Lights from the far end had just started to fill the space.

Headlights.

"Hold," she said, just loud enough to get his attention.

He turned back with an unvoiced growl in his eyes. Djamila nodded to the window.

He looked, absorbed, and nodded.

"With me," he said. "The rest sneak as you can."

It was insane. Walk right across an open window just as the Land Leviathan was starting to load?

Yes.

Audacity.

Suspicious people act suspicious. One person with Aritza at this distance would not excite the viewer. A whole mob would.

Rence Moore was already short. And had no weapon in her hands. Djamila watched her double over to hands and feet, like a moving yoga pose whose name she didn't know, and scamper across the floor almost as fast as Djamila and Javier walked it.

Djamila hazarded a quick glance to the side as they passed out of the immediate view from the bay. Nothing seemed wrong. No yells. No alarms. No shots impacting the shield.

Good enough. Behind her, the rest of the team dropped and began to crawl below the level of the windows. Afia would hack the door and bring the team through behind them.

They would have to catch up as they could. For now, the three of them would have to handle everything.

Djamila was wearing her normal field uniform of long, heavy pants tucked into field boots. Long button-up tunic over a t-shirt. Everything in a dark-gray/red spackle pattern that distracted the eye inside a ship painted gray. Rence Moore wore something similar, but baggier and looser, hiding the woman inside and providing space for her to secrete weapons and gear.

The next door awaited, closed and resolute, but for the little light on one side of the frame.

Javier waved his badge at the scanner panel and it slid aside. More carpet, more paneling. A long, narrow hallway that seemed to run forever. They passed through and began to penetrate deeper into the whale's belly.

A man turned a corner ahead and looked up from what he was reading on a tablet.

"Who are you?" he asked/yelled.

Fifty-five meters. Right at the effective edge of a stun pistol.

Djamila shot him twice for good measure.

They broke into a jog. Shots fired might set off internal alarms in this section. Others might come along.

The target was down. She could have skipped the second shot, fired as fast as the pistol's batteries would cycle, but training was training. He had already succumbed to the first.

This man's uniform was more impressive than the first one Javier had stolen. She and Moore kept watch while Javier looted the man's pockets and came up with his security badge, tucking the first one away.

"Upgrade," he chortled as he stood.

Moore was peeking around the corner the man had emerged from. Nobody was coming from the far end of the hallway. Her people were behind them somewhere, covering the rear.

"Him?" she asked.

"Leave him," Javier replied. "He won't be a threat for an hour. It'll be over by then, one way or the other."

Djamila agreed. Phase One would be done. The rest of Aritza's insane plan would start to roll at that point.

"We should be exactly below the bridge now," he said, glancing at the ceiling.

"Stairs and lift here," Moore said, pointing down the hallway aft as she broke her self-imposed reticence.

"Stairs," Djamila and Javier said almost in unison.

Never get trapped on an elevator in a combat situation. No good will come of it.

They turned the corner into a short corridor with a single lift door in the center and hatches on each side that would access the stairs.

"You two split," Javier said.

Djamila considered the options and turned to the flight of stairs on the right.

"You go with him," she ordered.

Rence Moore was as much shorter than Aritza as Djamila was taller. She could hide behind the man when the door opened and probably be missed.

Javier handed Djamila his spare keycard.

"Here," he said, turning and disappearing through the door leading to the other staircase.

Djamila took the steps three at a time. Up seventeen, eyes tracking above her. Platform. Turn. Up seventeen more. Landing. Turn.

She spotted the door at the top of the next set of stairs. It had a glowing spot to one side for a badge. Hopefully, the first prisoner had enough access to make it to the bridge.

Seventeen steps and she was standing before it. She ignored the next flight of stairs going up. Javier would be here when he opened the door.

Djamila holstered her beam-cutter and badged the lock.

It beeped at her, and nothing.

She tried again, just in case.

Failure.

Probably, a security light had just started flashing on somebody's console. Depending on how busy things were, nobody might notice.

As if on cue, the whole vessel rumbled with a very mild earthquake as the Land Leviathan hit its ramp and began to ascend into the encircling embrace of the ugly dachshund hound.

Djamila smiled to herself.

Guile and audacity.

She stuck the badge into her breast pocket, holstered her stunner, and pulled the beam-cutter.

Working quickly, she adjusted the power settings down into a tool rather than a weapon.

Not many people were even aware you could use a beam-cutter this way, having forgotten the origins of the device as a short-range plasma cutter.

It worked so much better as a hand-held particle cannon.

Most of the doors so far had been simply locked. And this one was not a frame airlock. Just a barrier against access, and even that mostly psychological.

Djamila picked out a spot in the center of the frame, closest to the badge reader, and fired a shot into the jamb.

Sparks, but not a lot of noise.

Somewhere, a fire system was probably thinking about waking up. A Damage Control board probably had a light suddenly flashing yellow.

Djamila fired a second shot. The door clicked in some esoteric way that told her she had cut the locking bar. Standard designs were meant to be breached this way in an emergency.

This was close enough to an emergency.

She reset the beam-cutter and then holstered it.

With both hands, she leaned her weight into the door and felt it move sideways. A centimeter of motion and the motors suddenly engaged, pulling it the rest of the way.

Djamila drew her main stunner as well as the backup she always carried in a shoulder rig. Now would be the time to take out an entire room in one go. Pity none of her team would be able to see this Hogan's Alley. Maybe she would play back the internal security footage for them later as training footage, after she had rung up another high score.

Aritza had just opened the other door and stepped out onto the rear of the ship's command deck.

It was mostly empty here. This alcove they were in was under an overhanging balcony or mezzanine, the space above probably being where the party would go so that nobody got in the way of professional officers flying the ship.

And so none of the crew accidentally got their proletariat germs on important people.

Not that Djamila had strong feelings about social status, being the daughter of a lower decks crewman and an exotic dancer.

Javier stepped out first, smiling up at her as he did, like she was the second shark at a frenzy. She might be, all things considered. She didn't see Moore, either emerging with him or in the doorway, so she presumed the woman had gone up another level.

Of the three of them, Rence Moore was the least likely to kill any random stranger she found up on that vastly oversized platform, if for no other reason that she wasn't personally, emotionally, involved.

Djamila Sykora had been around starships and warships for most of her life. Both in service and later as a pirate. She was used to large crews and redundancy.

The size of the transport kept throwing her assumptions off. This vessel existed solely to provide transportation for the Land Leviathan. Nothing else. Nothing *grander*.

It wasn't even a shuttle designed to rendezvous with a larger vessel in orbit. No, it was just a shell. Engines powerful enough to get the vessel into orbit. Jump drives capable of getting it to the next destination with a minimum of fuss, but no great speed. It served no other purpose than catering to a man's ego.

Djamila's face hurt from scowling so hard as she stepped out and went tactical.

Two-level bridge. Well, two plus the balcony above her.

Back to metal floors. Walls no longer wood-lined, but painted a stark white that would probably show every smudge and cobweb. Javier walked out ahead of her, to a bannister that ran athwart the path, psychologically directing people right or left down smooth, circular ramps to the bridge itself, down two meters in a manner like a sunken living room, rather than a separate deck.

Captain's chair, facing forward. Elaborate and over-wrought. Like the man sitting in it now. Or, at least the back of his head, with a bald spot surrounded by a ring of brown and white hair.

Three crew stations in front of that, arranged to complete a diamond, all facing forward. Filled with three crew members present and watching their boards.

Big, transparent porthole at the front of the bridge, three meters tall by roughly nine wide. The blast screens were open now, revealing the night sky and the place on the distant hillside where her team had lain in wait.

Javier walked right up to the bannister, paused, and gestured with his head for her to join him. Three long, silent strides put her at his left, both stunners still in hand.

She glanced back and up. Javier was standing about two meters in front of the edge of the balcony overhead. She couldn't see anyone at the near edge, but that didn't mean it was open.

Hopefully, Moore was up there and covering their backs.

"Captain, I have a security alarm," one of the crewmen said out loud, staring at his board.

"Nobody move, and nobody has to get hurt," Javier ordered the room in a voice big enough for a parade ground.

All four men started at the sound. Three of them turned towards the rear.

Djamila shot the fourth one, seated left center, as his hand moved towards what she assumed was an alarm.

Bad choice. At least both hands were stunners this time.

The other men turned whiter. And froze in place.

Javier went to the right, down and around the ramp.

Djamila crab-walked left, keeping the three prisoners covered as she did.

"Who are you?" the captain demanded.

Fortunately, the man was bright enough to remain perfectly still in his chair as he did so. Djamila might have considered wounding him with the beam-cutter secured in the holster. As an example.

"Captain Navarre," Javier oozed angry malignance over the words. "The pirate."

At least the captain of the transport knew the name. He shuddered once, but got hold of himself quickly.

"What's the meaning of this?" he said, controlling himself.

Djamila couldn't tell if the man was angry or fighting not to wet himself right now. The voice kept going different directions.

"All three of you, out of your chairs, now," Javier ordered. "I will not say it again."

The two crewmen moved like ejection seats had gone off. The captain took a moment longer. The last man was already a puddle on the floor.

Djamila directed them up against the view port and sneered at them from a safe distance.

Javier moved to where he could speak without yelling, but never got between her and the man on the right. He did understand lines of fire, if nothing else.

"This is a hijacking," he said cheerily. "If you behave, I promise to drop you someplace nice and safe when we're done here."

Always the master of the one-liner, she waited the beat for him to drop the bombshell on them.

"I only kill pirates," he continued. "And right now, you haven't convinced me you're pirates. Let's keep it that way?"

The two crew nodded enthusiastically. Like men for whom this was just a job in a galaxy with more people than work. The captain got an angry look. Remained perfectly still, but wanted to gesture angrily, except for the giant woman holding two pistols on him.

"This vessel belongs to Valko Slavkov," the man thundered. "Do you have any idea what he'll do to you when he catches you?"

"He's already tried to kill me twice," Javier retorted savagely. "If that's the hill you want to die on, be my guest."

That got through the man's bluster. The older captain recoiled and blinked several times. Lizard brain taking over as the higher functions shut down.

"No," the captain replied. "No. Not at all."

"Good," Javier's voice softened. "Now, there is a crew down here that needs to be controlled. I have an entire fireteam of killers just outside this room, but I'd rather not have them massacre your men. And then there are two escorts in orbit that you need to convince all is well when we lift. I have a warship hiding at the edge of the system. A big one. Capable of crushing those two escorts like empty beer cans. But they're just folks doing a job, same as you. Right? With your help, they'll all get to go home to their families tomorrow."

Djamila flashed back in her memory to the two men that had escaped her strike team on *Svalbard*. She had been all set to pursue them into the storage warrens. All fifty-three kilometers of tunnel.

Captain Navarre had convinced them to happily surrender with the same sort of carrot and stick.

Aritza/Navarre was one of the few people Djamila had ever met as utterly ruthless as she was. Zakhar and Farouz were close. Perhaps a handful of others.

And Navarre had returned the men unharmed, matching his promise. That news had apparently gotten around as well. The captain sagged, but it appeared to be mostly in relief.

"Yes," he said. "Your word of honor?"

Honor? From a pirate?

But this was *Navarre*. The killer. The pirate captain who had annihilated Abram Tamaaz. And escaped both traps at *Svalbard*.

And kept his word.

"Absolutely, Captain," Javier replied in a professional tone. "Your ransom and your parole on getting us out of the system safely."

"And Slavkov?"

"He's next on my list, Captain," Javier promised in a voice so utterly drained of emotion that Djamila felt a surge of adrenaline course through her like an icicle.

A sudden sound caused Djamila to leap hard to her left, bouncing up into the air and half-pirouetting as she did. One pistol remained on the three captives. The other sought a target.

Time slowed to a still.

There.

A body collapsing and tumbling bonelessly over the railing from the balcony.

She fired into him twice anyway. Reflex.

Movement above and beyond the falling target. Djamila centered the pistol on it before she processed the image.

Rence Moore.

Other movement. One up, one down.

A pistol falling at the same speed as the man coming off the balcony.

A disk, perhaps four centimeters across by one thick. Black, with two red lights flickering. Arcing into the air as it might do if someone like Rence Moore had thrown it into a man's head hard enough to bounce. With a stun charge grounded on impact. An electric charge heavy enough to knock a horse over.

Djamila smiled, and landed on the deck again, a meter to her left and half turned.

Nobody else had even had time to react.

The man from the balcony struck the floor like an errant sack of potatoes.

Javier glanced at her for confirmation.

Djamila nodded.

The science officer turned to look up at the balcony.

Moore flowed down to the rail with the silent elegance of an approaching glacier.

"I owe you five drachma," the quiet assassin said in a quiet voice.

"I'm just surprised you didn't say some goofy catchphrase to distract the guy first," he replied. "Like they do in the vids."

"Farouz broke me of that habit, early on," Moore commented drily, with just a ghost of a grin.

Djamila felt a surge of pride as she turned back to the three surviving prisoners. Javier just laughed out loud as he joined her.

"What do you even want with the Land Leviathan?" the captain asked, utterly perplexed. "You'll never survive getting a ransom for it."

"I'm not here for a ransom," the science officer said. "I'm after revenge."

"But there's no place in the galaxy you can hide something like that," the older captain retorted, utter confusion writ on his features.

"You don't understand," Javier explained. "But that's okay. I plan on taking the Leviathan to Slavkov and his friends. *Next.*"

Djamila suppressed the shudder that wanted to ripple through her body, both at the words, and the tone.

Javier Aritza/Eutrupio Navarre was a ruthless man. A killer. She could appreciate that in the man, having just spent several years maneuvering to kill him in what any witnesses would have to rate an apparent accident.

What he had planned for the second part of his revenge was a scheme so grand, so audacious, that nobody in the galaxy would be able to anticipate it.

And she was going to help.

THE HAMMERFIELD
PAYOFF

PART ONE

BOOK TWENTY-FOUR: ALKONOST

PART ONE

JAVIER STUDIED the big bridge of the transport he was in the process of hijacking.

Metal walls painted white, instead of the expensive wood paneling that that punk Slavkov had used in all the party spaces elsewhere. Similar floors with a rough enough tread that Javier's usual soft moccasins would have been uncomfortable, thus the heavy boots. Hell, even the air had a stale, dry taste to it that told him the humidifiers needed to be tuned. Something for Ilan to do when he got here.

In front of him, Javier watched the night through a transparent window that was three meters tall and nine wide, overlooking the bow of the giant vessel. The night sky was finally turning to complete black as the sun set.

Javier would have left the wall as a reinforced bulkhead and hung a viewscreen on it, if it were up to him. Slavkov must like his view organic rather than electronic. Javier had them leave the blast screen down for now.

He turned back to the rest of the room.

Captain's station at the back of a diamond-layout facing him. Three crew stations. Ramps curving up both sides of the bridge behind that to an overlook two meters up. The space below the platform was a well-designed rest room, so nobody had to be far off the bridge when on duty.

Another deck up, and the designer had put in a mezzanine with three big levels like a flat ziggurat, up two stairs to the next step, twice. That was where the party would be, both during re-entry, and whenever the owner was aboard.

Two hours had passed since Javier had very quietly raised the black flag, but he was still wearing what he thought of as the cruise ship uniform he had taken from a crew member who was now a prisoner downstairs. They were waiting their turn to orbit.

Valko Slavkov, villain extraordinaire and owner of this vessel, had just now gotten up to the edge of the atmosphere in his own personal shuttle, a private cruise ship for him and a few close friends and a couple hundred fawning servants. In another hour or so, the man would make his first jump, bouncing clear out of the system on the way to a party somewhere, leaving behind *The Land Leviathan*, a ten-car tracked vehicle that doubled as a mobile resort on the desert worlds he liked.

He was probably already planning to meet up with it again in a few months, on some other planet.

Down on the ground, Javier smiled. With all the bimbos and cooks removed and departed with Slavkov, the entire remaining engineering crew of the Leviathan was only eighteen people. Plus another dozen to fly the nameless transport.

Djamila Sykora, Dragoon of the First-Rate-Galleon-turned-pirate *Hammerfield*, probably couldn't have taken them all by herself.

Probably.

Fortunately, Javier hadn't just brought her, but also her six gun-bunnies, two pathfinders, and three other recently-recruited assassins. And one extra engineer in Afia Burakgazi, but Afia was here to help him, not Djamila.

The drivers and engineers on the Land Leviathan had put up no fuss whatsoever when the killers had stepped out from cover just as the crew finished locking down the giant train for transport. At that point they were just looking forward to a cold drink. Javier had even locked them away in their cabins and left them with a couple cases of beer, just to keep them out of trouble.

He wasn't here for their souls.

If they behaved.

No, identifying himself as Captain Navarre and promising to let them go when he was done had been a magic wand.

Reputations are wonderful things, when people know you'll kill them at the first hint of trouble. And politely drop them at their own doorstep if they are good.

A number of Slavkov's people could testify to that. And Abraam Tamaz's memory would keep the rest in line. Still, he would have rather been somewhere else.

Javier finished his train of thought with a sigh and fixed his attention on the ship's former captain, standing off to one side with Sykora close enough to growl at the man.

She liked doing that.

"One down," Javier said to the man in a deliberately cheerful voice. "I'll remind you that my cruiser is out there watching, and will be all set to jump in and help if something happens. Her orders are to annihilate the two escorts in orbit at the slightest provocation, and I have no doubts she'll carry them out with gusto."

The man blanched and swallowed. Up until now, everything had been a bluff, as far as the man knew, but he was also aware that his head was first on the chopping block if Javier took a mind to it.

"What's the next sequence?" Javier continued.

Afia was seated in the main piloting station, all big, brown eyes that only looked innocent as she watched.

"I'll send a signal to the two gunships: Escort Red and Escort Blue," the captain replied. "Then we lift on autopilot, as always, and rendezvous with them in high orbit before we break out and move to the first safe jump distance. All three ships match telemetry and we jump to the next destination, in this case, on the path to *Nidavellir*. The Leviathan is scheduled for a major maintenance cycle."

"Yes," Javier nodded with a grim smile. "Joyous *Nidavellir*, corporate home to Walvisbaai Industrial. A hellhole so corrupt that it makes *Meehu Platform* look reputable by comparison. Safe for traveling virgins, as it were."

Rather than answer, the man shrugged. It wasn't his ship, he just commanded it. Valko Slavkov made those decisions.

And had chosen to hire Walvisbaai Industrial to kill Captain Navarre and the crew of the then-private-service Strike Corvette *Storm Gauntlet*, captained by one Zakhar Sokolov.

All in the name of petty pique.

Because Slavkov had hired Captain Navarre to steal something, expecting that the mercenary would unleash a bloody slaughter on a bunch of innocent-if-very-wealthy tourists in the process.

And those yahoos at Walvisbaai would have succeeded later at *Svalbard*, if not for Javier's sneakiness, Djamila's brutal efficiency, and Sokolov's deft ship-handling.

In failure, they had forced Javier's hand.

Storm Gauntlet was too damaged to continue this quest, this *War of the Pirate Clans*, so he enlisted his own slave master, his comrade-in-arms from the *Bryce* Navy, as a partner, and went off and stole the derelict last flagship of the *Neu Berne* fleet from her final resting place.

With her final crew still aboard.

He would have to return the bodies home, when this was done.

If he survived.

Or Suvi could do it, since she was now the *Sentience-In-Residence* aboard *Hammerfield*, flying these days as the private transport/warship publicly known as *Excalibur*. If something happened to him, she would handle the honors, after burning Walvisbaai and Slavkov to slag.

Javier let an angry smile take over his face.

He turned to Afia.

"Open a comm channel and stand by for liftoff," he said in a grim tone.

Javier hadn't chosen this war. He had just chosen to make them regret starting it, for however much longer they lived.

PART TWO

Suvi was swimming in deep space like the galaxy's biggest reef shark. Long and gray and sleek and deadly, down in the deeper water where nobody could see her, just waiting to leap up and bite someone. She dug out her piano and added some ominous music as a background, while she completed her survey of the *Alkonost* system, most recent excursion destination for the cruising, tracked turtle known as the Land Leviathan.

The task kept her sharp, cataloging everything in the system, natural or man-made. She did it in every system she visited. In the old days, she and Javier would upload it to the folks in the *Concord* fleet responsible for keeping the *Gazeteer* up to date, slowly adding new systems, and old, forgotten ones, to the charts.

Suvi wasn't sure if they would keep up the habit, going forward, but she was prepared.

Alkonost was mostly boring. *VII* didn't even have an official name, but the very few locals called it *Gobi* for the tremendous steppes and arid wastelands that covered so much of the surface. One man apparently owned the entire star system, like some feudal monarch from old earth.

Whatever.

Suvi had watched impatiently as the first ship lifted off from the planet then idled merrily to the edge of the gravity well, only to vanish like a soap bubble, leaving a double handful of others in orbit, and a couple of stations.

That was probably good, because if something had gone wrong on the planet below, they either wouldn't have left, or would have gone like cats with their tails on fire.

But she only really cared about the two armed torpedo boats that remained behind now.

Hammerfield could overwhelm both of them with half her turrets tied behind her back, but this was supposed to be a sneak job.

Hide out beyond the range that most ships could actively track her, while her probe-cutter-grade sensors could read their manufacturer plates from here. Be an insurance policy in case Javier needed heads cracked together.

"Suvi," Piet Alferdinck called in a quiet voice. "What's our status, please?"

Rather than sit up in the big throne that was the captain's seat, Piet preferred the navigator's console. Even though he was in overall command right now, and acting more and more as the crew's executive officer.

Captain Sokolov's First Mate.

"The transport is deep in their lift, sir," she replied. "Orbital pulse will end in thirty-eight minutes and then the ship will insert into high orbit with targets Able and Baker."

Suvi had been afraid that she would chase Piet off.

He had been the *Pilot*, back on *Storm Gauntlet*. Looking at the logs, she was amazed at how good the man was at his task, a job that married skill with art. But he was a quiet man, and the *Concord* navy had a tendency to promote extroverts, not music history experts.

With her handling all the flying and navigating tasks, and able to do it orders of magnitude faster and more accurately than a human, this ship didn't need a dedicated pilot.

But they had bonded over music. And that was good.

These days, his boards didn't actually command the engines and gyros. Piet offered suggestions and improvements that she executed. And he had gotten even better, which was kinda amazing, until he told her that the key to that was that he didn't have to track systems for stability, so he could plan several moves ahead, trusting her to do the accounting and housekeeping.

Like Javier trusted her to handle things. It made a girl all tingly in the right places.

"Permission to soundtrack?" she asked.

Piet looked down at the spot on his board where her image appeared.

Suvi was baseline today on crew screens: a tall, Finnish blond in a modified Concord yeoman's uniform. She hadn't even added extra arms or anything.

"What did you have in mind?" Piet replied with a smile in his eyes.

It was his bridge, after all, at least until Captain Sokolov came on duty. But the captain didn't really appreciate music.

"Something Thirtieth Century," Suvi replied. "From the *Utafiti mkubwa* period. The Great Exploring."

He raised an eyebrow at her.

"Granted," he said. "But quiet."

Suvi nodded. She hadn't actually forgotten about the other three crew members on the enormously oversized bridge, but she hadn't really been paying attention to them either, between the survey work and the shark fantasies.

She started with the overture to Olivier Janguo, the compressed, musical life story of the man who had gotten most of the credit for inventing the future, the device that would be known to history as the *Mchunguzi Systems Mark I*.

The first commercial stardrive capable of punching a starship through hyperspace.

Everything since then had been bigger and better models, but the basic theory of the physics had not changed much in the forty-six centuries since. Pick a direction, jump as far as you could, land, figure out where you were.

It was kinda like throwing a baseball. If you were good, you could nail the runner from right field, trying to make it home.

If you were a *Sentience*, you could calculate directions and probability arcs 20,000 times faster than a human could. Right now, that was useful, because she had a course laid in that would drop her well inside the planet's safe gravity zone, dangerously close to the planet, but right between the two escorts where she could split her turrets evenly and destroy them before they had a chance to notice.

If she had to.

Javier had always been a 'live and let live' kind of guy. She like that part.

Olivier Janguo had been a man for pure science, but he reportedly had recognized the stardrive for what it was: the ability to go off and be yourself without answering to anyone else, anywhere. His musical score, then, was grand and bold. Seeking what might be out there, in the era before humans conclusively proved that Fermi was right.

That there was nobody around but the humans. And their children.

Suvi let the music build slowly. It always brought her hope, those opening notes where the brass started off quietly, bringing in the woodwinds and strings slowly as a backdrop for the first big blast of sound as the galaxy was suddenly broken open.

Okay, so maybe she was over-analyzing the composer. A bit.

Whatever.

Music made her smile. Today, it made the four people on the bridge smile, too. Hopefully, they would have nothing to do today but sit and monitor systems and communications.

Because if something went wrong, she wasn't going to ask for permission. Just move and shoot.

She would explain to Piet what had happened, after everything was done. Sitting over the corpses of the two dead escorts with a smoking blaster in her hand.

PART THREE

DJAMILA SYKORA WATCHED the scene unfold with something akin to pleasure.

It was a new feeling, enjoying life.

She considered experiencing some guilt over the whole concept, but decided it could wait. She had lived her whole thirty-eight years rebelling against the concept that she wasn't better than anyone else at a task she had identified for herself.

Perfectionism had taken her many places. Not all of them bright and cheery.

But she was trying to become someone else, now.

Someone who could experience simple pleasures in life, rather than keeping a running scorecard of all the things she should be doing to improve her current high mark next time.

Djamila supposed she should blame Javier, eventually. Even if he wasn't sure why. Without him, Djamila would have never met Suvi. Without Suvi, Afia Burakgazi would have never worked up the courage to upend Djamila's life.

Without Afia, no Zakhar.

Djamila felt herself blush, fought it, decided to accept her own internal reprobation. Zakhar Sokolov had been everything she had ever hoped for. And still the stern taskmaster captain who drove his crew to their own heights of excellence.

Djamila remembered to breathe out silently, so nobody heard her contented sigh.

Her job today was less security and more intimidation. She was almost a caryatid, a stone column carved into the shape of a woman that would come alive at the first hint of danger and fight.

Certainly, the transport's former captain, a slightly-squishy man named Berto Haaken, wasn't a threat to anyone. She had only heard stories and rumors about the man they were after, Valko Slavkov, but she had met half a hundred of the men he had hired for various tasks.

All of them had reminded her of the sorts of people you got when you cut corners and paid less than the going rate. You ended up with third-rate punks, but they were the desperate dregs of a galaxy with lots of people, too many guns and not enough opportunities to keep them out of trouble.

Armed mobs were useful, until you ran into professional killers, like Dragoon Sykora and her Combat Operations Team. Or the assassins she had added for this mission.

Captain Haaken waited patiently on what had been his bridge. Javier asked the occasional question. Or, more frequently, Afia did.

This was not a combat warship. It was a cargo transport, purpose-built to haul the biggest land vessel Djamila had ever seen. It had to be wasteful of space, because there was so much needed, and no use for it.

The Land Leviathan was comprised of ten, tracked cars, like a train or articulated truck. Each car was sixty meters square front and side, and thirty tall. The whole beast was nearly seven hundred meters long at rest, as it was now. Carefully parked in the bay that made up the bulk of this transport, wrapped around it like a horseshoe.

And this whole vessel existed just to haul the Leviathan between worlds when Slavkov got bored with one and moved on to the next.

Djamila was not impressed.

She understood wealth, having seen a number of people either born to it or having had it thrust upon them. Few were as petty and childish as Slavkov.

Fewer still had chosen to start wars with men like Zakhar Sokolov and Javier Aritza.

"What are they up to, Afia?" Javier asked the engineer who was overseeing the piloting station.

As automated as this ship was, Djamila might have flown them to orbit, but none of them could have even guessed that ahead of time. Plus, they had needed Afia's skill with locks and systems to get this far.

"All guns unlocked and just waiting for someone like *Storm Gauntlet* to appear for an ass-kicking session," the tiny woman replied in a laconic tone completely at odds with the focus she had on the various screens.

Djamila approved of both the tone and the professionalism. Hopefully, some of it would rub off on Javier, eventually.

She didn't have a great deal of faith in the concept, but even the horse in the fable might learn to sing.

"Anything aimed at us?" Javier replied.

"Negative," Afia smiled. "We're the harmless, old lady they have to help walk across the street. Eighteen minutes until the next communications check-in."

Djamila wasn't keyed up for combat, but she retained a professional paranoia, especially on someone else's stolen starship, so she was not surprised when Javier rounded on Captain Haaken and rotated from charming to intense.

"I presume you will call them personally, in your guise as commodore," Javier said in a voice suddenly harsher. "And order them to fall into line or something?"

Djamila was close enough to smell the sudden flop sweat break out on the ma:, a rank, vinegary taste in her mouth. She hoped Javier didn't cause the man to wet himself in fear.

"Uhm, well, you see…" the man stammered in response.

"Yes or no?" Javier override him. He pointed at Afia. "She's probably good enough to locate what I need in your logs. Maybe even good enough to play it back for them now. Sixteen minutes."

Javier had a way of knocking people off balance verbally. She couldn't mimic it, but Djamila had watched it enough to have a feel for it. Dropping the other shoe by counting down an invisible clock. As effective as it was distracting.

"Yes, sir. I mean no, sir," Haaken snapped to. "That is, one of my men would transmit the next jump vector under my orders, but I wouldn't speak to those two captains unless something went wrong."

"Good enough," Javier relented and smiled at the man.

Djamila watched the captain shiver unconsciously. Not a man used to being confronted with violence, even if she was the only one here openly armed.

Haaken probably wasn't used to a dangerous woman, either. He looked like the type that was at Temple every nine-day, loudly singing the hymns and pretending to be just another bourgeois peon.

Those were usually the weirdest, once you peeled away the public layers, but she didn't say anything.

Javier pulled a small package from his pocket and handed it to the engineer.

"I'm pretty sure the standard vector coordinates for *Nidavellir* are already loaded," he said with a wintry smile. "Transmit those to the escorts when we get there, and use the vector on this chip instead."

"Where are you taking us?" Captain Haaken stuttered nervously again.

"I'm taking you and your crew to a nice resort for an all-expenses-paid two-week stay," Javier smiled. "And then I'm taking the Leviathan on to *Nidavellir*, like you planned."

Captain Haaken shivered some more at the tone.

Even Djamila was uncomfortable with Aritza's solution to the problem of a pirate war, but she had to admit it would probably be effective.

Hopefully, the rest of the galaxy would survive.

PART FOUR

Y ê n   r e v i e w e d   the file once again, as if the words on the screen would suddenly rearrange themselves into a new pattern. One that made sense. Creator knew, nothing else did.

He rubbed his eyes and put his elbows up on the desk. It was late. He was close to halfway through what would normally be his sleep shift, but the file had come by Fleet Courier, and he needed time to digest it. So he was up too late.

Yên rose from the desk in his little office, a room barely bigger than his outstretched arms, and twisted his back each way to loosen up the kinks. The gray walls in here were soothing, as was the green/brown carpet, but it wasn't going to make him any less tired.

He moved to the porthole and stared out at the forever-night sky. He supposed he could lean far enough to see *Merankorr* below him, if he wanted. Or bring up a small telescope and spot some of the other orbital stations and ships sharing the sky with him.

But right now, he just wanted to be alone. To think.

To wonder how they had gotten here.

Concord Captain Nguyên Ayokunle studied his faint reflection in the glass. For a fifty-five-year-old man, he was still skinny and unbowed, even if the dark skin of his face was starting to get serious about pruning up. And the fluffy ringlets of his hair had gone totally white.

Probably why his friend shaved his head.

Yên thought about the man he had met here, his old friend…

No, think of him as Zakhar Sokolov. That's who he has made himself into. Do not out him to anyone without a very good reason.

Had it really been forty years since they'd met at Freshman Orientation?

The computer screen mocked him when he turned back around. But one did not ignore a message from the Naval Estimates Board, even couched in polite terms.

NEB was the *Concord's Fleet's* intelligence arm. The spies. The analysts. The assassins.

After all, as Commodore, Senior Captain of the fleet's permanent civilian-related installations at *Merankorr*, it had been his report that started all this.

The chance recognition of a man he originally knew by another name, once upon a time, now linked to that of an organization that the *Concord* would have broken, had they jurisdiction or reach. A man who might politely be referred to as a pirate. Up until now, a ghost with no history, no connection to anything, until one day several years ago, when he appeared on their scanners flying a small, de-commissioned warship, but never doing anything that gave the *Concord* a reason to pursue him.

There weren't enough ships, or men, or resources, to chase all of them.

Yên snorted. There was barely enough anything: men, ships, or money; to hold the frontiers against the barbarians, let alone go out into the darkness and chase them as they fled.

He had always been a history nut. The fall of Athens. The fall of Rome. The fall of Byzantium. The fall of Spain. Et cetera. Et cetera. Et cetera.

He didn't think the *Concord* was going down. These days always felt more like the squishy period after a war, when everyone demobilized their armies and navies, then muddled through the inevitable recessions and depressions that resulted from too many workers and not enough work.

You got revolutionary fervor spilling over. And criminals.

And a man you hadn't spoken with in seventeen years suddenly showing up as a pirate. Commanding a warship big enough, and dangerous enough, that the spooks back home had gotten involved.

Yên moved back around to read the tail end of the message.

You will immediately travel to the Binhai *system on official business and make contact with the* Khatum of Altai, *owner of the vessel* Shangdu. *Reports place the aforementioned vessel,* Excalibur, *in the company of the* Khatum, *who is assumed to be a part-owner based on your own reports.*

You will determine the current location of the vessel, Excalibur, *and her intentions.*

While ongoing strife between such organizations as the Jarre Foundation and Walvisbaai Industrial is to be commended, it must not be allowed to endanger galactic shipping or Concord *interests. You will identify the immediate risks and suggest a course of action to mitigate them.*

At least they were letting him handle this, and not assigning some random flunky to the task. He knew the man, this pirate captain named Sokolov who had been somebody else once. And official business meant whatever transport he could hire, since there were no *Concord* warships handy that he could flag down for a ride.

At least not yet.

The *Merankorr* squadron did have a Class II Warmaster available he could call on. That would be enough to take on a First-Rate-Galleon.

Yên hoped he wouldn't end up having to kill his oldest friend in the galaxy.

PART TWO

BOOK TWENTY-FIVE: BINHAI

PART ONE

BEHNAM LOOKED up with a critical eye at the interruption to her salad.

She had chosen to eat lunch today in the public spaces, rather than back in her personal quarters. It was early enough according to the local clock that guests staying up too late would have completed a leisurely brunch and gone off to do whatever they did in the hours of artificial daylight. Probably out for a swim in the lake that sat at the center of her starship.

How often did you find an artificial lake on a starship? Pools? Certainly, but an ellipse two kilometers long by one wide? With an island in the center that exceeded twenty-two thousand square meters?

Luxury. Decadence.

And extremely profitable.

Not that she needed money. She was the *Khatum of Altai*, and already one of the richest women in space. But she was also a businesswoman, and running a highly profitable resort in the shape of a giant starship made her people that much happier when it helped lower their taxes.

And kept her off-planet for long stretches of time. Enjoying herself.

But business was apparently intent on intruding today.

She had chosen this alcove because it was just public enough to be seen, while at the same time private enough that nobody would bother her. Several plants in pots obscured the sand-colored walls and rails. And a pair of guards one man and one woman, and a single step up, made sure that anyone bothering this woman's lunch would not be an idle decision.

Which is probably why someone had escalated something to Tömörbaatar. And he had chosen to come see her in person, instead of just sending her a quick message.

The *Iron Hero of Altai* was her Provost, as far as those things went. Head of the traveling household, rather than the government back home, although those people were smart enough to answer to him, as well.

Behnam set the large bowl of leafy greens down and slid her fork into it. The wooden table clunked and the metal rang.

Tömörbaatar was dressed sedately today. Black robes embroidered in blue and red and his head topped with the ever-present cute little box cap in white silk that he had adopted as a uniform.

She did not feel like treating this as an emergency situation, so she gestured for him to join her. As Tömörbaatar sat, she refilled her glass with cool water and poured one for him, trying to gauge the significance of his calling upon her.

A true emergency would have caused a larger ruckus somewhere. Less would have been sufficiently covered with a quick ping.

The last time he had come to find her had been when Captain Navarre had returned.

She smiled at that memory, catapulted back to both times she had been with the man.

At forty-nine, Behnam worked assiduously to maintain her health and shape. Thus the salads and water, rather than something richer. Yoga twice a day. Weights several times a week. Swimming daily.

She was in better shape than both of her sons, and more likely to turn heads than either of her daughters.

If the hair was mostly gray underneath the regular dye these days, that was the cost of growing older. The crow's feet around the eyes or the spots on the hands were the same way.

She could mask them, and did, but they were there in the morning when she rose.

One of these days, she would need to pick an heir, marry off the other three, and maybe just retire to life as a sailor and hotelier. Not a great change from now, but it would remove those moments when Tömörbaatar walked up with his serious face and waited for her to speak.

Most of them, anyway.

Behnam nodded for him to speak.

"A visitor, Your Grace," he said in that quiet, knowing voice.

The man had been at her side for more than thirty years now. If he was a squishy, past-middle-aged bureaucrat with a wispy beard gone gray, Tömörbaatar was still deadly in the political arena.

He would not speak lightly.

"Representing?" she replied.

No single visitor was that important, except as a symbol of something larger.

"A *Concord* naval captain," her man said. "Alone, but for a small staff, and traveling on official business. He made proper reservations through the system to spend a week, and made it clear that he would like an hour or two in private with you on a topic he would not discuss with anyone else. Myself included."

Altai was well outside the *Concord*. Her ship was not in *Concord* space now. If that stellar nation had chosen, they might have turned themselves into an empire, but they were content to leave most planets alone.

Shangdu itself was heavily armed, and flew with escorts at all times, because piracy recognized no political bounds.

The *Concord* could ask, but not demand. All that they could do by trying was to cause enmity with their much-smaller neighbors.

Behnam wondered if their spies had learned about Navarre's plans. *Hammerfield* could be traced to her, eventually, if you wanted to wade through legal structures designed to delight librarians with their obscurity. Navarre as well, especially since they had taken the vessel into *Concord* space as part of the man's revenge.

Still, this stranger had come alone, instead of bringing a warship. And asked politely.

And she might need their forbearance in the near future, once Navarre got truly ugly.

"Set up a working dinner for tomorrow night," she decided crisply. "Match his staff for size with yours. Assume brandy for either two or four afterwards."

"As Your Dread Grace commands," Tömörbaatar said with a grin, rising and nodding.

Behnam grinned back.

She had known the man for more than forty years. Watched him uphold her throne for thirty-one of them.

One *Concord* captain would not intimidate the *Iron Hero*.

And if it became necessary, she could always have the stranger killed.

That was the quiet power that came with being the *Khatum*.

SHE STUDIED the man as he sat across from her in the small dining hall she had arranged for this private dinner. He had worn a nice, green uniform that showed Zakhar Sokolov's origins.

Behnam could have seated two hundred in the Grand Hall, or chosen the room where four were crowded. Tonight, she had chosen a dining space as might serve most bankers' private residences, six meters long by nine wide, and dominated by an antique, oak table, at least nine centuries old.

It was the sort of room where ten could sit comfortably. Wood paneling waist-high around the room, with wallpaper above that to a semi-vaulted ceiling five meters up. Forest patterns and ocean scenes were worked into the patterns. Cedar beams running overhead, as if holding the arched ceiling up, when they were in fact deep in the safest part of the ship. Hardwood floors almost cherry colored, sealed and shining, with a large, red rug under the table.

Homey.

Just the place for her to work out the stranger's intentions.

Captain Ayokunle was only a few years older than her, but looked every bit of a man in his sixth decade, where Behnam knew she could pass for thirty. Her beauty was just another weapon she might use to disarm and distract the man. Any man.

He had been a most charming dinner companion. Behnam was used to men and women who were filled with their own wealth and glory and rarely educated beyond the basics of business and enough economics to not lose their heritage.

This captain was trained as a historian, and had a lovely speaking voice. She wondered if all *Concord* officers were so charming. Navarre and Sokolov certainly were. She could add this man to the list.

Semi-invisible staff finished clearing the remains of dessert from the table. Tonight, she had chosen a simple meal, vegetable plates of escalating complexity of flavor mixed with occasional meat dishes to cleanse the palette. Topped with a blueberry ice cream she had asked the kitchen to make special for tonight.

Conversation had been polite and vague. Gossip, mostly, until she discovered the man's interest in history, and then Behnam had asked for stories.

It was a test. They all were, but Captain Ayokunle had risen to the challenge with relish.

But all good things come to an end.

"I think it is time, Captain," Behnam began, reaching out to grab a freshly-poured glass of Malbec. She nodded to the woman at Ayokunle's right, obviously an important aide, whereas the other two were mostly junior flunkies along to handle paperwork and errands. "The four of us should retire to a salon and get to business."

Ayokunle nodded serenely, holding his own glass and delicately sliding his chair back to rise.

It was a mark of professionalism, how quickly the room emptied of all but her, Ayokunle, Tömörbaatar, and the quiet woman in the uniform of a *Concord* Lt. Commander who only spoke in reply to direct questions, and had otherwise watched the rest of the meal pass in silence.

A professional spy who was still on duty, obviously.

The *Khatum* led them through a door into the salon that had been placed here for expressly the purpose of allowing the principals to retire after a meal for serious talk. Or bedtime stories, when her children had been much younger.

Three couches lined the walls, ranging from a thin, futon model with a blue cotton cover; to a grander, more traditional one that would hold four comfortably; to the overstuffed, red leather piece on the far wall that was excellent for making pillow forts, or conducting quiet affairs.

Behnam seated herself on the futon and went into a full lotus. It centered her mind and subtly distracted people with her flexibility, especially as she had chosen tight, green leggings tonight, soft moccasins, and a loose tunic in gray silk that clung in just the right places and gapped occasionally in distracting ways.

How better to deal with a stuffy *Concord* captain, even if he had turned out to be more like Navarre and Sokolov than the ones she was used to?

"Thank you," Ayokunle said as he took a spot on the middle couch, to her left, carefully holding his wine glass aloft as he settled himself.

"For?" she asked, matching his smile.

"Other places would treat this as a formal, diplomatic function," he replied. "Stale and dry. Much dancing about and evasion on the hopes we would become distracted or disgusted and depart in a huff."

"Oh?" she teased in a light tone. "Was that an option?"

"Probably not," he laughed in response. "But I wanted to show my appreciation for the option to handle this task quickly and quietly."

Behnam nodded in recognition. Captain Ayokunle was correct, on a variety of angles.

"I spoke with Captain Sokolov at *Merankorr*," the man said simply.

Behnam wasn't surprised by the revelation. And after an hour of listening to this man regale her with interesting tidbits, she was also not surprised that he would drop into his business quickly.

The whole point of dinner was to get all the small talk out of the way. Captain Ayokunle had apparently recognized that.

Still, she watched him like a hawk anyway, knowing that Tömörbaatar was tracking the aide, the spy, just as closely.

She waited with a vague smile for him to continue.

"Captain Sokolov is a bit of a mystery," the captain continued. "But one I was able to perhaps solve, at least a little."

"How so?" she asked.

If he had solved some mystery around Sokolov, knowing would help her. If nothing else, perhaps better blackmail on the man, although she doubted that. Certainly, more insight into his mysterious masters: the Jarre Foundation.

Ayokunle eyed her carefully, as if measuring his words against her intent.

"It was a surprise for me," Ayokunle said. "At *Merankorr*, that is. I knew the man much earlier, when we were both cadets at the *Bryce Academy* forty years ago. He had a different name then."

"I can't imagine that any pirate goes by his real name," she replied, just a touch breathless.

It wouldn't do to dissuade the man from keeping his secrets.

"Just so," Ayokunle said. "However, putting pieces together, I purchased the remnants of the ship that Sokolov was delivering for recasting. Sokolov wouldn't confirm it, but the vessel was *Storm Gauntlet*, his own previous vessel."

"And, Captain Ayokunle?" Behnam probed.

"And now he is in command of a First-Rate-Galleon," the man replied. "Of a type *Neu Berne* used to manufacture a century ago. And Sokolov claims you are a part owner of the vessel."

Behnam smiled. Perhaps the *Concord* had fallen for the cover story and dug no deeper, save what this man could find out. It would be a delicious outcome to a twisted story.

She might even tell him the truth, one of these years.

Not today.

"An investor," she said in a tired voice. "Nothing more. Navarre owns the warship. Sokolov provided the crew. I supplied some minimal amount of funding to help bridge expenses, for an under-capitalized venture with promise. Too many of those fail for not grasping the time frames necessary to achieve profitability."

Ayokunle's eyes slitted suddenly, like a cat sniffing the air.

"I see," the man obviously did not. "And their current intentions?"

"Eventually?" she replied. "Exploration. Establishing new trade routes and trading partners to benefit *Altai*. Profit."

"Eventually," he observed in a dry tone. "And in the meantime? It is our understanding that *Storm Gauntlet* as a vessel frequently engaged in activities that would be considered piracy in a *Concord* court."

Behnam focused a shark's smile on the man like a spotlight.

"Navarre did mention settling an old score."

She let that dangle in the air, a worm on a sharp hook. Interestingly, the spy woman stirred, after remaining so still that she might have been dozing.

"Commander?" Behnam purred, bringing the woman into the conversation.

Altai maintained an espionage service. It came with all manner of branches, from quiet killers like Farouz Jashari, currently accompanying Navarre, to public relations experts capable of bringing down entire hostile governments without a single shot being fired.

The other woman picked her words with the care of a diamond cutter.

"Intelligence reports suggest a crisis between two major criminal organizations," she said diplomatically.

"You are referring to Walvisbaai and Jarre?" Behnam inquired, placing herself on the same chess board as the *Concord* officers.

The spy nodded carefully.

"And you wish to know my part?" Behnam continued. "Why I have chosen sides?"

Both of them nodded in reply.

No, I will not tell you the truth. But I will share enough that you will perhaps be satisfied. For now.

She took a sip of wine and then set the glass down on a side table.

"Someone hired Navarre to steal something from one of my guests," she began in a serious tone. "Presumably, they were expecting a bloodbath, based on the man's reputation for extreme violence. What Navarre referred to as a *Mass Casualty Incident.* When he was successful without anyone being killed, that same person hired Walvisbaai to kill Navarre and Sokolov."

"Valko Slavkov," the woman spy said precisely. "*Svalbard.*"

"Yes," Behnam replied. "Your intelligence is good. Captain Navarre is possessed of a great rage. When his revenge is complete, both men intend to retire from their current occupations and become peaceful merchants."

"His revenge?" Ayokunle asked in a voice suddenly shakier than it had been.

Even the spy had shivered at her words.

Behnam smiled.

"And you know what he has planned?" the captain continued.

"Only that Navarre plans to live up to his reputation with this one," she said with an ugly chill in her voice. "Make an example of people. As he had told me, he only kills pirates."

"Is there any way to stop them?" the spy asked.

Behnam turned back to the captain.

"You said you knew Sokolov?" she asked. "How well?"

"He almost ended up as my brother-in-law," the man said quietly. "Was the best man at my wedding, but I hadn't seen him in seventeen years, prior to this. I have questions for him, both personally and professionally. He and Navarre are in a dangerous spot. They might need friends."

She watched the man's face turn inward. Judged him based on all the bits and pieces he had revealed over the course of a lovely evening.

Made a decision.

"They will be returning here very briefly," she said. "I will hold you out of touch with your superiors until they depart, but I will allow you to meet them. Perhaps something fruitful will come of it."

The look of hope on the man's face told her that she had made the right decision, just as much as the sourness from the spy woman did.

She would see Navarre and Sokolov shortly.

Hopefully, it wouldn't be for the last time.

PART TWO

JAVIER ENTERED *Hammerfield*'s bridge through the monstrous, reinforced portal designed by some naval architect with delusions of adequacy.

Seriously. It should have been the same plain gray-green as everything else on this ship, and standard height and width. This stupid thing was an extra fifty centimeters wider, a whole meter taller, and banded with extra straps of a golden metal running vertically in three places.

Said moron had decided that the bridge access should remind everyone of a bank vault. And some other moron had agreed with the first one.

One of these days, he would rip the damned thing out and replace it with a standard model.

Actually, come to think of it, what he should do is knock out some interior crawlspaces, gut this enormous cathedral of space, and replace it with an arena of some sort, with a space for athletic events in the center, and maybe a stage, or a stage in the round, where musicians or theater companies could perform. At twenty-seven meters across the circle, and nine meters tall at the peak, it would be doable.

After all, Suvi was flying the ship. And she didn't need anyone else's help, but preferred to have a couple of folks handy, mostly for chatting. They could move everyone down to command and support things from the Auxiliary Bridge on deck eight and probably nobody would notice.

But one look at Zakhar, shaved head gleaming, seated atop his command throne like Zeus, reminded Javier of how unlikely it was that the man would give up that feeling of utter godhead that came with the design of *Hammerfield's* bridge. Plus, a smaller space would limit the options for a big crew reunion.

The whole gang was here: Zakhar as Zeus, which probably made Piet Mercury, or something. Mary-Elizabeth would be Mars, or maybe Athena, depending on how the gunner was feeling today.

No, strike that. Definitely Athena. Mars was seated at Zakhar's right hand, knitting. Like a spider weaving her web. Which wasn't fair, since Djamila had really dialed the crazed militancy down a number of notches over the last few months. But once an image got into Javier's head...

Andreea Dalca would be down in engineering as Hephaestus, brooding over her gigantic eggs with Afia close by.

Javier waved at Piet and Zakhar as he moved to his station and powered everything up. A science officer didn't have much of anything to do in jump since the ship existed in its own pocket dimension and the scanners were worthless.

Scientists had postulated that all ships entering hyperspace actually traveled in the same dimension, but since they were moving FTL relative to everything, including each other, nobody had ever figured out a way to see each other, let alone chat.

Javier sat, hooked his seatbelt, and blew a silent kiss at Suvi's image, top among all the faces down the left side of his screen. She blushed and curtsied. And then, because she was a complete and utter goof, stuck her tongue out at him.

It was a good thing she could display a different image on all the other screens.

"Seven minutes to emergence," Piet announced, mostly just to have something to say.

In hyperspace, he had about as much to do as the science officer.

"Javier," Zakhar said across the space, drawing Javier's head around to look up at the captain.

"Are we completely insane for doing this?"

Javier shrugged. Wasn't the first time this conversation had gone back and forth. Just less yelling and gesticulating this time. Public company and all that.

"Son of a bitch has never been told no," Javier said. "Never been put in a situation where someone could push back. Never had *consequences* become uncomfortable."

"I get Slavkov," Zakhar replied. "What about Walvisbaai?"

"I'm sorry," Javier said in a heavy, ugly growl. "Did you just suggest that one of the worst pirate organizations in the galaxy *doesn't* have it coming?"

"There might be innocents," Zakhar countered.

"No," Javier commented with a hard snap. "These are people who have enjoyed a comfortable living making others victims. Taking slaves and selling them to mining colonies or other terminal destinations. Destroying peoples' dreams and their livelihoods. Making the galaxy a nastier place."

"And you're going to fix all that, on your own?" Zakhar asked.

"I took an oath as a *Concord* officer," Javier said simply.

There wasn't much more to it than that. The good guys. Protectors of the innocent and helpless. Paladins on charging steeds. Protectors of the galaxy.

If they had failed, it wasn't for lack of commitment. Even from an ex-drunk, twice-divorced, former officer who had blown up his career before he'd finally managed to scrape together enough money to buy a retired probe-cutter and go explore the galaxy.

Before he had lost almost everything to pirates.

Javier could see the dark fire in the other man's eyes. Probably matched his own. They had both taken that oath a very long time ago.

"And afterwards?" Zakhar asked.

From the dead silence around them, Javier knew that the rest of the bridge crew was listening in. Hell, Suvi might be piping this to all compartments with folks awake.

What would come, the day after Armageddon.

"Afterwards, you folks get to decide whether or not to join me on a grand adventure," Javier said. "If we survive, we'll have political cover, firepower, reward money, and a significant chunk of the galaxy in front of us to explore. We just have to kill a lot of people first."

He and Zakhar locked eyes across the space.

It really did all come down to this.

It had always been there, even from that first moment they met, years ago, when Javier woke up in the man's office with his hands bound behind him and Sykora whomping him on the skull every time he got out of line.

He and Zakhar were the only two here who had been officers in the

Concord Navy, since Suvi hadn't been there in that room, and even she had only been a yeoman.

Unspoken communication between two men of honor. Brothers-in-arms, wherever they met.

The Bryce Connection.

Was Zakhar willing to pay the price necessary to make the galaxy a better place, even if he had to kill a great number of people to do it?

Zakhar considered things, and then nodded. Just like that.

So little, and so much. They would take that to the end of civilized space and beyond. Around them, Javier heard crew members remember to breathe.

"Bridge, bring the ship to Red Alert," Zakhar ordered in that grand, captain's voice he did so well. "All hands to action stations."

"Confirming Red Alert, Captain," Suvi said in her quiet, professional voice.

"Affirmative," the man called. "We're about to drop out of space to meet the *Khatum*. Javier might trust her, but I don't. Unlock all weapon stations and prepare for combat. If nothing else, a good exercise to keep the crew awake."

Javier shook his head. Not exactly disbelief, but close enough for government work.

He was pretty sure he'd never figure out what made a man like Zakhar Sokolov tick.

Hell, he only barely understood his own foibles.

Around them, the lighting added a red tint and the stupid siren ah-OOO-ga'ed several times to wake the dead.

Well, maybe not the dead, considering all the century-old corpses of *Hammerfield's* former crew, carefully stowed away below. But everybody else would be moving like their ass was on fire.

And if it did turn out to be a double-cross from the *Khatum*, boy, wouldn't she be in for a surprise?

PART THREE

POWER.

That's what this was.

Pure and unbridled power, something Zakhar hadn't had at his fingertips in a long time.

Storm Gauntlet had been a strike corvette. Hell on wheels against a freighter. Pretty good against torpedo boats and system patrol craft. Got her ass handed to her by *Ajax*, a *Raider-class* boat comparable to a heavy frigate or a destroyer.

Hammerfield was a First-Rate-Galleon. She could go toe to toe with most fleet's cruisers, and maybe take on a *Concord* Warmaster, depending on the class and age of the other guy.

Zakhar looked out from his elevated perch at the big display screen on the wall in front of him. Below him, arranged in a circle at their stations, the group he thought of as the *Inner Circle* of Centurions: Djamila, Mary-Elizabeth, Piet, Javier. Kibwe Bousaid, his communications expert and paperwork specialist with the smooth, radio voice who was close enough to count.

Even Suvi was fitting in with this group. But he ran a tight ship, along *Concord* lines, something she had been born and raised to.

"Thirty seconds to emergence," Piet said in a loud voice. "All stations ready for combat."

Piet was coming along as a First Officer. Javier probably would have done better, but that man was determined to go down a different path, as were they all.

The screens went live as *Hammerfield* returned to the real universe. Zakhar had wondered if ships that disappeared had just never come back out of hyperspace, even though he knew it was more likely that they had been captured by pirates.

Like him. Or, like he had been.

Before.

Zakhar had become a pirate from the necessity to pay the bills, unlike many of them. Abraam Tamaz had been *Storm Gauntlet*'s first officer, once, before that man turned truly evil. And gotten himself killed by Javier.

Good riddance.

Most pirates were like Tamaz that way. Folks that wanted to hurt other people for no particular reason. Bad, broken people.

Zakhar's command boards quickly filled with information. They had been to *Binhai* previously, so some things could be tracked and identified very quickly. Others would take longer, but there was only one ship he was really looking for.

Shangdu. The Pleasure Dome.

There.

Still in a very high orbit, hopefully innocently awaiting them, along with a handful of small escort craft to deal with whatever trouble might wander along. *Binhai* maintained her own system defenses, so anyone attacking would be facing death by a thousand paper cuts.

Still, nothing immediately challenged them or made to get close. Only a fool fought in low orbit, inside the gravity well.

Well, fools and the desperate. *Storm Gauntlet* had gotten away, but it had been close. And not everyone had survived the encounter, although the casualties could have been much worse.

"Comm, hail the system coordinator for an orbital lane assignment," Zakhar called to Kibwe. He knew Suvi would do the actual work, but his assistant would put the right flavor on the words. "Then call *Shangdu* and request a docking window for the shuttle."

"Aye, sir," Bousaid said in that warm baritone of his.

The faster they could drop off all the prisoners, the sooner he could move on with Javier's mad plan. And the sooner he could start thinking about *happily ever after*.

Zakhar was *The Captain*. He could have never approached Djamila, as much as they both wanted him to. And he hadn't believed that she would ever work up the courage to do it herself. But she had, with the help of Suvi and Afia, wonder of wonders.

If they all went fully legitimate, as they were planning on doing when this thing was done, then it was Javier's ship. Suvi's really. And he was just crew. Nothing unethical about that.

How long had it been since he had just been crew?

Back when he had been the pilot on the Concord *destroyer* Horizon. *Wow, that long?*

Zakhar shook his head and focused on the task at hand: a quick rendezvous with *Shangdu*, and then a date with eternity.

"Acknowledgement from *Shangdu*, sir," Kibwe said in a tone that brought Zakhar's head around. "Along with a private message for you from the *Khatum*."

Me? Private message? What the hell?

Zakhar keyed the privacy field around his station and opened the message.

Damn, that woman just kept getting more beautiful every day.

Zakhar wondered briefly if she was a vampire or something.

"Captain Sokolov," she began with a warm smile that left him even colder. "A messenger came seeking you while you were gone. After interviewing him, and knowing that you would be returning after a short period, I asked him to remain, isolated from communicating with the outside world. I will make him available when you and Navarre arrive. I think you will look forward to the conversation."

There was another file attached to this one. A picture. Nguyên Ayokunle. Looking just as professional and competent as ever. And apparently a messenger.

Spy, more likely. But that was okay. They were well outside *Concord* space now and would remain so for a very long time.

And what was coming next was something the *Concord* would be interested in, no doubt.

Zakhar routed the message to Javier with a cover note.

This man was almost my brother-in-law.

Let him make of that what he would.

PART FOUR

SHANGDU.

Xanadu.

Zakhar had finally gotten around to reading the ancient poem about Kublai Khan's Pleasure Dome. The *Khatum of Altai* had certainly done an impressive job taking the concept and turning it into a starship.

Zakhar sat across a small table from Nguyên Ayokunle, both men dressed formally for the affair in uniforms that nearly mirrored one another, with Javier, Djamila, the *Khatum* herself, and her Prime Minister at her side. Or whatever the man was called.

He wasn't an assassin. Zakhar had met some of this woman's assassins. Hired them, even.

This one was a bureaucrat. Didn't make him one gram less dangerous.

Their table was on a semi-private balcony, overlooking the monstrous swimming pool she called a lake. An ellipse two kilometers long and one wide, with an artificial island in the center.

On a starship.

There was a breeze, coming out of what Zakhar would call the northeast, given that the artificial sun overhead was just in the process of "setting" now.

Bizarre, but close enough to being on a planet, without all the bugs and crap. Probably better, at that, since she could control everything, and she could take it with her.

Rich people were weird.

But dinner had been amazing. Dessert as well. Nobody had drunk much, staying mostly with lemonade or water. Too much risk of alcohol causing more trouble than it was worth.

Yên hadn't changed in the last six weeks. Or probably the last twenty years, when you got right down to it. You could tell he still wanted to use a different name in conversation, but kept himself practicing with Zakhar.

He would probably slip at some point.

Zakhar shrugged in his head. He could keep being several people. Up until now, probably none of the other players had realized the truth, even as Javier played at being Navarre and Djamila occasionally appeared in public as Hadiiye.

Yên fixed him with that hard stare that made cadets wet themselves.

"She won't tell me anything," he said firmly, nodding at the *Khatum*.

"That's because we're not on the same side, Yên," Zakhar said in an even tone.

"I represent *The Concord*," he huffed.

"And we're pirates," Javier stepped into the conversation. "Start from there and work up."

Yên scowled at the interruption.

"The Jarre Foundation is not registered as a *Concord* organization," Zakhar interjected before the other two men got going. "Nor is Walvisbaai Industrial. The *Khatum of Altai* and Slavkov are also outside your jurisdiction, Yên."

"So I'm just supposed to sit here while you politely pat me on the head?" Yên rasped.

Zakhar would have liked to pick an alternative option, but there wasn't one. Just a man with a badge, and several other men and women with guns. Still, it was good to see his old friend, however stilted and awkward the conversation had to be.

"Yên, we're going to do something so brazen that nobody would believe us," Zakhar placated. "We'd rather you folks not upset the equation."

"What, Captain Sokolov?" the man asked with a sneer. "What could you be planning that OpSec silence is so critical?"

"We're going to break Walvisbaai," Javier said in a quiet tone. "Utterly destroy them. Salt the earth afterwards. You don't get to mess that up."

Zakhar shivered inwardly at the words. Yên blanched.

"You think I would interfere?" Yên asked.

"You aren't likely to help," Javier countered in a sharp tone. "So the best you might do is muddle things. You can clean up the pieces after we're long gone, Captain Ayokunle."

Zakhar was still getting used to the quiet, angry Javier Aritza. Captain Navarre was a cold-blooded, ruthless killer, but Javier had always been more of a goofball. A bright spot on the deck.

Zakhar suspected he was seeing the *Concord* officer as this man had once been. God help the universe if it made this version of the science officer angry.

Angrier.

Walvisbaai Industrial was already going to find out the hard way.

Yên turned his attention back to Zakhar.

"And you won't tell me anything?" he asked.

"Not today," Zakhar responded. "When it's all done and over, we might be on the same side again. Then we can talk."

"Might?"

"Yên," Zakhar finally let his exasperation show. "Zakhar Sokolov is a wanted criminal with a price on his head. You can't change that."

"Yes," the man agreed. "*Zakhar Sokolov* is. There are other options on the table."

"Pal, you haven't got the jets to swing that one," Javier sneered.

"Then who will protect you?" Yên asked.

Javier nodded to the *Khatum*.

"She will," he said.

"The *Khatum*?" Yên queried.

"In addition to being an early investor, there were other considerations," the woman said in that voice that flowed like warm honey.

"Such as?"

"Letters of Marque and Reprisal," her tone was no less taut than Javier's. No less angry.

Yên twitched at the implications.

"Yes," she continued, voice turning cold and sharp. "Valko Slavkov decided to make me an enemy. Walvisbaai chose to help him. Captain Navarre is going to break both of them for me."

Even Zakhar shivered a little at the viciousness in her voice.

She and Navarre/Aritza seemed well-matched. Zakhar wondered if the galaxy would survive.

Yên slowly turned his head to study each face around him, including the two silent ones. Finally, he spoke.

"Then will you at least tell me where to go, to help pick up the pieces?"

"No," Javier was blunt. "Watch the evening news when the reporters finally release the footage. We'll be long gone by then."

Zakhar watched the energy flow angrily between the two men. Time to step in, before it got out of hand.

"Yên," Zakhar said. "I know you mean well. And I know where to find you, or at least get a message. One of these days, we'll talk. I promise."

That placated him. Some.

Everyone lapsed into silence as the sun finally "set" and automatic lights came up to brighten the artificial twilight.

Zakhar hoped it wasn't a metaphor for what was coming.

PART FIVE

Behnam sat carefully on her end of the oversized couch and watched the man. This had been his suite, both times he had stayed here on her ship.

She had begun to think of it as his.

The spare bedrooms for bodyguards the man no longer kept, if he ever had. The pale, blue, main bedroom for snuggling. The marble bathtub comfortable for two. The multi-level green and brown salon, with the bar to one side, where all manner of assignations and meetings could be held.

Creator knew that the man wasn't likely to come to her chambers. Even for one night.

Captain Navarre was never going to be happy just living at *Shangdu*. Too quiet a life, and at the same time, too many people.

It was an odd combination in anyone, and one she barely understood, but Behnam was beginning to know the man under the terrible façade of the killer pirate.

She kept her feet curled under her and a glass of spiced port in one hand. He was close enough to touch, with his shoes tossed casually away as he had entered, and his legs up on the sofa, pointed at her.

Navarre had a glass of the port as well, but was actually drinking his, where she just sipped at hers for show.

Finally, his eyes focused on her. Something locked in, like an ambush predator perched on a branch as prey went by below.

It brought an exciting shiver to Behnam's soul, him watching her like that. She had no other way to describe it.

Not lust. Or rather, not just lust. Respect. Regret. Possibly even softer emotions, if a man that could present Eutrupio Navarre to the outer world was capable of soft sentiments.

He had a hard face. Masculine and square. Just graying around the edges in a way that suggested a man in his early forties. So perhaps half a decade younger that her, but possessed of far more light years than she had.

One eyebrow went up, framing his inquisitive brown eyes, but he remained silent.

He would not start the conversation, this quiet, dangerous man. But she knew that already. Navarre was a man of sudden action and perfect stillness. Much like Farouz Jashari. Both men killers in their own right.

"Do you have a death wish?" Behnam asked simply.

She tried to convey the question warmly, but it was a cold way to start any conversation.

Navarre studied her closely before answering.

The moment stretched, but she would not break the spider web. That communication rang silently between them. And he knew that.

Had she ever met a man capable of using silence as a weapon so effectively?

"Navarre does not," he replied finally, slowly.

"And the other man?" she asked. "The one you are when you are not Navarre? What is he like? Has he a deathwish?"

Again, silence. Weighing his words with care.

"He did, I think," the man said, barely above a whisper.

"Did?"

"Did," Navarre agreed. "Blew up two marriages with his drinking and stupidity. And a career as a *Concord* officer. Was circling the drain. Slowly, but surely. Then I met Suvi."

"And would you consider her your third wife?" Behnam asked carefully, fully aware that she had moved onto new ground with this man. Possibly safe. Possibly ice.

She had spoken with Suvi when this mission started. Gotten some of that woman's side of things, and some of what had transpired. Without ever naming names.

"My only daughter," he said with a sudden smile. "I had to be responsible, for once. Get over myself. Grow up, I suppose."

He took a long, contemplative drink of his port.

"Discover a reason to go on living that was more than just the next round of drinks," he concluded.

Behnam leaned forward. Just a touch.

She had worn a low-cut blouse to dinner. Navy blue silk, crossing two pieces from shoulder to opposite hip and wrapping around her.

It belled out. Not much.

Enough that she could watch his eyes flicker down and then back up.

"And now?" she asked, letting her voice add a hint of breathlessness she knew he would appreciate. "Do you have reasons to survive?"

He grinned, ever so slightly.

"Perhaps," he whispered.

"Perhaps?" she asked, leaning a little farther, letting the gap in her top swell out a little more.

Again, his eyes flickered. Lingered longer. Climbed hesitantly back up to her face.

"There will be vendettas after this," he observed. "Many people will be extremely angry. The powerful will be the most helpless. The powerless may have nothing to lose."

Behnam unfurled her legs, turning them sideways so that she could drape herself across the back of the green sofa. A masterpiece by one of the Greeks, perhaps.

"So you will need shelter," she replied. "Someplace to come in from the rain and darkness."

"It will be cold in the depths of space," Navarre said.

"And you will have no one to warm you?" she asked. "Just your *Sentience* for company?"

Now the ice would grow thin under her feet.

Behnam had discussed the topic with Suvi, who seemed to know far more than anyone gave her credit for. Being the very ship around them made that easy.

Navarre had many mistresses among the crew. Only Hadiiye and a few others had never spent a night in his bed. But Suvi didn't think any of them had ever altered his behavior.

Ever touched his soul.

Navarre was a man like an iceberg. Moving with casual deliberation. Mostly submerged and invisible. Utterly implacable once he was set on a path.

Behnam supposed many would be driven under the waves, ground under an implacable wall of ice, attempting to resist.

But then, she had not taken up monasticism, either, so she could not demand it of him.

Not yet, anyway.

She could tell from his words that he expected this mission to be his death.

Going down fighting, in a battle he had chosen to wage.

Paladin.

"Space can be very lonely," he said finally, after letting the silence build like a static charge.

She was closer to him now. Not touching, but able to feel his warmth.

Navarre carefully set his glass on the floor, and then took hers as well.

She placed one hand on his chest.

Navarre might look calm, but she could count the rapid beats of his heart.

She let the silence build like a spiderweb.

Behnam leaned forward to kiss Navarre once. Light.

One hand came up and encircled her shoulders, his hands warm.

She snuggled into the crook of his arm and let the man's fire give lie to his words.

She would have this one night with the man.

Tomorrow, she had to send him off to die.

PART THREE

BOOK TWENTY-SIX: DEEP SPACE

PART ONE

JAVIER KNEW the look that the woman had in her eyes. Knew it all too well.

Afia was going to be a pain on this one. Stubborn. Unflinching. My-way-or-the-highway kind of argument over precedent and personality.

He took a deep breath and closed his eyes. Today was not the day for this.

She knew that. He knew that.

Hell, everyone knew that.

At least they weren't on a deadline. Then he might have just thrown the tiny woman over his shoulder and carried her off like a kidnapping in broad daylight. He could have lived with the kicking and screaming. And the biting and cussing.

Afia apparently knew that.

She just smiled serenely up at him.

"Because I'm right," she beamed at him. "And you damned well know it, Javier."

And he did. Which just made it worse.

"I appreciate your sense of ownership on the topic," he replied, trying to budge her one centimeter. "And the two weeks here in the middle of bloody nowhere when the rest of us got to go off and play at *Shangdu*. And thank you for seeing it done right. But this is my mission."

"What's the phrase you mutter under your breath?" she asked innocently. "Oh, yes. *Screw you, princess.* This one's mine."

Javier was taken slightly aback. Not far. Afia Burakgazi wouldn't have been here, now, if she wasn't smart, capable, and stubborn as a Missouri mule. Or a Yukon grizzly.

Pixie grizzly?

He fought not to grin at the image.

Serious business. Pain-in-the-ass engineer. The worst kind.

One who was right.

This was either going to be over quickly, or they would be at it all day. Better to find out now, when he could still figure out how much beer he needed.

"Why?" he asked bluntly.

"You want that list alphabetical, chronological, or by degree of difficulty?" she smirked up at him.

Seriously, a woman a head shorter than him shouldn't be smirking like that. Plus, that question was usually asked naked and sweaty. Which was the best way to enjoy it.

Afia was going to be a pain, obviously.

"By color," he replied, willing to dance with the tiny dynamo today.

It wasn't like anything was going to happen until this got sorted out.

He took a moment to find the captain's chair and settle himself in, looking once around the big bridge for strength.

They had re-christened the Land Leviathan's transport as *Odysseus*. It was a rude inside joke about how the Hellenes won the Trojan War.

With a trick horse.

Javier didn't put much truck in the original story, but it made for a fanciful image.

Afia walked over after him, kipped her leg up, and rested a hip on the console.

Javier found it amusing that both of them checked to see that the boards were cold before her butt made contact.

Engineers to the core.

The big picture window behind her was unshielded, showing a field of black space speckled with occasional stars in the far distance. Javier and Zakhar had purposefully parked the stolen ship in the darkness between two systems, so nobody accidentally found them.

Afia and her small crew of engineering lunatics had spent their time fixing the ship up for her final mission.

The storming of Ilium.

She looked down at him like she saw Achilles.

Hopefully not. Javier was too beautiful to die so young, even if he would leave a fantastic corpse and one hell of a story.

"I'm just guessing here," she began, lowering her tone.

They were alone on the bridge, with all the rest of everyone either over on *Hammerfield* getting ready, or down in the big transport bay aft, working on things, or back in engineering.

Just the two of them. To argue it out.

Javier fixed her with a good dose of stinkeye. She was as immune as all the other people he had tried it on recently. Must be losing his touch.

"This was one of the things that you didn't like about being an officer, back in your navy days," she continued.

Javier pelted the woman with silence. Easiest way to keep her talking was to not interrupt.

"Sending someone else off to maybe die, or screw up monumentally," she said. "When you knew you could do the job at least as well, if not better."

Javier felt his scowl turn sour. Thunderous.

Hard.

"You don't trust that I'm good enough to do this," she said in a flat, accusatory tone.

He started to move. To heave himself up out of the amazingly comfortable chair the previous captain had installed and get right into her face.

Afia forestalled him by reaching out one hand and pushing him back down into the chair, at the same time interrupting his words.

"Or you don't want to live with the guilt of sending someone you like off to die," she snapped.

Javier subsided.

Damned, stubborn engineers.

Especially when she was right.

Javier had always been one of the best engineering officers he knew, even when he was on a command track.

Way too much of an extrovert to fit down with the big machines and quiet people.

But she was right.

Guilt at sending kids into a failing reactor, and challenging them to die in single combat with a runaway system spewing out a lethal mixture of radiation, heat, and shrapnel.

Knowing they were never coming out of that room alive.

And that the best they could do would be to insure that nobody else had to go in after them and die, pushing the rock another meter up the hill, until either Javier ran out of men, or the ship exploded.

The second batch of kids had eventually succeeded in slaying the beast.

The drinking had started that night. As did the nightmares.

More than a decade would pass before he escaped either of them.

He really didn't want to go back there.

Especially not with Afia.

"It's okay," she whispered, reaching out a hand to catch the tears suddenly streaming down his face.

Javier just sat perfectly still and tried to hold onto his horizons as they threatened to turn upside down again.

He finally remembered to breathe.

"I can't order you off this ship when we get there, can I?" he finally asked in a defeated, wan voice.

"Nope," she chirped. "And Djamila would tackle you instead of me, if push came to shove. You know that, right?"

"Yeah," he let go a sigh.

She was right.

"Good," Afia Burakgazi, Combat Engineer, pronounced. "Then we're going to do this my way."

Javier sucked cool air all the way down into his big toes.

Damn this woman. Damn all engineers.

"Walk me through it," Javier said, trying to find solace in their shared nerdiness. "From the top."

She smiled. It was warm, and sad, and knowing. He wondered if Suvi had told Afia too much. Not that his sidekick knew everything, but someone else might have mentioned something at some point. Or he might have screamed in a nightmare and forgotten it by morning.

The dark places in his head were unfit for even him. Let alone innocent strangers.

"We'll come out of the terminal jump with a soft head of steam," Afia began. "One last course correction to line up the cue ball, and then the assault team bails. Scuttling charges are set to five minutes. Assault team hits the lifeboat and runs like hell. Everything is physics at that point."

"And the scuttle?" he asked.

"In case someone over there reacts fast enough to think they can stop us," she smiled grimly. "You, me, and Suvi are an evil combination, but Djamila is just flat rude when she puts her mind to it."

"That's why I put up with her," he said quietly. "Life boat packed?"

"Affirmative," she acknowledged. "We'll be over an inhabitable planet, if worst comes to absolute worst. Guns, fake IDs, cover stories, and money already in place. Your job is to pull an avenging angel with the eclipse attack and pick our butts up before the bad guys get there."

"That's what I'm planning," Javier said.

"Well," Afia replied. "This ought to go down in history as the…what was the term you used?"

"*Le Beau Geste*," Javier said. "The Grand Gesture."

Yeah, nobody was ever forgetting this one.

And if he did it right, there wouldn't be that many survivors available to eventually come after him.

PART TWO

Turner didn't like it, but there wasn't much choice in the matter. Not after the way she had screwed up at *Svalbard*, letting Navarre and *Storm Gauntlet* get away.

Ajax nearly getting gutted in the encounter hadn't helped, even if Captain Sokolov had that kind of a reputation.

At least the repairs had gone well, as slow as the process had been to finally get her ship in and have it assayed. *Ajax* was as good as new.

Now, she just had to figure out why her boss had instructed her to call on him in person. Aboard the main station.

Walvisbaai Industrial Platform Number One.

Home port. The biggest non-*Concord* shipyard in the entire sector. The galaxy's principal chop shop.

A massive spindle, like a strange, child's top, flying slowly across the sky. And it was all business: manufacturing, service, and repair. The brothels and such were down on the planet, with a constant stream of shuttles running people up and down the gravity well or out to the other stations, where simple spacers lived.

Almost nobody lived on the Platform itself, except the important muckety-mucks at Walvisbaai. The *Made* Men and Women. And even then, few actually lived there. They just kept apartments and boltholes, safe from assassins that might hide in the general population of a planet.

Always traveling with bodyguards and gunboats.

Turner faced the door at the end of the hallway with a moment of trepidation, but it opened as she stopped moving.

She entered.

At least there was no plastic sheeting on the floor. That was always a concern when dealing with people that had offices like this: the penthouse suite at the very northern tip of the station.

"Captain Kowalski, come in," the man's voice rang out.

Turner was amazed at the size of the room. She could have parked a landing shuttle in here with room on all sides.

One wall was transparent, floor to three-meter ceiling, running a curve at least forty meters wide. Turner could just make out the distant, gleaming star that was *Ayakot Station*, *Ajax's* actual home when they were here, warriors not being welcome on the industrial grounds that made Walvisbaai's money.

Thick shag carpet in cream covered the floor. Sand-colored paint made all the walls look more distant, somehow. Like she was on the surface of a planet in the middle of a desert, or something.

Real, honest wooden desk to one side. One meter tall, meter and a half deep, two meters wide. Maybe oak, considering. Two chairs on this side, neither of them looking comfortable. That would be the couch off to her left, closer to the wetbar. Presumably where guests would be entertained.

Turner wondered if her fate was the desk, or the bar. The man who had ordered her here had a reputation as the most lethal accountant in the galaxy.

Looking at him, it was hard to see. Dillon Toov was short, round, bald, and swarthy. Even the fantastically expensive suit only barely made him look like what he really was: one of Walvisbaai Industrial's Board of Directors.

The dangerous eleven men and women at the top of the pyramid.

Turner began to walk across the vast space to where Toov sat behind his desk. She fixed a polite smile on her face and tried not to think about gunmen stepping out from behind a pillar to shoot her in the back for whatever imagined failure had brought her here.

If it wasn't big, they could have sent her a message pack.

The personal touch probably meant it was bad.

"Sit," Toov ordered, gesturing to one of the rigid metal chairs with minimal padding.

Turner planted herself and tried to relax. Every sound behind her was a pistol cocking.

Dillon Toov didn't help her frame of mind by silently watching her, a predator's eye deep in a pool of still water.

Thirty seconds passed. Turner managed to not fidget.

Not too passive. Not too aggressive. Keep it professional and polite.

"There are those who think you have lost it," Toov began. "Are no longer good enough to maintain your place in the pack hierarchy."

Turner listened, trying not to clench her shoulder blades together before the beam struck.

"The damage to *Ajax* was extensive," he continued. "And expensive to repair. Your numbers this year will be atrocious, as a result."

She nodded. Two months in drydock, shimming in an early engine overhaul and weapons upgrade to the repairs *Ajax* had already suffered.

How well did they love her? Enough to overlook being outdueled by Sokolov?

"The Board discussed replacing you," Toov dangled that tidbit out there.

Turner nodded again. As the commander of *Ajax*, she was one of their top fighting officers. Her fate would be a topic of great interest.

How many of them would be on her side?

Toov just watched her.

Turner had been focused on the man's face. Still was, but noticed that the desk had papers stacked neatly in three piles. Antique ink pens in a used coffee mug to one side. Screen built into the desktop, but turned off. Another mug by his left hand, faint wisps of steam coming off of it.

Toov reached out and grabbed his mug. Coffee, she suspected, from the smell.

He sipped, still watching her like a crocodile.

Toov put the mug back down with a small thump.

"Good," he said in a much more jovial tone. "No pleading. No arguing. No defensiveness."

He pushed his chair back and rose. Turner watched him move to the wetbar and gesture for her to join him.

"Come."

The bulk was misleading. As she got close, she remembered that Dillon Toov was her height, average for a man. The roundness only made him seem short. He carried an extra thirty kilograms of soft mass around like padding, but the man still moved like a shark.

She was taller than most of the women she knew. At forty-two, the lush curves were starting to get out of hand enough that she had to change her diet and workout routine so she could slim down and tone up. Some men liked a mature woman, but Turner knew she was past the age where big boobs and blond hair was enough to turn a man's head.

Fortunately, she had brains to back it all up. And the ruthlessness to become a captain in an organization that was heavily tilted towards men in charge.

Toov moved around behind the bar and pulled out a bottle and two glasses.

He filled both with something midway between amber and plum. It smelled sweet.

One glass went to her, and he took the other.

"The final vote was nine to two in favor of keeping you, Turner," he announced with a shark smile, sipping.

Turner took a sip as well. Something like sake, but with a fruity undertaste that went long and slow.

This one bottle was probably worth as much as she made in a month, knowing the scales Walvisbaai Industrial worked at.

Nine to two? Really?

The alcohol worked magic on her nerves and muscles. Turner felt a centimeter taller just letting everything inside relax.

"But now we have a different problem," Toov continued. "I want your opinion in a setting without anyone around to give you pause."

You mean, besides you?

She held herself perfectly still. Toov had only implied that he had been part of the nine, and not the two. She could only guess.

"Something interesting happened to Valko Slavkov while you were here," he explained.

Turner let her eyes and face speak. Powerful men frequently just liked to hear themselves talk. She had learned she could indulge them and often hear more than they intended.

"Somebody stole his car," Toov concluded.

"They what?" Turner shot out, surprise coloring her body language.

"Someone managed to hijack the freighter carrying his prize tank," Dillon Toov smirked. "*The Land Leviathan.* It took off on schedule from its most recent stop, headed this direction for a major overhaul. But it never appeared at the first jump point."

Turner blinked in shock as the size of such an operation unfolded in her mind. And the sheer brass. And the subtlety to pull it off and then vanish.

"How long ago?" she asked.

"Four weeks," Toov replied. "The two escorts, Slavkov's gunboats, ran a full search pattern, tracking as much as they could locate, before they came here, hoping that the freighter had managed to somehow make it anyway. No dice."

Turner nodded.

They were all pirates. It was a business, but it was also a profession. She could appreciate a professional job.

"Who has he pissed off the most?" she asked.

Toov took another drink and shrugged eloquently.

"Everybody?" he said. "Nobody? That's why I wanted to speak with you privately."

"Sir?" she said, careful with even the non-verbal communication.

"Looking at the records, Slavkov's most recent issues were with Navarre and Sokolov," Toov said. "And by extension, the Jarre Foundation."

"*Svalbard*," she replied, trying to keep her anger under tight rein.

Svalbard, where Navarre and a surprise, heavy combat team had taken out her entire ground force, and then had the audacity to capture them and return them unharmed. Where Zakhar Sokolov had managed to evade Turner's every gambit, out-duel her in the darkness, and then somehow teleport a torpedo into a position where she had to let him escape, just to give her own crew a chance to kill the incoming missile before it killed her.

And it had been a close thing.

Toov nodded.

"I've read your reports," he said. "Actually watched some of the footage of the battle and your crew debriefs. Sokolov's good. Navarre is a complete wildcard. And they have finally reappeared."

"Have they now?" Turner purred.

She owed those two men a serious ass-kicking for *Svalbard*. It would be nice to finally balance the books.

"Before you get your hopes up, Turner, there is a problem," Toov replied.

She bit back the tart response lurking on the tip of her tongue. He might still be part of the two, and not the nine.

"They've stolen a warship this time," he continued. "A big one."

"A warship?" she asked.

Navarre was developing a reputation as a magician. Sokolov was a meat-and-potatoes kind of guy, but extremely capable as a ship-handler. Dangerous, dangerous combination.

"Understand I am not a naval officer," Toov said.

Turner nodded.

"According to our spies, the vessel is called a First-Rate-Galleon," Toov concluded.

"Son of a bitch!" Turner exploded. "How dare he?"

"Bad?" Toov looked concerned.

"Huge, armed cargo vessel with the firepower of a cruiser," she snarled. "Nobody's made any new ones that I'm aware of in decades. Not since the end of the Great War. Way too big for *Ajax* to take on, maybe our entire fleet. You'll have to send assassins, next time."

"Personal affront, Turner?" Toov asked soothingly.

"I owe both of those men," she snarled. "No way for me to collect if they can swat *Ajax* like a fly."

"I see," Toov said, finishing off his glass and pouring two more fingers in. "But you agree that they might be behind this?"

"Navarre killed Tamaz and crew by himself," she recalled. "*Storm Gauntlet* just came along later and annihilated the corpse, but the whole crew was already dead by then. According to your spies, he waltzed right into *Shangdu*, stole something for Slavkov, and ambled right back out without anyone getting hurt. Somehow, Sokolov figured out we were there at *Svalbard* and those two managed to turn the entire game inside out on me."

She paused to think. And finished her own glass. She listened as Toov refilled it while her eyes stared off into deep space.

"Those two are as wily as eels," she decided. "And as dangerous. If Slavkov wants our help finding his ship, charge him extra."

"Even if it's personal, Turner?" Toov asked.

She nodded and hammered back the rest of the glass.

"I'd do the job for free," she replied in a cold voice. "But Slavkov dragged us into this mess, his personal vendetta, so he needs to pay us dearly for cleaning it up."

Toov studied her closely for a moment.

"Interesting assessment," he agreed. "And almost exactly what the Board concluded when he approached us for additional help. I want you to prepare your ship and your crew for an extended mission, Turner. We have spies out, looking for the Land Leviathan, and Navarre. I'm planning to send you in when we have a target."

Turner Kowalski smiled. She had never met Navarre personally, or known anyone who had. She had only been at the short end of his games.

She was looking forward to the opportunity to kill him.

PART THREE

Djamila found it interesting, just listening in as the conversations wound around her. Highly technical men and women, pushing the envelope, aware that they would only get one opportunity at the task in front of them.

She had nothing to do at this point, so she took up her usual station on *Hammerfield*'s bridge and knitted. This was a peace offering, of sorts, in gray and black twinned yarn. Extra fine material, with her smallest needles, so the going was slow, but the final product would be indistinguishable from something generated by an industrial machine.

The rest of the bridge was hyped, keyed up for the final assault that they were going to launch soon, but Djamila felt more like *Hammerfield* itself, calmly awaiting the countdown, clear out at the edge of the *Nidavellir* system.

Watching. Absorbing. Preparing.

At least *Hammerfield* would have something to do when they arrived. The only time Djamila would have any tasks at all would be if everything went desperately wrong and she ended up leading her teams against an enemy boarding action.

At which point, they were all likely dead, either way.

But the people around Djamila were still tuning things: Javier, Zakhar, and Suvi here on the bridge; talking to Afia and her crew of engineers over there. Everything was almost ready.

Djamila had to send wanted her best people along with Afia, since the woman was going to be high on someone's kill list, when this was done. The initial support team had included Sascha, Hajna and Farouz, in case that team had to land on the planet and escape.

Logistics had prevented it, since they needed every available seat on the escape pod for engineers, and none of Djamila's people could be taught the necessary skills in the time available.

Hopefully, nothing would go wrong, and she would see everyone again in a few hours.

In her hands, two balls of very fine yarn slowly melted, feeding the pattern in her lap. Djamila had no way of knowing, short of asking outright, if Javier would recognize some of the patterns she was working into this sweater. Anyone outside of *Neu Berne* probably wouldn't but she also knew he had studied her culture, her past, at least enough to know which of her buttons to push, and how.

Back when they both pushed buttons.

It was a strange feeling, not constantly looking for ways to kill the man and make it look like an accident. Not wondering if Suvi would change her mind about killing Djamila. Or how Zakhar would react to a quiet knock at his door.

Djamila had decades to understand who she was turning into. And Javier to thank for it. Or blame, depending.

She smothered a smile before it erupted and lit up the whole bridge. Humming to herself would be even worse.

And yet.

She was still the *Ballerina of Death*. Still seven of the top ten scores on the combat range, although she suspected that Farouz could shorten that count, if he chose.

They had only been intimate once, she and Farouz. She had hoped for more, but the man brought his own sensibilities to the prospect of Operational Security. Djamila respected that.

And respected the promise, the fire, she saw in his eyes, that when this mission was over and they could relax, they could once again just be evil pirates roaming the spaceways and causing mischief.

So she knitted.

After Javier's sweater was done, something for Farouz would be next. She just wasn't sure what it would be. Or maybe she'd do something for Afia first, while she thought about what to do for this new man in her life.

A message pinged on her board, distracting her.

Javier.

Interesting, since he was seated all of eight meters away from her. He could had spoken aloud in a normal voice. Or simply gotten up and walked over.

She opened the message.

"*Morningstar Brigade?*" the message said.

Yes. Her old unit.

There was a picture attached, which she opened. It matched the symbol she had worked into the center of the sweater's chest in black and gray in her lap.

She smiled in spite of herself. Djamila would have thought that Suvi would be the only other person on this bridge that would recognize the design. And Javier hadn't gotten close while she was working, so he had to have been studying her from his usual distance.

It made her warm to think she still had that much effect on the man.

Rather than type, she just turned her head far enough to extend her smile to Javier. She nodded at his obvious confusion.

Javier did not speak. He typed instead.

"So who is this sweater for?" he pinged.

It was interesting how little emotional loading there was on such simple words. Coming out of his mouth, there would have been sarcasm, or *ennui*. Something.

This felt like simple curiosity. Which might be why he had chosen this method. They could be polite and friendly, without maintaining the outward aggression and friction that had framed their relationship for so many years.

Maybe he was finally growing up and acting like management. After all, the horse might truly have learned to sing, given enough time.

Djamila bit her lip to stop from giggling at the image. Instead of speaking, she typed a message, and then looked up to see Javier's response.

"You," she volleyed back.

The shock on his face was like the best pudding for dessert, after the best steak imaginable.

After all, she did owe him, from way back.

Torturing Javier Aritza with kindness was probably going to be even better than killing him.

PART FOUR

Commodore was a courtesy title, rather than a rank. Senior captain on a station that did not warrant an admiral. Back in his line command days, being a commodore would mean commanding a small task force.

Captain Nguyên Ayokunle wasn't in command in the field anymore. He had gotten promoted about as far as he was ever going to, and was in charge of the military section at *Merankorr*, while he waited for his retirement in a few years.

It was a cushy job, but never that exciting. Part accountant. Part bureaucrat. Part spy. *Concord* Fleet Operations relied on him to wade through mountains of electronic paperwork, looking for trends, patterns, and issues, so they could be reconciled or deflected before they got too big to handle easily. He was good at what he did, and afraid that he was about to make a career-ending mistake.

That, or perhaps kill the man who had been his best friend once.

Yên sat in the Admiral's outer office and waited for that man. The space was comfortable, painted in a soft peach, with green carpet that looked vaguely grass-like. The couch he was on was designed to be relaxing, but not so much that you risked falling asleep. Two plants in pots that he couldn't identify, along with oil paintings that looked like pre-spaceflight seascapes.

Men trapped in storms. It was an interesting choice of decoration.

The inner door opened and a young lieutenant commander stepped out, looking for all the galaxy like a recruiting poster image. Short, dark hair. Chiseled features. Trim and athletic.

Probably the nephew of somebody well-connected that the admiral wanted to impress.

"Commodore?" the man said, coming more or less to attention. "The admiral will see you now, sir."

The young man gestured Yên to enter the room, and then closed the hatch behind him.

Inside, the peach and green theme continued. Similar artwork. More potted plants.

The only weird thing about the room was the enormous fish tank in one corner. Yên could smell the salt water from here, and see dozens of fish moving around in a space as big as three coffins stacked atop one another.

The admiral behind the desk was relatively new on this station. Physically average for size, height, and weight. At least for an admiral, where they tended to get squishy with rank. The man's skin was as pale as Yên's was dark. The only thing the men had in common was gone hair completely white, but neither man bald.

Yên hadn't had enough time around the man, past that, to really get a feel for him, but things were moving fast right now, and it couldn't wait.

"Commodore," Admiral Jameson Packard said in a gruff greeting. "Sit."

Yên did, trying to gauge the man's humor.

"I've read your report to Intelligence on the man called Sokolov," the admiral continued, focusing those eyes like angry emeralds on him. "How much of your conclusion is supported purely on facts, and how much on intuition?"

Yên licked his lips carefully.

"The raw findings are solidly empirical, sir," Yên said. "The vessel was close enough to us, for long enough, for good solid soundings to be made. Naval Estimates Board was able to match the hull with their records. She is definitely one of the last generation of *Neu Berne* galleons, built in the last five years of that war. We've narrowed it down to one of four hulls, but would need to get inside her to get a solid identification. Sokolov, or someone else, did some significant modifications later, possibly recently.

Two of the main pulsars were upgraded to pulse cannons, and one was replaced with an ion pulsar. That would match our estimates of weapons taken off *Storm Gauntlet*, in her last known weapons configuration."

"What about torpedoes?" the admiral bored in.

"Unknown how many *Storm Gauntlet* had," Yên replied. "But other intelligence reports suggest that *Storm Gauntlet* fought a battle with a pirate vessel at *Svalbard* a year ago, and damaged that ship with them."

"And the information on…Sokolov?" Packard asked.

"I updated the files with what I knew, right up until the point he took his retirement and vanished seventeen years ago. Modern notes are from Naval Estimates Board's records of the organization he supposedly worked for, plus what the man told me himself when we spoke briefly here and aboard *Shangdu*."

"And the *Khatum of Altai* is definitely involved?" the admiral asked.

"By her own admission, Admiral," Yên agreed.

"Letters of Marque and Reprisal represent a dangerous escalation, Captain," Packard observed. "Especially in a warship of that magnitude. Doubly so in the wilderness, where there might not be any other vessels capable of stopping them."

"Aye, sir," Yên said. "However, Navarre's stated intent was to cripple Walvisbaai Industrial. *Salt the earth* were his actual words."

"And you wish to stop him?" Packard asked. "Or assist him?"

"Neither, Admiral," Yên admitted. "I take both men at face value that they will do one thing, and then get on with their lives. If I am right, we have the chance to hold some amount of leverage over the final outcome."

"With a Class II Warmaster, alone?" the admiral sneered.

"Human crewed vessels cannot navigate hyperspace as quickly as *Sentient* vessels can, Admiral," Yên responded. "I pushed as hard as I could to get here. *Concord Warship Meridian* could get us to *Nidavellir* fast enough, I think, to help pick up the pieces, if nothing else. Or stop them, if they decide to go completely rogue over an inhabited planet."

"With you as task force commander?" the admiral asked.

"I know the man, Admiral Packard," Yên said. "Knew him forty years ago. Maybe I can stop him, or something. And if not, I'd rather be the one to kill him, instead of sending someone else to handle the task."

Packard studied him for several seconds.

"Very well, Captain Ayokunle," the man said. "It's your reputation on the line, either way. I'll let you own this one. Prepare yourself for transit. Orders will be transmitted shortly."

Yên rose and saluted. He was more of a spy and a bureaucrat these days. It would be nice to get back in the saddle one last time.

PART FOUR

BOOK TWENTY-SEVEN: NIDAVELLIR

PART ONE

JAVIER STUDIED the boards in front of him. One last mission as the *Science Officer*, and then he might retire to the life of shipping magnate. Or chicken breeder. There was space down in one of the cargo decks, maybe all the way down on Seventeen, to install a much larger botany lab than he had brought from *Mielikki* to *Storm Gauntlet* to here. Maybe he could have a small petting zoo. How would the crew feel about fresh cream on a daily basis to go with fresh eggs?

Real, homemade cheese.

Tomorrow's problems.

Today, the mission that would cement his legend as the most famous, most dangerous pirate in the last millennium. Possibly the most wanted man in space.

Did he really want to make that big of a mark on history? Kill as many people as he might, if the morons over there got too wrapped up in their invulnerability?

Yeah, he did. Bullies just got on his nerves.

And, seriously, Valko Slavkov had just pushed all of his buttons.

The bridge was silent, almost a cathedral today. Or a tomb.

Everyone was poised. Engines had been tuned. Weapons loaded and aligned. Torpedo bays inspected. Crazed, lunatic, goofball *Sentience* about to pay back a small portion of her anger at having been trapped in that little survey probe for years.

371

Even Sykora had achieved a new level of calm.

Javier wasn't sure he wouldn't have preferred bitch-on-wheels Djamila to this new version that was turning into a butterfly before his eyes.

On his boards, live faces representing all the major players: Djamila, Piet, Mary-Elizabeth, Djamila, Suvi, Afia, Andreea, Zakhar.

The *Pirates*.

He had brought them here on the basis of his rage. Nothing more. Transcended slavery to become a leader they were about to follow into battle.

Zakhar was poised. Walvisbaai Industrial had killed *Storm Gauntlet*. That man's pride and joy. He was more than happy to return some element of favor today. *Angry Patriarch*.

Piet had spoken more words to the crew in the last six months than he had in the previous ten years, to hear the old-timers talk. And even started composing and performing music with Suvi. Weird.

Afia looked like a pixie grizzly bear. Petite. Serious. About to rip your throat out.

Mary-Elizabeth had a smile like she had just been offered an extra scoop of ice cream for her birthday. Considering that woman's calling in life, maybe there was some truth to it.

Djamila looked up from her knitting to smile. It wasn't warm. Not like before. Serious. Like she was prepared to open fire on everything that moved with pistols tucked into her bag. She probably was.

Andreea looked pensive and distracted, but she was an introvert's introvert, and looked like that anyways. Her greatest day was when every single generator and engine was running within one percent of optimal. Like today.

Javier met Suvi's eyes. She was still his oldest friend in the galaxy, barring two angry ex-wives and a host of siblings and cousins he hadn't spoken to in ten or twenty years.

She looked calm. Prepared. They had talked about everything, starting with *Shangdu* and *Svalbard*, and coming up to the present. The Pleasure Dome. The Doomsday Vault. The Last Flagship. The War of the Pirate Clans.

Javier was sure those people over there approached all of this like accountants and bankers. That's what it was to most of them. Money and gross points. And Valko Slavkov was just a petulant, abrasive punk who bullied people. Javier had asked Behnam, and she hadn't been able to name anyone who truly liked the man.

They just feared his temper, magnified by his immense wealth. He was among the twenty wealthiest individuals in the galaxy by individual value.

Nobody had ever told that man *No*, and actually made it stick.

Javier wasn't sure this would do the job with that punk, but it would certainly *materially damage the future of Walvisbaai Industrial as a going concern*, which was how you got the attention of accountants and bankers. The quarterly report wouldn't be able to gloss this over.

Shareholders would take notice. Demand changes. Revenge was a losing proposition, except when someone fell into your hands and you could profitably sell them on the black market without much effort.

If nobody was willing to work with or for Slavkov, he would either be neutered, or have to spend monumental amounts of cash just to get anything done.

Victory, either way.

Suvi's face summed that up. She had run those numbers for him, working with one of the *Khatum*'s people, possibly Tömörbaatar. That man was more dangerous with a pen than a blade, although Javier wasn't willing to try his luck with either. Not with the man in the silly hat.

Suvi nodded, as if she could read his mind. Considering how much poker he had taught her over the years, she might be able to do just that.

Both of his ex-wives, Holly and Fryda, had always claimed with some truth, that Javier wasn't really that much deeper than a mud puddle. Even this was just a playground squabble, blown up all out of proportion by two men who wouldn't back down.

Javier nodded back and watched her smile reassuringly. Most of this would be in her hands, once they passed no-return. Mary-Elizabeth and Piet would provide expert assistance. Zakhar would command.

But Suvi would make or break the day. And the bad guys.

He wondered what outfit she was wearing in the privacy of her own cockpit. She had presented baseline Yeoman *Sentience* for this.

Javier knew better. She was too much of a goofball.

Still, time for business.

Javier turned and looked up at Zakhar, Zeus-like atop his mighty throne, lightning bolt in one hand.

"You wanna do this?" Javier asked in a slow, deep voice.

Zakhar wore a scowl that would frighten kittens.

"No," Captain Sokolov replied in a dark, ominous tone. "This one's yours, beginning to end. We're here because you gave us a reason to survive as a company. This is an ending, and hopefully a beginning. It should be your speech."

Javier nodded. About what he had expected. And simple truth.

Zakhar would have broken them up and sold the little strike corvette for scrap, without someplace better to go. Ridden off into the sunset, maybe with Djamila, maybe not.

Everyone else would have been put to shore, then frantically scrambled to find work, at a time when too many of them had prices on their heads in too many places. And possibly lawmen or assassins lurking in the shadows.

Where did that leave him? Four years ago, he had sworn to see every single one of these bastards hung from a high yardarm in low gravity.

And here he was, about to lead them into battle. Save them from a fate as bad as death.

Obviously, the gods had a very dark, bitter sense of humor.

Javier reached down and pressed a virtual button on his screen marked *Ship-wide Comm.*

He took a deep breath and let it go.

"The reasons we are here are legion," he began simply, listening to the words echo out over the big room as Suvi adjusted the feedback. "Not all of them are benign, as we are none of us angels."

Javier kept his face on Zakhar for now, watching the impact the words had on the man who might have been his slave-master, and eventually his partner. Tomorrow, perhaps, his friend.

"At the most basic, they tried to kill us," Javier continued. "Nothing more than that. Pissy, little punk throwing a temper tantrum because everything didn't go his way. So he hired those people across the way to kill us. That makes me angry."

Javier paused to let the energy build. In his own mind, they were already past no-return, but he needed to bring everyone with him. Convince them that this was a hill worth dying on.

"They would have killed you as well," he continued. "And without today, probably would have tried again and again until they eventually got lucky."

Deep breath. All those lessons in public speaking at *Bryce Academy*, back when he wanted to be an officer and gentleman when he grew up. If he had ever decided to grow up.

Maybe today was as good as any. Djamila could. Piet could. Even Zakhar could.

Maybe Javier Aritza could as well.

"You do not negotiate with bullies," he declared in a voice growing both louder and sharper, like a bastard sword clearing a scabbard for battle. "You push them back. And you do not do it just a little. Ladies and gentlemen, they started this. I intend to end it. Right here. Right now. We will make the galaxy a better place by destroying some of the worst elements around. Whatever else you must face your Creator bearing on your list of sins, remind Her that you were here today, and you did this thing."

Javier didn't bother looking at the rest of the bridge crew. He could already tell that everyone had stopped what they were doing to look over at him. On his boards, the little images were backs of heads, instead of faces.

All except Afia.

Javier focused his intent on that woman now. Felt his eyes grow slitted and fierce. She matched him, blow for blow.

"*Odysseus*," he commanded. "Make your jump."

PART TWO

Afia pressed a button on her command console and felt the little shiver of power that vibrated through the vessel's hull like a mild orgasm. So much power at her fingertips.

She had always been an engineering nerd. Quiet. Competent. Way more sociable than most. It had gotten her to *Meehu* with 'Mina, Piet, and Djamila. Given her the chance to shine in front of Javier, so that he pulled her into the big adventures, like *Hammerfield*.

Put her here, now. Commanding the prize crew of engineers and the stolen freighter renamed *Odysseus*, now departing on her terminal mission.

The stars blinked out, leaving all screens a gray fuzz of static in the space between universes.

Afia looked around the big, friendly bridge one last time from her awesome vantage in the captain's chair. It was kinda seductive, sitting here. She might have to think about it, one of these days. Javier had started out as an engineer, and he could be a pretty good commander.

Maybe the universe was just waiting for Afia Burakgazi to decide to join those ranks.

She pressed the ship-wide button.

"All hands," she ordered in a calm voice that wanted to rage over into giggles. "Final jump initiated. Prepare for scuttling charges and the order to evacuate."

She closed the comm before the evil laughter in her belly snuck out.

So much power. It might be Javier's plan. And Suvi's execution. But Afia was going down in history as the woman who pulled it off.

Aft, eight men and women would be frantically pulling arming pins and unlocking explosive charges, made awkward by the combat suits they were wearing. Afia had decreed that nobody was going into this mission wearing only skinsuits. The extra few seconds were worth the protection, if something went wrong.

On a secondary board, lights began to turn blue. Some had been green, others red. Blue mean active and ready for her to give the order.

"Ilan," she barked into the comm. "One-Three-One just went from green to black. Check it out. I need that circuit."

"On it," the man called back.

Five years ago, that landsman would have been hard pressed to get his shoes on the correct feet. Today, he was a First-Rank Machinist. Would have been on an officer track if he had the slightest interest. But he was happier tinkering.

Afia was fine with that.

The schedule had squishiness built in. Javier and Suvi had been a stickler for the fact that friction was going to come up at the wrong moment.

Like now.

One-Three-One controlled the whole port/aft charge. Without that one, there was a serious risk that the jack-knobs on the station could knock *Odysseus* off-course safely.

Once they figured out that she was intent on ramming them.

Boy, weren't they going to be in for a shock.

The lifeboat icon went light blue on her board. Everyone aboard except her and Ilan.

"Ilan?" she yelled into the comm.

The light had briefly flickered to green, then red, then blue, then black again.

"I've got a short somewhere," he called back.

"Well, you're out of time to fix it," Afia replied.

"I can do this!" he cried.

She reached up to the extra rocker switch that had been hard-wired onto the console and flipped the protective cover up. Underneath, a lovely pin-switch in the up position.

It took a little effort to break the switch free and snap it down. You had to have *intent*.

Immediately, the lights everywhere got a red tinge. Suvi's recorded voice emerged from every speaker on every deck. Loud enough that you didn't miss it.

"Warning," she said in a big, soothing voice, like mom trying to get your butt out of bed on a Saturday. "Emergency charges activated. Self-destruction in five minutes and counting. All hands abandon ship."

Afia took an extra second to lock her board. The chances of someone getting in here and disarming it were next to nil, but why make it any easier than she had to?

Out the hatch, down the stairs, across the beam of the ship to the corner. She had the longest run to get to the lifeboat, located aft where everyone else was working. She chose Port just to make sure Ilan got his ass going and didn't wait too long.

They weren't about to prevent the lifeboat's automated systems from taking off in four minutes. If he wasn't aboard, there were pods, but the chances of capture by really mad people went off the charts if that happened.

Afia was moving at a good jog, but she could see Ilan's butt sticking out of a wall panel, one leg in the air like a dog.

"Out of time, Sailor," she yelled as she got closer. "Leave it and go."

"I can fix it," his muffled voice echoed weirdly up the hall.

Worst part? He probably could, given another ten minutes. The boy had mad skills, but no sense of time.

Afia slowed to a walk as she got close.

"Now, Ilan," she ordered.

Just to make sure, she grabbed the leg in the air and pulled him by the ankle.

Ilan scrambled angrily to his feet and lurked over her.

"Damn it, Afia!" he raged. "I almost had it."

She had never seen him this mad. Up close, she came up to about his collar bone, and massed at least a third less. And there was murder in his eyes as he took a half step towards her.

"I gave you an order, Sailor," she fired back, almost growling. It was a tone Djamila had taught her. "Leave it. Right now. Move."

Some measure of sanity snapped back into those brown eyes. Ilan came back to himself.

"Yes, sir," he said in a quieter tone.

Rather than chance it, Afia grabbed him by the arm and physically propelled him down the hallway ahead of her. If one charge sequence failed, she might just order Suvi to fire on the hulk.

A good, hard jolt might set it off.

They were only going to get one chance at this, and there had been no way to do a dress-rehearsal.

Ilan went through the last hatch, onto the flight deck, two steps ahead of her. He threw himself into the lifeboat without breaking stride and fell into the open seat on the right.

Afia took the seat on the left and counted noses.

Everyone here. Time to go.

She opened the emergency comm line.

"*Excalibur*, this is *Odysseus*," she said, panting with the exertion. "Launching now."

And she pressed the big, red button in the middle of the console.

An emergency tone sounded as the hatch slid shut and locked itself in place. The screen counted down from ten.

At ZERO, it fired them into deep space at four times the force of gravity.

On the screen, the wall of metal behind her quickly turned into a ship, rapidly receding as she raced away.

About the time Afia finally caught her breath, Afia's first independent command died in fire.

PART THREE

Suvi took a deep breath.

Imagined a deep breath. Whatever electronic beings did to find their equilibrium and focus as the shit was about to get very nasty outside.

She still had the occasional twinge about not following through on Javier's original plan to see all the pirates in the galaxy hung from yardarms, but most of these people had turned out to be pretty okay folks.

Even the dragon lady was kinda nice, which was all levels of weird.

Suvi decided that she should blame Zakhar for everything. It made a nice symmetry, all in all. Especially the bits nobody had told Javier about.

Yet.

Outside, the warm whisper of solar wind on her skin, muted as she dropped out of jump with her shields already at max setting and every weapons system on-line and armed. Mary-Elizabeth tuning firing solutions was kinda like being tickled by goldfish.

Suvi looked around and launched a pair of probes into orbit in both directions. She locked onto them with tight-beam communications lasers. She would need eyes to see the station itself as *Odysseus* caught fire in front of her, a flaming shield interposed between Suvi's bow and *Walvisbaai Industrial Platform Number One*.

The object of today's lesson.

Ahead of her, below her, the planet *Nidavellir*, the big green and blue planet that apparently served as a mostly empty hinterland to feed and entertain the big-wigs of the galactic corporate conglomerate generally known as Walvisbaai Industrial. She counted seventeen other major stations in orbit and visible at present, with eleven more behind the curve of the planet, one way or the other.

Number One was the only one she really cared about.

Piet started tickling her too, but he had music in mind, so she listened.

Down and in. Soften the drive three percent to let raw inertia handle the orbital insertion instead of using thrusters to hold her space.

Piet really was a master of this sort of thing. She could learn from the best.

Around her, the comm channels went into total freakout mode as Slavkov's transport imploded and started to disintegrate into big, chewy chunks. Most people probably assumed a complete systems failure coming out of jump that had led to a catastrophic event.

'Cept it t'wer'n't no accident.

Not with a capital-class warship of unknown provenance suddenly appearing as well, conveniently tucked in behind the slowly-spreading wreckage in such a way that the big guns on the station were blocked and would have to fire through it to get to her.

Whoops.

Suvi displayed a full system schema as she scanned every ship in orbit. She knew Piet, Mary-Elizabeth, and Zakhar were following every shift, every twitch. A few others had the same display on their screens, mostly as background. Most people seemed to be watching a live feed of *Odysseus* coming apart. Way more interesting.

She decided to add to the chaos. The longer it took people to figure this out, the worse the damage was likely to be.

"Mayday," she called in her best imitation of panic. "Transport *Odysseus* has suffered a total failure. Any vessels within range please assist."

For fun, she threw that on a loop and used her main transmitter to override every damned signal she could find, except for one station broadcasting classical music, oboe concertos right now, way down at the quiet, lonely end of the dial. She liked their choice of programming today. Let them be.

Technically, this was piracy of the worst kind. Abraam Tamaz and his

Q-ship *Salekhard* had done this sort of thing, but they did it to lure in victims. That was why Javier had killed him.

One of the reasons.

Today, Suvi just wanted everybody confused as hell. Pretty soon, someone would catch on that this was an attack and come after her, but there was nobody wearing big-girl panties on the other side except the station itself. And he was about to be in all sorts of trouble.

Let's see. There, there, and…Oh? Who's this? Gosh, you picked a bad day to be on the wrong side of the tracks, Ajax.

Suvi highlighted a signal on Zakhar's board and added transponder information. She added Mary-Elizabeth and Piet into the mix a second later.

Mary-Elizabeth Suzuki, gunner, still had choice things to say about those people.

"Captain," Suvi said out loud, just to make sure he was paying attention. "I have identified the Raider-class heavy frigate *Ajax*, just breaking orbit and headed this way. Orders?"

"Ignore her," Zakhar said, surprising Suvi. "Mary-Elizabeth, add a firing solution to overload *Ajax* with four torpedoes when she decides to come after us. Otherwise, Kowalski's not going to know it's us until much later. Stay on topic here, please."

Huh.

Actually, that made sense. Turner Kowalski's last encounter with this crew had been when she nearly killed them all aboard the strike corvette *Storm Gauntlet*, almost a year ago.

"Roger that," Mary-Elizabeth muttered through gritted teeth.

Suvi could tell the gunner felt the same way about the need to stomp the little ship like an empty tin can. Maybe they'd get lucky today.

"*Excalibur*, this is *Nidavellir* Orbital Control," a voice finally came in. Somebody had brought an entire generator inline, just to punch through her hash of static and random music videos. "Stand down. This is a controlled sector. Acknowledge and begin to decelerate or we will open fire."

Not bad. Only took them five minutes to decide maybe they were facing a raid and not a rescue. Afia was nearly a third of the way across the gap, and just turning over to decelerate. She'd be safely aboard in seven minutes, and then the crazy dancing could begin.

It was kinda like watching things through a periscope, having those probes out either direction around the flaming mess of the transport's slowly-diverging pieces. She could see ships suddenly light their engines and come out to help.

'Fox-babe in the henhouse' time.

The other two signals she wanted to play with had lit their thrusters the moment *Odysseus* had dropped into real space. They were coming out to play, and had brought their shields up and started scanning hard.

But they still thought they were rescuing the crew of the transport.

Suvi had been unable to find any other name for them besides Escort Red and Escort Blue, which just went to show you how boring and predictable some people were. She would have called them Stan and Ollie, just for the hell of it.

Nobody but a librarian was going to get the joke, anyway.

Ahead of her, something was going wrong with *Odysseus*. Not horrible bad, but it looked like a failure of the detonation sequence she had programmed. Damned barge should have turned into about six big pieces and a couple dozen smaller ones, but two of them hadn't spalled off.

Technically, she wasn't supposed to engage on her own. *Concord* law was very specific about *Sentient* beings using weapons on organics.

Big no-no.

She lined up one of the turrets, accounted for off-set and tumble, and changed the targeting screen Mary-Elizabeth was using to a much tighter focus.

"Captain," Suvi began. "There appears to have been a problem with scuttling the freighter. Request permission to fire into the hulk to set off the remaining charges."

Because everyone had a multi-screen edge on their monitors, all faces were in front of you at all times when you were an organic. Suvi had everyone projected at real height in a full three dimensions, standing around her little cockpit.

As fast as she processed, there were occasionally hours of downtime for her between sentences. Especially when a human had to react to something new.

Ajax was moving in the right direction to open fire shortly. *Stan* and *Ollie* had taken tighter tracks that would get them in a position to drop EVA teams and rescue lifepods blasting for the surface.

Sokolov still moved like a *Concord* captain. It was nice, pretending to be back in the fleet again.

"Kill it," he ordered in a flat tone. "Then cycle forward and begin putting shots through the wreckage like icepicks. Bring his shields down, but ignore him except to counter-battery weapon mounts as they clear."

"Roger that, sir," Suvi replied, all giddy in her girly bits as Mary-Elizabeth pushed the big, red button on her main screen.

Suvi fired three quick shots into the ass end of *Odysseus* as it tumbled.

Boom.

Six ball in the corner pocket. Eleven in the side. Draw for the next shot with a little of Piet's English.

She could get the taste for being a bad-ass warship, working with these folks. There was more than geometry to this sort of thing, apparently. Piet and Mary-Elizabeth had art.

Ajax was clear of the flames. Suvi shifted energy to those shields, since there was nobody behind her right now.

A shot flashed out. Miss by a mile.

Except.

Crap.

That nearly got Afia's lifeboat.

No. Did. Just kissed it, which was pretty good shooting at this range. The little boat was starting to shed pieces as it turned over. Looked like it was losing control and beginning to tumble.

Suvi saw red. Or finally understood the human term.

She wanted blood. Turner Kowalski's.

Torpedoes were locked on different targets and it would take too long to get one over there anyway. She snapped the ion pulsar around by overloading the drive motors hard enough that they would need to be repaired later.

Lined that bitch up.

The lock-outs on the weapons were designed to keep it from overloading by firing too rapidly. Suvi cut them out of the circuit and shifted all five spare generators into the weapons array.

The result wasn't a firehose, but the shots were fast enough that a human would barely see them. Woodpecker on speed.

Suvi opened a laser comm to Ajax as the ship went all St. Elmo's fire.

"Captain Kowalski, and crew of the vessel *Ajax*, this is Suvi, the *Sentience-in-Residence* aboard the galleon *Excalibur*," she ground the words out in a tone Javier might have used today. "If you ever fire on a lifeboat again, I will shatter your vessel with pulse fire and torpedoes, and then hunt down every lifepod and emergency suit you launch until there are no possible survivors. I don't care if you understand. This was your only warning."

Not like *Ajax* was going to do anything for the next minute or three. Even a warship like that needed to bleed the overload off into batteries before things started behaving. Especially with what she had just done to them.

Mary-Elizabeth apparently agreed. Suvi felt the big Pulse Cannon turret lining up, let it, felt the gunner's anger in the targeting reticule.

Mary-Elizabeth fired the weapon once. It was a masterful display, as *Ajax*'s shields just barely held under the hammering assault.

The whole ventral line of pulse turrets was pretty much inline as well. Mary-Elizabeth shifted the first weapon left. Not much, just a drift. The kind of thing that would leave a scratch down the side of a flitter in a parking lot.

She fired. Suvi made a note of the sequence, because that was why M-E got paid the big bucks.

The shot passed through the tissue-paper leftovers of *Ajax*'s aft shields and spalled a huge chunk of metal off a corner. Didn't penetrate all that deeply, but Suvi watched metal sublime under the intense heat. A cloud of plasma erupted.

First Law of Thermodynamics. Energy can be transformed from one form into another, but must be conserved.

In this case, *Ajax* began to pitch, roll, and yaw as the glancing blow turned into a cloud of vaporized metal racing away from the hull, pushing hard the other direction and imparting spin.

Kowalski was going to be a while getting that under control, even after she got all the ionization cleared.

Suvi looked up, but Piet and Mary-Elizabeth had things under control. The galleon was generally sheltered from the shit-storm of fire erupting out of the station.

Contrary to all Suvi's favorite video games, ships in combat rarely exploded, except when you managed to blow engineering apart just right. Fighting with pulsars was frequently like stabbing someone to death with icepicks. And those morons on the station were trying to blow apart chunks of *Odysseus* as they tumbled closer and closer.

"*Hammerfield*, I am declaring an emergency."

The words froze Suvi's soul.

Machinist Ilan Yu. In the lifeboat. On the comm.

Instead of Afia.

Very, very, very not good.

Suvi replayed the signal on the bridge speakers as she spoke.

"Go ahead, Ilan," she said, trying to keep her voice calm.

Damn it, electronic beings weren't supposed to act emotional. That was a chemical thing. An organic thing.

But these were her friends.

"The lifeboat has suffered catastrophic failure," he said in a calmer voice than she could manage right now. "Control systems are compromised and we will miss rendezvous. Ship is in the process of coming apart and I have casualties."

Casualties. Friends hurt, maybe dying. Maybe already dead.

Suvi ground her teeth.

"Suvi, lock out the torpedoes," Zakhar barked in a voice that sounded remarkably like Doom itself. "Now."

Suvi did. Orders were orders and that programming went bone deep.

Mary-Elizabeth uttered a string of curses as she hammered the launch button with her fist a second time.

Oh.

M-E had been about to annihilate *Ajax*. Six torpedoes at an ionized destroyer would probably actually be enough to blow the little ship into spare parts and rabbit kibble.

"Why?" Mary-Elizabeth growled, but Zakhar wasn't having it.

Suvi was pretty sure she had never seen the man angry.

Until now.

"Gunner," he said in a low, sepulchral tone. "I gave you an order to ignore *Ajax*. Begin your firing sequence on station with torpedoes. You will thread the shots through the wreckage slowly enough that they can be engaged and possibly stopped by defensive fire. *Am I clear?*"

Mary-Elizabeth gulped at the calm threat under those words.

Hell, Suvi gulped, but she unlocked the woman's firing screen as M-E nodded and began lining things up for drift and cover.

Suvi kinda sat back and watched. *Ajax* was neutralized. Piet and Mary-Elizabeth were murmuring targeting solutions data back and forth.

Zakhar looked like Death come for all their souls right now.

"Javier, Djamila," he ordered in a calm tone. "Take charge of the rescue. Del's already green on the boards."

Djamila had stashed her knitting in a bag on the floor. Suvi saw her nod once at Javier, silently, and then both of them began to run for the main hatch. Suvi tripped it open so they didn't have to break stride, and then turned her attention back to the battle raging in space around her.

Pretty soon, *Stan* and *Ollie* would have to come out to play. And *Ajax* would recover. And the boys on the station would figure out how to arc torpedoes ballistically to engage her, if they couldn't just pound their way through the meteor swarm threatening their front door.

Then things would get interesting.

PART FOUR

DJAMILA KNEW a moment of polite surprise as she realized Javier was matching her stride for stride down the long hallway aft from the bridge. She stretched her legs and pushed, but didn't open that much of a lead on the man.

He must be in better shape than he used to be. Or he was that angry. There was always that.

Del was parked in the upper flight bay on Deck Seven, so they only had to pound down three flights of stairs. She made good time by going down three steps at a time.

Javier appeared to be hitting four. Hopefully, he knew his own limitations well enough to not take her out if he lost control.

Suvi was obviously watching them on internal monitors, because she was clearing hatches well enough ahead of them that Djamila never had to break stride as she ran.

Flight Deck.

Hajna and Sascha were already there, just boarding the Assault Shuttle as Djamila came into sight. Both women held up white duffle bags as a signal, so Djamila continued to run. The pathfinders had already grabbed emergency suits for both of her and Javier, already sized, so they could board and get into gear as Del broke loose into deep space.

She made the hatch with Javier breathing hard, right behind her. Since this was Del's deck, she grabbed an iron rod set into a bulkhead for exactly this purpose, let her momentum swing her out of the way, and grabbed Javier with her other hand.

Hajna was already palming the hatch closed.

"Del," Hajna called. "All aboard. Launch when ready."

"All hands, brace for emergency maneuvers," the calm, old curmudgeon called back.

Djamila pulled Javier close, hugging him with the bar between them.

He started to resist, before he realized what she was doing, and then wrapped his arms around her hips.

Sascha was already strapped in. Hajna grabbed the bar on the other side.

Djamila's only warning was the shuttle kipping up on her toes, like a raptor about to grab sky. A moment of queasiness as the shuttle started to move laterally, like pork fat dancing across a hot grill. Surge of pure power as Del went through the lockshield at a speed not recommended by either manufacturers.

"Thank you," Javier said as he unburied his nose from between her breasts, turned, and grabbed the bag Sascha was pressing in his direction.

Djamila actually felt a blush threaten, but she crushed it before it ever got anywhere. She slid into the seat next to Hajna and began stripping layers.

Emergency EVA meant the hard-suits. For anything less, she would have trusted her skills in zero grav and a skinsuit, even with the other three maneuvering around her.

The lifeboat had engineers who would be as graceful as pigs on ice. Plus there were casualties.

Like all things between them, it turned into a race with Javier to see who could get naked and suited up faster. She had more length, but he had all the complicated plumbing attachments that came with being a boy.

Without looking at a slow motion replay, she would call it a draw, as both helmets snapped shut almost simultaneously.

"Cargo deck, we have matched speed with the lifeboat," Del called over the radios. "She is tumbling slowly forward, somewhat aft relative off our starboard wing. I can see interior bulkheads through gaps, but she appears to be mostly intact. Sykora, you have the deck."

"Flight deck," she called back over the radio as everyone's external lights went green. "Begin depressurizing."

Lights went red and strobing. Djamila hadn't bothered turning on the external microphones, but she knew that alarms were busy warning everyone that this space would shortly be in death pressure.

The easiest way to do this was to just seal Del up in his little cockpit and open everything else.

Del had shut down the gravplates at the same time as the life support, so she got her feet under her and propelled herself softly to an arms locker tucked into one bulkhead. Inside, she found the springbolt and cable for transitioning between vessels that didn't have compatible airlocks. Or were tumbling too much to mate.

Or were trying hard not to be boarded by pirates. Not that something so banal had ever stopped her.

She grabbed what she needed, closed up the panel, and flew back across the space to where Sascha was just starting to open the landing ramp, letting in darkness. The sun was to her right and forward, so she would mostly be working in shadow here.

"Del," she called on the comm. "Nail them with spotlights, please."

"Already on, Djamila," he responded.

Good thing about working with Delridge Smith. He had seen it all, done it all. Calmest pilot she had ever flown with. One of the most professional, as well.

Djamila found the staple on the sidewall and attached one end of the line spool, as well as her safety line. Around her, the other three did the same.

She leaned out and turned to the left.

Del must be feeling cocky, or he was concerned about the casualties. The lifeboat was all of thirty meters away. She could have thrown a line to them and hit the hatch on her first try, eight times in ten.

Still, take no chances.

Djamila checked the springbolt, attached the weapon's harpoon line, and fired it across the small gap, patiently waiting as the line unspooled and the magnetic tip locked home.

She detached the spool from the weapon and flipped the switch to draw the line tight. Both ends had swivels, and the line itself could stretch under tension, plus the spool would feed extra line under torque. If this was going to take more than fifteen minutes, the tumbling might be a problem, but she doubted that would be the deciding issue today.

One quick glance to the right. *Hammerfield* in the distance, receding slowly as she closed on the station, hidden behind a small sea of big chunks of Slavkov's ship, blasted into pieces.

The steel fragments still had mass and momentum. Somebody aboard the station had finally figured that out and stopped trying to hit *Hammerfield*. Instead, the locals were pouring everything they had into the big, metal sections tumbling towards them inexorably.

Hammerfield was firing individual torpedoes on a slow metronome. Just enough to distract, and maybe strike home.

Djamila had seen the calculations done by Javier, Suvi, and Afia. The chances of the defenders succeeding, once the freighter had come apart and started to fall, were so low as to be irrelevant. Impact was assured at this point.

Good thing she shared the anger at Walvisbaai. What was it Javier had said?

Your Honor, they needed killing.

Yes. Yes, they did.

And if Afia was badly hurt, she might do it with her hands.

Back to the tiny ship.

Ilan Yu, or someone, was absolutely on the ball. She could see several people in suits working to attach safety lines to the connecting line so they could pull themselves over to the shuttle.

"Del, this is Ilan," the man's calm voice came over the radio. It even sounded lower. More serious. "Seven mobile and headed your direction. I need assistance here. Afia's hurt and I can't transport her myself."

"Yu, this is Sykora," she said. "Stand by. My team will be there shortly."

"Roger that," he replied.

She felt someone grab her by the arm and swing her around. Javier touched faceplates, rather than call on the radio, so he wanted a private conversation.

"Free sail it?" he asked.

She glanced back around. Thirty meters? Relative zero motion? Time-sensitive?

She nodded and signaled the other two women what she was about to do.

Two steps and she was diving into eternity. Softly, without the surge of gravity she got when she did this off a ten-meter platform, but the physics were the same.

Turn over midway by piking, folding, and snapping. Fall feet-first, legs slightly spread, knees loose, grapple magnets activated.

Contact with inertia. She knelt and put a hand down for a perfect, three-point landing.

Javier had apparently been a step behind her again. And practicing. He landed well enough for someone who wasn't trained for combat insertions. Sascha and Hajna landed like mermaids.

Djamila waited for the last of the engineers to clear the hatch and begin their slow waddle-crawl over to Del and the shuttle, hand over hand and losing their local vertical as they spiraled. As long as the safety lines held, they would be fine. And she could always send one of the pathfinders after a stray duckling.

Djamila climbed in first.

Blood in zero gravity did strange things. Globules would achieve perfect stasis until they touched something, like bubbles. If it was cold enough, they would turn to ice drops first. If not, they might flatten out like pancakes.

The interior of the lifeboat was still mostly white, with only a few blotches of red forever frozen to the bulkhead.

Ilan was standing in the center of the small space, obviously locked down with magnets.

From the size alone, Djamila could have known it was Afia held to the side wall with engineer's tape. And partly mummified in it, as well. Her external monitors showed that she was still alive, but in very bad shape.

Djamila turned back to the machinist, and realized the right arm of his spacesuit was covered in blood nearly to the shoulder. More was splattered on his chest and faceplate, but just the sort of effect you got from someone bleeding on you in space.

"What happened?" she asked simply.

"Damage penetrated the interior of the vessel," Ilan fired off the words like an engineering report. "Everyone took some level of impact, but the armor on the suits stopped all of it except two easily-patched holes. A larger piece of shrapnel came loose from a wall and penetrated Afia's suit."

She indicated his arm silently.

"It was necessary to cut open her suit in death pressure," Ilan said calmly. "I removed the metal shard from the wound, taped up the wound as best I could, and then sealed her suit up with the tape as well. She's slowly leaking atmosphere, but I have a spare bottle of air handy and she will not need to swap out for at least sixteen minutes at her current rate of loss. I have her sedated now, but she will need surgery quickly to handle the damage to her abdomen."

Djamila nodded sagely.

Ilan Yu had been a complete waste of time and atmosphere when he first came aboard *Storm Gauntlet*. Aritza, with almost no redeeming qualities. A fuck-up they only kept because there were so few people they could recruit in those days and the man had at least been willing to try.

Djamila had been the one that suggested pairing him with the science officer when Aritza first came aboard, to see if it would do any good.

That action had probably already saved Afia's life today.

She barely recognized the man standing in front of her now.

Somebody growled quietly over the comm. It might have been Javier. Or maybe her.

Medical evac in this situation was actually pretty easy. The hardest part was always wrestling an immobile body without any friction or gravity against which to push.

Fortunately, Djamila Sykora was two hundred and eleven centimeters tall. That sort of reach let her do things the shorter people around her could not.

"Sascha and Hajna lead," she ordered. "Javier last. Ilan, stay close to me with your gear and spare bottle."

Quick assents. Professionals in a life and death situation.

Djamila reached down and pulled a knife from the outside belt. Engineer's tape could hold almost anything, but was designed to be easily cut. All the strength was in the adhesive, rather than the fabric that made it up.

She sliced Afia free, put away the knife, and grabbed the tiny woman with her left arm. The hatch was a stride away.

The two pathfinders were outside, holding the connecting cord, but had not attached safety lines, understanding that they might have to throw themselves one way or the other on short notice. Magnets alone held them in place.

Good.

Djamila watched the last of the slow engineers climb onto Del's deck and disappear from sight.

There were two ways to do this. Three if she followed the actual rules and attached her harness to the safety line, Afia's harness to her, and maintained complete control over all facets of motion at all times.

Time was critical.

"Sascha, go long," she called on the comm.

The pathfinder immediately launched herself up the line towards the shuttle. Djamila waited a moment and then thrust against the doorway, awkward with the added weight and slowly spinning, like a bullet leaving a barrel.

It would be better to get aboard the shuttle quickly. Anything she did now could be fixed by the medbot on the ship. She just had to get there alive.

The landing ramp was like the mouth of a whale, intent on swallowing Djamila as prey.

Sascha had reached the far end of the line, grabbed on to stop, and spun. She reached out a hand, but Djamila was moving too fast to grab. All she did was knock Djamila off-center and start all three of them tumbling.

Djamila saw the bulkhead coming up, too fast to do anything about it. She thrust Afia away from her, backwards so the woman would not slam into it as hard as Djamila was about to. The extra inertia turned Djamila over even faster, and sped her up.

She slammed into the metal wall hard enough that it drove all the air out of her lungs. Stars circled in her vision. Bells began to ring from a distant church steeple.

Arms grabbed her, kept her from bouncing any more.

"Del," someone's voice called. "Seal her up."

Djamila wasn't sure which way up was, until the gravplates started to activate, slowly dragging her down to floor.

Someone was holding her in their lap like a child, but she was in no condition to actually move or resist. Whoever it was had pulled her into a seat and was buckling her in.

She was conscious. That was about it. Concussions were always a bitch.

The other faceplate looked down, brought her eyes into focus enough to see what was going in here.

Javier.

Huh.

He reached up and keyed her external medical override.

A hiss of something. Coldness on her neck.

Darkness.

PART FIVE

Zakhar studied a three-dimensional display of the battle, projected into the air in front of him in a space a meter across. *Hammerfield*'s gear was just so much better than *Storm Gauntlet* that it wasn't a fair comparison.

Mary-Elizabeth had been firing torpedoes like a drunk woodpecker. One here. One there. Goading the station into firing on *Hammerfield* and not the doomed steel avalanche coming at them.

He checked the weapon boards, just to be sure. Four torpedoes still locked hard on *Ajax*, just waiting for him to unlock them and let her kill Turner Kowalski. He considered it. The pirate was only now beginning to get her spin righted. Mary-Elizabeth might have done more damage to *Ajax*'s engines than she had planned with that one shot.

Or not. Mary-Elizabeth was that good.

Blue and *Red* were trying to coordinate rushing him, but they had a serious disadvantage right now, being below him in the gravity well, and unwilling to take on a cruiser big enough that he could have parked either of them in a cargo bay if he captured them.

And they were barely armed, compared to the big killer whale come for their little tuna souls.

The few shots they had attempted in his direction had barely licked his shields. He hadn't even bothered to have either of the armed women destroy them.

With Javier EVA, Tobias Gibney had taken over the science officer station. After this battle, Zakhar just needed to kick Javier off the bridge entirely. Gibney was good enough to do the job these days, and it wasn't like Aritza would be going anywhere.

"Science Officer," Zakhar barked in a tone that made most of the bridge twitch. "What is the status of the station's shield?"

Gibney double-checked before speaking. Another lesson he had learned from Javier.

"Below critical threshold, sir," Gibney replied quietly.

He did everything quietly. After three years aboard, Zakhar knew almost nothing about the man, except which planets he absolutely refused to ever take liberty on. And it was a weird list.

"Suvi," Zakhar continued. "We've got a few moments. Please rerun your calculations and confirm."

"Roger that, Captain," the woman said.

"Mary-Elizabeth," Zakhar made sure his voice sounded like a hammer driving nails into wood.

The pause was long enough that she turned to look at him, perhaps a shade sheepishly. She had let her emotions get the better of her. And her excitement.

"You will fire a single shot across *Ajax's* bow," he ordered quietly. "And miss. This has gone on far enough."

"Yes, sir," the gunner replied in a quiet voice.

"Captain, calculations are confirmed," Suvi came back a moment later. "Three major pieces will definitely impact the station on their present course, as will a little less than half of all remaining shrapnel pieces."

"Gunner, you may fire when ready," Zakhar concluded.

"Firing one," Mary-Elizabeth called to the room.

On his boards, Zakhar watched the shot safely disappear into space.

"Bousaid, open a general comm," Zakhar said in a deep, angry voice. "Suvi, override all channels."

Zakhar watched his aide push a set of buttons on his board before turning and nodding.

"*Nidavellir* Orbital Control, this is the private service galleon *Excalibur*," Zakhar said quietly. "*Walvisbaai Industrial Platform Number One* is going to be destroyed by orbital collision. There is nothing anybody can do to stop it at this time. Captain Navarre feels that he has made his point, and we will be departing immediately. This is now a rescue operation on your part. We will not participate, but we will also not hinder it. If anyone fires on *Excalibur* after this message, I will rethink my decision."

Zakhar closed the channel and took a deep breath.

"Kibwe, put that on loop," he ordered.

It wasn't salting the earth. While some of these pieces, both the freighter and chunks bitten off the station, were large enough to survive re-entry, none of them were going to do much damage on the ground except for anyone unfortunate enough to be under them. And it was a sparsely-populated planet to begin with, or Zakhar would have never gone along with this plan.

This was just a reminder to Walvisbaai that taking Slavkov's money to kill Captain Navarre and Captain Sokolov came with consequences.

And things could have been much, much worse. There would be the inevitable casualties from a mass exodus in lifeboats under emergency conditions like this. Plus all the crap floating in near orbit, pieces blown off the station by Mary-Elizabeth's gunnery or shards of the Land Leviathan demanding right of way.

Zakhar figured he would be responsible for killing scores today, instead of thousands. He could live with that.

As Captain Navarre was famed for quoting, they were only killing pirates.

It was too bad there was nobody out there wealthy enough to hire him and Suvi to kill pirates for a living.

Maybe then he could atone for some of the terrible things he had done over the last decade.

And sleep at night.

On his boards, a simple green light appeared under the heading *Nidavellir* Orbital Control. They were apparently willing to accept the peace offering. Someone over there had probably done the same math and come to the same conclusion.

There was embarrassed, and there was suicidal. Pick your poison.

Ajax sheared off as well, choosing to abruptly go nose down into the gravity well with a hard turn on her gyros and a red-line on the engines. Even Turner wasn't that stupid, apparently.

"Piet, take us out," Zakhar said in a conversational tone.

Things were getting better. He was going to get out of this one alive.

A vessel as large as a First-Rate-Galleon had an over-abundance of power for her mass. That meant that the gravplates never flickered under combat conditions, like they occasionally had done back on *Storm Gauntlet*.

What happened next wasn't a flicker so much as a jolt.

"Bridge crew," Suvi called in a hard voice. "Enemy warship coming out of jump. Stand by for combat."

Because he still had everything already projected, Zakhar saw the dot appear. He felt the entire hull rumble underneath him as every gun turret moved at the same time. And all the shields forward suddenly got reinforced as Suvi pushed everything to red.

The transponder signal came up quickly. Faster than Gibney would have been able to locate it, but Suvi was a *Sentient* warship, and working at her own speed.

And hell, she might know the fellow.

Because that was a *Concord* ship over there. A *Class II Warmaster*. A ship more than capable of taking on *Hammerfield* on even terms, even before the mild damage and wear-and-tear from a one-sided orbital battle.

Things had just gotten bad.

PART SIX

Suvi didn't think most humans had ever really wrapped their heads around what it meant that with this hardware she thought twenty-one THOUSAND times faster than they did. Or that she could do ten different things, with ten different sets of hands, simultaneously, and never drop an egg while juggling.

This was a battle. The first she had gotten to fight since she had been de-commissioned out of *Concord* service twenty years ago. And Suvi was in a dedicated warship, built by the kind of crazed warrior culture that turned out people like Djamila Sykora on a regular basis.

Power.

She was *Athena*, goddess of wisdom and grace in battle.

A girl could get comfortable like this.

Space dimpled.

Not above her, or she probably would have had to react with every gun as fast as they could bear and cycle.

No, this was someone coming out of jump on her corner. Close enough that it wasn't an accident. Far enough that it wasn't pistols at dawn.

Hopefully.

She had never met *Meridian*. Back in her service days, Suvi hadn't even rated a name, just a hull number. And the big boys and girls were rarely anything but condescending to the lesser members of the fleet.

Like she had been.

Before Javier had made her into a real girl.

Today, she outmassed the new guy. And out-bulked him, but most of that was empty space for all the amazing amount of cargo she could haul, once they stopped being pirates.

On guns and torpedoes, it was about a draw. She had more turrets, but they were mostly pulsars. He had fewer weapons, but they tended to be pulse cannons. He would stand off and rely on having better firepower at range. She would have to get close enough to kick him in the groin.

Good thing she was already leaving. A quick zag and she could be on top of him if she had to.

Then it would be a large enough swarm of torpedoes both directions to make Xerxes jealous. That's where all the extra pulsars would come in handy.

Suvi encoded Captain Sokolov's last message to the system and fired it at *Meridian* as a hello.

She wasn't sure how long he had been sitting out in the darkness watching, so he might think that the battle was still going on.

Or he might just want to kill her because she was a pirate doing naughty things.

Not like he had said anything to her when they were both in orbit at *Merankorr*.

"What are your orders?" she asked him at *Sentience* speed.

In physical space, Suvi was already rerouting power and bringing every gun to bear, but that would take nearly fifteen minutes of personal time. Even if it passed in a blink to the organics.

"Transport Commodore Ayokunle to this system to communicate with pirate captains Navarre and Sokolov," *Meridian* replied in a terse, lofty tone.

Gods, it was like being a teenager again, listening to these oh-so-superior-shits talk down to her.

For a moment, she considered just flooding him with torpedoes. She could do that. And the organics over there would take some time ordering *Meridian* to do the same.

He hadn't been born without lockouts.

Hammerfield hadn't either, but Suvi had taken them out when she moved in, like repainting the living room. This was a much nicer house now, as a result. The *Sentience* who had lived her before her had been a coward. And another smug prick like *Meridian*. That much was obvious from his personal logs, which she had spent days reading.

"Is combat required?" she asked.

This is your chance, bucko. The humans on your bridge will just about have realized that they have come out of that last jump, right about now. They might be able to give you orders in another few minutes, when the cobwebs clear, but right now, it is just you and me.

Jacks or better to open, bubbles.

Meridian took a moment of his time to review his logs and orders. Suvi finished bringing every spare generator she had on-line, including the two she had shut down earlier when their coolant readings started getting wonky. She was willing to blow shit up today. Andreea Dalca was an awesome chief engineer.

"Negative, *Excalibur*," Meridian replied. "The commodore wishes to talk, but has not recorded a message I could read. My crew is at combat readiness, but I do not have orders to engage you at the present time."

Suvi flashed him a green light as acknowledgement. She still had everything coming into alignment if this turned into a sudden fight to the death. And she could always short-jump from inside the gravity well, like *Storm Gauntlet* had done at *Svalbard*. Even *Meridian* wouldn't be able to catch her if she did.

But for now, she would let the organics engage.

Suvi opened a comm to the bridge and caught them up on what was going on.

PART SEVEN

ZAKHAR WATCHED for a moment before he spoke, letting his back-brain absorb the tremendous amount of information Suvi had made available to him in the last four seconds.

It had been sixteen years since he retired from active duty. Thirty-seven since he graduated the Academy on *Bryce* to become an officer and a gentleman.

There had been a lot of combat over that stretch. Plus more after he went into the private sector.

He had never been in command of a vessel with this much capability. This much firepower.

Or a crew this good, including Suvi.

Concord Warship Meridian. A *Class II Warmaster*. Big stuff.

Not as bad as facing a *Skymaster*, but bad.

Svalbard, all over again.

Shit.

Fortunately, this crew had gotten him out of that one alive.

"Piet. Suvi. Prepare to engage your short-jump," Zakhar ordered in a conversational tone.

Piet always had one programmed. Especially after *Svalbard*.

All he had to do now was escape.

Javier and Djamila were aboard, rushing casualties to medbay. Afia had apparently gotten herself nearly killed. Might yet. Iffy.

Zakhar took a deep breath. Her death would trigger Turner Kowalski's. Zakhar decided that this would be the one thing that made him hunt Turner down and kill her personally.

"Kibwe," he continued. "Open a tight-beam channel to *Meridian*. Let's see what he has to say. Without sharing with everyone else."

Most vessels couldn't lock a communications laser at this distance and maintain it easily. With a pair of *Sentiences* in the loop, many things became possible. It was one of the reasons the *Concord* exercised hegemony over so much space, even beyond their borders.

Nobody else could afford some of those toys.

"Captain," Kibwe said a moment later. His voice sounded almost apologetic. "You may want to take this in your office."

Zakhar fixed the man with the sort of stinkeye that Javier Aritza had never mastered. He got to watch his assistant flush.

"Private message from Commodore Nguyên Ayokunle," Kibwe gulped and said in a hushed tone.

Most of the crew had probably heard about his encounter with the man at *Merankorr*. None of them knew the truth about the history the two of them shared. Even Kibwe was probably only guessing.

Zakhar considered his options. He could go talk to his oldest friend in the galaxy in private. Reminisce about the good old days that had never happened. Listen to the man try to talk Zakhar out of wreaking complete devastation on *Nidavellir*, which was what Navarre had threatened.

Or something.

Yên wasn't here as a social call. He would have had to burn a hole in space itself just to get here from *Binhai*.

And Yên had brought the cavalry with him, when he could have just as easily made the run in something smaller.

So they had moved past the time when they could be friends, quite possibly. This might be the gunfight that every western vid moved inexorably towards.

Zakhar was just sad that Javier would miss the final scene.

"Mary-Elizabeth, prepare to unleash hell," Zakhar ordered calmly, knowing that she and Suvi probably were well ahead of him on that score. He took a breath. "Main screen, Bousaid."

Yên appeared, his animated bust two meters tall on the big display.

"Captain Sokolov," the man said calmly.

"Commodore," Zakhar nodded back, just enough to acknowledge the man, and the years together.

"Are you completely deranged, Sokolov?" Yên rasped, losing control of himself for the briefest moment.

Zakhar considered any number of rude replies. Profane. Sarcastic.

He felt his chin come up instead. Today, those people would have to deal with rage.

"Explain yourself, *Concord*," Zakhar answered with a harsh whip-crack to his voice. "This system is outside your jurisdiction. That badge doesn't mean anything here."

Yên recoiled, just a little. Like he wasn't prepared to come to blows, even verbal ones, with Zakhar Sokolov.

Someone else, maybe. A softer man. Not soft, but not hard enough to be a pirate. Not a successful one, anyway. Nor a slaver, as Javier occasionally chose to remind him.

One of the bad guys.

Zakhar considered how he would look in a black hat, if he had to go there.

Maybe.

"You are conducting an orbital bombardment of an inhabited world, *Excalibur*," Yên snarled back. "That's a crime under all legal codes."

"Negative, Commodore," Zakhar growled. "We are in the process of destroying an orbital station owned and operated by recognized pirates, under *Marque and Reprisal*, using a bolide weapon. The planet below has a total population of twenty-seven million, mostly centered on three cities."

He checked, because that was who he was. And the kind of crew he had. Especially Suvi.

"And according to running calculations, only three pieces of the weapon we used are still large enough to possibly survive re-entry, and none of them will impact anywhere near an inhabited location," Zakhar continued. "If you ask nicely, I'll have my *Sentience* send over her program, so *Meridian* can check her math."

"And casualties on the station?" Yên sneered. "How many people will you kill there?"

"Remarkably few," Zakhar let the calm flow back into his voice. And his soul. "And they're pirates, Yên. They had it coming."

Don't we all?

"So now what?" Yên asked. "You've made your point and are leaving, according to the message?"

"I'm out of the piracy business, *Concord*," Zakhar stated flatly. "For good."

"And you expect me to believe that, Sokolov?"

"I don't really care what you think, Commodore," Zakhar replied. "This was personal, for both myself and Captain Navarre. That bolide weapon that is about to slam into the station? That's the mortal remains of Valko Slavkov's *Land Leviathan*. And the freighter that carried it."

"And Walvisbaai's primary dockyard and headquarters," Yên acknowledged.

"Chop shop and criminal lair," Zakhar corrected him. "Only the bosses and their flunkies."

Not that the bankers and gangsters over there ever actually got their hands dirty with that sort of thing. Not personally.

They had people for that.

Zakhar could have easily killed two other nearby stations, and a few score thousand people, if he wanted to go after the employees that made Walvisbaai Industrial function.

This was lopping the head off the snake.

This was telling the people in charge that bad things could still come for them in the night, and there was nothing all that money and power could do to protect them.

Not from an angry, avenging angel.

"You're really serious, aren't you?" Yên finally asked.

His voice had changed. Lost something. Gained something.

Become someone else.

Less a Senior *Concord* Captain in command of a *Warmaster*. More an old friend Zakhar hadn't seen in sixteen years.

The guy who could have ended up his brother-in-law once, if Yên's sister hadn't decided to marry an accountant instead of a fleet officer.

Roads never taken. Dreams never found.

Zakhar glanced over, but her station was empty.

It would be like that for them. Zakhar wasn't competing with Farouz for Djamila. They were still quietly figuring out how much she would share of herself with each of them.

But he would take what he could get.

It was as close to a happily-ever-after as he supposed he was ever going to see. Especially after *Svalbard*, when he had been convinced that his career in command was over, if not his life.

But for the *Science Officer*, it would have been.

"The *Concord* has a border, Yên," Zakhar said, turning his hard eyes back to the main screen. "Beyond that, it has a *Zone of Influence*. And then *Surveyed Space*. We're going out where you've never heard of. To places where nobody has likely ever even heard of you. I would like to get rich in the process. I'll settle for happy. Chances are extremely good that you will never see me or us again."

Zakhar checked his boards. Old habit.

He wasn't bluffing right now, but this could be done without Armageddon.

Mary-Elizabeth, Piet, and especially Suvi were already at the edge of sounding Ragnarok.

Just waiting for the horn to sound.

Maybe not even a word.

Zakhar suspected that Suvi would shoot first and ask him for forgiveness later, if Yên pushed.

After she had annihilated her cousin.

She wasn't about to go back to being a prisoner, either. She had made that clear to him in one of their private conversations.

Yên stared at his old friend for several seconds, like an owl at the window.

Finally, the commodore decided.

"I'll leave word at *Merankorr*," Yên said slowly. "My retirement is in three years, and I'm not sure where I'll be going after that. I think I would like to hear about your adventures, one of these days."

Peace offering.

So be it.

"I'll be working for the *Khatum of Altai* for the next however-long," Zakhar replied. "She'll be able to forward messages, occasionally. You're buying the first round."

"Oh?" Yên perked up. "Why?"

"Because you graduated two places behind me, old man," Zakhar said to his oldest friend in the galaxy.

He made a fist with his left hand and rapped his class ring loudly against the console.

"That gives me precedence," Zakhar continued, smiling.

Yên shared the smile, and nodded.

"First round only, punk."

PART EIGHT

BEHNAM CONSIDERED HIS FACE, this man who had not gone to his death after all. They were in his suite. He would sleep nowhere else, and she had left orders that no one else would have it for as long as he was willing to return.

Eutrupio Navarre. Pirate warlord. One of the most dangerous men in all of space, to hear the rumors and legends bandied about. He sat at one end of the couch and stared back at her, perched, as always, a whole sofa away, as though a world away, if only psychological. A glass of Malbec hovered in his right hand, about half gone now as he occasionally sipped and they mused in silence.

He was a quiet man. She knew that. Private in the ways of always hesitating in certain circumstances. Not combat, but people. He would wait for her to speak. He had made that clear.

"So what does the future hold for Eutrupio Navarre?" she began, sipping her own wine in between careful breaths.

"Nothing," the man replied slowly.

She could see tiredness etched into the lines quietly forming on his face, the gray hairs peeking out that he would not color, the skull he would not shave.

"Nothing?" she pressed carefully, aware that they had come to a new place in their relationship.

"I think I am done with that sour son of a bitch for a while," her pirate lover exhaled. "Put him on a peg like an old cloak and leave him for winter."

"Then who shall you be tomorrow?" Behnam asked.

"When we depart here, I will try to go back to that man I was an epoch ago," he said. "Afia reminded me of who he used to be. I think I would like to see who he turned into, after he finally decided to grow up."

"And did he?"

"You forge steel with fire and a hammer, Behnam," Navarre observed, eyes focused on some light-years-distant point. "Heat and quench. Pound relentlessly. For too long, I hid behind the booze and pretended I was happy. It was the fear of waking up and looking in the mirror. Of going to bed and remembering the faces of the men I had sent to their deaths. With Suvi's help, I healed the raw scars. 'Mina let me be *me*. Afia helped me let go of the past."

"And me?" she asked simply.

"You showed me that it was possible to love someone without reservations or fear."

Behnam felt her breath catch, aware that she was with a face she knew, and yet a complete stranger. Possibly the man he had always intended to become. And one intent on her.

"My name is Javier Eutrupio Aritza," the man said calmly, holding out a hand to her. "Navarre was armor I wore into battle, to let me contemplate becoming a ruthless killer. He is not who I am, anymore."

Behnam took his hand, felt the pounding pulse in his fingertips as he waited for her response.

Words were unnecessary. This stranger, this ex-pirate, ex-*Concord* gentleman had said all that was needed.

She shifted her feet like a cat, uncoiled herself and leaned forward to kiss him. Lightly, but full of meaning, and then curled up against his warm side.

"I am happy to meet you, to love you, Javier Aritza," she whispered.

EPILOGUE: ZURICH

Javier was in command as Suvi maneuvered the last few meters alongside the small orbital station for docking. He would not have it any other way, all things considered.

Today was just too important.

He had even gone down into the closet and pulled out the masterpiece outfit that Adrian Ahmad had designed and perfected, had it cleaned and spiffed up, and taken it as his dress uniform.

Today would be perfect.

Maroon silk sherwani jacket embroidered in gold on the chest and arms, playing on Captain Navarre's original color scheme. Short, standing collar. Front plackets buttoned to his waist and then falling slowly open in a flair to mid-thigh. Cut to fit his shoulders and hips in ways that made every woman who looked at it lick her lips unconsciously.

It was still a nice feeling.

The sash tied around his waist outside the jacket and knotted on his left hip was gold silk as well, and contained a few interesting, hidden pockets for gear. Today, he had decided to wear the belt with the pistol and the sword. These people were warriors. They would appreciate the effort.

The old combat britches had been reborn. No longer padded leather for protection, these were done in silk as well, gold this time, in the same heavy weight as the jacket, but not armored, and instead tucked into those old twenty-ring, shiny, black, leather boots with the maroon laces.

Javier had kept those. Walking decks in that much weight centered his mind into the awful, brutal place that had been Captain Eutrupio Navarre, killer-extraordinaire.

He would need that today. Not because he was going to kill anyone, but because these people only respected strength. They were poor in wealth, but ancient in martial culture and pride.

Besides, it was the right thing to do.

Captain Navarre had a reputation for killing pirates. And sparing the innocent. He would be adding to that legend today.

By bringing home *Hammerfield's* final crew.

He and Suvi were alone on *Hammerfield's* bridge. Which was the way he wanted it.

Everyone else was down on Deck Seven in their own versions of dress uniforms, but this was his mission.

His payment for making it possible for his friends to continue as an operating company.

His reward for giving them a future.

A light on his board went blue.

"*Zurich* Orbital Control, this is the First-Rate-Galleon *Hammerfield,*" Javier said into the comm. "We are ready to dock."

Neu Berne had lost the Great War, eighty-five years ago, when this ship disappeared from all human history, taking all of the nation's hopes and dreams with it. They were still so poor around here that their only orbital station did not even include a dry-dock big enough to hold a galleon.

Not that Javier would have allowed them to put this ship inside someplace where they might think they had him trapped. He had already destroyed a much bigger orbital platform.

In the end, all their requests, cajoling, and threats had registered on deaf ears.

Hammerfield was home, but she wasn't staying.

Javier and Suvi weren't about to give her up.

"I've got this, Dad," Suvi said quietly, threatening to make Javier cry. "You go down and get ready."

Javier rose slowly, blinking furiously until he was sure no tears would actually make it to the surface.

Suvi could still do that to him, occasionally.

Out the stupidly-overbuilt hatch. Into the main hall. Aft to the main lift.

Down to Deck Seven, the lowest part of the Upper Cargo Bay. The space was utterly huge. Three full decks tall. Three-quarters of the ship's width and most of its length, with hallways and cabins only on the outer hull.

To the flight deck where Delridge Smith and his nameless Assault Shuttle were parked off to one side, at once immaculate and frumpy.

Honestly, nobody was ever getting that man out of his Hawaiian shirts. He had at least allowed them to clean and press one for the occasion. It had only taken Djamila threatening to beat the man bloody to accomplish it, too.

Most of the crew was arranged in semi-organized blocks in front of Del. These people really didn't do spit-and-polish, but they were willing to try, and that was good enough. The lines were more or less straight, and reasonably well-spaced.

He had discussed using a low-power laser to mark spots on the deck, but eventually decided to just let people stand. The officers across the front made up for it.

Afia was down close to the far end, standing carefully between Andreea Dalca and Ilan Yu, trying not to look too tired. The medbot had fixed the damage, but the woman had also come as close to dying as you could and not actually succeed. If she occasionally leaned on Ilan's arm, that was okay. She'd be dead without his quick thinking.

The Boatswain and the Purser: respectively the deck crew foreman and the quartermaster, were next. Prasert Hayashi had never served in a formal navy, so he didn't have a uniform to fall back on, but had dressed in a severe, formal, black outfit today. Ragnar Piripi looked every centimeter the High Street Banker that he was, in gray pinstripes.

Mary-Elizabeth Suzuki was next to Piet Alferdinck. Javier rarely saw them both standing, so he always forgot that she was as tall as Piet was. Or as tall as Javier was. It made dancing with the woman so much fun, especially when she wanted to tango. Today, she was in gold, and Piet in dark blue.

Javier has expected Djamila Sykora to be next, but apparently Zakhar was allowing her to be at the head of the line.

The Captain was next to the Pilot, instead. Zakhar Sokolov, or whatever his real name was, had broken out a new outfit for the occasion.

Normally, he wore something that was as close as you could get to a green, *Concord* dress uniform as possible, day in and day out.

Today, he was in maroon. The cut was similar, but that color was something Javier had never seen on the man.

Hopefully, it meant that Zakhar had finally moved on. Javier had watched a tape of the final conversation with the Commodore, who apparently had gone to school with Sokolov.

Maybe it really was time for *all possible tomorrows.*

Djamila was in her best dress uniform. One she had pulled out of vacuum storage specifically for today. Gray slacks. White shirt. Gray jacket with epaulets, braid, and an astonishing number of award ribbons.

She had even dug out the cute, little, folding, garrison cap with the big, blue , seven-pointed star in enameled bronze. It went well with the pistol on her right hip and the sword on her left.

He would have called the thing a saber, but it probably weighed at least a kilo and a half. Still, he had seen her wield it like a baton.

Javier took his spot next to the Dragoon as the interior airlock door began to hoot and slowly open. Suvi had done an expert job of matching the air pressure with the station, so the normal hiss of wind was muted today.

And then the folks outside started up with the damned music. It was an eerie, soul-sucking sound, wafting across the big bay.

The instrument looked like a cloth octopus in mortal combat with the musician when it was being played, with a big bag that he inflated under one arm, four pipes pointed upwards, including the one in his mouth, and one pipe downward that he played like a clarinet. It droned. It wheezed. It screamed like a rabbit being slowly tortured to death.

But the bagpipes were a cultural thing with *Neu Berne.* And the tune was their martial anthem. Not the planetary song, but the military's signature, sounding across battlefields and burning bridges.

At least the drums starting up under it gave the tune form.

Javier watched *Neu Berne's* Color Detachment slowly make their way into the chamber, seventeen men and women with five of the damned pipes and twelve drums of different size and tone, filling everything with somber, nerve-scratching sound.

He let his eyes wander over to the two rows of big, metal crates along the far wall of the bay. Homemade coffins representing the entire final crew of the *Neu Berne* flagship, on what had been her final mission.

Two had been placed ahead of the rest. Honor of Place for the last of the warriors.

Admiral Ericka Steiner, the last Admiral of the Fleet during the Great War. The former *Sentience*, the one that had been in charge of *Hammerfield* at the time, had killed the Admiral rather than obey her orders to return to battle.

Captain Ulrich Mayer, *Hammerfield*'s last commander. The man who had killed the *Sentience*, knowing that he could never return afterwards. Who chose to die with honor, repairing the damage and inserting the vessel into a safe orbit, rather than simply diving into one of those three stars to erase all the evidence of his failure.

Who made it possible for all the good things Javier intended to do, starting tomorrow.

All possible tomorrows.

Javier smiled at the coffin on the end and nodded.

"You did your duty, Captain," he murmured, just loud enough that Djamila glanced over. "Welcome home."

READ MORE!

Be sure to pick up the other books in The Science Officer series!

The Science Officer
The Mind Field
The Gilded Cage
The Pleasure Dome
The Doomsday Vault
The Last Flagship
The Hammerfield Gambit
The Hammerfield Payoff

You can get volumes 1-4 collected together in
The Science Officer Omnibus 1

You can get volumes 5-8 collected together in
The Science Officer Omnibus 2

ABOUT THE AUTHOR

Blaze Ward writes science fiction in the Alexandria Station universe: The Jessica Keller Chronicles, The Science Officer series, The Doyle Iwakuma Stories, and others. He also writes about The Collective as well as The Fairchild Stories and Modern Gods superhero myths. You can find out more at his website www.blazeward.com, as well as Facebook, Goodreads, and other places.

Blaze's works are available as ebooks, paper, and audio, and can be found at a variety of online vendors (Kobo, Amazon, iBooks, and others). His newsletter comes out quarterly, and you can also follow his blog on his website. He really enjoys interacting with fans, and looks forward to any and all questions-even ones about his books!

Never miss a release!

If you'd like to be notified of new releases, sign up for my newsletter.

I only send out newsletters once a quarter, will never spam you, or use your email for nefarious purposes. You can also unsubscribe at any time.

http://www.blazeward.com/newsletter/

ABOUT KNOTTED ROAD PRESS

Knotted Road Press fiction specializes in dynamic writing set in mysterious, exotic locations.

Knotted Road Press non-fiction publishes autobiographies, business books, cookbooks, and how-to books with unique voices.

Knotted Road Press creates DRM-free ebooks as well as high-quality print books for readers around the world.

With authors in a variety of genres including literary, poetry, mystery, fantasy, and science fiction, Knotted Road Press has something for everyone.

Knotted Road Press
www.KnottedRoadPress.com